ROTHERWEIRD

Andrew Caldecott

Illustrated by Sasha Laika

Jo Fletcher

BOOKS

Jo Fletcher Books
New York • London
an imprint of Quercus Editions Ltd.

© 2017 by Andrew Caldecott
First published in the United States by Quercus in 2019

ISBN 978-1-63506-153-6

A catalogue record for this book is available from the Library of Congress.

Distributed in the United States and Canada by
Hachette Book Group
1290 Avenue of the Americas
New York, NY 10104

Printed and bound in Great Britain by Clays Ltd, Elcograf S.p.A.

10 9 8 7 6 5 4 3 2 1

www.quercus.com

For
Rosamond

PRINCIPAL CHARACTERS

Outsiders from wider England

Robert Flask	A historian
Jonah Oblong	A historian
Sir Veronal Slickstone	A businessman and philanthropist
Lady Imogen Slickstone	His 'wife'
Rodney Slickstone	Their 'son'

The town of Rotherweird

Aggs	A cleaner
Angie Bevins	A schoolgirl
Deirdre Banter	Owner of *Baubles & Relics*, an antique shop
Professor Vesey Bolitho	Astronomer and Head of South Tower Science
Collier	A schoolboy
Godfery Fanguin	Former teacher and biologist
Bomber Fanguin	His wife
Marmion Finch	The Herald
Gorhambury	The Town Clerk
Gregorius Jones	Head of Physical Education at Rotherweird School

Boris and Bert Polk	Co-owners of *The Polk Land & Water Company*
Orelia Roc	Niece of Mrs Banter, assistant in *Baubles & Relics*
Hayman Salt	Municipal Head Gardener
Rhombus Smith	Headmaster of Rotherweird School
Sidney Snorkel	The Mayor
Cindy Snorkel	His wife
Hengest Strimmer	Head of North Tower Science
Angela Trimble	School Porter
Mors Valett	The town undertaker
Vixen Valourhand	A North Tower scientist

Rotherweird Countrysiders

Bill Ferdy	Brewer and landlord of *The Journeyman's Gist*
Megan Ferdy	His wife
Gwen Ferdy	Their daughter, a schoolgirl
Ferensen	A nomadic close neighbour of the Ferdys
Ned Guley	A schoolboy

Elizabethans

Calx Bole	Wynter's servant
Hubert Finch	Rotherweird's first Herald
Sir Robert Oxenbridge	Constable of the Tower of London
Geryon Wynter	A mystic
Thibo Fortemain	
Master Malise	Child prodigies
Hieronymus Seer	
Morval Seer	

CONTENTS

ILLUSTRATIONS

Old History

One for sorrow: Mary Tudor, a magpie queen – dress black, face chill white, pearls hanging in her hair like teardrops – stands in the pose of a woman with child, her right palm flat across her swollen belly. She knows that what she carries is dead, if ever a baby at all.

'This cannot be true.'

On the polished table lies a single parchment, a summary by her private secretary of ten reports from different corners of the realm. A courtier lurks in the darkness, faceless, a smudge of lace and velvet. The palace has the atmosphere of a morgue.

'I have seen the reports myself, your Majesty.'

'You think them cause for celebration?'

'*English* boys . . . *English* girls. We are blessed with a golden generation.'

'All born within days of each other – you do not think that a matter for concern?'

'Some say it is a matter for wonder, your Majesty.'

'They are the Devil's spawn.'

Unnatural creatures, she thinks, sent to mock her barren state and sap her faith, their gifts in science, philosophy, alchemy and mathematics grotesquely developed for minds so young. *Prodigies* – such an ugly word. She glances down the unfamiliar names: seven boys, three girls.

'Place them where they can do no harm,' she adds.

'Your Majesty.'

'Find us an unforgiving island and maroon them there. They may not be taught or cosseted.'

'Your Majesty.'

The courtier withdraws. He knows the queen is dying; he knows from the ladies of the Privy Chamber that the pregnancy is false. He must find a sanctuary where these children can learn and mature beyond the jealous royal gaze. He will talk to Sir Robert Oxenbridge, a man of the world and Constable of the Tower of London, where the gifted children are presently held.

He scuttles down the dim corridors like a rat after cheese.

Sir Robert watches the children playing on the grass near their billet in the Lanthorne Tower, and then surveys the strange miscellany of objects gathered from their rooms – *abaci*, sketches of fantastical machines, diagrams of celestial movement, books beyond the understanding of most of his adult prisoners, let alone these twelve-year-olds, and two wooden discs joined by an axle wound around with string.

The Yeoman Warder picks up this last object. 'Designed by one of the girls. It's a merry conceit, but requires much practice.' He raises his wrist and lowers it in a languid movement and the conjoined discs miraculously climb and sink, higher each time, until they touch his fingers.

Sir Robert tries, but under his inexpert guidance the wooden wheels jiggle at the end of the string and stubbornly decline to rise. He is nonetheless captivated.

'But there is this,' adds the Yeoman Warder, holding out a board, on which are pinned the bodies of two bats, slit open to reveal their vital organs. Threads and tiny labels crisscross the corpses.

'Not pretty, but then, the path of medical advancement rarely is,' replies Sir Robert, without complete conviction.

'He is different, Master Malise. Remember, one serpent in the Garden was enough.' The Yeoman Warder points to the lawn below and Sir Robert sees the difference – the boy stands aloof, not from shyness but a natural arrogance.

He recalls the queen's opinion that they are the Devil's spawn, but the playful inventiveness of the discs-on-a-string decides him, and the thought that when the old queen passes, the new dispensation will not favour banishing talent on superstitious grounds. Sir Robert turns his mind to an old friend, Sir Henry Grassal, a kindly widower. He owns a manor house in one of England's more secluded valleys and has the wealth, learning, time and inclination to provide the needed refuge and, no less important, the education.

As befits a veteran soldier, he plots a strategy. Even a sick queen has many eyes and ears.

April 1558. A wooded country lane.

It is early morning on an obscure tributary of the main highway. A covered wagon drawn by a single horse of no distinction appears, and stops. A ladder is lowered. Mud-stained urchins emerge, seven boys, three girls, and huddle on the roadway for warmth as broken sunlight knifes through the canopy. Each child clasps a silver penny bearing the faces of the queen and her foreign king and a lordly motto: *PZMDG Rosa sine spina – Philip and Mary by the grace of God a rose without a thorn.*

A second wagon appears, very different to the first. The slats on the side are polished to a shine, the wheels fortified with iron rims, the harnesses of finest leather tether four horses, not one. The wagon halts on the opposite side of the clearing and once again steps are lowered to deliver ten children – but these are mirror-opposites with clean complexions and clothes cut to fit. Like two teams from different worlds, haphazardly drawn together in the same game, they eye each other across the glade. Sir Robert points at one cart and then at the other, urging each group to cross. The children understand the instruction and its immediate purpose, although none can fathom the deeper reason for the switch.

This is not a mission for strangers. The carter fought with Sir Robert Oxenbridge in France and trusts his former captain in all things, but he has never heard children speak this way, exchanging complex chains of numbers and shapes with foreign names, even discussing the arrangement of the heavens. He crosses himself, uncertain whether his new charges are cursed or blessed.

Sir Robert, riding alongside, notes the gesture and its ambiguity. He still judges the children virtuous, save for the boy with the surgical interests, Master Malise – such joyless eyes.

They descend from the valley rim and Oxenbridge points far below. A single plume hangs in the air.

'Rich man's smoke,' he says, knowing the difference from a campfire, 'from the tallest chimney at Rotherweird Manor – our destination.'

He smiles at the carter. Had there ever been a gentler act of treason?

JANUARY

I

First Interview – The Woman

'The usual terms?'

Her irregular employer rarely deigned to answer questions directly. His slender fingers drummed the tabletop. 'Longer and more remote than usual.'

'Time is no problem,' replied the actress. 'They don't write for women my age any more.'

He still repelled her – that unnatural white bloom to the skin, the merciless eyes – but there were compensations, and not only the money. She had stayed on a yacht, better described as a floating mansion, in the South China Sea, a chalet in the Dolomites and a *palazzo* in Florence, all his properties, and she had heard talk of others. She picked up his second qualification.

'You said "remote"?'

'Very – but in England.' She would have registered disappointment, but for the intensity of his reply and the surprising notion that England could boast anywhere truly remote. 'You're discreet. You impress the locals. That is all.'

The actress smiled. Impressing came naturally to her. 'The same role, same costumes?'

'Of course.'

Here the interview would normally end, but she could not resist the burning question. 'Where in England?'

'Rotherweird.'

She failed to suppress a look of surprise. 'But they let nobody in. They're apart, they're different.'

'I appear to be an exception.'

'Your money is the exception.'

'True – period glaziers, wood restorers and plasterers come expensive. Prepare to be lady of an Elizabethan manor house.' He stood up before continuing; *no more questions*, the gesture said. 'One detail – can you play maternal?'

'Play maternal' – he had such an unsettling way of putting things. She nodded, knowing her beauty did not touch him. The dynamic between them had always been wholly transactional.

His cold left hand clasped hers – the wrist birdlike, the grip like iron. 'Done then,' he said, handing over a cheque by way of advance – a colossal sum for playing in public a wife he had never had.

2

Second Interview – The Boy

The boy stood outside Vauxhall Station facing the bridge across an array of traffic lanes, pedestrian lights and bus stops. It was bitterly cold and still dark at 6.20 in the morning. He would be on time. He fingered the switchblade in his pocket. If the meet turned out to be some kind of pervert, he would pay.

Ignoring the underpass, he vaulted the railings instead. A young suit stumbled towards the station, looking the worse for wear. Noting the bulge in his jacket pocket, he toyed with taking him, but decided against. He was off his patch, and alone.

The hand-drawn map directed him to the riverside flats west of the bridge with the instruction 'Press P' at the point of arrival. He peered up – posh, real posh. The boy feared that 'P' meant parking, having no intention of getting into a stranger's car, but this 'P' sat on top of the row of silver buttons. Anxiety turned to excitement. He smelled opportunity. Someone rich was looking his way. The world might label him a victim of his background, but he was not a victim of anyone or anything; he was himself, a force, going places. But the tag did have its uses: here was another fool, determined to cure him.

He pressed the button and a smooth voice spoke from the grille: 'Go to the lift. Press "P" again.'

The door clicked open. Where the boy came from, lifts were rare and never worked when you found them. They were places for meets and dealing and graffiti. This lift had a carpet that swallowed your shoes, and cut-glass mirrors. The ascent was silent, its movement undetectable as the numbers beside the door flared and faded.

The boy walked into a lobby and gawped at the stunning view, sallow light staining the river as the city began to stir. There were more cars now, and the occasional bicycle. Above the table in front of him hung a picture of the same river in evening light with a small brass plate – *Monet 1901*. Beneath it a bronze frog stared straight ahead.

The boy was right to be apprehensive. He had been watched. The tall man bent over the telescope had fair, almost albino skin, close-cropped silver hair and a high forehead. The lines in his face were fine, as if age had been kept at bay by some rarefied treatment. His hands were long, almost skeletal, the fingernails manicured. His Indian-style jacket, dark trousers and open-necked silk shirt mirrored the easy elegance of his penthouse flat. The boy did not know it, but he had chosen the art and furniture himself; he frowned on wealthy men who used advisors for taste.

He polished the telescope lens, replaced the cap and turned to the internal cameras. The boy was crude, but build and face held promise. He pressed the internal intercom: 'Bring him in – and remove the knife.'

The boy was disarmed by a young man with a minimum of fuss; he knew when not to mix it up. He was ushered into an office with computers standing in ranks on a glass table on one side of the room. In company with the modern were artefacts and pictures that meant nothing to him, except that they screamed 'money'. His host sprang from an armchair and the boy revised his expectations: this was no do-gooder. The lips had a heartless curl to them.

Unsettled, he sought to assert himself. 'What am I 'ere for?' He was used to staring people out – barristers, magistrates, child psychiatrists, social workers, policemen, rivals on his patch – but he evaded these remorseless eyes. Worse, the man did not speak.

The boy was used to dealing with people who came to the point – twenty quid, two kilos, guilty or not guilty, who to cut; business talk.

When it did emerge, the voice was as firm as the handshake. 'A drink, perhaps?'

'I'm not 'ere for a drink.'

'Coffee for me,' said the old man, 'medium sweet. And macaroons for our friend – with nothing to drink.' The assistant left the room. 'I appreciate your coming,' continued the man.

'My coming for what?'

'Do sit down.'

The boy did so, noticing that each chair arm ended in a predatory animal's head.

The man searched his face before offering a hint of a smile, apparently satisfied. 'What are you here for? A fair question. Call it a role more than a task.'

The boy hated smart talk. His nostrils twitched at the mild oily fragrance to the old man's hair.

'You play a part – understand?'

'I dunno what you're on about.'

The man held up a list of the boy's convictions – Court, date, offence and sentence. 'Impersonation, forgery, obtaining money by deception . . .' The list covered several pages – an unedifying mix of dishonesty and violence.

The boy played the victim card. 'Things have been 'ard. 'ad no chance, did I?'

'You had plenty of chances. You just got caught.'

Now the boy knew he was here to be used, not cured. 'Whaddya want, then?'

'I have lost something rare and valuable. You need only know it was taken from me long ago.'

'Then you gotta pay.'

'I haven't *got* to do anything.'

The assistant entered with a tray and the fragrance of fresh baked macaroons permeated the room. The boy grabbed one. His host followed, picking up his with a slow, easy elegance.

'If I get no money—' interrupted the boy, his mouth half full.

The old man sipped his coffee, quite unhurried. 'You reject my terms before you've heard them?'

The boy bit his lip. ''ow much then?' he asked.

'Enough for a son of mine.'

Son of mine! An expletive died in the boy's throat. Perhaps, after all . . .

''ow much is that?'

'Think thousands.'

A posh phrase came to him: *son and heir.* 'You got other kids?'

'My wife and I are, regrettably, not blessed.'

So he wanted a son – but *why* choose him? 'What about my probation officer?'

'The adoption papers are ready. You have only to sign.'

'All this to find – what?'

The old man ignored the question. 'You will be transformed – new name, new clothes, new voice.'

From his host saying nothing of substance, the conversation was now moving alarmingly fast. 'What if I refuse?'

'Make that choice and you'll find out.'

'We'd be staying 'ere?'

'For a month or two, while we polish you up, then to a country town. You've never been to the country. Experience is a form of power, Rodney.'

'*Rodney?*'

'"Rodney" suits him, don't you think?' the old man said to the assistant, adding, 'With work.'

'Yes, indeed, Sir Veronal,' the assistant agreed.

Sir, Sir Veronal – the boy had never met a 'sir' before, nor indeed a 'Veronal'.

'Why are you doing this?' asked the boy.

'I'm a philanthropist,' explained Sir Veronal. 'I give.'

Not without taking, thought the boy.

'And when I make generous offers, I like an answer.'

The offer was a no-brainer, but the boy's desire to win ran deep. 'You *might* be on, if you tell me what I'm looking for.'

The lines on Sir Veronal's face fleetingly looked like scars. 'It's something you'll always have, even when it's gone. Mine was stolen.' Sir Veronal rose to his feet. 'Naturally, there are conditions. Violence is usually an admission of failure. As they say on the medicine bottle: use only as instructed. And remember, I hire you to *listen* – in school, in the street, wherever.'

'School—?'

'Children know more than adults think, but they lack discretion.' Sir Veronal smiled; *discretion* was too rich a word for the boy in his present state. 'Meaning, when to keep their mouths shut. You must become adept at worming your way in.'

A beautiful woman glided into the room, tall, middle-aged, with marble-white skin and dark hair held back by a golden slide. Her eyes had a striking tint of violet, and she had a way of standing as if she had practised the pose for maximum elegance.

She spoke quietly, but with a penetrating clarity. 'Welcome home, Rodney.'

'Lady Imogen,' explained Sir Veronal.

Rodney held out a tentative hand as Sir Veronal allowed himself another smile. The unruly colt was broken.

'We want an English boy of breeding, style without ostentation. First we clothe you properly. Then we start on that voice.'

The boy nodded obligingly. His benefactors were clearly mad, and there for the taking. *Play along*, he said to himself, *just play along*.

3

Third Interview – The Teacher

Jonah Oblong's career as history teacher at Moss Lane Comprehensive – his first post – was dramatic, but short. When asked about his predecessor, the Head had looked at his shoes and muttered, 'Fled to Australia.'

Oblong soon understood why. The class boasted seven different first languages, three intimidating bullies and four pupils with parents hostile to the idea of their offspring learning anything they did not know themselves.

Then there was the problem of Oblong's appearance, which lay not in the face, which was pleasing enough, but in the bandyness of his legs and their disproportionate length. With the gangly build came clumsiness, an attribute that, whilst endearing in other contexts, did not assist in the pursuit of class discipline.

Oblong began well – his re-creation of the Great Fire of 1666 with a cardboard city in the school car park achieved a hitherto unknown interest in England's remote past – but the mantle soon slipped. His division of the class into Roundheads and Cavaliers led to two broken windows, and a King Canute demonstration caused a flood.

Conventional methods fared no better. After three minutes beside the blackboard, Conway, head of the Wyvern Shanks gang and no respecter of authority other than his own, interrupted. 'Can't we do the World Cup?'

'It's not history.'

'Why not?'

'It hasn't happened yet.'

'What about the last one?'

'*Bor–ring*,' whined two girls at the front.

'It's not on the syllabus.'

'He don't know,' crowed Conway, 'Ob-bog don't know who won.'

'Brazil . . . ?' guessed Oblong.

Guffaws all round.

Conway's water bomb hit Oblong on the shoulder, and something snapped in that gentle psyche. Oblong took the plastic water jug from his desk and poured the contents over Conway's head, just as the School Inspector walked in. Sensing his fate, the class behaved faultlessly for the rest of the lesson and said 'sorry' (in so many words) at the end – even Conway.

At the Employment Exchange, he was labelled overqualified or underqualified for every vacancy except teaching, where the lack of a single reference was proving fatal. The woman behind the counter handed him a dog-eared copy of the *Times Educational Supplement*, adding with a wan smile, 'You never know.'

He invested two pounds from his diminishing reserves in a small cappuccino and went to the local park. The *TES* revealed a demand for scientists and an even greater demand for references. He persevered to the last page of the classifieds, where a square edged in black like a funeral notice advertised the following: *ROTHERWEIRD SCHOOL – History teacher wanted – modern ONLY – CV, photograph, no references.*

Like everyone else, Oblong had heard of the Rotherweird Valley and its town of the same name, which by some quirk of history were self-governing – no MP and no bishop, only a mayor. He knew too that Rotherweird had a legendary hostility to admitting the outside world: no guidebook recommended a visit; the County History was silent about the place. *So: a hoax more likely than not,* Oblong concluded.

Nonetheless, he sent in his application that morning, declaring a desire 'to share with my charges all things modern and nothing fusty and old'.

To his astonishment a reply came back by return:

Dear Mr Oblong,

We are impressed by your credentials and priorities. Present yourself for interview in the New Year, 4.pm., 2nd January (pre-term, quiet). Train to Hoy; thereafter a test of your initiative.

Yours most sincerely,

Angela Trimble, School Porter

He checked the trains online and found Hoy well served. The station was unexpectedly quaint, with a lovingly preserved clap-perboard signal box. Oblong hailed a taxi.

'Rotherweird don't do cars,' responded the taxi driver with a toothless smile.

'I've an interview at four.'

'In Rotherweird? Who are you – the Archangel Gabriel?'

'I'm a teacher.'

'Of what?'

'History.'

The taxi driver looked amused. 'Take a bus to the Twelve-Mile post and then the charabanc.'

'Why can't I take a taxi?'

'The charabanc meets the bus; it don't meet any taxi. Sorry, mate, Rotherweird isn't like other places. Bus stop over there.'

The bus stop sign had a separate plate beneath the more con-ventional destinations: *Rotherweird bus for charabanc, according to need.* The bus – an old Volkswagen camper van – arrived minutes later.

'You coming or what?' the driver shouted rudely out of the window. Oblong clambered in.

The van hastened through rolling hills and farmland until,

spluttering after an extended climb, it reached a huge spreading oak. Oblong looked round. He could see nothing of note. The driver jabbed a finger in the tree's direction.

'That's the Twelve-Mile post, that's the Rotherweird Valley, and you owe me six quid.'

Oblong paid up. The camper van disappeared in a belch of smoke back the way it had come.

At all points of the compass, hills basked in midwinter sunshine, yet the valley below lay hidden in fog. He was standing on the rim of a giant cauldron in which, somewhere, lurked Rotherweird, and an interview. He found it curious that a place so determined to resist modern transport should insist on a modern historian. He heard a whirring noise, followed by a disembodied voice – a deep, cavernous bass – and snatches of the song it was singing:

> 'Not all those who wear velvet are good,
> My child,
> Beware those who like silver, not wood,
> My child . . .'

Out of the mist lurched an extraordinary vehicle, part bicycle, part charabanc, propelled by pedals, pistons and interconnecting drums. The double bench in the back had a folded canvas hood for protection. The driver wore goggles, which concealed his face but not a shock of flame-red hair. On the side of the charabanc, written in florid green and gold, stretched the words: *The Polk Land & Water Company* and underneath in smaller letters: *Proprietors: B Polk (land) and B Polk (water)*.

Smoothing greasy fingers down the front of a grease-stained shirt, the driver introduced himself as Boris Polk. 'Seven minutes late – my apologies – damp plugs and visibility nil.'

'It's only that it's gone three and—'

'Time equals distance over speed. I'm not to be confused with

'That's the Twelve-Mile post, that's the Rotherweird Valley,
and you owe me six quid.'

Bert – we're identical, but he's first by five minutes. I invent and he administers; he has children, I do not; I chose land and he chose water, which is interesting, 'cos—'

'I've an interview – my *only* interview—'

'Interview!' exclaimed Boris, raising his goggles to examine his passenger more closely. 'I haven't had one of those since the summer of . . . the wet one, now when was that . . . ?'

'It's at four.' Oblong pointed at his watch for emphasis. 'Four, Mr Polk, that's less than an hour away.'

'Is it now? "Time equals distance over speed" is another way of saying there isn't goin' to be no distance – not with you standing there like a totem pole – because there isn't goin' to be no speed.'

Chastened, Mr Oblong heaved his case into the back and was about to follow it when Boris resumed, 'My dear fellow, you're a co-driver, not a fare. We don't waste energy at *The Polk Land & Water Company*. Pedal like the clappers, and she goes like the clappers.'

'Right,' said Oblong.

'My patented vacuum system creates thrust – without engine noise, please note – so energising the lateral coils, and—'

'Hadn't we better—?'

'*Avanti!*'

The dominant Oblong gene was a tranquil one, as attested to by an ancestry of minor diplomats (the sort who write out table plans in copperplate writing, but make no decisions of moment). However a rogue chromosome occasionally surfaced, as in One Lobe Oblong, a pirate hung by the French in the 1760s. And now a deep-buried wish for adventure stirred in One Lobe's descendant, encouraged by the breakneck speed, the wheeze and whoosh of the vacuum system and Boris' penchant for taking bends on two wheels rather than four. The fog enhanced the feel of a fairground ride, briefly thinning to reveal the view before closing again. In those snapshots, Oblong glimpsed hedgerows and orchards, even a row of vines – and at one spectacular moment, a vision of a walled town, a forest of towers in all shapes and sizes, encircled by a river.

The light was failing fast when the charabanc finally lurched to a halt. Fog swirled like smoke from the river below.

'Old Man Rother,' explained Boris.

A bridge reared disconcertingly into the dark, at right angles to the town, to judge from the yellow smudges of lit windows.

Oblong clambered out. 'What do I owe you?'

'Nothing, and good luck, *and* be yourself.'

He added a cheery wave as Oblong set off up the slope of the bridge, cobbles turning the arches of his feet. Mythical stone birds and animals stared down from the parapet. At its summit, the bridge curved sharp left and descended to a forbidding gatehouse, its portcullis lowered. Rotherweird Town had been built to keep its enemies out – or its inhabitants in.

He shouted and waved his arms until, with much clanking, the portcullis withdrew into the battlements. Through the open arch a broad street ran north, signed the Golden Mean.

A statuesque blonde sat on a wooden bench by the gatehouse wall, improbably reading by a gaslight on an elegant hook above her head. She stood up. Mid-thirties, Oblong thought, and not to be trifled with.

'I suppose you're Jonah Oblong.' The voice was deep, the tone no-nonsense.

'You must be Angela, the School Porter,' guessed Oblong.

'Miss Trimble to you.' She added, 'Horrible evening!' as if he were responsible.

Oblong heard a violin, faint but distinct, practising a daunting run of arpeggios with aplomb.

'Strong on music,' he said, to win her round.

'Strong on everything – this *is* Rotherweird, you know.'

Oblong glanced at his watch.

The gesture did not impress. 'There's modern history for you, always in a rush. Until you're staff, you don't go in – and you're not staff until you're hired.' She opened the oak door behind her. 'You'd do well to remember we're most *particular* about history.'

She escorted Oblong into the Gatehouse and down a stone passage to a second oak door, reinforced with crossbeams and studded with rusty nails. She lifted the knocker, a grotesque face, and let it fall.

'Do come in,' said a reassuringly friendly voice.

A large table had been pushed against the near wall. A sentry-duty rota hung above it. Two ornate oak chairs faced him, probably imported for the occasion, judging by the dinginess of the rest of the décor. Both were occupied, one by a short, rotund man with small eyes and lank, dark hair; and the other by a tall angular man with a beaky face, a bald crown and bushy white eyebrows. The small man's clothes were expensive; the tall man's might have been so once, but were now beyond any respectable second-hand stall. Oblong sensed they did not like each other.

Facing the chairs was a stool. Oblong obeyed the small man's instructions to sit. He felt like a man in the dock.

The tall man extended a hand and introduced the short one. 'Mr Sidney Snorkel, our Mayor. He likes to participate in appointments. I am Rhombus Smith, Headmaster of Rotherweird School.'

'We take the teaching of the young most seriously in this town,' interjected Snorkel in an oily, sibilant voice. 'We like our teachers focused. Chemists do not teach French. Sports masters do not dabble in geography. And modern historians—'

'—keep to modern history,' chipped in Oblong, remembering the advertisement.

'In class and in life,' said Snorkel, before embarking on a series of *staccato* questions: 'Dependants?'

'None.'

'Hobbies?'

'I write poetry.'

'Not *historical* poetry?'

Oblong shook his head.

'Published?'

'Not yet.'

Snorkel nodded. Oblong's literary failure to date was apparently a good thing.

'It consumes *all* your spare time?'

Again Oblong nodded.

'You realise you teach modern history and no other history *whatsoever*?'

'Keep to the subject, I understand.'

'Any questions for us?' asked Smith politely.

'Questions?' echoed Snorkel, but impatiently, as though his mind were made up, despite the absence of any enquiry about Oblong's gifts as a historian or a teacher (being, of course, two very different things).

Oblong asked about lodgings – rooms to himself, rent-free, with a cleaner thrown in. He asked about food – breakfast and lunch, also free. He asked about pay – generous, albeit in Rotherweird currency. He asked about dates.

Snorkel answered this question, as he had all the others. 'Term starts in ten days – arrive four days early to settle in. You'll be Form Master to Form IV and modern historian to all.' Snorkel stood up. 'He'll do,' he said, adding in Mr Oblong's general direction, 'Good evening – I've important guests for dinner.'

Miss Trimble entered, helped the Mayor into an immaculate camelhair overcoat and they both departed.

Rhombus Smith closed the door. 'You can say "no", but I'd rather you didn't. Mr Snorkel is so very hard to please.'

'I've not been interviewed by a mayor before.'

'The price we pay for avoiding those idiots in Westminster.'

'He interviews everyone?'

'Oh, no. The modern historian is a *political* appointment.'

'Sorry?'

'Curiosity about the past is your game, but we're forbidden to study old history – by law.'

'Why?'

'Ha, ha, that's a good one – I'd have to study old history to find out, wouldn't I! So just remember to keep it modern. 1800 and after is the rule, and *never* Rotherweird history, which incidentally you shouldn't know anyway. Now, my boy, is it a yes – or do you need another five minutes to think about it?'

Oblong had no hint of a prospect anywhere else, and he firmly believed in the old adage that a good headmaster never runs a bad school. He accepted.

'*Splendido!*' exclaimed Rhombus Smith, shaking his hand warmly. 'My motto is, scientists teach while we in the arts civilise. Isn't that right?'

Oblong nodded weakly as the Headmaster hunted through various pieces of furniture before retrieving two pewter tankards and a large bottle labelled *Old Ferdy's Feisty Peculiar*. 'Ghastly job, manning the Gatehouse. This keeps them sane.'

The beer was indeed memorable: earthy, the taste layered. Rhombus Smith raised his tankard by way of a toast. 'To your happy future at Rotherweird School.'

'My . . . happy . . . future,' parroted Oblong without conviction.

The Headmaster opened a window and peered out. Through his fertile mind, courtesy of an eccentric but photographic memory, flashed several obscure literary passages descriptive of fog. 'Who's your favourite weather author?' he asked, closing the window.

'Shakespeare.'

'Myself, I go for Conrad. Men of the sea *get* the weather. Favourite weather line?'

Oblong floundered.

'How about Mark Twain – climate is what you expect, weather is what you get.'

So it went on, literary small talk, during which Oblong warmed to Rhombus Smith's passion for the nineteenth-century English novel. Between quotes, the Headmaster provided other details. Oblong was joining a day school, which took children only from the town and the surrounding countryside. 'Probably more talent than you're used to . . . you'll be kept on your toes,' he added.

Oblong found Boris and the charabanc where he had left them.

'You got it then.'

'How did you know?'

'The hesitant spring in your step.'

Going uphill, Boris pedalled less furiously and the pistons moved more languidly, leading to a less fraught journey, until the near-accident happened. As the charabanc eased round a hairpin bend near the Twelve-Mile post, a large black saloon car loomed into view, headlights on full. Boris swerved and pulled on the brake; the charabanc slewed sideways, ending up across the middle of the road. The black car screeched to a halt.

'What the hell's that?' exclaimed Boris.

'A Roller,' stammered Oblong.

'I don't care if it's Elijah's flaming chariot, you don't drive down the Rotherweird Road like that.'

Boris marched towards the car, which disgorged a tall elderly figure who moved towards Boris with surprising grace.

'You – what do you think your horn's for?' The man spoke without emotion. His clothes exuded the same aura of wealth as the car. 'Get off the road – or I'll drive you off.'

'Drive *me* off—?'

The man returned to his car, which started to roll forward. Boris barely had time to realise the threat was real, flick a gear and reverse into a meadow before the Rolls Royce accelerated away.

In place of the more usual flying silver lady Oblong glimpsed a gilded weasel atop the radiator.

'Never known it, never—'

'I don't care if it's Elijah's flaming chariot, you don't drive down
the Rotherweird Road like that.'

Normality returned. The bus to Hoy was waiting, with the same charmless driver. Mr Oblong waved farewell to Boris Polk. Further exploration of Rotherweird would have to wait.

Rodney Slickstone slouched on the back seat between his adopted parents. The countryside had no appeal, still less the thought of dinner with a mayor, but the car changed everything – the touch and smell of leather, the dappled surfaces, the running board and the predatory purr of the engine. Driving a ridiculous vehicle off the road confirmed Sir Veronal as a man worth following.

The actress's thoughts were different. She could not discern why her employer had such a fanatical interest in Rotherweird. Everyone knew the place was an anachronism, and the inhabitants irrationally hostile to the outside world. She disliked the boy and disapproved of playing Sir Veronal's wife to secure his adoption, the purpose of which was equally obscure. Yet she did like playing live drama, whose future scenes, like the town below, remained shrouded from view.

Boris Polk parked the charabanc in one of the sheds of *The Polk Land & Water Company* and hurried across the courtyard to his rooms, a troubled man. Outsiders very rarely came to Rotherweird, and when they did, they came nervously and with respect. The driver of the Rolls Royce, by contrast, had exuded an arrogant sense of entitlement. Only one explanation came to mind: he had just met the Manor's new owner, although he could not fathom this outsider's motivation for such a lavish investment in a place where he knew nobody. The re-opening of the Manor troubled him.

The townsfolk knew nothing of Rotherweird's past, but in the valley's rural community, secrets appeared to pass down the generations. He had particularly in mind the secretive neighbour of his friend, the brewer Bill Ferdy, who was known only as Ferensen. In the loft Boris kept his singular (in both senses) carrier pigeon,

Panjan – Snorkel's henchmen intercepted all communications between town and country, the inhabitants of the latter being regarded with deep suspicion by the Town Hall.

He wrote a short note addressed to Ferdy:

Ferdy, Tell Ferensen I think I've met the Manor's new owner – a disturbing experience – Boris

He rolled the message into a tiny canister, which he attached to a harness on Panjan's chest. The bird's scruffy appearance belied a sharp intelligence. A whisper of Ferdy's name sufficed. The note contained no request for advice and no suggestion of what to do. Nor did he expect a reply. The countrysiders revered Ferensen, but he never came to town and few there even knew of his existence. Nonetheless Boris went to bed, more at ease for having shared his experience.

4

A Sale

Behind the front window of *Baubles & Relics* on the Golden Mean, Rotherweird's only antique shop, a bewildering array of objects jostled for the attention of passers-by. A hippopotamus head peered down at an elephant's foot; a Victorian microscope stood between two turbans; assegais hung from the webbing of snowshoes, and a giant marionette of Father Time rode a rocking horse, arms and scythe suspended from the ceiling with fishing line. Mrs Banter owned the shop, but her niece, Orelia Roc, ran it, gathering stock from junk shops and house sales in the outside world. The visual wit in the display was entirely Orelia's.

On the night of Mr Oblong's interview, aunt and niece sat beside the small fire at the rear of the shop, balancing sales and acquisitions, as ever a fractious exercise.

'That,' shrilled Mrs Banter, pointing at the hippopotamus head, 'is a disaster.'

'It's a talking point.'

'How many times—? This is a *selling* shop, *not* a talking shop. And remember, I only stoop to trade to give you work.' The familiar lecture was interrupted by a knock on the door. 'Tell them we're closed. Can't people read?'

There was something of the gypsy about Orelia Roc, alluring and intimidating at the same time. Her hair was dark, long and curly; her eyes mischievous and a deep hazel. Men admired from a distance, but to her disappointment few attempted to get to know her. She wore brass bangles, a worn pair of jeans, a T-shirt and a frayed woollen scarf. By contrast, Mrs Banter's jersey was cashmere; her shoes glossy patent leather. She lived in a prestigious tower-house in the north of town. Such was the imbalance in their rewards from the business.

Orelia had been much closer to her late uncle, Bartholomew Banter, than his wife. He was her mother's brother, an architect with a genius for inserting arresting new structures into Rotherweird's tangle of houses, towers and walkways.

In widowhood Mrs Banter gave her social ambitions full rein, working her way into Snorkel *soirées* and onto the board of the Rotherweird Riparians, a town charity where the well-heeled preached more philanthropy than they practised. Keen to open a luxury store, Mrs Banter invested in a vacant property on the Golden Mean, only to baulk at the capital outlay and the cost of staff. When her orphaned niece returned to Rotherweird and offered the compromise of an antique shop, which she would run for modest pay and rooms above the premises, Mrs Banter agreed to a two-year probation period. Antiques, after all, traditionally attracted the well-to-do. Although in the event Orelia's choice of merchandise veered more to the eccentric than the antique, the shop quickly moved from barely washing its face into profit and Orelia stayed on, despite the cultural gulf between her and her aunt, who had a gift for materialising when the grander customers called, but not otherwise.

Nearer thirty than twenty and in need of adventure, Orelia had no intention of allowing their mystery visitor to escape. Through the spy-hole in the front door, the man outside appeared and disappeared disconcertingly, but the wide-brimmed hat and the laced leather boots were familiar.

'It's Hayman.'

'You mean the tramp?' said Mrs Banter, knowing full well who it was.

'Hayman Salt.'

Orelia opened the door. 'Hey man,' she said, her traditional welcome to the curmudgeon, with whom she had a good *rapport*.

Salt, head of Rotherweird's municipal gardens department and its chief plantsman, manoeuvred his bulk through the doorway. In the warmth of the room he steamed like a kettle. The unflattering title bestowed by Mrs Banter had been applied by others, but he was no tramp, having both a respectable home and employment, but in several respects the description fitted: a face ruddied by weather wore the tramp's ambiguity of expression, flitting from careworn to carefree; his shaving lacked skill; and his mane of greying hair was unkempt. A darker reason lurked behind the jibe: Salt would periodically disappear into the countryside for what he called 'field trips'. Town rumour suggested that he even fraternised with countrysiders, and visited their homes.

However, there could be no disputing his quality as a plantsman. The town's formal beds and the less manicured Grove Gardens boasted a range of hybrids unique in England, each immodestly marked with a metal nameplate ranging from *Hayman's Arum* to *Hayman's Zinnia*. Yet humour leavened his vanity; when the Mayor complained about the lack of a tribute to him, *Snorkel's Petunia* appeared, the petals a hideous mix of orange, yellow and green and the scent putrid. In Rotherweird, where scientific prowess was commonplace, nobody thought to ask how Hayman Salt could be so prolific a creator.

His visits to *Baubles & Relics* had a common purpose – the sale of archaeological finds from Roman military buckles to coins of modest value, unearthed during his excavation work. He would come in his lunch hour, declare his goods, haggle with Mrs Banter and seal the deal with a glass of her sickly sherry.

'You're dripping!' shrieked Mrs Banter.

He tossed his hat and coat to Orelia, who felt a hard object bounce off her hip – a trowel. She checked the other pocket as Salt squeezed into the middle chair by the fire: a sheaf of polythene bags – but hardly the weather or time for planting or lifting?

Without his usual small talk Salt produced from his jacket pocket four coloured stones in red, blue, brown and white, the colouring faintly mottled, but rich, each perfectly round and matched in size. Orelia noted tension in Salt's shoulders, as if he wanted both to keep the stones and be rid of them.

The two women peered at the merchandise. Mrs Banter saw profit. Orelia felt an intangible presence.

'Where'd you find them?' asked Mrs Banter.

'Ten guineas each, take it or leave it.'

Orelia saw the stones as elemental – fire, water, earth and air – and her reaction to them triggered an instinctive insight: they were not decorative, they *did* something.

Mrs Banter misread Salt's brusque response as a new negotiating technique. 'Beads are two a penny. Still, I'll allow they're pretty – three guineas each and a guinea for thinking of us.'

'They're beautiful,' added Orelia, taking issue with her aunt's meanness.

'Two guineas for thinking of us,' added Mrs Banter with a grimace.

'Ten guineas each,' repeated Salt with an edge to his voice.

Mrs Banter, pale with irritation, conceded.

Salt's old self resurfaced as Orelia poured the drinks. 'Trick or treat!' he exclaimed, giving Orelia a handful of bulbs from his other pocket. *'Hayman's Croci!'*

With a greenish tinge to the roots and blue blotches on the papery outer skin, the bulbs held promise of unique blooms to come.

Mrs Banter declined to offer the 'tramp' a second glass. As Orelia showed him out, he whispered, 'Odd things, those stones. Get rid of 'em far away if I were you.'

Mrs Banter, whose haughty exterior concealed a mind like an abacus, turned on her niece as the door closed. 'That show of sentiment cost me twenty-six guineas.'

'He knows when to hold a price.'

'They're very probably stolen.'

'Aunt, *really.*'

'You don't know where he goes at night.' Mrs Banter sprinkled her conversation with references to her customers' more secretive movements, especially after dark. 'Knowledge is influence,' she had once declared obliquely to Orelia when challenged about the habit. As Orelia bemoaned the loss of her uncle's restraining influence, Deirdre Banter moved on to practical matters. 'The label will say *Ancient Rotherweird comfort stones.*'

'Being what exactly?'

'Mediaeval worry-beads.'

'Right.'

'Price on application. You have to be above trade to understand trade – if only your mother had taught you that.' With this swipe at her late sister-in-law, Mrs Banter pocketed a fistful of notes from petty cash and joined her waiting rickshaw taxi.

Orelia labelled the stones as instructed and chose an inconspicuous place, hoping to buy time for further investigation. She chose well. Nobody showed any interest and with much else to occupy her, she thought less and less about them.

Salt's discomfort did not ease. Suppression of the truth could be as bad as a lie. He did not know what the stones did, but he did know where he had found them and that was disturbing enough. He prayed that they would end up in someone's jewellery box, unloved and unused.

5

Oblong Tries to Learn the Form

Oblong's attempts at reconnaissance were not productive. Maps confirmed the valley's secluded position and its one access road but were otherwise stripped of detail. The town itself did not even appear. The Rother too seemed shy of the outside world, emerging from the base of the northern hills, only to plunge underground once more near Rotherweird's southern boundary.

Guidebooks described Rotherweird's community as 'secretive and hostile; visitors should expect to be turned away or ejected at dusk without transport'. A unique plant, the Rotherweird eglantine, grew haphazardly under the oaks of the Island Field, a large meadow south of the town surrounded by a tributary of the Rother, but outsider botanists were barred access. The run-down camper van, the surly driver and the portcullis were no doubt part of the same deterrent strategy.

A detailed list of instructions headed *Outsiders and Countrysiders* promptly arrived in the post. 'Outsiders' covered anyone from the outside world and 'countrysiders' anyone from the Rotherweird Valley who did not live in town. Neither outsiders nor country-siders were permitted to stay overnight, imported teaching staff being the one exception, but the rules still denied Oblong lodgings on the Golden Mean or Market Square. According to a footnote he *did* qualify for the town's special festivals, of which only two were mentioned: *The Great Equinox Race* and *Vulcan's Dance*.

A large package followed, containing two gowns, one with a purple stripe on the sleeves (Form Master) and one with a green stripe (history teacher). The covering note read:

Regalia enclosed - check for size.
  Yours most sincerely, Angela Trimble.

PS And no old-world accoutrements such as computers or talking machines. We study by the book and we talk face to face.

When the afterglow of the gowns had worn off, nagging questions took root. *Why* had Rotherweird School chosen him? Why had it not asked for references? Why had Rhombus Smith not mentioned his predecessor? Had he or she been an outsider too? But these thoughts did not deter Oblong, they intrigued him. He wrote that evening to Rhombus Smith:

Dear Headmaster,
Please send last year's reports, and suggested history subject(s).
  Yours, Jonah Oblong

The requested reports came by return with a covering note in a cultured hand:

Dear Mr Oblong,
How delightfully enthusiastic. Material as requested. Great Depression?
With kind regards,
Rhombus

The reports divided between pupils from the town (white paper, and the great majority), and countrysiders from the surrounding valley (green). The former were honoured with Christian names, the latter listed only by initials at the end – again, a whiff of discrimination. The Form Master's name had been erased, as had that of the previous teacher of modern history.

Oblong decided against the Great Depression and in favour of the American Civil War, a subject on which he had expansive notes and which should have something for everyone. He immersed himself for the next week in the causes and the opening engagements; he would have time enough in Rotherweird to master the rest.

6

Strange Company

Oblong returned, as instructed, four days before the start of term. The journey followed his first – train to camper-van to charabanc – but with frost on the ground and a cloudless sky. Through rolling fields, orchards and occasional farms, Rotherweird Town with its two peculiar bending bridges and a forest of towers danced in and out of sight. A rocky escarpment rose sheer from the riverbank on the northeastern side, its prominence emphasised by the town's single church, whose crenellated stone tower dominated the skyline. Further east, beyond the river, stretched a forbidding expanse of marshland, relieved only by a single prominence to the south on which stood a watch tower, now deserted and, to judge from the absence of any track or road, unreachable.

For variety Boris delivered him to the North Gatehouse this time, leaving Oblong free to progress down the Golden Mean to the School, over whose entrance hung a cast-iron book attached to a pair of spectacles. Beyond he could see a series of interconnected quads, the open spaces laid to grass.

The Porter's Lodge, its walls honeycombed with pigeonholes, guarded the gateway. Miss Trimble was on duty. *If dressed less severely, with her hair let down, in both senses, she would be attractive, in a Junoesque way*, mused Oblong. He tapped the glass.

'Ah,' she said, 'back for more!' as if greeting the proverbial bad penny.

Feeling more like a new boy than a teacher, he trotted behind her to the form room. The quality of the equipment and prevailing tidiness impressed. Wallcharts illustrated the evolutionary stages of the frog and the chicken pox virus, but in a degree of scientific detail unusual for the age group. Miss Trimble appeared embarrassed by their presence and hastily rolled them up. Her unease prompted the thought that he must have *two* predecessors: the Form Master (clearly a biologist) *and* the modern historian. He checked the exercise books for biology and history. Although, as in the reports, both their names had been excised, their handwriting was very different. Detecting the scent of suppressed scandal, he gently challenged Miss Trimble, who replied curtly that Rotherweird School did not 'do nostalgia' and advised him to concentrate on present colleagues.

'Most are back, and they all like their tea. The staffroom is over there – through the big oak door and left. Then back to me for your lodgings.'

Silence descended as Oblong entered, and a sea of unfamiliar faces examined him from head to foot.

An early middle-aged man in a tracksuit broke the ice. 'Boris said to keep an eye out. I'm Gregorius Jones, PE – healthy mind in a healthy body – and your posture, if I may say so, is deplorable in one so young. I do a free staff Pilates class on Tuesday evenings if you wish to arrest your physical decay. But now it's introductions . . .'

Most were cursory in their welcome, though not rude. The warmest greeting came from a jovial man, conspicuous for a surprisingly successful combination of large ears and aquiline nose.

'Meet the one and only Vesey Bolitho,' said Gregorius, 'Head of the South Tower Science Faculty and our resident astronomer. Vesey and I share a common interest in heavenly bodies and perfect motion.'

'Delighted – I always welcome a stray visitor to our strange cosmos.' Bolitho lowered his voice. 'It's sad the statutes do not permit at least a Middle Ages historian. Galileo, Brahe, Copernicus –

such men are my heroes. I teach their teaching, but nobody can teach their times. Still, one black hole is better than several. Do drop by one evening – I have a decent telescope near the South Tower. Meantime' – he gestured to the seething mass of teachers – 'circulate like a planet if you wish to be a star.'

In Bolitho Oblong detected a welcome sense of mischief.

'And make your friends from the South Tower,' whispered Gregorius Jones.

'Why so?'

'Their science is nicer.'

Oblong circulated, struck by how colleagues addressed each other by surnames. An old-fashioned formality flourished in Rotherweird School. Least welcoming was Hengest Strimmer, a youngish man with half-moon glasses and curly dark hair, of precocious talent, presumably, being head of the North Tower Science Faculty. A colleague, Vixen Valourhand, slim and slight with short hair, hung back, looking more bored than hostile.

Strimmer declined Oblong's proffered hand.

'Remember the last historian,' Strimmer said to Jones. 'Fifty guineas this one doesn't make next term.'

Vesey Bolitho returned, and Gregorius Jones went with him. Oblong did not resent his isolation; respect had to be earned. He decided to explore. The Music School had the latest in recording technology. The modern language faculty in Babel Building and the imposing gym were no less blessed: so, a remarkably endowed school with no visible tribute to any benefactor. The South Tower Science Faculty boasted a large dome, Vesey Bolitho's observatory.

Access to the North Tower Science Faculty proved less easy. In a remote quad a long iron fence with sharpened railings offered only one narrow gate, presently open but festooned with a rosary of padlocks and the off-putting sign, *North Tower Science Faculty: Academic Appointments only.*

Deciding he could stretch reconnaissance to an academic

appointment, Oblong slipped through, only to leap back. The mastiff's jaws missed his thigh by inches. Teeth bared, revealing mottled black and pink gums, the dog snapped, growled and snapped again. Strimmer emerged from the gloom.

'Can't you read?'

'Sorry, I thought—'

Strimmer put on an infantile voice. '"I'm an outsider, I've no time for their petty rules".'

'I'm just puzzled as to why this Faculty is so well defended.'

Oblong shuffled forward, the dog lunged, Strimmer smiled and Oblong took a pace back. The mastiff reverted to nuzzling the back of Strimmer's right thigh, programmed apparently to love his own and to attack anyone else who crossed the lintel.

Oblong dangled a toe. Another snap.

'Call yourself a historian? The wise guard their valuable resources.' Strimmer patted the animal's head. 'He eats test tubes for pleasure.'

Oblong denied Strimmer the satisfaction of an immediate retreat. 'Perhaps you knew the last modern historian?'

'Well enough to know they'd choose an imbecile to replace him.'

Discretion finally triumphed over valour. Oblong returned to the Porter's Lodge. 'I met a charming man with a charming dog.'

'It can be hard to tell them apart,' responded Miss Trimble with the flicker of a smile.

Maybe he could make a friend or two in this unusual school. The thought emboldened him. 'What does the South Tower do?'

'They design light entertainment for the outside world, from toys to telescopes.'

'And the North Tower?'

Miss Trimble turned her wrist and glared at her watch. 'You'd best be getting on,' she replied. She provided keys, an address (3 Artery Lane) and a succinct summary – first left, third right, second left, fourth right, down a cul-de-sac, left again at the end, right, left, right, left, almost to the town wall.

Oblong found himself engulfed in the bustle of a market town without cars. Bicycle rickshaws, lovingly decorated and powered by Boris Polk's vacuum technology, served as taxis, their occupants in this season swathed in brightly coloured blankets. Their bells and the warning cry 'Rickshaw!' formed an integral part of Rotherweird's street music. Between them darted conventional bicycles, front baskets filled with books or produce. Clothes had colour and variety for both sexes with a bewildering array of different styles, be it hats, trousers or coats. Rotherweird's designers, keen to be self-sufficient and original, had gone their own way.

Shops, now closing, declared their wares or services on swinging hand-painted signs. Streets bore their names on rectangular iron plates set in the walls, painted white on dark green. While the Golden Mean, running north-south, was direct and generous, side streets were narrow and rarely straight. In darker alleys half-timber houses bent towards each other in greeting. Towers of oak and plaster dominated architecturally with several joined by suspended covered passages, some tall and thin, others short and stubby, many twisted by time, all with windows. At lower levels too, bridges joined buildings, creating below them havens from bad weather, settings for gossip and betrayed secrets. Elaborate balconies hung from the lower levels of the more prosperous towers; exterior staircases wound up to doors in the oddest places. In daytime, with such a varied skyline, light and shadow constantly shifted at street level.

In Market Square, the hub of the town, shops and stalls clustered around the imposing façade of the Town Hall, one of the few buildings built of dressed stone. The shops were owned by townsfolk, the mobile stalls by local countrysiders whose names were emblazoned across the awnings. As dusk eased into night, the stalls, also vacuum-powered, were being guided home to their respective farms. The portcullis rose punctually to allow their escape: countrysiders could not lawfully stay beyond seven o'clock.

Market Square was, in effect, a roundabout, thanks to its central tower, set on stilts and hung with oak shingles, whose four-sided clock, halfway up, chimed citizens to church and municipal meetings. Higher up, the tower bulged to accommodate the enormous single bell that gave the structure its name: Doom's Tocsin.

Number 3 Artery Lane proved to be a misnomer, less artery and more an insignificant vein in Rotherweird's complex circulatory system. Oblong's rooms occupied the highest habitable level of a ramshackle tower, reached by a creaking wooden staircase that had not quite rotted through. He had a small kitchen and bathroom as well as a comfortably furnished bedroom and study. The panelled walls were stained dark. From his study window, he could see the foaming rush of the Rother.

His spirits rose when he saw a vase of paper flowers, supplies in the kitchen and a laid fire in the study. He was on tiptoe on a chair, arranging his books, when he was ambushed by a croaky woman's voice.

'I'm your general person – people call me Aggs.'

Oblong clung on as the chair tipped back. Two firm hands righted him and he turned to find a short lady with frizzy white hair and teeth like tombstones. Late middle age, he guessed.

'I does all the School town lodgings,' she continued, describing the reach of her empire with a sweep of the hand, 'you and Thingummy and Mr Whatsit over there.'

'Hi.' Oblong shook Aggs' proffered hand. She had a grip like granite.

'A floor to yourself – how about that?'

'Very nice, very suitable.'

'Suitable for what?'

'Study and repose.'

'Study and repose! You keep to that and I'm an Austrian,' retorted Aggs with a knowing wink.

Oblong, sensitive to the demands of overtime, suggested she need not stay so late.

'Need tells me my hours, Mr Oblong, and in my book, welcomes and farewells come first.'

Oblong asked what a general person did.

'What you makes of 'er. Cook, cleaner, washer and spy,' chortled Aggs, as she put on some toast and the kettle. 'We're gonna be friends.'

'Aggs as in Agatha?'

'Agapanthus. Even Mr Smith don't get that right. Now you get some fuel inside you or you'll get those books all wrong. Some goes by height, some by subject and some alphabetical – I'm a subject person myself. Why put pillows in with saucepans?'

As he obediently consumed his second tea, Aggs delivered instructions on working fridge and cooker, a weather forecast for the coming month, a list of essential shops, the opening and closing times of Rotherweird's only pub, *The Journeyman's Gist*, and, to conclude, an assurance that he would have no trouble with Form IV. He had only to turn up at eight-thirty on the first day of term – *gowned*.

'Were you my predecessor's general person?'

'Not one of mine, if he ever had one.'

There are good liars and indifferent liars and a few, like Aggs, whose lies were so obvious, they could hardly be called liars at all. Her face, tuned to candour, went awry. Eyebrows arched and nostrils flared as she looked at her shoes.

Oblong decided against inflicting further misery. She was clearly acting under orders.

For two days Oblong kept mainly to his rooms, in part to avoid worsening weather, in part from shyness, and in part from a determination to be fully prepared for his first class. Aggs had stocked his cupboards with an array of supplies, so there was no pressing need for more shopping.

On his last free evening Oblong decided to be more adventurous, only to encounter two buildings with a declared hostility to visitors.

The first hid behind a high wall displaying intermittent signs in red script: *Prohibited Quarter – ROTHERWEIRD MANOR – KEEP OUT*. Despite this injunction, heavy restoration work appeared to be in progress. The second, a fine building open to view, boasted an equally forbidding message in a plaque set in the wall, which read: *Escutcheon Place* and beneath it: *Marmion Finch, Herald of Rotherweird. NO VISITORS*.

The exterior of Escutcheon Place was a heraldic work of art: stone snakes wound their way up oak beams either side of the imposing double front door; four griffins cast in lead stood guard along the top cornice; shields were set above each window, and a magnificently florid 'R' for Rotherweird adorned the double doors.

In the Manor and the Herald's house – apparently the town's oldest properties, and both barred to visitors – must lurk the reason for Rotherweird's peculiar constitution, he decided before rebuking himself. He had a contractual obligation to keep to 1800 and thereafter, if addressing the world beyond the valley, and to treat Rotherweird history as off-limits entirely. Here he must live in the moment. Private speculation could only lead him astray.

At intervals along the Golden Mean and the other major streets, open stairwells with extravagant names like Jacob's Ladder and Blind Man's Stair spiralled up like helter-skelters. Oblong passed several before realising that they gave access to an open aerial walkway, Aether's Way, which straddled the prosperous western quarters of the town at various levels. He ascended, and found rows of craftsmen and traders huddled in competitive groups – each with a shopfront and an elaborate iron sign. Some of the signs were static, others had tiny metalwork doors opening and shutting; chemists' jars emptying and refilling, lettering changing colour; clock hands rotating; models walking, flying and flapping wings.

Intermittently he chanced on more grandiose façades sculpted with scenes illustrative of particular skills: Rotherweird's Guild Halls. Oblong set about collecting them and noting their whereabouts. In the coming week he discovered ten – the Carvers, Glassblowers, Bakers, Timekeepers, Tanners, Milliners, Metalworkers, Toymakers, Masons and Mixers. Only two eluded him.

On Aether's Way the traders were not unfriendly. Word appeared to have travelled fast, with, 'Evening, Mr Historian!' swiftly becoming a common refrain. He found it invigorating, watching other walkers pass below as he tried to assemble the working pieces of this extraordinary town. One tower – *Vlad's*, Rotherweird's distillery and purveyor of spirits, whose shopfront opened onto Aether's Way – boasted brass bubbles at uneven intervals on the tower's sides. The window display was impressive for the variety of bottles, in shape and colour, and their contents – whiskies, gin, brandies, and wines both ordinary and fortified.

Rotherweird's sole pub, *The Journeyman's Gist*, was his final port of call. The inn sign depicted a traveller, hand to ear, as if garnering intelligence, above the name of the landlord, Bill Ferdy, whose brew, *Feisty Peculiar*, had so impressed. In keeping with the prevailing style the walls, a mix of white plaster and dark oak beams, enclosed one large room with several tables set between a crowded bar at one end and a blazing fire at the other. On one side were wooden stalls where board games were being played. Rugs softened the flagstone floor.

A powerful man with a friendly face addressed him from behind the bar in a country burr. 'Who be thou then? I'm sure to be asked.'

'I'm the new teacher.'

'I'm Bill Ferdy.' The landlord's handshake nearly dragged Oblong behind the bar. 'Not 'istory, by any chance?'

'Spot on,' said Oblong.

'About time – it's in the statutes: we can't be without one for more than a term. Anyway, thank the Lord you don't look like that Flask fellow.' Bill Ferdy put his finger to his mouth in a gesture of self-rebuke. 'Whoops – mum's the word. The first pint is on the house, Mr Historian.'

'Why *The Journeyman's Gist*?'

'Gist be old English for foam and bubble and yeast. And the nub of things. As any journeyman wants, right?'

Oblong nodded as Strimmer walked in with his fellow North Tower scientist, Vixen Valourhand. Strimmer elbowed Oblong aside.

'Manners, Mr Strimmer, manners,' said the landlord.

'He's a historian.'

'And I'm a landlord and you're a scientist – *so*?' Ferdy placed his sizable fists on his hips.

Rather than provoke a fracas, Oblong retreated to a far corner and tried with little success to recreate his walk in verse. At least he now had a name for his fellow historian: *Flask*. Between verses he caught the stare of an older man sitting in shadow at the far end of the room, though he appeared more inquisitive than hostile.

When he next looked up, his observer had gone.

'They were never going to risk another Flask,' muttered Strimmer into his beer, flicking his head in Oblong's direction, 'but that idiot—?'

'Once bitten, twice shy,' agreed Valourhand.

Strimmer assumed that his former pupil, a physicist and now the most junior member of the North Tower staff, was still in thrall to him, despite his ending a brief physical intimacy with brutal abruptness. He had been attracted by her cutting turn of phrase, the green-grey eyes and russet hair, Vixen being a School nickname awarded as much for her independence of spirit as her colouring.

'But why let a bloody outsider into the Manor? What's Snorkel playing at?' asked Strimmer.

'The outsider paid through the nose. I've seen his car – black, shiny and big. Trough-time for Snorkel, that's why.'

His eyes glinted. Valourhand knew the look: Strimmer sensed opportunities.

'How did Flask know an outsider would take over the Manor?'

'Flask always said, "Find the past to read the future." Perhaps he was right.'

'Pseudobabble,' replied Strimmer dismissively.

'Flask also said he would take the town over, which makes sense – why else would an outsider come here? Our independence attracts him; he wants to rule.' Valourhand saw the flaw in her own argument but kept it to herself – rule here, but to what end? He did not need the money; he did not know the people. Was it a valueless exercise in conceit? She thought not; she had glimpsed his face through the window of his Rolls Royce and he did not look that type.

Strimmer underestimated Valourhand. She led a double life of which he knew nothing, and she had her own ambitions, albeit with no settled direction. She had had her own conversations with Flask, and had kept selected details to herself. She wondered what else Flask had discovered, and how it connected to his disappearance.

Behind the ornate walls, columns and architraves of Escutcheon Place lived Marmion Finch, holder of the town's one hereditary office, Herald of Rotherweird. Finch after Finch after Finch had ranged through these lugubrious corridors.

His known duties as recorded here and there in the weighty twenty-four volumes of Rotherweird's *Regulations*, had an air of quaint formality. He regulated the carvings that decorated the town's roofs, balustrades, door-knockers and weathervanes – different families had exclusive rights to different emblems – and he controlled quality too, his *imprimatur* being required for the elevation of any apprentice to master carver. He had a right of veto over new structures, although by convention he rarely exercised it. He kept the registers of births and deaths. He calculated the dates of feasts and rituals, a task requiring no more than a rudimentary grasp of the lunar calendar.

And the office imposed other burdens, unknown to Rotherweird's citizens: Marmion Finch held the town's only copy of the *Rotherweird Statute*, under whose disturbing terms the valley had obtained her independence, and he alone had read it, being exempt from the *History Regulations*. He kept and guarded the historical records, shelves and shelves of them, in the *archivoire*, the great library in the heart of Escutcheon Place, which only he was allowed to enter.

He stood alone in other ways too, having succumbed to his father's insistence that he marry for social connection, not love: Mrs Finch had turned out to be a snob, in rapture to Snorkel's circle. Under her influence, his son and heir had acquired similar priorities; as a consequence, his work became his life.

On the evening of Oblong's tour, every volume of the *Rotherweird Regulations* stood open, covering the six tables in the bays of the *archivoire*. He had scoured them all in vain for a law prohibiting the Manor's reopening or, failing that, its sale to an outsider.

He did not like the outsider's showy car, or his face or the weasel motif, which had reluctantly been passed for use in the restoration. Worst of all, he did not understand Sir Veronal Slickstone's motivation, although Snorkel's was clear enough.

In the gloom of the rearmost bay of the *archivoire* lurked a row of shelves that held two deeply contrasting collections of sixteenth-century books, one on conventional science and philosophy, neatly bound in beige leather and beside it, black-bound, an altogether more arcane mix of works on poisons, torture, heresies, assassination, breeding patterns and the philosophy of power. Both had once resided in the Manor.

Books reflect interests; interests inform personality and personality decides a course of action. Instinct told Finch that these collections had been assembled by opposing forces, and if that were the case, the Manor had at different times been home to both the virtuous and the malevolent. He had the uncomfortable thought that its closure all those years ago must mean that the latter had triumphed and somehow remained a threat . . . but *how*?

When flummoxed, Finch spoke out loud improvised words in nonsensical chains. It calmed him and aided contemplation, so he did so now: 'Worm . . . cast . . . spell . . . struck . . .'

7

Another Point of View

In the Manor, Sir Veronal reviewed progress. Masons, carpenters, carvers, roofers, gardeners and glassmakers had done their work admirably.

His morning's work at the Town Hall had also been encouraging. Rotherweird's *History Regulations* prohibited both archaeology and the ownership of any historical pictures of, or publications about, the valley. Equally, nobody outside Rotherweird was permitted to write about the place, thanks to an ancient Elizabethan statute. So the greater the secrecy, the greater the secret, surely.

Research in London's antiquarian bookshops had uncovered one page in a small book, dated 1798, which had slipped the net. The author described himself as *Ambrose Claud, The Vagrant Vicar*, and had recorded his one visit to the Rotherweird Valley in these terms:

After two pleasant days in Hoy I was unable to resist the challenge of Rotherweird. I passed two nights walking down the valley and two days sleeping in the security of her outlying woods. I had allowed my beard to grow and wore my least imposing clothes. On the following day the weather came to my aid. The rain was so torrential, I was able to slip in unnoticed before the portcullis closed. The innkeeper was warm-hearted, but wary. All I gleaned from my visit came from him. It appears that a statute in the reign of Queen Elizabeth I endowed the district with its special status. He let slip that according to legend there was a terrible reckoning between settlers and the local inhabitants from the surrounding countryside – so terrible that special measures were needed. Even today I heard one of the former dismiss one of the latter as a 'countrysider'. The rest of England they regard with even deeper contempt. The origins of this sense of superiority remain obscure, save that the level of learning is peculiarly high: I found myself discussing Newton's Principia Mathematica with a storekeeper in the market square! The next morning I was rudely ejected, despite the cloth.

Sir Veronal turned to the Mayor's original letter, oozing with deference and greed.

Dear Sir Veronal,

I write with due humility as Mayor of Rotherweird, the only self-governing town in Britain. We are obliged by law to treat history with suspicion, but have an ancient Manor House whose renewal we feel would appeal to a man of your refined tastes. I would require financial assistance to secure the necessary consents for an outsider like you, but trust this would be no obstacle.

I must emphasise that you were brought to our attention by an impeccable source.

I look forward to your early reply.

Your humble and obedient servant,

Sidney Snorkel

Sir Veronal binned begging letters on principle and nothing here invoked an exception until that word, 'outsider' – it penetrated his blocked memory, although he could remember no *individual* outsider, only the fact that he had hated them all. This one word, in conjunction with the peculiarity of Rotherweird, had brought him here . . . slender evidence for such a huge investment.

After an additional donation to the offshore Snorkel Foundation, the Mayor identified his 'impeccable source' as one Paul Marl, a disclosure of little assistance since, apart from a Yorkshire postman and a fisherman from Hull, neither of whom had anything to do with anything, no other person of that name existed in England, let alone Rotherweird.

Sir Veronal re-read the passage from Ambrose Claud's travelogue. He needed a source of intelligence, and the Vagrant Vicar had unwittingly shown the way.

Mrs Banter, proprietor of *Baubles & Relics*, lived in the smart quarter of town, some way from the shop in a house that resembled its owner in physique: solid in the body (the main building), long in the neck (the tower), with two beady eyes at the top for observing everyone below (two powerful telescopes with infrared lenses, which between them covered most of the main streets and squares).

Occasionally by day, and invariably at night, with its enhanced potential for indiscretion, she ascended to the tower's top floor to conduct a round of 'observations', recording the results of note in a growing array of notebooks. Knowledge of people bestowed power over people. One notebook was devoted to the Manor; despite the shield of its perimeter wall she tracked the progress of the chimneys, rebuilt in old brick, and the reroofing in contemporary Elizabethan tiles. She detected a fastidious mind and considerable wealth at work. She noted the convoys bringing materials in and debris out, as well as occasional visits by the shiny black engine-powered car with the gleaming radiator and the golden weasel on the bonnet.

There would surely be an opening of the restored Manor, an occasion for her to shine, and cement her social position.

8

Term Begins

Children and teachers tramped the same journey, from home to the noticeboards in the main quad of Rotherweird School, although only the former were subjected to Miss Trimble's fastidious eye for deportment and dress.

'Shoulders back!'

'Socks up!'

'Shirt tail showing!'

And repeatedly, *'Gum!'*

Oblong found his twenty-minute walk excruciating. Children dressed in black and brown emerged from doorways like bees, only to give him as wide a berth as his fellow teachers.

The majesty of his gown brought some compensation, and at the noticeboards, as in the staffroom, Vesey Bolitho gave support. 'You'll feel like a moon in an asteroid belt, but in no time everything settles.'

The noticeboards brought home to Oblong how few teachers he knew – and yet all the pupils appeared to know him. He heard the name 'Flask' muttered among the sniggers behind cupped hands.

Form IV had sixteen pupils, eight of each sex. As they drifted in, they said, 'Good morning, sir.' Some even said, 'Good morning, Mr Oblong, sir.'

He made his opening address on the American Civil War. He did not get far. 'Girls and boys, you cannot imagine the carnage of this war, the complexity of its causes, the width of its consequences. Guess how many young men died?'

'Seven hundred and fifty thousand,' said a girl at the front. 'Approximately.'

'Thirty per cent of all Southern white males between eighteen and forty,' added the boy beside her.

Oblong gulped, unsure who was teaching whom, but by the end of the lesson he had the unsettling feeling that Form IV regarded outside history as essentially fictional. They had engaged with the statistics, but not with America as a real place.

Morning drizzle turned to sleet by early afternoon and as darkness fell, the sleet thickened into snow. By the time Oblong made it back to his lodgings, the flatter roofs and more neglected pavements were white. Indulging one of the few gifts learned in his partly rural childhood, he lit a fire and worked through a pile of essays before cosying up by the hearth with an anthology of pastoral poetry, which made his own efforts seem inept. Below, the river boasted flecks of white where snow had settled on projecting driftwood. In such conditions the knock on the door was wholly unexpected.

He admitted a stout man in his early sixties in corduroy trousers, leather ankle boots, a mustard-yellow tweed overcoat and a black felt hat with fur trim, Russian-style, which he removed as he held out his hand. Oblong recognised his observer in *The Journeyman's Gist*.

'Oblong?'

He had a hearty, enthusiastic air. His eyes twinkled. His hands were never still. Throwing his coat over the back of a chair to reveal an equally tatty tweed jacket, he heaved a canvas bag onto the table, from which emerged several bottles of *Old Ferdy's Feisty Peculiar*. 'Best anti-freeze in town,' he said with a smile. 'Fanguin at your service, Godfery Fanguin.'

Oblong looked blank.

'Don't tell me – Snorkel has expunged my name. Thirty-five years of loyal service and what do you get? Eternal anonymity! You see before you a veteran of Rotherweird School. Form IV is Fanguin. Fanguin is Form IV. Or rather, *was*.'

Oblong shook Fanguin's hand warmly. 'Why give up?' asked Oblong. 'I didn't ask to be Form Master.'

'I didn't ask not to be. Call it the price of an ill-judged friendship.'

'Not Flask?' blurted Oblong.

Fanguin ducked the enquiry. 'I'm looking at a bottle, and a bottle is looking at me. In polite society only a glass stands between us.'

Oblong returned from the kitchen to find Fanguin dipping into the fancy notebook in which he kept his completed poems.

'Not for school, I hope. Children are balladeers. They crave a rattling good metre, nifty rhymes and a grotesque storyline.'

'I try to get to the bottom of things,' replied Oblong huffily.

Fanguin slapped his thighs and guffawed before pouring out the deep ochre beer. 'Well I messed that one up, didn't I! The Fanguin school of small talk – nought out of ten, bottom of the class. Talking of which, how are the little perishers?'

'They're fine.' Oblong softened: Fanguin's *bonhomie* was infectious. 'I rather think they miss you.'

Fanguin seized on the compliment as an opportunity to go through his former pupils, one by one, so skilfully done that Oblong had no inkling what was happening. 'Ned Guley – nice boy, if quiet.'

'Attentive,' said Oblong.

'Single child . . . I trust you're not—?'

'Well, actually I am.'

'But parents alive, surely?'

'Only my father, and he's in a home.'

And so it went on, with Oblong disclosing far more about himself than Fanguin revealed about the class, including his age, his lack of a permanent home, his literary ambitions and his limited experience of teaching, not to mention much else in life.

At the end of this review, Fanguin moved from the classroom to the staffroom. Oblong's good reviews for Rhombus Smith, Vesey Bolitho and Gregorius Jones were greeted with approving nods, likewise his less flattering notice for Strimmer.

'Jones is the odd one,' said Fanguin, whose discretion was slipping under the influence of the *Feisty Peculiar*. 'He could be an outsider like you.'

'Really?'

'We discovered him on a field trip in Rotherweird Westwood. He was running like a man possessed, with no apparent destination – primitive clothes, no money or papers, not even a name except Gorius. Rhombus took him in, upgraded his name to Gregorius, and after a year or two made him our first Head of PE – noble savage turns gym master! A coup as it turned out. Everyone likes Gregorius Jones.'

'Why do you all have such outlandish names?'

'Do we?' Fanguin sounded genuinely surprised, but almost everyone Oblong had met had at least one strange name, and some two. In all things Rotherweird went its own way.

After his eulogy to Gregorius Jones Fanguin clambered to his feet and raised his glass. 'I give you Form IV, past and present,' he boomed before downing what remained of his fourth bottle. Oblong, still on his second, followed suit.

As he sat down Fanguin made an offer. 'Can I help with anything? I do mean anything.'

'What does the North Tower do?'

Fanguin's *bonhomie* waned a fraction. 'They design weapon technologies which Rotherweird sells discreetly to the outside world. Due to our limited facilities and manpower, it's mostly blueprints, with occasional prototypes. The South Tower by contrast designs toys and distractions, also for worldwide distribution. Strimmer regards Bolitho and his team as juveniles; Bolitho regards Strimmer and his acolytes as moral degenerates. The Town Hall does nothing to discourage the enmity: it encourages competition, which in turn increases the revenue from both.' Oblong squirmed in his chair. 'You've another question, I think.'

'You know how you always take over from someone? In my case, there's you and the other one – Mr Flask. I've seen exercise books with the names rubbed out – I mean, as if it's . . .'

'Dead man's shoes?' suggested Fanguin. After weeks of evasion, the bluntness shocked. 'Well, let's say Robert Flask left abruptly.'

Oblong blurted out his next question. 'The Mayor implied he taught early history against the rules.'

Fanguin, whose eyesight had appeared impeccable, began polishing a pair of spectacles with a spotted handkerchief, a theatrical performance designed to give maximum effect to his reply. 'Oh no,' replied Fanguin, 'Robert Flask didn't teach old history – he did something far worse. He went in search of it.'

'I see.'

'He wasn't called Flask for nothing – liked a jar of the *Old Peculiar*, did Robert. But after he vanished, I never heard a squeak. Thin-air job. Nobody knows where he went.'

Oblong tried again to elucidate Fanguin's own fate. 'But why is your name scrubbed out too?'

'I did the decent thing. I didn't report it.'

'Report what?'

'Flask broke cover one morning and told the form some most inappropriate things about history.' Fanguin paused. 'Still, as you're his and my successor, you'd best have this.' He handed Oblong a small plastic bag bound with elastic bands. 'That's Robert Flask's notebook – what's left of it.'

'How did you get it?'

'His general person found it in a drawer.'

'Not Aggs?'

'Hair like a bottle-brush, teeth like tusks and a heart of gold.'

'Why did she bring this to you?' muttered Mr Oblong, remembering her denial of any connection with Flask.

'I was Flask's best friend – and the young Aggs looked after me in my bachelor days.'

'Where could Flask have gone?'

'Something was up. He moved from nice rooms in the School to a seedy back street. A few days later he'd vanished – puff of smoke. Guess he'd had enough of Rotherweird.' Fanguin peered at his watch, hurriedly put on his coat and hat and shook Oblong's hand with alarming vigour. 'Be sure to keep in touch. You have much to contribute, I feel certain of it.'

With that, Fanguin rolled precariously down the steep staircase and out into the night.

Oblong went straight to the package. The pages of the notebook had been ripped out. Inside the front cover the name 'Robert Flask' had been written in ink with the address of his first lodgings – Exterior School Tower East, third floor – but was otherwise blank. On the back inside cover was written the following in ink in stilted handwriting:

STOLE CAR
ASC 1017

The banal entry hardly justified Fanguin's theatrical presentation. Oblong was not interested in vehicle theft – still less a vehicle this old – but he hid the remains of the notebook in his sock drawer, just in case.

Fanguin plodded home, finding it hard to resist the urge to self-pity. He lived for his class, and his dismissal had left him bereft. He liked the outsider, although Oblong lacked the charisma required for high-tier teaching. The contrast with Flask could hardly be greater. Flask had played the fool to get the post, only to display a ferocious intellect as he set about befriending Rotherweird's more maverick citizens and chasing down her remote history.

Fanguin hoped the notebook might hold a clue as to why and where Oblong's predecessor had disappeared. If Flask had been onto something of importance, and he could discover it, might he not get his post back?

In this endeavour he expected competition. Flask's other close friend, Strimmer, whom Fanguin cordially disliked, was not a man to leave stones unturned if what lurked beneath might offer him power. Flask, ever playing off one friend against another, had hinted to Fanguin that he had confided important information to Strimmer.

Another matter troubled Fanguin. His downfall stemmed from a notorious history lesson in which Flask had encouraged Form IV to investigate the town's origins. The pupils reported this crime to Fanguin, who decided not to report his friend to the Headmaster or the Town Hall – then Flask vanished, the truth seeped out and Fanguin paid the ultimate price for his loyalty. But why would Flask, hitherto so careful as to what he said to whom, commit professional suicide in such a flagrant way? Hopefully in the new historian's hands the strange notebook would yield the answer.

He felt a familiar tickle in his throat, an irritation that alcohol caused, cured and then caused again.

The Journeyman's Gist had endured a quiet night, custom halved by the weather. Bill Ferdy, the landlord, put out the fires, cleared the glasses, squared the accounts, discharged the staff and locked the tills. He helped himself to a pint of Sturdy and sat by the fire. With conditions treacherous, sleeping overnight in the pub appeared sensible, even though it was illegal for countrysiders. Nobody would know. He had already warned his wife, Megan, of the possibility.

He reflected on his good fortune. He had the only pub in town, and was more tolerated than any other countrysider. He grew his own hops and brewed his own beer. He had three delightful children – Gwen was unusual, true, but her mathematical gifts were a source of pride. He was dozing when there was a knock at the door – 1 a.m., long past closing time. A tall man with strangely neutral colouring stood in the doorway, his dress expensive, and not to Rotherweird tastes.

'Bill Ferdy?' He spoke impersonally as if making an arrest.

'Bar be closed, I'm afraid.'

'I drink only the best.' A leather suitcase stood in the snow beside the man's feet. Bill Ferdy was not in the mood for confrontation – he decided to hear him out. The man sat down at the nearest table. 'The name is Slickstone.'

'Is that a first name – or a second one?'

'I am Sir Veronal Slickstone, and I'm here to make you an offer. Eight hundred thousand for the pub, no strings.'

'Pence?' laughed the landlord.

'Guineas,' replied Sir Veronal with the straightest of faces.

Bill Ferdy gawped. The lease was renewable every seven years, and not worth a fraction of his visitor's offer. 'It's a bit sudden. The pub has been in our family since—'

'The best offers are sudden. The secret is accepting before they vanish.'

'Give me a day or two.'

'No time.' Sir Veronal took several brown envelopes out of the bag and a one-page agreement, in duplicate. 'Here is a ten per cent deposit, and your copy of the contract. You have only to sign.'

Bill Ferdy reflected. Gwen was unlikely to take up the reins, but one of her brothers might. Nor had he any idea what to do with such money – all he could think of using it for was repairing and restoring the more dilapidated parts of a pub that would no longer be his. That triggered a thought.

'Would you keep *The Journeyman's Gist* going?'

'I would keep the pub.'

'With Ferdy beer?'

'I would keep the pub, but for this price I do not expect questions. Yes or no?'

The blunt reply brought Bill Ferdy to his senses. He was landlord of the only pub for miles, which brought happiness to many, and therefore to him. It was without price.

'Thanks, but no—'

'I always get my way, Mr Ferdy.'

Ferdy suppressed a surge of dislike. A 'Sir' can buy anything, he seemed to be saying, including the right to threaten strangers. 'I'm locking up,' he replied curtly.

Without a goodnight his visitor strode off into the night.

Old History

1556. The Tower of Knowledge.

Here in the tall tower in the grounds of Rotherweird Manor Sir Henry Grassal works, grinding glass and observing the heavens.

Here too, in daytime, a swineherd admits two children.

'These be the two with the gifts,' he says. 'They are peasant stock, all earth, dirt and feral looks. Born together, ever together,' added the swineherd.

'What gifts?'

'The lad finds and names all that moves. He knows the differences between everything living. And she brings them alive with her knife.'

Sir Henry smiles. 'I know she does.' The mysterious carvings on the dead plum tree at the edge of the Manor gardens have long puzzled him: butterflies, bees, animals and insects, all vital and painstaking. One moonlit night he has caught them at work, the boy and the girl; she with her knife, he investigating every cranny in the bark for signs of life.

'They live by the pigpens. Their mother is dead and their father is a sot.'

By their best estimate they are ten years old. He gives them new names, Hieronymus and Morval Seer, which he announces by placing a hand on each head as if baptising them. 'Seer means a person who sees more than is visible.' Sir Henry likes outlandish names, names from his travels. 'Now you will live with me.'

Two idyllic years follow, filled with learning, security and physical wellbeing. Sir Henry, a polymath and widower with no surviving children, invests in them his considerable emotional and intellectual reserves. Reading, writing and the spoken word occupy much time, but he also encourages their original interests, with Hieronymus studying lifecycles and biology and Morval drawing whatever her brother finds. Clothed, fed and washed, they are transformed in appearance too.

Notebooks fill. Morval's knife cuts woodblocks and sharpens quills. At fourteen she has mastered ink-making, using plant sap for fluidity of line. Sir Henry brings back tiny quantities of lapis and cochineal. The two children are bound by complementary talents as well as kinship and shared adversity – his knack for questioning the natural world, focused but practical, and her instinctive gift for reproducing the appearance of things, eye to hand, every vein on an insect's wing, every line on a human face. Remembering their Copernicus, they see themselves as twin moons bound by a common sun: Sir Henry Grassal.

1558. The Rotherweird Valley.

Hieronymus and Morval Seer are in the orchard with Sir Henry studying the structure of flowers – where the fruit will grow, how and why. Down the hill judders a cart with hide awnings, an ordinary sight, but for the outrider, scabbard bouncing on the thigh, fine saddle, the velvet cap, the air of authority.

'New friends,' cries Sir Henry, but for once he will be wrong.

They stand in the Great Hall, ten children in a line, every one of them twelve years of age. The old man with the kindly face opens his arms. 'I am Sir Henry Grassal, and this is Rotherweird Manor, my home and now yours. You were in peril but are no more. For reasons that are forgivable, your queen mistrusts you. So do not stray beyond this island. You will have more than enough to occupy you here, doing justice to your abundant talents.'

Of the ten, only Malise wilfully mistranslates the invitation. *I will indulge my talents*, he muses, *by taking your house, your island and your power*. He watches the captain of the escort, Sir Robert Oxenbridge, watching them, feeling relief that he will be leaving. Grassal's face is kindly, but weak; Oxenbridge's hardened, a soldier's look.

Two children walk in, a boy and a girl, their own age.

'Meet Hieronymus and Morval Seer, born in this valley the time that you were born, and with equal gifts to your own,' says Sir Henry.

Malise feels jealousy in the air from the other girls and a corresponding interest from the boys. The girl has an astonishing beauty, and innocence too: Eve in the garden. He feels a new kind of desire for a new kind of power. The effect of her brother on the new arrivals is less pronounced. He appears studious to the point of remoteness.

March 1559. London.

Geryon Wynter tires of London, and London tires of him. The vigilance of the new Queen's Council inhibits his researches into the darker reaches of knowledge. The right books are elusive, and spies insinuate themselves into the city's society like worms in cheese. Strangers peer in his windows; servants talk more than they should.

The fifth son of a clergyman, the corruption of Wynter's learning stems not from exposure to vice but to an excessive preaching of virtue. Listening to his father's interminable services and sermons, he concluded in childhood that gods are created by man to inspire in life and to comfort in death. But where are the new gods? Isn't it time to start again? And what might the recipe be?

He isolates the most potent elements in his father's belief: prophecy, a code of behaviour, the Passion and resurrection; the rest he finds insipid. He tracks down Latin translations of Greek texts and then learns Greek himself and rifles these works for their invented deities and the fabulous stories that give them permanence. He is drawn to the monstrous – gorgons, furies and three-headed dogs – and how these classical gods meddle in the affairs of men, and vice versa.

But there is more to the young Wynter's life than hunting down mythologies. He tests, dissects and explores. He is a scientist, focusing on the destructive forces, from gunpowder to untraceable poisons.

An extravagant ambition takes shape. He will create a new god, even gods, with the sinew and scientific reality to survive and flourish. He does not know how, but believes this to be his destiny. For the present, however, he has more mundane challenges.

There is the issue of servants. They cook and clean, but are dumb souls. He craves an intellect to share the burden of his research. He trawls prisons and courts and after many months is rewarded at the Middlesex Assize. It is the charge that catches his eye: theft of a book by night (*A Miscellanie of Peculiar Weapons*), and the defendant's demeanour. The squat, ugly young man fences with the visiting judge, showing more wit than sense.

'It is a serious business to assail a man's house in the early hours.'

'It is a serious business to leave a book shrouded in dust.'

'Not this book, perhaps.'

'Weapons are a subject for study. Wars are won by them.'

The Judge can tell from the accused's clothes that the upstart has more learning than money. The sentence has limits – first offence, and a man who can read, which gives him what the poor do not receive, the 'benefits of clergy'. Yet Judges have a knack for finding a way.

'Brand him in the brawn of the thumb, unless he pays ten shillings within the week – your own ten shillings, mind.' He addresses this last to the defendant.

Wynter stipulates his terms for a retainer in the Court cells, the young man accepts and Wynter pays the fine. He renames him, an act of ownership, Calx Bole – Calx for the chalky whiteness of his skin, Bole for his corpulent torso. Bole prefers to cook and clean himself, rather than have other servants between him and his new master.

At night they research together the location of *tumuli*, burial mounds in the English countryside, from Saxon round barrows to later, more sophisticated sites. They identify the Rotherweird Valley as especially rich in these untapped sources of hidden treasure. Wynter even gains access to the Winchester copy of the *Anglo-Saxon Chronicle* in its present home at Canterbury. It makes interesting reading.

He sells up his London residence in favour of a manageable house near Hoy, a village above the Rotherweird escarpment. The mouse-haired Mrs Wynter has no say, as this is not in her husband's book a domestic matter. Bole's surliness soon dissipates. He wears the gratitude of a rescued dog.

So here is Wynter, this cold but clear February afternoon, watching Bole dig beneath the rim of a semi-circular prominence on the western side of the Rotherweird Valley. Their labours have yielded a silver spoon and a hollow torc, damaged but in fine gold. Wynter, seeing the vestiges of an old road entering the hollow below them, descends the steep slope and makes a most unexpected discovery.

Set in the ground is a white tile, incised with a tiny flower. The palm of his hand prickles as he holds it close.

'Stand there,' he says to Bole, who does so, and promptly disappears.

A magical door! Wherever it leads, destiny has handed him a base ingredient for creating his new god: a mystery to wonder at. He peers at the tile. The exquisite workmanship suggests reverence and confirms that someone has entered and safely returned. Is the tile itself the door, or does it mark a deeper gateway? Hell or Paradise?

He closes his eyes and follows his servant in.

*

Hell and Paradise both lie beyond the tile, it turns out. He and Bole explore, map and analyse, but only the open ground and only in daylight. It is a fantastical but dangerous place. Wynter takes a close interest in the locals now. Someone else must know this secret.

He visits the tavern in Hoy for the chance of stray intelligence, and again destiny is kind. The carter talks to a gardener who talks to a farmer who confides in a tinker who speaks loosely. A wagon of children, finely dressed, was unloaded last year at Rotherweird Manor; and Sir Henry Grassal has turned schoolmaster in his dotage. They reputedly have unusual talents. Wynter smells opportunity. He gleans what he can of Sir Henry – kind and therefore vulnerable, knowledgeable and therefore easy to lure. He crafts a letter to fit.

Sir Henry finds Wynter's house pleasing, though no manor. The walls are panelled with carved oak. His host has a library and well-turned furniture. Wynter shows his knowledge without flaunting it. Mrs Wynter says little, but is considerate and kind. She compliments him on his riding and his horse.

Yet Sir Henry feels on edge. The servant has a predatory menace. Wynter's manners are *too* polished, over-perfect, like a diplomat striving for a treaty. In the library several shelves have their books double banked – forbidden texts behind, or just too little space?

At the end of a fine lunch, in terms of food and drink at least, Wynter dismisses his servant and his wife. He eases into the subject, but Sir Henry senses a well-worked design: again the diplomatic game.

Wynter slices two peaches with a silver knife. 'I have designed a new dwelling. I call it an ice-house. It will keep ripe fruit to the spring. We have a pond, shallow enough to freeze solid. Talking of early fruit, you teach, I understand.'

Ripeness in Spring: a code for his prodigies, all innuendo and nothing express – Sir Henry is on his guard.

'I like to pass on what I will shortly lose,' replies Sir Henry, who favours an epigram to block a probing thrust.

His hair curls silver as wire; his hands are knobbled with veins and stippled with freckles, and yet the face harnesses vitality. *He is in his early sixties*, Wynter guesses, *but not to be underestimated.*

'Such a resource,' Wynter whispers, as if to convey his ability to keep a secret.

An ill-chosen word, Sir Henry thinks, wearying of the game. 'The light fades. I must take leave of your excellent hospitality.'

Sir Henry is glad to have kept his cards close. As he steadies his horse, a breeze ruffles the hedge. Faces appear and disappear in the shaking leaves, faintly demonic, some with cheeks puffed out, some drawn in.

'Mr Bole's topiary,' smiles Wynter.

'*Incubi* and *succubi*,' adds the servant with a grin, only to earn a glare of rebuke from his master. This is not the desired impression.

Sir Henry is pleased to reach the bridge to Rotherweird Island and home.

FEBRUARY

I

Slickstone's Discovery

'Tonight we go exploring, you and I,' said Sir Veronal, handing the boy a coat and a notebook.

'What do I do?' The boy was broken in. He desperately wanted to please.

'You note the streets, you write them down.'

The actress watched. She had never felt so superfluous. At least in her other roles for Sir Veronal she had been permitted to speak. *Make your own part*, said her inner thespian voice; *improvise*.

'Go to bed,' added Sir Veronal, dismissing her from the room.

They made an incongruous pair, the ramrod-straight old man and the slouching boy with a lantern. Between ragged clouds stars shone brilliantly. A thin film of frost added sparkle to pavements, roofs and cobblestones. They talked in whispers.

'Give me the names, Rodney.'

'On your right – Coracle Run; on your left – Blue Stone Alley.'

Sir Veronal closed his eyes from time to time as if striving to find significance in these outlandish titles. The boy sensed his master's frustration. They hurried on.

'Escutcheon Place,' said Rodney. Again it appeared to mean nothing. Then, quite suddenly, Sir Veronal froze, a hound catching a wisp of scent.

'What?' interjected the boy.

'Quiet,' hissed Sir Veronal, 'absolute quiet.'

No sound from anywhere. The old man moved right, then left. 'This way, and not a sound.'

With a new alacrity, Sir Veronal hurried through side alleys and streets, the boy struggling to keep pace, until they emerged into one of the darker sections of the Golden Mean. Shop-signs swung in the wind. Sir Veronal stopped. 'Lantern.'

They peered in the window at an array of strange shapes and objects.

'*Torch.*'

The pencil-beam swept to and fro like a searchlight. Stuffed animals, a Zulu shield, stools, chairs and carved walking sticks appeared and disappeared.

Sir Veronal pointed. 'There!' he yelped.

'Just stones,' said the boy, now bored.

'Such colours! I know them. I *definitely* know them.'

Sir Veronal spoke with an intensity that energised the boy. The stones must be rare and valuable to have this effect. 'I'll smash the window. Easy, easy—'

Sir Veronal struck the boy on the cheek with the flat of his hand. 'You wait for orders, you don't suggest them.'

For once in his life the boy did not retaliate.

'What's the number of this shop?'

The boy ran both ways, worked it out. 'Twenty-two, the Golden Mean – *Baubles & Relics*.'

'Relics . . .' Sir Veronal savoured the word. 'Maybe, just maybe. Now . . . *home*.'

For appearances the actress's bedroom had a connecting door to Sir Veronal's, but he had never used it, and she had never been tempted. Money and power might be a recipe for sex appeal, but not on foundations this glacial. Her lack of attachment mattered to Sir Veronal, not because it might make her available to him, but because other intimates might lure her into indiscretion.

She had attended business dinners, receptions and contract signings as Lady Slickstone. She had talked art, superficial politics and social niceties with his guests, but never probed. She always ensured she looked the part she played – the Ambassador's Wife – which was a dull, unstretching role, but work all the same.

In this strange town, with its carved gables, towers and soundless transport, she felt in Sir Veronal a sea-change – fresh energy, but with it, intense frustration, and what struck her as an adolescent-like lack of self-knowledge. She concluded that despite the lavish investment, Sir Veronal did not yet know why he was here.

Outside, the planting had been completed in advance of the first frost. Only the finer touches awaited the spring. She watched her fictional husband and son return across the lawn, her bedroom lights off, peering from behind the curtain. She knew from Sir Veronal's stride that something of moment had occurred.

A dangerous but invigorating impulse seized her: the desire to investigate. She changed in the dark, opened the window and shinned down the drainpipe. She had a key to the postern gate and the security cameras were not yet operational. The pair's footprints, as if painted green on shiny white paper, brought her to the Golden Mean and *Baubles & Relics*. Excitement gripped her, the thrill of going off-script.

She returned little the wiser, but intrigued. Something in this shop of eccentric curios had aroused Sir Veronal's interest. She decided to keep eyes and ears open. Might not Rotherweird redefine her role? If Sir Veronal's character was growing richer under the town's influence, why not hers?

2

Oblong's Discovery

The following night the snow returned, and Oblong had supper with the Fanguins. Although they had been introduced by first names, Oblong continued to call Fanguin 'Fanguin', and vice versa: this was the way in Rotherweird. Fanguin insisted on calling his wife Bomber; whether in reference to her generous dimensions or her frank way of speaking, Oblong considered it indelicate to ask. She had skin as white as flour and hair as black as coal. To accentuate the contrast, she wore bright red lipstick. With large, warm eyes and an earthy, combative spirit, she was instantly likeable, despite the forbidding effect of her colouring. She had a gift for drawing people out of themselves.

'Damn fine risotto, Bomber,' trumpeted Fanguin, having finished well before his wife and guest. 'She taught cooking, but they terminated her employment with mine, for encouraging Flask in his "investigations" – when I wasn't.'

As Fanguin had given him Flask's notebook, Oblong was sceptical about this denial, but anxious that it might be dangerous ground for an outsider, he timidly broached a different subject.

'This town is packed with clever people. I'm unclear why you elected Mr Snorkel as Mayor? When he's—?'

'—a reptile?' suggested Fanguin.

'Surely a toad,' Bomber countered. 'He rakes off squillions. Meet his wife, and you'll understand why.'

Fanguin paced the room. 'It's a good question. I'm not sure we ever did elect him. He just sort of happened, just as his father did, and his grandfather before that.'

'But we could unelect him, and we don't even try.'

Fanguin acknowledged Bomber's point before continuing, 'It's practicalities: rubbish disposal, water supply, clean pavements – plus, we all think ourselves so clever, we'd never agree on anything.'

'You've missed the big one,' said Bomber. 'Snorkel keeps us from our past. Our independence depends on *not* investigating it. Snorkel knows how difficult that is. He allows the traditional festivals, but goes for anyone who pries too deep.'

'Like Flask,' said Oblong.

'Like him,' added Bomber, wagging a finger at her husband.

Emboldened by her candour, Oblong blurted out – and instantly regretted – 'If it's so dangerous, why give me his notebook?'

'You're a blithering idiot, Godfery Fanguin. You'll be the end of us all. First it's Flask's job, then yours, then mine, now his.'

'I'm a biologist,' Fanguin protested. 'I want to know why we are what we are. Why have we so many gifted people? Why are we alone in England left to our own devices?'

Bomber turned on Oblong. 'If you have any sense, destroy that notebook.'

And with that warning the conversation moved to more mundane topics before Oblong said his farewells and headed home. Under fresh snow the towers looked forbidding: fingers with whitened nails pointing skywards, windowsills standing out like knuckles. In the narrow but unusually straight Lost Acre Lane a childish impulse seized him: he *had* to throw a snowball.

He kneaded the fresh snow, aimed at the street sign and missed. He stooped to make another, only to hear a light thump from the roof behind him. He came up slowly from his stooping position, but Lost Acre Lane was empty in both directions. He walked to the next narrow lane – Groveway – equally empty. A second light thump and a crunching noise followed, still above his head.

He feared a mischievous child had been lured onto the roofs by the snowfall and that he would have to play rescuer in a landscape of slippery slates. He cried, 'Hello?' in both directions, and to his astonishment a long, thin pole appeared over the roofline, held by a slight figure who planted it on the sloping tiles. The pole bent almost double, then slowly, crazily unwound. Airborne, the figure became a creature of grace, apparently flying to the roof directly above Oblong's head. A balaclava masked the face.

'Now look here—!' he shouted.

The figure vaulted back, delivering a perfectly aimed snowball in midair, flush on Oblong's upturned forehead. The impact, the residual effects of the evening's hospitality and his natural clumsiness did the rest: Oblong fell heavily backwards. By the time he was back on his feet, the vaulter had gone.

Dazed, the letters of the street sign slipped and slid in front of his eyes: Lost Acre Lane. *Lost Acre . . . Lost Acre . . .*

Then he saw it: *Lost Acre . . . STOLE CAR.*

Flask had used a simple anagram – but what had he found in Lost Acre Lane? What of the letters and numbers beneath – *ASC* 1017? If he were right, they had nothing to do with a car at all, while being too high for a house number. The letters seemed random. Nor could he see anything unusual about Lost Acre Lane.

He wended his way back to his lodgings. With a cup of coffee and a spoonful of Vlad's whisky to sharpen the wits, he sat and racked his brain for an hour, but without success. As he resealed the diary, he felt the edge of loneliness. The Fanguins had entertained him generously, but they did not offer the joshing camaraderie of a contemporary. Gregorius Jones came closest, crying 'Hi Obbers!' whenever their paths crossed, and joining him from time to time at *The Journeyman's Gist.* Yet Jones' hearty exterior hid an impenetrable reserve whenever any subject of substance threatened. Fanguin's account of Jones' origins suggested a personal tragedy, buried deep. At least he could now add to his list of close encounters the mysterious vaulter, too lissom for Jones, or any other man.

Last but not least, he could not escape Flask. He felt a failure in comparison. Flask had fought for his subject, penetrated the defences of the locals and befriended them. He had uncovered the past too, his findings presumably recorded in the missing pages of his notebook. He decided that he owed it to Flask to keep an eye out for further leads, and to the Fanguins to do so *very* discreetly.

Several blocks away, leaning on a chimney, Valourhand watched the burning light at Oblong's window. Rotherweird's roofscape was her alternative universe: she knew the take-offs, the landings and the sight-lines. She would never have thrown a snowball at Oblong's predecessor. Unlike the callow Oblong, Flask had presence.

'Dazed, the letters of the street sign slipped and slid in front of his eyes.'

3

Hayman Salt's Discovery

Hayman Salt had not been back to *Baubles & Relics* since his sale of the stones, although he occasionally sidled past to see whether they remained in the window. He welcomed adverse weather. Without it he could not risk a visit to Lost Acre, his private fiefdom, his great and special secret. A leaden evening sky threatening snow came a close second to fog in clearing possible observers.

He wore a cape with a black hood and carried no provisions beyond his whisky flask, his idea of panacea. Rotherweird's one cobbled road ran from the two gatehouse bridges into the surrounding hills, but there were older, less conspicuous paths.

Salt crossed the wooden footbridge at the southwestern corner of the Island Field before plunging into a tangle of branches between two pastures. Here the snow had fallen more heavily. Drifts had formed in the hollows of the exposed northern and eastern slopes, but the landscape's loss of profile did not hinder him. Every tree remained distinctive to his botanist's eye, as good as a signpost. He elbowed and kicked his way through dense undergrowth into an open space with a sunken road beyond. Over the centuries, sheep, cattle and human feet had worn away the topsoil. The sides of the road were steep, the earth dark, peaty and rich. Salt walked on until he reached the basin of a large bowl with a circle of ancient beeches on its rim.

In the centre of this hollow, little affected by snow thanks to the canopy above, Salt scuffed away the dead leaves to reveal a white marble tablet a metre square and incised with a single flower. He stood on it and disappeared like a flicker of old film. He felt the familiar rush of head to feet, but uniquely, his instant arrival in Lost Acre was not painless. He sank to his knees, grimacing, joints wrenched, eyeballs smarting, air squeezed from the lungs and ears buzzing with tinnitus. Instinctively he checked the tile, which was intact. There must be some disturbance to the forces that powered it.

He slowly raised himself to standing. No snow here – the night sky sparkled with a crystalline quality undiluted by artificial light. The constellations were inverted in comparison to Rotherweird, but otherwise true to Rotherweird's time and season. Salt took deep satisfaction in being the only human visitor, Lost Acre's sole guardian and explorer.

He had in fact quickly moderated the latter role in the interests of self-preservation, now keeping to a square mile of grassland from the white tile to the stream below. Lost Acre's fauna mixed and matched, blossom with teeth, finned animals, bird-winged butterflies. Many of these freaks had proved to be both carnivorous and hostile. Salt had yet to discover the cause for this bizarre intermarriage of life forms, but the consequential dangers were clear. He had once ventured over the stream to the outer margins of the forest, only to be snared in thread-like wire and attacked by a creature so monstrous that its features still haunted his dreams. On another occasion he had climbed high into the rocky uplands on Lost Acre's misty rim, until predatory birds had driven him down.

In this chosen area of relative safety he mapped the ground botanically, lifting what he needed for his cultivars back home.

Salt had not been in for more than a month, not since his discovery of the mysterious stones. Tonight he had come for the snowdrop bulbs, with their distinctive yellow-purple spots around the neck of the flower, which would appear in Rotherweird as *Hayman's Galanthus*. He had already harvested *Hayman's Croci*, source of his present to Orelia Roc. Here both species were now inexplicably flowering out of season.

He used a small crystal light, anxious that a more conspicuous lantern might attract unwanted visitors, and worked away with his trowel, careful not to harm the colony's potential for further expansion. Before long, Salt became uneasy. The grass had grown unnaturally tall when it should be dying back. He even found stalks re-flowering among unusually heavy seed-heads. He kept his gloves on. Winged seeds from the forest were everywhere, far from their natural habitat. Some burrowed when disturbed, others snapped or flew away. He wondered whether Lost Acre's capacity for cellular rearrangement had brought with it a structural instability.

Within ten yards of the tile he found the first clutch of eggs, stippled brown and yellow but near transparent. From what he could make of the embryonic creatures inside, they were winged. In six years of visits, Salt had never found a single nest in the grass, but it now appeared that the avian lifeforms had abandoned their traditional nesting sites in the forest. Yet Salt could see no sign of earthquake, storm or drought. The earth felt no different. The silhouettes of the trees below appeared unchanged. He concluded that these behavioural changes did not reflect past disturbance but rather, apprehension of some future threat.

His concerns did not end there. He had found the stones nestling together within a few yards of the white tile, where he could not fail to find them. He had never encountered a malignant object before. To an atheist with no belief in the supernatural, the sensation had been inexplicable. He already regretted the sale, fearing he had been manipulated into bringing the stones to Rotherweird. If that was right, some other human either lived in Lost Acre, or travelled there from Rotherweird, and had him under observation.

These anxieties provoked Salt to break a golden rule. Bagging his bulbs and pocketing his trowel, he set off across the grassland, leaving old frontiers behind. The grass snagged at his waist, occasional tree seeds snapping at his heavy trousers, but he strode on, noting another disturbing oddity. The forest, normally a chorus of squawks, howls and warbles, stood mute as stone.

An easterly wind got up. The swaying grass and the moonstruck seed-heads conjured an impression of seafoam, Salt the swimmer, sometimes with the current and sometimes against it. In the scissory swish Salt thought he heard a hissy mumbling in Latin: *Et quis est, et quis est?*

'And who is this?' As a botanist he kept up his Latin, having excelled in the subject at Rotherweird School. Latin made the curriculum for its contribution to scientific treatise and linguistic logic, not for any doors it might open to the past, which were kept firmly shut. Salt, seeing nothing untoward, dismissed the words as a trick of the wind and hurried on.

He reached the extraordinary tree some twenty minutes later. It was large and squat in the bole, its two dominant bare upper branches stretched out, splay-fingered, like a haunting ghost in a child's cartoon. Beneath the highest branch, on the forest side, a patch of sky disobeyed the laws of physics, blocking out the starlight, all a-shimmer, but dark as water in a deep well. Salt instinctively suspected a kinship between this phenomenon and the stones.

Moving closer, he tripped over an iron bar, encrusted with rust, with what looked like a scooped cup near the protruding end. He disengaged it from the grass, again getting that sense of a malignant presence. A jumbled Christian motif came to him: the Tree of Knowledge of Good and Evil. Part of Lost Acre's appeal had been its freedom from any moral compass, a place whose inhabitants lived by the laws of nature, a choiceless universe. But an iron bar required hands, a furnace, mined materials, a designing intelligence and a purpose. Only the corrosion gave comfort: the bar had been cast long ago.

Salt froze. A stop-start movement in the grass, following his route from the white tile, looked too measured for the wind, more like a creature of stealth, stalking him. He tested the bar as a defensive weapon, only for it to snap like a biscuit. He peered hard. The twitching shadowplay suggested a sizable animal, the speed and decisive line a good sense of smell or sharp sight, or both. Another Latin word hissed from the sward – *nuntium habemus*: we have a messenger.

Salt realised he would not outrun his pursuer and anyway, flight would suggest he saw himself as a victim – a sure way, he suspected, of becoming one – so better to make a positive gesture without obvious hostility. He shook the light to a fierce glow and held it aloft.

Neither quadruped nor biped, neither human nor weasel, the creature that stood up to face Salt presented an uncanny mix of the two: animal in the pinched snout, the fur, the pricked ears and the predatory teeth; human in the eyes, hands (other than the clawed nails), the intelligence of the gaze, the pinkish patches of skin between the russet hair and the rough leather clothing. It held a spear, well balanced for throwing as well as thrust.

Salt had often wondered how Lost Acre's species, all of them hybrids, mixed and matched, and whether as a human he might be vulnerable to mutation. To those conundra he now added a new question: accident or design?

'*Sum Ferox*,' said the weaselman.

The creature's composite nature might not have shocked Salt, but its use of classical Latin did. What had the human half been, to have that first language? *All the same, a name well chosen*, thought Salt. Even though the creature held the spear upright, more on guard than the offensive, the face could not have been more predatory.

'Hayman Salt.'

To his amazement the weaselman shifted effortlessly into English. 'We need help,' said Ferox. 'There will be great turbulence.'

'Why?'

'*Saeculum.*'

Salt examined the creature's face. He saw cruelty and guile, but also anxiety. '*Saeculum* – you mean a cycle! That explains . . .' Salt gestured to the seed-heads in the meadow.

'Someone must go from here to there at the ripe time.'

Salt wondered if he had misheard. Ripe, or *right*? He had no chance to enquire for Ferox suddenly shouted, his head whipping round to face the forest, '*Fugite!*'

Salt needed no encouragement: luminous discs were emerging from the forest. Ferox seized Salt's crystal light and pointed back towards the tile, the path still visible like the wake of a ship. Salt understood: *I'll draw them off, you go.* As he ran, a glowing fungal disc flew past his head, offering a glimpse of recessed eyes and a thin crescent of shark-like teeth.

'*Saeculum,*' bellowed Ferox after him by way of a final reminder, but Salt did not look back until he was well away. He could see the weaselman fending off the attacking fungi with a warrior's

'*Sum Ferox.*'

grace, spinning and ducking, the spear dancing around his waist and head. With each successful strike, a light went out.

His journey back was even more painful than his journey there. He sank to his knees and groaned. Usually the tile quickly recharged. Unsettled, he waited and tried again, but the tile did not respond; it was feeling uncharacteristically lifeless to the touch.

The door had closed behind him.

Saeculum.

He paced the clearing, raging in the dark as snow continued to fall. He resorted to the only solace to hand, his whisky flask, swigging deeper with every new failure. He speculated that the stones' removal might be connected to the closure of the waypoint, even to Lost Acre's cyclical crisis. The theory only made his bad humour worse.

Now drunk, he kicked at the tile, connected only with fresh air and fell on his back, cracking his head. He closed his eyes and let the balm of the cold drift over him.

'How did you know he'd be here?' asked the first voice, which Salt recognised as Bill Ferdy's.

'A feeling in my bones,' replied the second voice.

'He weighs a ton.'

'He's a fool,' said the second, now half-familiar.

Salt came to as he was swung over someone's shoulder. He groaned.

'Hat . . . anything else?' resumed the second voice.

'Can't see nowt,' replied Ferdy.

'We'd better get him home quick,' said the second. 'In twenty minutes we'll have a blizzard.'

Salt, barely conscious, registered the remark and identified the second voice – Ferdy's neighbour, Ferensen, the man with a mysterious ability to predict warmth, frost, rain and snow hours ahead with uncanny accuracy. Behind his back, countrysiders called him the Rainmaker.

'Let me be!'

'Quiet – you've caused quite enough trouble already,' said Ferensen firmly. From his upside-down position Salt could make out the old man and his white hair.

'I didn't ask for your help,' cried Salt, and passed out before Ferensen could respond.

The Ferdys' farm came into view as the snow slackened, rows of hop-poles emerging from the gloom like a fleet at anchor. On the hill beyond the farmhouse stood the strange hexagonal tower where Ferensen lived, its position given away in the blanket of snow only by the firelight behind the windows.

'My place?' said Ferdy. 'My Megan does a mean pick-me-up.'

'Not half as mean as mine,' replied Ferensen, 'and I need to talk to him.'

Bill Ferdy deferred to Ferensen, as he always did, but his tenant's answer to how he had known Salt would be in that particular place – 'a feeling in the bones' – struck him at best as incomplete. He sensed trouble ahead.

Ferensen's tower comprised a single room where he thought, studied, exercised, cooked, watched the stars, stored books, slept, washed and lived. He would descend to the main house when in need of a bath or company. The room had the appearance of an intricate memory test, so cluttered were its contents.

Three sides of the hexagon had floor-to ceiling-bookshelves (and it was a high ceiling) signed in ornate gilt letters at the top: *Natural*, *Antiquity* and *Affairs of Men (various)*. Two adjacent walls accommodated a single bed and a contraption that served as a shower. The last wall, opposite the doorway, boasted a generous fireplace, wide and deep, with a wooden mantel carved with grotesques in the best Rotherweird tradition. Round it, like an audience, ranged a long sofa and several high-back Jacobean chairs with basketweave seats. From the ceiling, open to the rafters, hung charts of the heavens, the oceans and Rotherweird Westwood, the latter liberally marked with the location of rare fauna. Horizontal poles, held aloft by pulleys, held sticks, coats, hats, capes, a beekeeper's suit and a parachute. This miscellany suggested a reclusive polymath with no regard for the *History Regulations*.

The fire had an open grate on a stone hearth, its flue coiling along the wall like a snake before disappearing through the roof, whose exterior featured a bewildering mix of solar panels and nesting boxes awaiting the advent of Spring. The higher books were accessed by large movable steps with solid sides not unlike a mediaeval siege-engine in appearance.

'Throw him down here,' said Ferensen, pulling the sofa up to the fire, 'and let's get those outer clothes off.'

Salt started to sing:

> *'I remember the Duke of Buccleuch,*
> *He was taller than me*
> *And brighter than you . . .'*

'God save us, what a racket! Ferdy, get me the *Black Bodrum Nightraiser Special,* third shelf up.'

Ferdy found the tin in a line of other tins, all with remarkable names. A pungent aroma of coffee permeated the room.

Ferensen brewed a pot on the fire. 'You don't deserve this,' he muttered, 'but needs must.'

Ferdy held Salt's head still as the old man poured. The effect was instantaneous.

'God save us,' spluttered Salt.

'It's all right, Bill; go and tell Megan you're back.' Ferensen added, 'You did well. Odds are you saved his life.'

As so often, the brewer was impressed by Ferensen's energy. Ferensens had lived in the hexagonal building as long as Ferdys had lived on the farm. They would disappear for decades, but a returning Ferensen always had a key to the house. The *History Regulations* prohibited the preservation of family photographs and diaries after the death of their owner, so nobody knew what ear-lier Ferensens had looked like. His father had known one, and his grandfather another before that. The house had been empty during his childhood, but after his father's death, this Ferensen had turned up. He had never mentioned his ancestors, and Ferdy did not ask.

Ferensens kept certain rules. They never went to town, and insisted on complete privacy. Their name – always straight Ferensen – was not to be mentioned by countrysiders in town, and this injunction was religiously obeyed. The Ferensens were *their* secret, contributing much to the rural community, with their unparalleled knowledge of horticulture, trees and animal illnesses. This Ferensen taught countryside children arcane sub-jects not on the School curriculum, with flair.

Bill Ferdy hesitated before leaving his friend. He had been wres-tling with whether to consult Ferensen about the strange offer made by the late-night visitor to *The Journeyman's Gist*. He needed advice, but did not want to trouble the old man. He let it pass.

'Where was I?' asked Salt, voice and intonation restored.

'You tell me,' replied the old man, hanging up their damp outer clothes on racks the other side of the fire, while surreptitiously checking Salt's pockets.

'Somewhere southish . . . ?'

'You can do better than that.'

'Near some beeches.'

'Imagine two lines running straight from the end of Old Ley Lane and Lost Acre Lane – follow them into the country until they meet.'

'Something like that,' conceded Salt.

'You promised me. Nobody goes in. *Ever.*'

'I only go to check on things.'

'It's unforgiveable – and highly dangerous.'

'I only got attacked once. Anyway, nobody can be now. Once I got back, the waypoint closed.'

'You sure?'

Salt was now moving into a hangover phase. 'Of course I'm bloody sure.' Salt peered into the cup. 'What the hell is this?'

'Coffee special enough to shake a sot from his dreams, but sadly, it can't cure ingratitude.'

Salt muttered a near-inaudible word of apology. Despite a mild nausea, his mental faculties felt enhanced. Ferensen's coffee was clearing his head like balsam. He had an insight: Ferensen alone with his books and his objects needed company.

'You should get a dog.'

Ferensen said nothing. Salt thought of Lost Acre's twisted fauna – birds with snouts, rodents with scales, carnivorous fungi – and a disturbing insight came to him.

'Ferensen the naturalist has no cat and no dog. I say something happened in Lost Acre – why you won't go back. Why you can't have animals here while you sleep.'

Ferensen flexed his fingers at the fire as if casting a spell, and then changed the subject. 'Ferdy brings news from town. There are strange events. The School historian disappears. The Manor reopens. Now an old way closes. Might they be connected?'

'There's another. In Lost Acre something is seriously wrong.'

'Lost Acre *is* wrong. It's an abomination. The closing is all for the good.'

'You want Lost Acre to die – its creatures, its plants?'

'What do you mean – die?'

'The ground was choked with seed. Fliers and crawlers are laying on open ground.' There were few pure birds or insects in Lost Acre; the orders mixed and matched so that one talked of fliers and crawlers. 'It's all out of season. They must sense cataclysm. I went further than I've ever been and I saw—' Salt stalled. His selfish desire for secrecy resurfaced. He did not want to share this discovery, even with Ferensen.

'I know what you saw.'

'I don't think so.'

'You saw a patch of slippery sky. I can show you on your map.'

With irritation Salt realised Ferensen had been through his clothes, but he could hardly protest. Ferensen spread out Salt's simple chart on a table. The drawing was competent, the annotations obscure, but Ferensen could read them.

'The "T" is the tile entry in the grassland. You have no annotations in the woodland because you have not been back, wisely taking my advice.' Ferensen turned his attention to the irregular lettered shapes, interlocking like misshapen Venn diagrams. 'Plant colonies. Weird mixes of our terrestrial species. Your letters approximate to our nearest relative. At a guess – here – grass of Parnassus, although in Lost Acre the flowers are red, not white, and the stems are sticky.' To Salt's astonishment Ferensen either knew or guessed most of the rest. Having made his point, Ferensen resumed, 'You have not marked the patch of sky, or the great tree that stands near it.' His voice quavered in a rare show of emotion. 'It's almost exactly here.' He placed a finger at the very edge of the paper.

Ferensen was right. Salt stuttered, 'How can you know? You haven't been in for years.'

'That patch of sky has been there for a very long time – at a guess, from the beginning, when primordial explosion or collision created Lost Acre. I call it the mixing-point.'

Ferensen's display of knowledge encouraged Salt to greater candour. 'I met an extraordinary creature, even by Lost Acre's standards – half weasel, half human.'

Ferensen's face clouded over as if an ancient pain had been dragged to the surface. 'Ferox,' he said.

Again Salt was taken aback, and again he asked the same question. 'How can you know?'

Ferensen ignored the question. 'He let you live. I'd like to know the reason.'

'He asked for help. He kept saying "*Saeculum*".'

'A cycle – the natural age-span of a person or a population.'

'Or a place,' replied Salt. 'I have a theory. Rotherweird and Lost Acre are indivisible. This valley has the only way in, and others before us knew, otherwise Lost Acre Lane would not be named and aligned as it is. Way back, government feared the secret would spread and Lost Acre's monsters might escape, so they gave us independence and banned the study of history. What they didn't know is that Lost Acre is volatile, and may self-destruct. What we don't know is what happens to us if it does.'

'*We* would be better for it.'

The odd emphasis was accompanied by a lack of conviction in Ferensen's voice. Not for the first time Salt sensed the old man was withholding as much as he revealed.

'Why does Ferox speak Latin?'

'He's older than you could possibly imagine.' Ferensen paused. 'The mixing-point confers great longevity – at a price. He must have said more.'

'We were attacked by creatures from the forest.'

'What sort of creature?' The question came with a strange urgency.

'Like the fungi you find on dead trees . . . only with eyes and teeth.'

Ferensen visibly relaxed as Salt remembered something else Ferox had said.

'Ferox seemed to think I was a messenger. He used the word *nu* – *nuntius*.' Salt suddenly felt wearier than he had ever felt in his life.

The last words he heard from Ferensen carried a tone of wry amusement. 'The effects of *Black Bodrum Nightraiser Special* are well established: instant recovery of consciousness, a short, sharp period of hangover and ten minutes of clarity, ending in a deep and restorative slumber.'

Seconds later the botanist began to snore. Ferensen poured himself the remains of the coffee. Lost Acre die – and all her creatures with her? Ghosts from the past assailed him. He, Ferensen, had a duty to try – but how, when he could not get in? And when the threat, whatever it was, seemed beyond human intervention? He recalled mention long ago of a black tile, which did not work. Suppose it opened when the white one closed? He determined to try to find it.

As for Ferox, whose messenger did he think Salt was? He could conceive of only one person – but not possible, *surely* not, God forbid not.

Ferensen stood up. He liked this weather, his tower cocooned in flakes of frozen moisture. He consulted his skin. The snow would stop in an hour. In three the sky would clear. Warmth and thaw were at least two days off. This he knew as fact, not opinion. Where had this gift come from? What had they done to him all those years ago?

'Like the fungi you find on dead trees . . . only with eyes and teeth.'

4

Of Invitations

Barely two weeks into term time Oblong received a message, unsettling in its terseness: Mayor's Office, 11.30 a.m. today. *Important.*

Oblong glanced at the rest of the post. Two fellow tenants were in receipt of a smart envelope with a heraldic device on the back – an upright hooded weasel clasping a staff. The thickness of the card inside left little doubt. *Typical*, thought Oblong, *locals get invitations, I get orders.*

In Rotherweird you measured your communal standing by how long the Mayor kept you waiting. Oblong was finally admitted to Snorkel's inner sanctum at 12.45 p.m. The large room exuded more money than taste. At the Mayor's end, the furniture was antique, but no one piece fitted with another. The paintings were over-polished; the pile of the carpet so thick that your shoes all but disappeared. Incongruously, a row of plastic chairs faced Snorkel's imposing desk. Snorkel invited Oblong to pull one up.

'Form IV had better be behaving,' said Snorkel gravely, 'because you'll shortly have a new pupil with most discerning parents. Smith will give you further instructions.'

Snorkel spoke as if he were the general, Oblong a private, and the Headmaster a lowly corporal overseeing the menial details.

'Is that all?' stammered Oblong.

Snorkel held up a thick, shiny cream envelope, identical to the two he had seen on the front doormat at Number 3 Artery Lane that morning.

'When yours arrives, accept promptly, dress properly and do not let us down. Our host was most particular about inviting you. I said he was erring on the inclusive side, but then I suppose it's a big house.'

The Mayor dismissed him with a lordly flick of the hand.

Oblong walked the streets, mulling over the cryptogram ASC 1017. He favoured a book and a page number, but knew no title with those initials – another brick wall. On his return home a creamy envelope awaited him.

Orelia thought she knew her fellow citizens by appearance at least, but the man in the doorway of *Baubles & Relics* confounded her. He cut a striking figure: tall, with an unsettling pinkish-white pallor to the face, and exotic dress – a shirt of Indian style under a heavy overcoat, hand-made brogues polished to a dazzling shine, mohair trousers with a crease as sharp as a knife and an ebony stick topped with a silver weasel's head. She thought him elderly at first sight, but revised her assessment as he strode vigorously into the shop.

'I was passing.' The voice was silky.

'There are labels for most things. Any queries – just ask.'

Her unusual visitor advanced two steps into the shop and stood stock-still. He looked high and low. His nostrils puckered. 'You had four stones.'

'Ah – the Rotherweird comfort stones.'

'Comfort stones?'

'A mediaeval parlour game.'

'I trust you still have them?' The voice edged higher, anxiety beneath the cool exterior.

She assumed he must be a friend of the Mayor. Outsiders hardly ever came here. She fetched the stones and he placed them in the flat of his hands and closed his eyes. Clearly this man, whoever he was, had no interest in parlour games.

Eyes snapped open. 'Price?'

'I'll have to ask my aunt.'

'Assume your aunt would say five times what you paid for them, cash preferred.'

Orelia decided she had discretion to accept generous offers. 'Two hundred should do.'

This time the smile was fuller. He produced four immaculate fifty-guinea notes from a crocodile-skin wallet. She gave him the stones, and the label too. 'Bag?'

He ignored the offer, glancing at the label instead. '"*Provenance unknown*" never cuts ice with me. Everything comes from some-where or someone. Please find out.'

He placed the label on the table and reached once more into his coat pocket and produced a blank envelope. 'Name?'

'Orelia. Orelia Roc.'

'As in the fabulous bird?'

'As in the fabulous bird.'

'Miss?'

She nodded. He wrote her name on the envelope and handed it over.

In what appeared to be a miracle of timing Mrs Banter appeared in the doorway, nose twitching in the presence of money, and outsider money at that. 'What are you selling?'

'The comfort stones, Aunt. This gentleman has paid most generously.'

Mrs Banter picked the label off the table. 'It says "price on application". That means application to *me*. Those stones are most unusual.'

'He paid two hundred guineas,' whispered Orelia, grimacing apologetically at the purchaser, who gave Mrs Banter an ambiguous, lopsided smile – dislike or amusement, or both?

'That's a deposit, not a price – these are rare stones, if not unique.'

'I assume by "deposit", you mean half the price.' The man took out his wallet and placed another two hundred guineas on the table. He did not relinquish possession of the stones. His manner brooked no argument.

'Done,' said Mrs Banter with a self-satisfied 'learn from me' look at her niece.

The stranger offered the same smile again and left.

'I'm not sure that was wise,' chided Orelia, but her anxiety did not touch an exultant Mrs Banter.

'Hold your nerve, and never take the first offer. Have we ever done such a deal? A hundred guineas a bead! Anyway, didn't you see the smile? He's a man of the world. He respects a woman of business.'

Orelia had interpreted the smile differently, but she said nothing.

Mrs Banter pocketed a hundred guineas and breezed out with an accounting instruction: 'Go light in the ledger and treat our little premium as a tip.'

Inside the stranger's envelope, distinguished by a hooded weasel gripping a staff, Orelia found an imposing invitation:

Sir Veronal and Lady Slickstone
At Home

∽

Saturday 27th February
Blue Lagoons and Canapés
6.30 p.m.

∽

RSVP
Rotherweird Manor

∽

Please bring this invitation with you

Everyone knew the Manor, a ruined Elizabethan building hitherto cordoned off from view. She had heard talk of a dodgy deal between Snorkel and a wealthy interloper. She recalled her unease with the stones and her suspicion that they combined to do something. She recalled Salt's similar misgivings. Had Sir Veronal felt the same way? If so, why pay so generously? His manner had been peculiar, as if he sensed a significance he could not articulate.

Nonetheless they had yielded a handsome profit and an invitation, so all in all, the sale of the stones had been worth it. Only one question escaped Orelia's attention. Mrs Banter rarely visited the shop in trading hours. How had she managed such immaculate timing?

Sir Veronal entered his library, an intimate room with fine panelling, locked the door behind him and placed the stones on his Renaissance desk. Against the fine marquetry they looked incongruous, beggars at a banquet. He had no inkling of what they did or where they came from, but he felt an inexplicable emotional response of piercing intensity. Half an hour of geological research had failed to identify their type, but he found the rarity encouraging.

Rotherweird had to be the place he had left all those years ago. He had come home. The next-door room would shortly be filled with his personal records; all he had to do now was retrieve his lost youth.

He pressed the frieze on the top of the desk, releasing a hidden compartment into which he deposited the stones, then turned to the last tranche of invitations lined up in their envelopes on the butler's tray, ready for the evening post. He hunted through and removed one envelope. He had overpaid; now it was her turn. He tossed the envelope into the blazing fire and watched the name Mrs Banter curl and darken before bursting into flame.

Beside the Herald's invitation to the Manor opening lay a much older letter, still sealed, which testified to his gravest duty: keeping

Rotherweird from her past. He ran his index finger over the medallion of red wax, feeling the lines of the ruff, the pleats of the skirt, the orb and sceptre in the outstretched hands. Elizabeth I, *Gloriana*. The tiny face wore a no-nonsense expression, and rightly so. The Great Seal of State adorned only documents of the highest moment. The ink, though faded, retained its clarity.

To the heirs and afsigns of Hubert Finch – only to be opened on fufferance of death, when the direft peril from the other place ftalks the fief of Rotherweird.

All Finch's ancestors had held this document, and none had opened it. His task was to ensure that remained the position.

He did not know the location of the 'other place', or indeed its nature. He had no inkling of the peril to which it referred. He knew only the importance of keeping both hidden from view.

The invitation had prompted him to check this ancient instruction. The reopening of the Manor disobeyed precedent and, he suspected, the *Rotherweird Statute*. Old houses hold the past; let them breathe and they exhale secrets – the very reason why his own house had always been off-limits to everyone save his wife and son, and the *archivoire* even to them. What had brought Sir Veronal to this backwater? Who was he? And the hardest question: why would a billionaire outsider choose Rotherweird of all places as his retirement venue? He sensed deeper currents and cursed Snorkel's venality.

He penned an acceptance. Time to enter the lion's den.

Vixen Valourhand chose an isolated part of the Island Field to practise her unusual choice of weapon. A line of pollarded willows yielded a row of stumps, varied in circumference and height off the ground.

Now or never, she had decided on receiving her invitation: her one chance to make an impression on Rotherweird society. Everyone who was anyone would be there.

With uncanny accuracy Flask had predicted the outsider's arrival, his wealth, the restoration of the Manor and even the holding of a party as a first step to seducing the town. He had added a layer of forbidden knowledge – the original owner had, centuries earlier, been a distinguished scientist and teacher, which only doubled the insult of giving the keys to the Manor to a plutocrat from wider England. *Protest*, he had suggested glibly, but that was easier said than done. Waving a placard would not do. She had to articulate an elegant demonstration and an equally elegant escape.

As to the first, she had invested much time in a costume with two linings and flat projectors between them. She had tried several different materials before achieving the desired effect. Additional features were designed to compensate for her lack of physical height. It would be a crowded room, and she must stand out.

As to the second, she expected security, hence the need for a weapon that would immobilise, but again, with style.

She kept her plan to herself. She had succumbed to Strimmer's cold good looks for a time, but conquest achieved, Strimmer quickly moved on. Independent action was her only weapon for making a point to her controlling former tutor.

Her thoughts returned to Flask and his delicate speciality, history, and how it worked the past to reveal the future. She reflected too on the price, for his discoveries had been quickly followed by his disappearance.

The light began to fail as she picked up the small device on the ground by her feet, cocked her wrist and aimed for the left hand stump, its profile not unlike a human leg.

Bill Ferdy's working day began with his arrival soon after dawn in a mobile market stall – the Ferdys shared one with other country-siders as an outlet for their excess farm produce – through the North Gate and down the Golden Mean to Market Square, followed by the walk to *The Journeyman's Gist*. Countrysiders freely gave each other lifts in and out, for not everyone sold in town every day. Winter, Ferdy felt, gave the pub added worth and purpose, a counterbalance to the elements and the season for *Feisty Peculiar*, his most potent brew.

The letter on the doormat could only have been delivered by hand, for no ordinary post ever preceded his arrival. That in itself was troubling.

On heavy-duty official paper beneath the date and the arms of the Rotherweird Town Hall it read:

Dear Mr Ferdy,

We write to inform you that on November 1st of last year your licence to sell liquor and foodstuffs expired by effluxion of time. No application to renew has been received by the Licensing Office. Accordingly your continuing trade since that date has been in breach of the law.

Further, on December 26th two packets of mixed nuts (hazel and walnuts) were sold one day past their sell-by date.

Your tenancy is hereby terminated on twenty-one days' notice pursuant to Clause 14(3)(x)(ii) of the Lease.

Provided all fittings and chattels are removed within twenty-eight days of today's date, and in view of your past service to the community of Rotherweird, no further action will be taken. If this offer is not complied with, you may expect to suffer the full rigour of the law.

Yours sincerely,

Secretary to the Licensing Committee

(Chair: S Snorkel Esq, Mayor & Chief Magistrate)

The charge was strictly true, but the authorities had accommodated Bill Ferdy's laxity in administrative matters for twenty-one years, sending a reminder two weeks after the expiry date, and Ferdy had always then complied. This year there had been no reminder.

His generosity of spirit brought slowness in joining up the dots of the dark intrigues of others. Only on reading the letter a second time did he register the change in tone and the unusual inclusion of Snorkel's name at the end. Then he remembered Slickstone's visit, and the brutal reality dawned: this time there would be no clemency.

He hit the bar with his fist and let out a single cry, that of an animal in pain.

The office of the Town Clerk, Gorhambury, lurked in a byway off the grander passages of the Mayoral Suite on the first floor of the Town Hall. Municipal staff theorised that Gorhambury – no one knew his first name, if ever he had one – had swallowed in infancy the twenty-eight volumes of the collected *Rotherweird Regulations* and had been digesting them ever since. He could recite from memory tracts of clauses and cross-references on subjects as diverse as planning and fireworks, transport and highwire entertainment. Snorkel might make the political decisions, but Gorhambury gave them life, for it was he who regulated the intricate machinery of the town's administration.

He looked the part: slight of build, with an incipient stoop, skin the colour of faded paper and a gaunt face whose expressions inhabited a narrow range between mild concern and deep anxiety. He wore three-piece suits (jettisoning his waistcoat only at week-ends), white shirts, dark navy blue ties unspoilt by any hint of decoration and brogues as shiny as liquorice. His work absorbed all his energies, leaving no appetite for love, fine food or the social whirl. He never complained, despite being taken for granted by the Mayor, and he brought to his interpretation of the law a firm sense of fairness and decency.

Files, immaculately ordered, filled shelves on the walls and cardboard drums with green plastic tops that dotted the floor like mushrooms. Lines of paper clips, colour-coded for different subjects, stood in serried ranks, awaiting commitment to the fray. Staples hindered efficient updating, in Gorhambury's expert opinion.

He did not have a lunch hour, but the Town Hall emptied between one and two, so providing a window for quiet study or off-the-record meetings – not that Mrs Banter's entry suggested any wish for discretion.

She swept in. 'Well – have you remedied this injustice?'

'Slow down, Mrs Banter.'

'You got my letter – they lost my invitation.'

'You were on the list.'

'Of course I was.'

'Only . . .'

'Only *what*?'

Gorhambury pushed Sir Veronal's short letter across the table:

We appreciate your list as an advisory aid, but the party is mine. Whatever your shortcomings, I do not make clerical mistakes – the unasked are not asked. Arrange security, as you know the faces, and deliver quotations including hourly rates well in advance.

The peremptory style and the detailed eye in money matters added to Mrs Banter's frustration. She and Sir Veronal had qualities in common; they would surely blossom in each other's company.

'You did mention me?'

'That would have been indelicate. I suggested the possibility of an "accidental omission" from the list we provided.' Gorhambury had no reason not to attribute Mrs Banter's omission to a clerical slip. She was a staple of Snorkel's evening *soirées* and surely a shoe-in for such a party.

He had rarely seen such misery on a human face. Parties in his view flourished while true civilisation burned, show-pieces for wastrels and torture for the diligent. This jaundiced view was coloured by self-interest, for who would talk to him? He did not do jokes. He did small talk about regulations. To date he had kept his invitation to himself. Mrs Banter's facial expression sealed it.

'Have mine.' He pushed the stiff white card across the desk. Mrs Banter ran her thumb over the embossed weasels, such *class*. 'I've security to organise – I'll be there anyway,' he added.

Mrs Banter's scruples evaporated. Snatching the invitation, she managed no more than a '*dear* Gorhambury' before rushing out, lest her benefactor change his mind. The fresh air tickled her conscience. At the Rotherweird Bank she transferred a paltry three guineas to the Town Clerk's personal account. He was only a clerk, after all. The gift went unnoticed. Gorhambury had little time for his own affairs.

Uplifted, all senses heightened, Mrs Banter passed the queues at *Farthingales* and *Titfertat* and headed for her dressmaker.

5

The Black Tile Opens

Lost Acre's fauna divided into three kinds: the pure species, untouched by the mixing-point, the random constructs from species that entered the mixing-point at the same time and the few creatures fashioned by her human visitors. Ferox was aware of two bouts of activity by humans – the one that created him, around the time of the Roman invasion, and the second, centuries later but still centuries ago, when they wore leather and velvet with ruffs around their necks. The man-made creations had mostly failed or been hunted down. Only he from the first period, and the cat and the monstrous creature in the forest lair from the second, had survived, so far as he knew.

Ferox considered himself fortunate. He and the weasel had complementary minds and characters. His human half had welcomed the enhanced smell and sight of a paradigm hunter, as had the weasel the human's wider intelligence. They did not coexist, they merged. From his human days he missed only the companionship, the legion's joshing camaraderie. Among Lost Acre's occasional visitors he had made just one friend, and he had not been seen for centuries.

He had been in Lost Acre in 1017 and so recognised these symptoms – the violent swings in the weather, Nature at her most defensive, burrowing, reproducing, storing up food, all the strategies of survival. He remembered too the moment of salvation, for *moment* it was, not a gradual improvement, but a spell, a flash of divine intervention. Had he known the mechanism, he would have tried to replicate it now. In his ignorance he could only watch the ways in and out and hope for a role to play.

He smelled the misshapen cat before he saw it, slouching through the grass, one of his kind, an amalgam of cat, boy and fire, but a creation from the age of leather, velvet and lace. It returned to Lost Acre through the white tile from time to time, but was rarely seen. Ferox dipped into the grass, trusting to his other senses. The cat tried the white tile and predictably failed. Ferox took the closing to be another sign of Lost Acre's degenerating fabric. To his surprise the creature did not give up but descended to the stream, picking its way through a network of webs gleaming like wire. Beyond lay the black tile and its guardian, too dangerous a place for even Ferox to venture.

The first use of the black tile in centuries sent a ripple of energy through Rotherweird and Lost Acre, although it registered with only a few.

Ferox felt it.

Sir Veronal, sitting in the chair in his study and surrounded by the recently installed records of his commercial empire, felt it: a stab of pain behind his left temple, a symptom of the slight tear to the microscopic membrane in his temporal cortex that the mixing-point had created and which served to suppress his early memories. They still lay undisturbed, like bubbles on an ocean bed, but in sleep and over time they would rise, one by one, to squeeze through this tiny hole and release their messages. Picked up by neurons and transmitted across the wider brain, they would eventually cohere to reveal to Sir Veronal his youth, and a second chance to fulfil his destiny.

Something else stirred too, a prickling in the fingers and an atavistic sense of lost power regained. Instinctively he reached for the hidden drawer and the stones.

*

Form VIb was Rotherweird School's one problem class, inhabited by mature pupils whose academic standards were below the norm. Gregorius Jones, the PE teacher who had welcomed Oblong on his first arrival in the staffroom, had recently been promoted to Form Master, an inspired appointment, for he encouraged the sporty and gave the artistic licence to flourish.

He would enter every morning with the same *brio*, disconcertingly stopping every three yards to do a sequence of squats before addressing his class (he taught no academic subject) with the same liturgy: 'On your chairs! Ten small jumps, arms out on every other one – no pleasure was ever had by an agile mind in a dilapidated body. The Temple of the Spirit is the classroom. Where's the Temple of the Body?'

'The gym,' answered the class in chorus as Jones led the way there for a brief ten-minute warm-up.

On this particular morning Jones hung from the rings, high above the mat, supported by only one foot.

'I call this "the hanging wasp",' he proclaimed, upside down, slowly waving his arms.

Suddenly a tremor disturbed Jones' usual flawless performance; he jerked twice and fell.

Miss Trimble, whose porterage duties extended to first aid, dismissed the class and tended the unconscious gymnast: nothing more serious than concussion, a badly bruised shoulder and a cut eye. She worried briefly about brain damage after he muttered repeatedly the words '*vespa pendens*'.

In ten minutes he was his old self. 'Well-known technique,' he declared, 'you show them how *not* to do it. My minor injuries will make them concentrate.'

She asked a pupil, who revealed that *vespa pendens*, 'the hanging wasp' – Jones' name for the exercise – had led to his fall. Jones was widely characterised as brawn without brains, yet he had muttered Latin when dazed. Come to that, 'the hanging wasp' was a peculiarly imaginative name for a supposed dullard to conjure. Unlike the other men who drifted through the porter's lodge, never shy about their cleverness or station, Gregorius Jones offered more than met the eye. Intrigued, she resolved to investigate.

Hayman Salt stood in the wood and imagined the scent of bluebells, *Endymion non-scriptus* – an elaborate name for such an unassuming plant. They would soon be everywhere, a brand new carpet without sign of wear. In years gone by Rotherweirders would come here for the beauty of it, but none did now, save perhaps Rhombus Smith and his wife – too far for most to walk, too many competing pleasures. This was old, forgotten England. Come spring, there would be few bees; birds and insects too were terribly diminished in number and variety.

An old rage burned – so many startling gifts, so much knowledge gleaned along the way, and yet what a mess Mankind had made of everything.

But who was he to rage against anyone? He flipped between Rotherweird and Lost Acre for his own entertainment and profit – the world's most extraordinary playground, with the most exclusive membership: himself. Ferensen might chide him for going in, but who was he to talk? He knew Lost Acre inside out.

He could never get a straight answer as to who the Ferensens were or where they came from. This Ferensen acted as the country-siders' Mayor in all but name, as Snorkel's rule neglected them. He had green fingers and a green mind, curing cattle, constructing water wheels, saving trees and reviving lost streams. Ferensen kept a courteous distance from those he helped, perhaps the consequence of his cerebral way of thinking, perhaps some undeclared sadness. His mystical gift also set him apart: Ferensen the Rainmaker, who disliked the warmth of the summer sun.

Yet Ferensen alone might make sense of the tangle of recent events. Salt could not understand the imminent closure of *The*

Journeyman's Gist, which Ferdy had revealed to him in confidence. No less worrying was the reopening of the Manor and the rush of invitations to anyone who was anyone. What was Snorkel thinking of? Who was this 'Slickstone'? And why had not a single country-sider been asked? Several were significant players in Rotherweird society, after all.

These concerns had prompted this early-morning meeting, arranged via the usual chain from Boris Polk to Bill Ferdy (via Boris' pigeon Panjan) and on to Ferensen.

While Salt thought of Ferensen, Ferensen, crossing the field towards him, thought of Bill Ferdy. The removal of his friend's livelihood had been an inexplicable strike at an institution that had served Rotherweird well for centuries, not to mention costing Ferensen his main source of intelligence.

Salt and Ferensen shook hands with an old-world formality before Salt came straight to the point. 'The workmen have finished and the invitations are out, but he never shows himself, and nor does his wife. Why keep yourselves hidden and then ask half the town in?'

'Your outsider is after impact. He wants to win you over.'

'He's as rich as Croesus and has Snorkel in his pocket – why does he need us? And why would he need a pub?'

'Information – where else are people less discreet?'

Salt had not considered this possibility. Ferensen had a gift for lateral thinking.

'Are you going to this party?'

'After *Snorkel's Petunia*? You must be joking.'

'I need a spy with an eye for detail, but we need to play safe – it must be someone who doesn't know me.' Salt nodded, still irritated by Ferensen's lack of openness. 'It's too much of a coincidence: the Manor opens, this man arrives, Lost Acre goes into crisis.'

'And Flask disappears,' added Salt.

'Ah, yes, your historian. I'd like to have met him.'

'I'm not sure you would – he was a slippery customer.'

Their breath coiled in the cold air. 'More rain in twenty minutes. Come back and cheer Ferdy.'

They wandered across the meadow, debating Nature and her decline. Then, casually, Ferensen let slip his news. '*Saeculum*,' he whispered.

'Sorry?'

'The black tile has opened – and it's in use.'

Salt struggled to remember. Ferensen had mentioned the black tile on the snowswept night of his rescue. He felt a surge of excitement. His way into Lost Acre, the white tile, had closed, but maybe he could save the place after all. 'By whom?'

'Or what. It may be an accident. Let's hope so . . .'

'How do you know?'

'In the bones.'

'Where is the black tile?'

'I believe it's in the forest somewhere.'

'Where is it *here*?'

'I don't know. It's never worked in our time.'

Salt read the emotion in Ferensen's face as neither fear nor anxiety, but something deeper: despair. Yet again he felt Ferensen was dealing in riddles and half-truths. How could he know of the second tile's existence without knowing where it was? And how could he feel it open 'in his bones'?

6

Sir Veronal Holds a Remarkable Party

Fortune favours the rich, or so it appeared on that Saturday evening. After days of intermittent showers, Rotherweird lay bathed in the crystalline light of that peculiar timbre that follows rain, and it was warm for the time of year. Most shops closed half an hour early. From five-thirty few adults of any note in the community could be seen. They were inside, wrestling with cosmetics, hair-driers, costume choices, scruples and mounting excitement.

Conventional wisdom construes an invitation to drinks at 6.30 p.m. as requiring attendance from 7.00 p.m. onwards, but this invitation had an air of stiff command. They must be on time.

The Manor, the oldest and grandest property in town, had been sealed off for generations, but few had thought to ask the glaring question: why had Snorkel changed a policy of centuries in favour of an outsider?

Sir Veronal arranged for the route from Market Square to be marked by rose petals strewn on the pavement. Form IV's pupils carried out the task for a golden guinea apiece. The Headmaster had no say in the matter, and no explanation was offered for their selection. Two were excluded on Sir Veronal's insistence – the countrysiders, Gwen Ferdy and Ned Guley.

As the hour hand on Doom's Tocsin slid past six, partygoers wound their way north, Snorkel having engaged the Town Hall's lowlier employees to escort them with lanterns. Faces of all ages peered down as the uninvited sought participation, however minor, in this seismic event in Rotherweird's history. Without (in most cases) meaning to patronise, the invited waved back, as guests to villagers at a country wedding.

The Mayor led the way in a powder-blue shirt and silvery tie under a Victorian frockcoat, his wife beside him in a stylish black confection sprinkled with crystals.

The guests halted at the main gate, ominously still closed. Some had counted on coloured balloons on the gateposts; others on a full orchestra; but all were taken aback by the lack of any festive welcome and the swivelling eyes of security cameras.

At half past six to the minute the gate swung open, revealing a tantalising glimpse of an inner archway leading to manicured lawns and topiary hedges, all bathed in an artificial light with no apparent source.

The rush through the archway slowed as the first arrivals took in the grandeur of the Manor and the quality of the restoration. The brick glowed a gentle but ripe apricot-pink. Old cement and new repointing merged seamlessly. Stained glass gleamed in the leaded windows. Heavy black nails pockmarked the massive oak front door.

Nothing suggested a ruin revived. Espaliered pear trees, pressed flat against the walls like candelabra, implied the loving care of centuries. Gravel pathways fringed with herbs wound in intricate patterns. Sculptures posed in arbours and archways, finely executed, contemporary with the house and often grotesque in design.

Slickstone had added one personal signature: hooded weasels with half-human faces adorned topiary hedges, the single flag above the central keep and the weather vanes at either end of the house. For an outsider, these grotesques had a disturbingly 'Rotherweird' feel in Finch's expert opinion. He had checked his secret records from their inception in 1572 and found no trace of a Slickstone.

The Manor's front door remained closed with no visible sign of any hospitality. A man in a small tent collected coats, shawls and hats in return for a ticket. Heaters designed as dragon mouths breathed spouts of fire along the approach.

Orelia arrived late to avoid her aunt; she also wished to observe her host and his house before he could raise the provenance of the stones with her again, as she felt sure he would. A tap on the shoulder caused her to turn.

'Orelia?' Salt truly looked like a tramp in this august company. 'Spy for me,' he whispered with an urgent look she found unattractive. She congratulated herself on keeping from him the sale of the stones. 'Just do it,' he repeated, and slunk away into a side street.

Salt's interest in Slickstone was new. She wondered what had provoked it.

Her mind turned to the party. She had watched early guests pass her window, but none stirred a flicker of romantic interest. An adventure might be a passable substitute. She resolved to carry out Salt's request, but more in her interests than his.

Oblong felt no less disengaged. His new friends – the Fanguins, the Polks, Jones and Rhombus Smith – acknowledged him politely, but no more. He understood: this was their hidden past, not his. He withdrew to an arbour, rubbing his hands against the cold, with a sinister satyr for company.

'Strange do,' said a husky female voice.

'Hi,' stuttered Oblong.

Orelia wore dark trousers with a cream silk shirt under a red tartan coat, simple but effective. 'Orelia Roc – I'm the lowly shop-keeper in *Baubles & Relics* – the closest we're allowed to get in this town to your naughty subject.'

Oblong blushed. He had passed the shop and noticed her good looks, which had deterred rather than encouraged him from entering. 'Father Time on a rocking horse – that's what I call style!'

'Too stylish, my aunt says – neither have sold.' Orelia tossed her hair. 'But this is a strange do: costume says a party; demeanour says a wake. We need a drink.'

But still none came. Feeling like strangers in their own town, the guests remained orderly, faced with the imposing perfection of the Manor and gardens. A reminder, reflected Rhombus Smith, on how a silent but forceful Form Master can impose better discipline than the voluble.

A single footman in a tailcoat emerged to present Gorhambury with an earpiece, an elegant variation on a megaphone and a list of guests. The earpiece sputtered into life, delivering instructions in a mechanical voice without pleases or thank yous: 'One by one, or couple by couple. Announce them, alphabetically, as on the list.'

The footman withdrew, leaving the main door open to reveal a small lobby with a crimson curtain beyond. 'Accompany, announce, return for the next,' continued the voice. Gorhambury accepted his orders meekly, passing them on to the guests through the megaphone. Conversation revived with the news that they would soon be inside.

'I go first,' said the Mayor.

'You are an "S", your Worship—'

Snorkel ignored him, seized his wife by the arm and marched through, Gorhambury following just in time to get out the words, 'The Lord Mayor and Lady Mayoress.'

Snorkel had lavished considerable time and effort on a speech of welcome for his new benefactor, but it dried in his throat. Above him the ceiling soared to a hammer-beam roof from stone walls masked by oak panelling and fluted columns decorated with swags of fruit and acanthus. A colonnaded staircase led to a raised balcony at the back of the room, where Sir Veronal stood, silent and alone. He wore a bottle-green velvet smoking jacket over a silk shirt buttoned to an Indian collar. He looked immaculate. In a minstrels' gallery above the entrance a Renaissance consort held their instruments at arms' length, as motionless as the waiters with their trays of Blue Lagoons and silver salvers laden with canapés. A huge fire blazed, the mantle supported by two stone giants on bended knee. Paintings of museum quality alternated with sumptuous Renaissance tapestries.

The immobility of host, waiters and musicians conjured a gothic fairy-tale, a banquet frozen at the moment of service. The absence of any electric light enhanced this otherworldly feel. Candles guttered and glowed from chandeliers of gilded wood, high and low, their light so warm it flattered skin, hair and costume.

'Bow, Sidney,' whispered his wife, Cindy Snorkel, quite overwhelmed.

Snorkel nodded deferentially as Gorhambury accelerated.

'Mr and Mrs Abner . . . Mr Anvil . . .'

The room filled alphabetically, couple by couple, as if into the ark; no newcomer daring to break the silence as Sir Veronal held his elevated position, still mute and motionless. Deeper feelings surfaced among the guests – pride at the architectural gem in their midst, tempered with unease as to why this mysterious sumptuary had chosen them. Rotherweirders understood the corrosive qualities of power, living under a mayor who took more than he gave, and they had an abiding suspicion of outsiders, but they were not immune to the siren voice of luxurious hospitality.

Sir Veronal's art collection added a *frisson* – portraits in historical costumes, subjects from mediaeval history, foreign cities. The *History Regulations* were ignored in oil, stone, silk and wool. Rotherweirders appreciated the craftsmanship, but were thrown by any hint of history in the subject-matter. Period costume morphed into fancy dress, real-life places and events into mere imaginings.

Gorhambury checked his list to discover only one absentee, a junior scientist from the North Tower whose no-show would surprise nobody who knew her. Mrs Banter he announced without mishap; with her natural *hauteur* she would have been on everyone's list.

As the last guests entered, the door behind Sir Veronal opened to admit Lady Imogen, stunning in a crimson dress with a light jewelled tiara in her hair, followed by a boy in a grey suit. The actress had never played with so many extras on such a lavish set. For the moment she had no desire to go off-script – an easy scene, maybe, but so uplifting to hold centre stage in such a set piece. With a half-smile, radiant but subtle, she hinted at welcome.

Sir Veronal stepped forward and extended his arms, the almost balletic fluency of the movement at odds with his age. 'Townsfolk of Rotherweird, Lady Slickstone and I give this modest party to thank you for the opportunity to resurrect our manor house. I hope we have repaid your trust.'

Orelia watched Snorkel wince at Sir Veronal's choice of words. 'Our' and 'repaid' – there was subtext here. The voice rang clear, more mellifluous than she remembered it. 'Be so kind to give us your names – we will try to talk to you all.' Sir Veronal turned to his supporting cast. '*Nunc est bibendum!*' he added.

He might as well have waved a wand. Waiters launched themselves with silver salvers, musicians struck up. The Blue Lagoons loosened whatever inhibitions remained, and the volume upped to loud in moments – party time.

Rodney surveyed the guests with contempt. They so lacked his master's class. He shuddered to think what their children would be like. He hailed a passing waiter. 'Get me a sausage and one of those blue things, and be sharp about it.'

Outside, unseen, a lithe hooded figure with a backpack vaulted the perimeter wall through a small gap in the field of the security cameras and slipped into a remote corner of the garden.

Rhombus Smith did not *do* parties. They made his dimples ache, grinning at people he barely knew or understood. The Rotherweird history on view intrigued him more than the imported masterpieces. Were the fireplaces original? What of the panelling? And if original, who had been the first owner? What had condemned this architectural gem to purdah for centuries? Then there was the strange feature high above the fireplace: the initials HG rubbed into GW. Layers on layers, that was the trouble with history – once you disturbed the surface . . .

His fellow guests intrigued him too, for festival unmasked them. Drifters drifted, content with free drinks and small talk. The driven pursued agendas. Snobs swivelled their necks like periscopes in search of worthier company. The unhappy imbibed at pace. Peacocks (and peahens) displayed. There remained the unclassifiables: take Strimmer, dressed like a mourner and waiting for others to come to him, yet apparently on edge. *Why?* he wondered.

One of the unhappy, clutching his third Blue Lagoon, approached. 'Evening, Rhombus.'

'Fanguin . . .'

'School – all well?'

'You're sorely missed.'

'Take me back . . . please.'

'Not in my gift, sadly, but English Lit is full of private tutors for whom things come right in the end.'

'Not for tutors teaching newts and amoebae.'

'Nature is understudied at Rothwerweird School thanks to the Mayor's low view of countrysiders. I'd support you behind the scenes.'

Fanguin swayed slightly. Someone believed in him. 'You're a sport, Rhombus,' he gulped before rushing off to canvas the suggestion with his wife, who tartly replied that alcoholics did not thrive in the teaching profession, so first things first.

Another unclassifiable joined the Headmaster: Professor Bolitho, who had cultivated a beard for the occasion, with Oblong in tow.

'Call this a cocktail?' protested the Head of the South Tower, scowling into his drink as if it were stale milk.

'A Blue Lagoon,' replied Oblong, displaying a schoolmasterly tendency to inform when no information was needed.

'I know what it bloody well is. I expected more *verve*.'

'Vesey is Professor of Mixology as well as Astronomy,' explained Rhombus Smith.

Bolitho clapped Oblong on the shoulder. 'Come to the South Tower at six tomorrow and I'll show you a true cocktail.' Bolitho pointed at their host. 'See how he swoops.'

The image fitted: Sir Veronal, the predatory bird in his gilded cage, shaking all hands but picking targets for closer attention with care – but for what? Rhombus Smith watched and realised that Sir Veronal was swooping on history, starting with Orelia Roc, assistant in the town's only antique shop.

'Miss Roc.'

'Sir Veronal.'

'You were admiring my Holbein.' The young nobleman in the portrait wore a crimson tunic and an expression of mild superiority. 'As I might have looked, had I lived then. Talking of provenance, what about my purchase?'

'School excavations.'

'Were they together or apart?'

'Together.'

'In a container?'

'Loose in rotten sacking.'

She spoke so spontaneously that Sir Veronal accepted the answers as true, or at least honest, and moved on to a heavily built man with an almost square head, a goatee beard and piggy eyes. He wore official costume, finely cut but entirely black save for a cream shirt and a red sash. He held a glass of water with a slice of lemon, a faintly comical mix of the puritan and the extrovert.

'Gurney Thomes?'

'I am he.'

Sir Veronal smiled. At last he had a guest who expected more deference than he gave – but his hopes of progress were soon dashed.

'Master of the Guild of Apothecaries?'

'That is so.'

'You work with the North Tower.'

'Indeed we do.'

'I have an interest in the sciences.'

'This is always gratifying.'

Oblong, the only historian on view, became Sir Veronal's next choice for prolonged attention, intercepted as he hunted for a refill. Sir Veronal beckoned to Rodney and the boy ambled over. Everything about him was precocious – his way of talking, his height, his patrician looks, his confidence. Oblong preferred children open to influence, but this boy's presence had something he could not place.

'Rodney, this is Mr Oblong, your Form Master, as from next week.'

'It's a privilege to meet you, sir. My father considered a private tutor, but we decided that class culture would have its moments – in the right hands.' The boy's tone wavered between sycophancy and insolence.

Sir Veronal took control. 'I need a private word with our local historian.'

Rodney offered a shallow bow and moved on.

'I'm only a modern historian.'

'The seeds of the present lie in the past. You can't study 1800 and leave alone what precedes it.'

'I suppose that depends on the rules.'

Sir Veronal picked up a candelabrum. 'Follow me,' he said.

Oblong obediently followed him up to the balcony and through the door behind. Shadows danced along the passage wall. Etchings, pen-and-ink drawings and a single painting flickered into view, the subjects all grotesque. Sir Veronal stopped by the painting, which featured a witch surrounded by a menagerie of monsters.

'All Goya, but this is the treasure – a long-lost "black painting" taken from the plaster walls of Goya's house and transferred to canvas. The other fourteen are in the Prado.'

After a descent and several turnings they emerged in the library, a square room with high round windows and oak shelves filled with antiquarian books. Oblong noted the fine marquetry desk, in period with many of the books, a room stocked with forbidden fruit – or was it literature, rather than history? *Or*, he belatedly asked himself, *can that line ever be effectively drawn?* Sir Veronal lit another candelabrum – he appeared to dislike the gas light; candled sconces projected from the shelves at intervals. A snuffer lay on the mantelpiece.

He shimmied up a ladder with a sprightliness belying his age, lighting candles as he went, before handing down a small, leather-bound volume.

'Marlowe's *Faust* of 1592 – it's based on the German *Faustbuch*. Next door Goethe's *Faust* – the first edition of 1808 and the second of 1829, the last version that Goethe himself edited. For all the flaws, it's the greatest play written: Paradise is dull; Hell is exciting, but at a price.'

Sir Veronal descended and ushered Oblong up the ladder. A Shakespeare first folio stood between the Goethe volumes and the complete works of Dante.

Sir Veronal listed other delights. 'Moving right – Webster's *The Tragedy of the Dutchesse of Malfy* and *The White Devil* printed by Nicholas Oakes. He also printed the "pied bull" quarto of *King Lear*, which I do not have . . . yet.'

And so it went on until Sir Veronal came to the point. 'I have one glaring absentee: a *History of Rotherweird*.' Sir Veronal's face came closer. 'I see only two reasons why these people hide their past. Treasure they wish to keep, or a danger they wish to avoid – or perhaps both.' Sir Veronal paused. 'I am generous to those who help me.'

While wanting to impress his new mentor, Oblong did not want to go the way of Robert Flask. He shrugged uncomfortably as Sir Veronal resumed his attack.

'How can a historian live here for six months and know nothing of the town's history?' The grey-green eyes bored into Oblong. Sir Veronal changed tack. 'What of your predecessor?'

'Mr Flask was dismissed.'

'How curious – why?'

'He did what you're asking me to do.'

'And what did he discover?'

Oblong regretted it as soon as he spoke, but he felt intimidated. 'Something in Lost Acre Lane – but I don't know what.'

'How did you find that out? From whom?'

'I forget, Sir Veronal – a comment in the pub, behind my back.' Oblong heard the lack of conviction in his voice, but he could not get Fanguin into further trouble.

Inwardly Sir Veronal's pleasure at the indirect vindication of his acquisition of *The Journeyman's Gist* curdled with his irritation at the historian's priggish respect for the rules. Oblong clearly knew more.

'You can't offer me a morsel and then withdraw the plate,' said Sir Veronal gently, although Oblong caught frustration, even menace, as he was ushered back to the Great Hall without ceremony. Politely packaged, the message was blunt: unless and until you open up, you're unworthy of these treasures.

Orelia had watched Sir Veronal head up the staircase with Oblong. A good spy would follow. She did not get far.

'Orelia, *my dear!*'

Orelia had never seen her aunt look so merry. She glowed in a new dress as bedecked with sequins as the rest of her was with jewellery and was regaling a silent Gorhambury who, by contrast, looked like an undertaker. Her aunt gestured flamboyantly at her niece. 'Doesn't she look splendid? The moral is: a good trade gets its just desserts. She induced the sale; I upped the price.'

Was it the Blue Lagoons or the headiness of the occasion, or was she merely basking in reflected glory? Whatever the reason, warmth peeped through. For once Mrs Banter appeared proud of her niece.

Eventually Orelia negotiated her own release as Rhombus Smith generously rescued Gorhambury. She ascended to the gallery, non-chalantly examined a painting and slipped through the doorway. She paused halfway down the passage; here disturbing pictures spoke of miscegenation and pain, fine for a museum, but a grim taste for the home of a man with the money to choose.

'I thought I saw someone slip in,' said a male voice behind her, footsteps following.

'Libraries are for enquiring minds,' muttered an authoritative voice from the opposite direction – Sir Veronal's, she guessed. The new historian had apparently disappointed him.

She seized a nearby candle and took the only escape route, a back stairwell that curled up into the dark; it was uncarpeted, incongruous in the prevailing ostentation, and cordoned off by a purple rope as thick as her arm. She skipped over the rope and went up, pausing around the first bend, hands cupped round the candle flame, for fear that the creaking steps would betray her.

'I'm sorry, Sir Veronal, we were checking for intruders.'

'Nothing so exciting,' replied Sir Veronal.

Voices and footsteps faded away. Candlelight danced along the walls. Once out of sight of the passage, this insignificant back stairway testified to neglect, doubtless how the Manor had been before the sale: panelling cracked, the boards grey-orange with dust, cobwebbed beams, and windowless. She turned six times, enough to pull a good cork, before emerging on a landing where the neglect continued. Sir Veronal's roofers had been here, but not the painters or other craftsmen, and she could see why: with low ceilings, mean rooms and meaner windows it was more a roof space than a top floor. She could only stand in the central passage. A crude fold-up trestle table held a chipped saucer and a half-burnt candle, which she lit. With a candle in each hand and her bag wedged beneath her arm, she wandered on.

In the last room a sizeable pockmarked grey tube hugged the wainscot. She discarded her initial thought of piping – the floor had no basins or radiators – and crouched down. She bent her fingers round, and the cylinder moved. At one end she found a handle, not easy to see, some way in. She pulled, and with effort it gave way – a lid, in effect – and from inside she extracted a wrap of material, over six feet high and much longer. The tapestry unrolled like a carpet, its colours untouched by dust, wear, damp or even, it seemed, time.

Orelia had a sixth sense for objects, something more than just the eye of her trade. She was confident that the work was feminine, and of the same vintage as the house. Indeed, she could see Rotherweird Church, the Manor and what was now the North Tower, free of the clutter of buildings that now surrounded them.

Her eye settled first on the homelier scenes – a man entertaining another to lunch, two horse-drawn wagons with children, a conventional burial scene, a school class in progress. Yet she could not avoid the horrors elsewhere – a man recoiling from a telescope, eyes bleeding green and scarlet thread, as beside him a hairless monster was hunted down. Beyond a scene teemed with barred cages, perfect cubes, some empty, some housing monsters; others held a mix of man and animal or animal and bird.

She rationalised the confusing narrative as a blend of local legend and fantastical imagination.

Orelia had a camera in her bag, a habit born of her work – you never knew what you might encounter: an object to buy or an object connected to another you were trying to sell. Now she took advantage, photographing the whole in sections, moving the candles to ensure she caught the detail.

She rolled the tapestry up and replaced it, gathering herself before returning to the party.

A passing guest jolted Miss Trimble's arm, spilling her drink, and moved on, oblivious.

'Allow me.' Gregorius Jones appeared, dabbing her sleeve with a silk handkerchief. 'Gorgeous suit,' he said.

Miss Trimble's usual reaction to such a forward compliment would have been a cold shoulder or worse, but Sir Veronal's strange welcome had given her an idea. 'Help me, Mr Jones, what were the closing words of our host's welcome?'

'*Nunc est bibendum* – Now's the time to . . .' Jones paused before adding lamely, 'Do something or other.'

Now she knew he spoke Latin and understood it, though the cause of his coyness about acknowledging that fact remained a tantalising mystery.

Orelia meanwhile resumed her watch on Sir Veronal, whose next target she foresaw.

She barely knew Marmion Finch – nobody did: a peppery recluse by general repute who made decisions on matters of arms and carvings with Roman impartiality, as had his father and grand-father before him. Even Snorkel kept a respectful distance from Escutcheon Place. Finch's surname was inapposite; he was more owl than finch, eyebrows so full as to be feathered, nose hooked, and that blink – both eyes at the same time. He sporadically flicked his ear in another avian gesture. Speckled brown suit, speckled brown waistcoat, brown shoes. He stood beside Mrs Finch, a small woman wearing expensive jewellery, in her late forties or early fif-ties. Everyone had heard of Rotherweird's Herald, but few had met him. His wife by contrast moved in high society and had endowed their only son with airs and graces as Finch's heir apparent.

She hurried over to reach him before Sir Veronal.

'Ah, it must be Miss Roc, the young woman with an eye for old things.' *Blink. Scratch.* Finch smiled and clasped Orelia's right hand with both of his. There was a beguiling quality about him.

Finch instinctively felt the same way about Orelia. He spoke with a mellow up-and-down musical voice. 'Talking of old things, why welcome your guests in Latin? He's not a schoolmaster. And why not a single family portrait or photograph on view?'

Orelia saw the point. The Great Hall told her no more about Sir Veronal than a museum would about its curator.

Finch's eyes darted from masterpiece to masterpiece – a Donatello, a Breughel the Elder, a Rembrandt, a Holbein – but all were unknown. How could any single man assemble such a remarkable collection? Finch looked at Lady Imogen. 'And why are we here?'

'Your chance to find out,' whispered Orelia, as their host glided up.

'Oh, Sir Veronal,' gushed Mrs Finch, like Mrs Banter a member of Snorkel's circle and therefore in thrall. Orelia caught a nuance: Marmion Finch and Mrs Finch were not well suited.

Sir Veronal ignored her and opened with a compliment. 'I do so admire Escutcheon Place. From the style and the pilasters I would say 1600 or thereabouts, and the first significant dwelling after this one.'

'You may admire only from the outside. So say the *History Regulations.*'

'What do you keep there?'

'I process applications for arms, refusals, postponements, appeals, challenges and designs.'

'Harmless fun?'

'Like cricket and Scottish dancing.'

'Then why close the house off?'

The exchange had the air of a courtroom duel with Sir Veronal as the cross-examiner, and Finch as the wily witness.

'We don't do antiquarians.' *Blink, scratch.*

'No historical records? No snapshots of Rotherweird's childhood?'

'No.'

This time the blink was out of synch. *He's lying*, thought Orelia.

Their host clearly drew the same conclusion. 'We should start a trend for more openness,' he said, before moving on.

'You weren't very friendly,' said Orelia.

'Too witty to woo,' replied Finch.

Orelia laughed as Mrs Finch scowled. Few in Rotherweird practised self-mockery. Orelia glimpsed between the buttons of Finch's shirt a tiny golden key attached to a chain. She was wondering what secrets that key unlocked as Finch abruptly assumed Sir Veronal's role.

'Has Sir Veronal been to your shop?'

'Once.'

'And did he buy?'

Finch had been secretive; she suddenly felt that way herself, shrugging her shoulders – better to lie by gesture than words.

'And Robert Flask?'

'Once or twice – always after old books under the counter.'

'Miss Roc, I hope we may meet again.' The Herald paused, before quoting Sir Veronal. 'And begin a trend to more openness.'

Orelia blushed. Marmion Finch was sharp as a razor.

At the other end of the room Mrs Banter, having left Rhombus Smith, was searching for new company when a footman appeared from nowhere. Voice and costume suggested superiority to the many other servants on view.

'Mrs Banter, follow me please.'

Mrs Banter almost fainted with excitement. The summons to meet her host had come at last. He stood at the other side of the room, looking elegantly bored. Opening lines and subjects raced through her head. 'My pleasure,' she replied breathlessly, noting the twist of gold braid on the servant's tailcoat. Sir Veronal had sent the *head* footman, no common waiter for her.

But then, horror of horrors, the wretched man led her firmly in the opposite direction to the entrance to the Great Hall. When she tried to turn back, an iron grip seized her arm.

'I am Mrs Banter,' she protested as if her name were a cure-all.

'This is a party for the *invited*,' said the footman in a flat, businesslike voice.

'You're hurting.'

'Am I?' He did not relax his grip for a moment.

Mrs Banter's cheeks burned. She felt the eyes of the world upon her. 'How dare you! I demand—'

He guided her into the coatroom. 'You will give me your ticket.'

She meekly handed it over. He retrieved her coat and led her through the porch into the night air. 'You have three minutes. Do not let us see you here again. Sir Veronal does not give second chances.'

Mrs Banter strode back to the gates. Despite struggling for a brave face, the tears came. She found a bench in a nearby alley and collapsed, head in hands, her mascara running. Such humiliation!

The actress watched as the woman was escorted out. She looked harmless, and well heeled. A guest revealed that she owned *Baubles & Relics*. The actress had another tiny lead.

Oblong found that the appeal of his company diminished in proportion to the drink consumed. Feeling increasingly isolated, he wandered outside. A lopsided cat scuttled across the lawn, arousing Oblong's sympathy but also his muse: a three-liner, unsurprisingly free by his standards, came to him:

> *O Felix,*
> *How did the double helix*
> *Fashion you?*

He took out his notebook, and his spirits rose.

*

Sir Veronal's fourth swoop proved more rewarding. 'Ah – Mr Strimmer.' The scientist shook Sir Veronal's hand. 'You've barely moved all evening. You find my guests dull?'

'A fair proportion,' replied Strimmer.

Sir Veronal smiled. A kindred spirit at last. 'A view I'm inclined to share.'

Strimmer had never encountered such a penetrating gaze, or such directness. Sir Veronal's skin had the sheen of a new-born mouse. This was not the kind of man he had been led to expect.

'You're a physicist?'

'Add to that inventor, passable chemist and engineer.' Immodesty came naturally to Strimmer.

'What does the North Tower do with such talent?'

'We develop destructive technologies for sale to the outside world.'

After so much uninformative froth from his guests, this hard data refreshed Sir Veronal. 'You approve of such science?'

'The world is groaning with unnecessary people. We serve the need to cull.'

'And the South Tower?'

'Waste of space, unless you like baby science – games and star-gazing.'

'You must have known Robert Flask.'

'Flask was a weirdo, but bright for an outsider and always digging,' replied Strimmer.

'Digging for the past or the present?'

'The former – he didn't much care for our rules.'

'Any finds?'

'He never admitted to anything concrete.'

'Did he ever mention Lost Acre Lane?'

'Not to me. It's not one of our better streets.'

Sir Veronal looked hard into Strimmer's eyes. He was telling the truth. 'The Mayor accused Flask of encouraging his class to explore the past – a strangely self-destructive act.'

Strimmer had himself been puzzled by this aspect of Flask's behaviour, hardly in character for such a calculating man. 'Flask liked to be ambiguous – and you're right, his vanishing is another puzzle. Did he jump before he was pushed – or was it a rush of blood?'

'Or was he permanently removed?' added Sir Veronal.

Strimmer's head jerked skywards, Sir Veronal following suit. A few yards away a ribbon of smoke had curled into the Great Hall from under the entrance doors and risen high into the rafters, where it had contracted into a roiling ball of darkness like a miniature weather system.

Sir Veronal hurried up the staircase to the minstrels' gallery and summoned security. 'There must be an intruder – find him!'

But it was too late: as servants scurried, the cloud exploded in a blinding flash with a sound of divine intervention: angelic brass announcing the last trump.

Inside Sir Veronal's nerve centre, the screens went blank.

As the fanfare faded, the entrance doors swung open. A slight young woman materialised in a billowing white costume, her short hair dyed turquoise and frozen into spikes. On the costume, molecular structures, theorems from Hooke's to Fermat's to Einstein's, came and went, together with a sequence of the early Fibonacci numbers in a visual cavalcade of man's scientific achievements. In the candlelight she glowed. Over her right shoulder the contents of a sack appeared alive and keen to escape. In her other hand she spun a slim golden rope with weights attached.

'Look at you – with your snouts in the trough and mitts in the gravy. Have you no shame?' Her amplified voice sounded high and husky at the same time. As she spoke she rose higher into air, her boots miraculously extending into stilts. The guests backed away towards Sir Veronal's end of the Great Hall. Suddenly her costume turned black, the scientific symbols giving way to currencies in a molten red colour. Her script matched the visuals: the virtue of science slipping into the murk of material greed.

'We don't want your money,' the apparition continued.

'Get her,' cried Sir Veronal.

The crowd, reduced from animated partygoers to shuffling automatons, made way.

'This house is no business of yours,' added the intruder.

As the head footman, Mrs Banter's earlier escort, burst into a run, she loosed the bolas. The small balls whipped round his ankles, tightened and locked and he hit the stone floor hard, chin first. He did not get up. She conjured up a second bolas, apparently from fresh air. She began to spin it, as if inviting someone else to try.

'So rude to interrupt,' she said.

'It's ruder to come uninvited.' Sir Veronal's party voice had gone. This was business.

'But I am invited.'

She flourished an invitation as her costume began to return to its original state.

Snorkel strode forward, puffing his chest like a bullfinch. 'Now look here, whoever you are, it's your Mayor speaking—'

'Snorky Porky.'

Snorkel was barely able to look at her. 'How dare you make such disgraceful assumptions about the good Sir Veronal!'

'Scientists do not make assumptions. The words "the good Sir Veronal", on the other hand, do.'

'Sir Veronal has given assurances and—'

'Assurances of what? This wake is a desecration. This house belonged to a great scientist. *Shame on you all!*'

So bizarre was this apparition and so outlandish the behaviour that few were prepared to accept she could be one of their own community until an altogether quieter male voice intervened.

Rhombus Smith stepped forward. 'You have made your demonstration. I suggest it's time to leave.'

Sir Veronal felt an uncontrollable rage begin to build. His hands itched, and a long-buried memory stirred. He gasped for air. Something profound was happening, cellular change. An inner voice prompted him, *You have power. Use it.*

'Help,' shrilled Miss Trimble, resolute in all things save small furry animals, 'what's in that sack?'

'Weasels, Madam,' replied the intruder, 'thousands of 'em.'

Miss Trimble wobbled. Gregorius Jones offered support, but the threat of weasels did not materialise; the girl had another surprise in store. She loosened the cords of the sack and with a whoosh of wind every candle in the room went out. Above their heads and on the walls a thousand red eyes glowed briefly and went out.

Then, from the darkness, a bolt of raw energy jagged from the elevated gallery straight at the girl. Only razor-sharp reflexes saved her: she leapt aside as the double doors behind her shattered in a flash of blue flame, leaving the hinges hanging loose. Her lower right stilt blew away, leaving a mesh of metal – fortunately for Valourhand, the artificial stilts ended in rubber pads on which her feet rested, insulating her.

For seconds there was total silence, then bedlam as screams and oaths rang out, interspersed with guests calling out the names of their partners.

In the gallery Sir Veronal collapsed. Servants carried him from the room.

Outside, Oblong's poetic reverie was rudely interrupted by an explosion, a blackout and another explosion before an androgynous figure ran past him, shed a ruined costume to reveal a bodysuit, seized a pole from a flowerbed and vaulted effortlessly over the wall.

A memory surfaced: the vaulter and the snowball in Lost Acre Lane.

The actress surveyed the extraordinary scene. At first unsure whether to act in real time or role-play, she chose to respond as a wife chosen by Sir Veronal would: decisively.

'New candles! Musicians – do what you're paid for!'

In minutes a degree of visibility returned. The girl was nowhere to be seen, nor was Sir Veronal. Drinks began their rounds again. The consort resumed, not entirely in tune, and Snorkel did his best.

'Ladies and gentlemen, forgive this minor interruption – a regrettable stunt, but nothing more. Let us show our honoured host we can rise above it.'

They tried, but the spirit of festival had been broken. Wall candles were relit, but the high chandeliers hung beyond reach with the Great Hall so full. In the gloom Rotherweirders wondered whether the young scientist had spoken the truth, despite her deplorable manners. Were they selling out to an intruder? Had they besmirched the memory of the original owner, whoever he was? The opulence of the occasion turned sour. In dribs and drabs guests began to leave.

Vixen Valourhand paused by an iron weathervane, her vaulting pole beside her. She felt invigorated. She had *delivered*. Rotherweird's citizens had been in awe of *her*, their reaction to the outsider exposed for what it was: subservience lined with greed. She recalled with equal satisfaction Strimmer's expression, shock laced with a dash of admiration.

That was Valourhand's superficial report to herself: an alpha for the demonstration and the escape. But a darker message bubbled away: the outsider had lightning hands, and he had aimed to kill. A mechanical attachment might be the obvious answer, but in that split-second before the bolt fired she had seen electricity crackling between his hands, as if he were coaxing it out. She thought of how Nature sourced such energy – cat fur, eels and thunderclouds – and could find no parallel.

She planted her pole and vaulted high over the street below. She had to get back to her rooms before the streets filled with Sir Veronal's returning guests.

7

Reporting Back

Orelia would have missed Mrs Banter, but for an observant fellow guest. 'Your aunt is down there and she doesn't look well.'

Hardly Mrs Banter's natural habitat, but there she sat in an insalubrious alley, slumped on a bench, head in hands. 'How can I—? How could he—?' she sobbed.

'Think of it as a silly demonstration.'

'Demonstration?'

Orelia escorted her aunt home and tucked her up in bed, Mrs Banter still fulminating at the injustice of the evening, an apparently disproportionate reaction to the protest, which Orelia put down to the Blue Lagoons.

Having returned to the shop, lit a fire and turned off the lights, Orelia's own mood darkened. Head in hands, staring into the flames, she reflected on herself and Rotherweird, concluding that something rotten lay at the heart of both. At the party Strimmer had given her the once-over as if she were merchandise at a cut-price sale. The other men of her age were certainly clever – but to what end? Her thoughts turned to the fresh-faced outsider who had attracted their host's special interest. He had charm, of a sort, but seemed untouched by life. The only men she felt true affection for were older – men like the Polk brothers, Salt and Fanguin – and mostly married, and they did not appeal in the way she wanted. She found solace in the bolt of raw energy that had destroyed the great oak doors with no visible explanation for its occurrence or its accuracy. She thought of the stones and their elemental colours. Maybe, just maybe, adventure truly did beckon.

A knock, urgent and familiar, interrupted her thoughts and she opened the door to Hayman Salt. She had never seen Salt so animated.

'What happened?' he gasped. 'They're shell-shocked – but nobody's telling.'

'There was an incident.'

'What incident?'

She bridled at the greed in his face.

'Tell me why you're so interested and I might tell you what happened.'

Salt tried a more complimentary tack. 'I asked you because you're more observant than most.'

'That's how I know I'm being exploited.'

'You're not the only ship in the sea,' growled Salt, turning to leave.

Orelia wanted to retaliate, but could not see how. She tried a long shot. 'I sold the stones.'

A palpable hit. *He's not much of an actor*, she thought as the big muscles in his face did not move, but small ones did.

'Bully for you, and at a thumping profit, knowing your aunt.' Orelia said nothing, and Salt's nonchalance quickly passed. 'All right – tell me. Who bought them?'

'Trade secret.'

'Where did you sell them?'

'In town.'

'I told you not to.'

'You expressed a vague hope. Anyway, my aunt makes the decisions.'

'Look, this may matter—'

'I sold them to the Lord of the Manor.'

Salt looked like thunder. 'What?'

'He came in person and went straight for the stones – no interest in anything else. Now, you tell me what they're really for.'

'I haven't a clue what they're bloody for.'

'So why the panic?' Orelia had half an answer: it had to be where or from whom he had got them. Since Salt was neither a thief nor a fence, it must be *where* – but no place remotely worthy of his grim expression came to mind. She would have to coax it from him.

But before she could try, Salt seized her by the arm. 'You're coming with me.'

'Sorry?'

'Now!'

'Where?'

'You'll know when we get there.'

To bring home to Salt that she was following him only to relieve her boredom and not out of obedience, she made him wait while she changed.

Salt's sulk showed no sign of easing. He turned his collars up, pulled his hat down and walked so fast that Orelia had to jog sporadically to keep up. He marched through an insalubrious part of town to a row of municipal potting sheds, nondescript lean-tos set against the western wall, and unlocked the most neglected. He disappeared.

She shuffled after him, tripping over a pile of wooden crates.

'Quiet!' Salt's first word in twenty minutes.

He produced a torch and revealed a stone wall, glistening with damp. The air was heavy with mulch, a smell redolent of autumn, not spring. The beam caught a vertical line of bolts seconds before Salt extinguished the torch. A metallic noise rasped in the dark as Salt yanked them back.

'Watch your head,' muttered Salt, more afterthought than caring advice.

She understood: this place was another secret that Salt did not wish to share. How many more was he hiding? But his disclosure of this refuge suggested the stones really mattered, even though – and she believed him on this – he didn't know what they did.

An archway appeared, she crouched, descended several steps and emerged on the riverbank at the foot of the town wall, the Rother lapping below them. From the gloom he rolled out a coracle, Rotherweird's standard form of river transport, made of willow and tarred hide; it resembled an upturned umbrella without the shaft and was the devil to propel and steer.

'Into the coracle,' he ordered, and she found herself obeying without a murmur.

The vessel barely accommodated the two of them but still skimmed across the water, the botanist paddling with a surprising deftness. 'See,' whispered Salt immodestly, 'I could win the Equinox Race if ever I wanted to.'

He hauled the coracle ashore and rolled it into the undergrowth. Hidden nearby waited a Polk vehicle, a quarter of the size of the charabanc, with the letters *RMGD* on the side in gold letters – Rotherweird Municipal Gardens Department, Orelia realised after a moment's thought.

With a pagoda of flowerpots rattling in the back, Salt drove the foreshortened truck across a field to join the main road north. After a good seven miles by Orelia's reckoning they branched left onto a modest country lane and began to climb. The smudge of the Milky Way spread above them.

'We need Bolitho,' she said, gesturing skywards, but Salt ignored her, leaving Orelia no alternative but to enjoy the drive for its own sake. She had travelled further afield than most townsfolk, but like them, she knew little of the immediate countryside. Here and there she saw the lights of distant windows, marking outlying farms on the valley's upper slopes. Salt pulled up at a gateway in a stone wall. Beyond she could see in silhouette the stringed poles of a large hop garden, and all about, fruit trees.

'The Ferdys?' she asked.

'We're not here to see them. From here you walk: you go past the Ferdys – without knocking or attracting attention – and up the hill to the tower. Knock before entering. Whomever you meet, whatever is said, it's between you, me and this gatepost.'

'And why must you go first?'

'I've got business that isn't your business.'

Intrigued and irritated in equal measure, Orelia jumped down from the vehicle.

'Knock – remember,' repeated Salt.

Orelia ignored him and started walking.

'Women,' muttered Salt as he drove off down the lane.

'Men,' muttered Orelia.

But there had been progress of a sort: Salt's reaction to the sale of the stones confirmed her instinct that they combined to do *something*. Might the inhabitant of this mysterious tower know what?

The air had turned chill and she was glad of the heavy woollen jersey she had pulled over her silk shirt. In the meadow beside her, two greys whickered softly to each other, tails swishing this way and that. The land rose again, and over a brow the town of Rotherweird came into view. Her citizens looked down on country-siders, yet here the countrysiders looked down on them. The per-spective was striking. The town looked recent compared to the ancient beeches and oaks before her. As she walked, her breath steaming, she wondered what lay behind the antagonism between town and country, and reproved herself for never questioning more closely why Rotherweird held such a unique status with no MP, no bishop and no county.

She found Salt's vehicle parked between a barn, herring-boned with oak beams, and a horse-drawn dray painted on both sides in green and gold letters: *The Ferdy Brewery: Fine Ales and Fine Everything.* She should have guessed that this mystery person would be part of the Ferdy household, bearing in mind that Salt was a regular at

The Journeyman's Gist and Bill Ferdy the one man with a firm foot in town and country.

Below the barn lay a farmhouse, two storeys, with a handsome porch, generous windows and rose canes, shaped by years of pruning, tied to the walls. A rough lawn curled down a slope to a small pond. Orelia quietly skirted the house and walked on to the tower in the lee of the hill beyond. Only close to did she see its hexagonal shape, faded brickwork and leaded windows. She had thought follies a creation of the eighteenth century, but this building looked older – indeed, older than the farmhouse. She could not comprehend how Salt's mysterious friend with his equally mysterious tower could connect with the four stones.

From outside she could hear Salt trying to defend himself against the probing questions of a second, gentler, male voice. The drama of the duel removed any guilt Orelia might have felt for eavesdropping.

'You find four stones, right by the tile, and don't tell me!' Despite the recriminatory message, the unfamiliar voice stayed calm, in sharp contrast to Salt's.

'I didn't like them.'

'Where are they now?'

A pause. She could imagine Salt's tortured face. 'I sold them.'

'They're corrupting and dangerous. We have to retrieve them.'

'To a shop, a nothing shop. I told them not to sell here – but you know shopkeepers, once they catch the scent of profit . . .'

'Again, why not tell me?' The unknown character maintained his tone of mild rebuke.

'I didn't want one of your lectures. And you take and never give. It's always questions and never answers.' By now Salt sounded furious – with himself, thought Orelia.

'I plead guilty to that. But it's for your own good. You don't know what you're dabbling in. You *really* don't.'

'There you go again – rebuke without explanation. Anyway, who are you, you Ferensens? One disappears, then decades later another turns up, yet never a woman, and never a child.'

Orelia was intrigued. Ferensen: an offbeat name in an offbeat home, and quite unknown in Rotherweird Town.

'You must talk to the shopkeeper.'

A long pause. Orelia knew why: Salt was prevaricating. 'That won't be easy.'

'Why not?'

At this point Orelia had had enough. She sacrificed the 'knock' of her instructions for a more dramatic entrance. 'Because *I* sold the stones,' she announced, taking three firm steps into the room.

The two men gaped as she took in a miscellany of objects – Inuit snowshoes, a Seljuk carpet from Konya, a Fang mask from Gabon, among other oddities. She saw travel in Ferensen's eyes and weatherbeaten face. Light of build and no more than five feet ten tall, with ears out of proportion to the face, his features were otherwise fine. Despite the silver hair, he had the alertness of a man in his prime. She sensed something else, something unnatural, an unease that parallelled her first reaction to Sir Veronal, although the two men could hardly have been more different.

Salt spoke first. 'Meet Orelia Roc, the assistant in *Baubles & Relics* and seller of stones.'

Ferensen shook her hand. 'Ferensen,' he said, 'just plain Ferensen. We need composure and imagination to unravel this little problem.' He placed three glasses on the mantelpiece and poured a generous measure into each from a dusty bottle with no label. Orelia caught the smell of brandy and apples.

'If anyone asks, he doesn't exist – nor does his tower,' said Salt.

She ignored the remark, sat down by the fire and rubbed her hands.

'You sold the stones to ... ?' asked Ferensen.

Orelia instinctively trusted Ferensen, not just for his age, but his air of patience and wisdom. 'The Manor's new owner bought them.'

'See,' said Salt, 'that's what I was trying to tell you.'

Orelia interrupted. 'The stones do something, don't they?'

'They do many things—'

Salt found Ferensen's candour with Orelia deeply irritating. He'd said nothing about the stones' purpose to him, but the edge to the old man's voice suggested more to come if he kept quiet. But only three words did.

'—to living things.'

The phrase hung in the air. *They do many things to living things.* Obscure, but laden with malignant possibilities. Living things: themselves, the water plants, the rose tapping at the window, the owl hunting the meadow. Many things. On his last visit to the tower the *Black Bodrum Nightraiser Special* had spared him a hangover, but had also impaired his powers of recollection. Ferensen had said something about his map of Lost Acre, something relevant to what he was saying now, but the detail would not come.

Ferensen remained his practical, unruffled self. 'Tell me, Orelia, what did you make of the Lord of the Manor – as a customer?'

'He would have paid anything.'

'She was at the Manor for the party tonight,' interrupted Salt.

'In the Great Hall?'

She nodded. Ferensen's face clouded. There was pain there. 'A fireplace with giants on bended knee?'

She nodded again.

'Pomegranates carved in the panelling, smooth as skin itself.'

She exchanged glances with Salt. How could Ferensen know? The Manor had been off-limits for centuries. Maybe in childhood he had made it over the wall. His possessions certainly suggested an adventurous spirit. She was already engaged by her mysterious host.

Ferensen listened politely to her narrative, asking no questions until, while describing his strangely hostile initial reception, she finally mentioned his name.

The effect on Ferensen was electrifying. He sprang from his chair. '*Veronal?* Veronal *Slickstone?* You're sure? You're *absolutely* sure?'

She produced her invitation.

Ferensen fell back in the chair. 'God save us.'

'What's wrong?' Salt asked before turning to Orelia. 'That's the trouble with Ferensens. They sow puzzles, but they never explain.'

'I should have *known* it was one of them, and I should have expected *him*.'

'One of whom?' asked Salt.

'Never you mind.'

'See what I mean!' Salt threw up his hands in exasperation as Ferensen followed up with a volley of questions about Sir Veronal's height, voice, facial features, skin colour and manner. Orelia did her best.

Ferensen shook his head and returned to the sale. 'In the shop – how was he?'

'He went straight for them. He had no interest in anything else.'

'How did he react on seeing them?'

'He seemed mystified. He wanted to know where they came from. When he first held them he shut his eyes as if they might tell him something. But they didn't. He was disappointed, but he still paid up.'

'Then there is hope – unless he finds a way in.'

'To Lost Acre?' asked Salt.

'To his memory,' replied Ferensen, 'where his past is locked away.' Ferensen made a calming motion with his hands, as if blessing a baby. 'On with the story – and please, call him Veronal. That is his name.'

Ferensen did not react again until Orelia mentioned the lightning bolt and how it had nearly reduced the intruder to ash.

'Blue-silver, blinding, fast?' he asked, 'with an after smell of spent firework?'

He was right. There had been. She nodded.

'Stands to reason,' was all he said. He picked a mottled stone egg off the mantelpiece and tossed it from hand to hand. 'Who did he talk to?'

'Chosen targets, I'm sure, anyone who might know of our past. I heard him ask Fanguin about Flask. He chose Oblong of all people for a guided tour, and then moved on to Finch.'

'Oblong, Fanguin, Flask ... they're all strangers to me. One at a time, please, Miss Roc.'

Ferensen refilled their glasses as Orelia gave three potted biographies. Oblong was the school historian, an outsider. Flask had been the School historian, therefore an outsider too, but Fanguin's friend. Flask had disappeared and Fanguin had lost his job because Flask had encouraged pupils to dig in breach of the *History Regulations* and Fanguin had failed to report him.

'Anything else of note?' asked Ferensen.

'Slickstone has a son,' added Orelia.

'Not his own, can't be. He must be adopted. You see, he's looking, and he wants to look normal while he looks.' He paused. 'But that's enough of that for one evening.'

As midnight was announced by various clocks, Ferensen warned that the rain would return in fifty minutes. He said goodnight, apologising to Orelia for being obscure, only to add to her frustration by counselling inaction for the present.

'How does Ferensen know Slickstone?' she asked Salt.

'He tells you nothing.' After railing against Ferensen for being uninformative, Salt then refused to divulge anything to Orelia about his own private business with Ferensen. The evening, she felt, had promised much and delivered little.

On the way home Salt made the oddest remark: 'Imagine a new world where Man could start again. What would we preserve? What would we cut down? Would we be more careful with our discoveries?'

As they parted in the street beyond the potting sheds, Salt

repeated a warning. 'You've never heard of him, remember –
Ferensen the Rainmaker.'

Hard to forget, as rain began to fall exactly when Ferensen said
it would.

That night Orelia could not sleep for the bombardment of questions and an underlying unease. 'Rainmaker' – what did that mean?
How had Ferensen come by this peculiar gift? What was this new
world he and Salt had hinted at? Why had Sir Veronal been drawn to
the stones? She recalled the monsters and the cages in the Manor's
tapestry: make-believe or reality? The answers to these questions,
she suspected, would explain Rotherweird's independence of the
rest of England and the enforced concealment of her past. But what
would happen if this security lock failed? What powers had been
so deeply hidden from view?

Similar questions jangled in Salt's head as he stirred a mug of
cocoa in his house and remembered what Ferensen had said on his
earlier snowbound visit including his description of the slippery
patch of sky in Lost Acre known as the mixing-point. He thought
of the stones doing many things to living things, the strange tree
with its spread-eagled arms, and of Lost Acre's bizarre and dangerous fauna. A horrific possibility occurred. Sleep did not come
any more easily to him.

Sir Veronal reclined on his bed. The four bedposts were carved
with a veritable bestiary – pelicans taking flight from the mouths
of dragons, snakes entwined with butterflies. Three huge tapestries
hung from the surrounding walls on the theme of summer, autumn
and winter. Nobody asked about the absence of spring; it seemed
an indelicate question.

His servants had never seen the phenomenon before – he was
known to them as a cold man, but this explosion of energy had
been spontaneously prompted by loss of temper.

The actress kept vigil. She had been closest to him when the lightning had flowed from his fingers like magic. The dark smudges on his fingertips confirmed that this dramatic outlay of energy had caused his coma. Had a device, hitherto unknown to the world, been installed beneath his skin? Had it malfunctioned, or had he intended to kill?

She feared the answer might connect with his obsession with Rotherweird. She decided that a Jacobean revenge play had begun, and in that thought she found a new justification for further investigation. You cannot play Lear without exploring how life with the late Queen had been before the play commenced. She could not play Lady Slickstone without knowing more about Sir Veronal's past. This town had to hold the material she needed.

At about midnight Sir Veronal surfaced, sharp as ever. 'The woman – I want all there is to know.'

His Head of Security was already briefed. 'There are two science faculties in Rotherweird School – the North and South Towers. What they do beyond teaching is something of a mystery, but they fund the town. The South comes within the School's jurisdiction and the North works with the Apothecaries' Guild. The woman is Vixen Valourhand, by all reports a withdrawn personality but a brilliant scientist. She teaches chemistry and particle physics.'

Sir Veronal sat up. 'She got the better of you.' He decided against further rebuke. 'Did Strimmer know what she was up to?'

'The Great Hall cameras suggest he was both surprised and unsurprised.'

Sir Veronal greeted this ambiguous answer with a knowing nod. 'What about him?'

'I would say, sir, he's a man to have on your side – devious, ambitious, and without scruple.'

'Did any acceptances not turn up?'

'None.'

'Any present uninvited guests?'

'Mrs Banter. She owns *Baubles & Relics*. You may recall we showed her out – firmly.'

Sir Veronal strummed the headboard with his fingers. 'With Mr Gorhambury in charge of security? It's too much of a coincidence. Get into his bank account and check for money. Then get Snorkel on the job. I want retribution. This town has lessons to learn.'

The actress blew out the candles and withdrew to her room. She sensed that the Second Act of this drama was already showing more promise than the first.

Strimmer stood with a hand on each side of her doorway. Valourhand sat by a mirror, halfway through the laborious process of restoring her former appearance, cheeks running turquoise with dye, short hair still spiky. She had morphed back into jeans and T-shirt.

'You might have told me. You could have got yourself killed.'

Valourhand knew the remark reflected irritation at the lack of consultation rather than concern for her welfare. 'I was faster.'

'Whose idea was all this?'

'I give credit to Flask for the general idea, but the detailed execution was mine.'

Strimmer wondered what else Flask had said to Valourhand and kept from him. 'So,' he said, 'either our interloper has invented a new weapon or he has unnatural powers. Whichever, he's more than the Snorkel palm-greaser Flask said he was.' Strimmer's tone turned suspicious. 'In your delightful speech, you said the Manor's former owner was a great man. Who told you that?'

'He was a great *scientist*. It was Flask – who else?'

'If Sir Veronal is after information, as I think he is, he'll be interested in what we know. But I'm against asking him here first. I'd lose the high ground.'

Always 'I' and never 'we', thought Vixen, as Strimmer continued, 'You weren't there, but Slickstone left the party for a good twenty minutes with the strangest possible companion.' He paused for effect. 'Oblong.'

Valourhand remembered the historian loitering outside the house as she made her escape. She had had enough of Strimmer. 'Night,' she said, indicating the door.

Strimmer returned to his study, the highest room in the tower, and locked the door. He reflected less on Valourhand's performance than on her surprise disclosure, gleaned from Flask, that a scientist of distinction had inhabited the Manor. This prompted a recollection of something Flask had revealed to him – a study of the buildings and their materials showed that, church apart, the North Tower and the Manor were the town's oldest buildings by several decades, close in age to each other. Flask had pointed out the unusual height and rounded shape of the North Tower roof. Strimmer now theorised that the North Tower had always had a scientific purpose.

Back in his room he tapped the spaces between the crisscrossing beams in the ceiling of his study with a broom handle. The noise confirmed what the roofline suggested (if you analysed without fear of the past, as Flask invariably did): a cavity above. Strimmer reasoned that any access would have come from the middle of his room, where the desk presently stood.

To his astonishment, on the application of firm pressure, an otherwise invisible hinged panel opened upwards. Armed with a torch, he hauled himself up into an extraordinary room. Half the perimeter was lined with tip-up seats, deeply set so their occupants could sit without being cramped by the slope of the ceiling. In the middle stood a magnificent chair, almost a throne, with clawed feet. With increasingly excited rubs from a shirt-sleeve, there emerged from the dusty wall paintings of stars, signs of the zodiac, numbers and algebraic formulae, and a sealed window decorated as a golden door, apparently opening onto infinite space.

A wheel with a handle sat low in the floor beneath the window.

He tried the wheel and felt a tremor beneath his feet. The entire floor must once have revolved. The phenomenon left no doubt: he stood in an observatory, and one centuries old.

He descended again to bring up a damp cloth and a powerful lamp. Further details emerged: nine sets of initials had been erased from the twelve seats, leaving three survivors (HS, MS and TF), all pupils, presumably.

On the revolving section where the telescope must have stood, he made another discovery. A small wooden tile, no more than eight inches square, had been inserted flush between adjoining floorboards. Rendered near invisible by centuries of dust, a damp cloth revealed a fine marquetry inlay of a sun and two moons about the initials HG with a cross beneath. Under a magnifying glass a tiny monogram emerged in the corner, a conjoined H and M. Strimmer deduced that the three surviving students were probably friends, as they sat together. He attributed the survival of their initials as testifying to their innocence of whatever disgrace had expunged the record of their colleagues' existence.

The cross on the inlaid tile suggested a memorial, most probably to their teacher. The H and M reflected the first initials of the two survivors. A question emerged whose potential Strimmer found exciting rather than sinister: was the disgrace of the majority connected to the death of their teacher?

A slight distortion in the floor caught Strimmer's eye. The beams of his study ceiling were mirrored in the observatory floor, but floorboards rather than plaster filled the gaps. Under the eaves a board had come loose, the edge standing a little proud. Strimmer sank to his haunches to lift it. Below a hidden receptacle held a book.

The title, embossed in gold on the spine, was mysterious: *The Roman Recipe Book*. A disturbing woodblock provided the sole clue as to its anonymous author: a devil sitting on an ornate chair, with yet another monogram beneath his feet. The posture – elbow on knee, hand on chin – implied a thinker, and the intensity of his gaze spoke of ambition. Strimmer had on rare occasions consulted antique scientific books in the basement of Rotherweird Library. He judged this to be many centuries old. Opposite the frontispiece he found a manuscript inscription in tiny letters, the ink faded to a purplish brown:

I

Was

Bound

Bearing

Mysterious

Recipes

He flipped through the pages, thirty-two, without a word on any of them. Each displayed four separate identical squares lined like a stave of music, save that the lines numbered six, not five, and ran vertically. In each square – though always on different lines and in different places – were four coloured circles of red, white, blue and brown. Beneath them appeared on one side recognisable creatures, or parts of creatures – a boy's head, a claw, a feather – and on the other, a composite. Grotesques, finely drawn, danced on the margins, some tailed, some clawed, some winged. A few pages featured elements, too – fire, lightning, water. Uniquely, the last page beneath the stave showed only ordinary people in silhouette: a soldier, a maid, a jester and other stereotypes. The draughtsmanship was exquisite and the colours vivid, but other than the title, there was no word to be seen.

Was it a songbook, with some long-lost notation? If so, why go to such extravagant lengths to hide it? He toyed with the motion that the diagrams were a speculative early guess at DNA, the building blocks of life, but these inked body parts and monstrosities with their mix of man, beast, bird and insect were hardly real.

Strimmer doubted that the book had any contemporary value

'Grotesques, finely drawn, danced on the margins,
some tailed, some clawed, some winged.'

beyond its age and binding, but the obscurity of the title, the tantalising inscription and the illustrations tickled his interest. He replaced it, re-securing the offending board, just in case. He had not forgotten Flask's disappearance.

Marmion Finch, chastised on the way home by Mrs Finch for overfamiliarity with a woman half his age (Roc) and underfamiliarity with the new force in Rotherweird society (the Slickstones), took refuge in the *archivoire*. Valourhand's performance had shown style and pluck, but it was her underlying message that had intrigued him. A great scientist had lived in the Manor – what kind of scientist? Had he owned the sinister black-bound books, or the orthodox books in beige? Maybe he had owned both? Had he uncovered the mysterious threat that had led the redoubtable Elizabeth I to abandon the Rotherweird Valley to its own devices?

He fingered the golden chain round his neck. *Ghost ... train ... times ... change ...*

8

Retribution and Forgiveness

Orders for Gorhambury were usually delivered by an underling in the form of notes written by the Mayor's ferocious secretary, whose style was quite as peremptory as Mr Snorkel's: 'Last month's tax revenue – S's desk – now!' or 'Mayor's rickshaw – scratched paint – deal!'

The habitual exclamation mark was present in today's injunction: 'S's office – 10 a.m. sharp!'

The secretary, her hair wrenched back with combs, her painted eyebrows dark and pencil-thin, gave a curt nod of approval as Gorhambury arrived on time. She stood up, smoothed her skirt over her knees and opened the door.

Something was horribly wrong. He had not been kept waiting.

Snorkel's massive partners' desk sat in the middle of a powder-blue carpet like a ship at sea. He flourished a bank statement – Gorhambury's own personal account – with a credit for three guineas highlighted in pink ink.

'Well?'

Gorhambury peered at the entry, too bewildered to protest at this invasion of privacy.

'001426 – three guineas credit – I've no idea. I never accept money from strangers.'

Gorhambury might have added that he was never offered money by strangers. He and Marmion Finch were the town's incorruptibles.

'Don't lie to me, Gorhambury!' Snorkel suddenly exploded in

self-righteous indignation. 'You've a pension, a bicycle-tyre allowance and an indecently generous overtime rate. How dare you sink so low!'

Gorhambury suppressed the observation that his overtime rate worked out at less than his ordinary rate as his encyclopaedic memory tripped into action. The transfer matched the date of his meeting with—

'*Mrs Banter* ring a bell?' added Snorkel with perfect timing, like many corrupt men a remorseless cross-examiner when pursuing the faintest whiff of corruption in others.

'I did her a favour. I got her an invitation.'

'Oh really – to what? You've never given a party in your life.'

'There was a clerical mix-up. She felt horribly left out, you see, and I felt sorry for her.'

'You refer to the Manor?'

'Yes, but I was going anyway, and—'

'Issuing invitations to other people's parties – that's positively regal.'

'She lives alone. It seemed kind.'

'Money is the evil of our time. It's a straight red, Gorhambury. Get your things and get out.'

'I've done eighteen years, three months and twenty-two days of loyal service – surely you mean a warning?' protested Gorhambury, 'to be reduced to writing under the *Employment Regulations*?'

'Red, red, *red!*'

Gorhambury slunk back to his desk, from which all municipal property had already been removed. Somewhere in that trampled soul, rebellion whispered. A year or so earlier, following a security failure, he had been given a spare set of keys to the main municipal buildings as the man least likely to lose them. They were still there, in a polythene bag taped to the underside of his desk. He pocketed them, together with a large leather notebook and a box of pencils from the Mayoral stationery cupboard. *In lieu of notice,* he said to himself. As he tramped home, he agonised over how he would pay the next month's rent.

Mrs Banter too received a follow-up dismissal after her ejection from Sir Veronal's party, the letter terse to the point of brutality, and no less wounding.

> Dear Mrs Banter,
>
> Gatecrashers are not welcome in the Mayoral Suite. Be so kind as to treat any current invitations in your diary as withdrawn, and expect no more in the foreseeable future.

A rubber stamp had appended a facsimile of Snorkel's signature. She detected the long hand of Sir Veronal Slickstone in this further humiliation.

Her emotions swung from one extreme to another: from hatred of the interloper and an urge for revenge to a burning desire for reconciliation and a relaunch into society. After hours of agonising reflection, she found a way to accommodate these contrasting ambitions. She had one point of leverage.

The next morning she delivered a note to the Manor, inviting Lady Slickstone to tea.

The luck fell to Valourhand. When Sir Veronal contacted the Mayor at dawn, demanding action, he insisted on clemency for the night's worst offender. A reprimand would do. Snorkel, smarting from the label 'Snorky Porky', which he feared might stick, argued for instant dismissal, to no avail.

Rhombus Smith delivered the reprimand in the manner of a complimentary rebuke. In his eyes she had enlivened the evening. He liked it when fact out-coloured fiction.

9

A Starry Night

The following evening, true to his word, Vesey Bolitho stood in the entry porch of the South Tower and welcomed Oblong with a cocktail. The first gulp almost laid the historian out.

'Mars' Mistake,' said Bolitho. 'Mixology is an art form. You wouldn't keep to the path in a beautiful park, so don't be a slave to the recipe book. Try the *Bolitho Beginner's Guide*. Pour in an inch of anything with a kick. Add one enhancer, as the mood takes. Splash something pale into something colourful or vice versa and add that too. Discard any undrinkable outcome. Then serve the survivors with a celestial name appropriate to final impression. Ice is optional, as in the planetary system. This has chilli sauce – for the shy ones.'

From the hallway they climbed to the observatory, Bolitho pausing for breath on every landing. The walls were circular, the ceiling domed, the telescope resting on a raised dais. The aperture to the sky was closed. A sea of paper obscured the floor. Bolitho apparently dismissed tables and chairs as spatially inefficient. The room was almost dark.

With the flick of a switch a skin in petal-shaped segments rose from the rim of the room towards the ceiling. A low eerie blue light descended: nightfall.

'How does the School afford equipment like this?'

'A goodly fraction of the world's inventions come from the two towers of Rotherweird School and the work benches of the

Apothecaries. Others claim the credit while we take our cut. You should see the science labs.'

Near the telescope stood a table crammed with glass discs, grinding wheels and metal scoops filled with coloured powders. 'Rock dust,' explained Bolitho. 'Up there swim the deeps, and these are my fishing rods. However, that's not why you're here.' Bolitho brandished a remote control like a wand. 'On the fourth day of Creation . . .'

As Bolitho spoke, the Almighty's work – suns, planets, moons, nebulae – appeared on the roof of the observatory. With a laser pen the astronomer embarked on a tour of this two-dimensional cosmos. He awarded some only a name; others earned an explanation or anecdote. The horse-head nebula in Orion was the creation of dust. Mizar in Ursa Major should be renamed 'the Drunkard's Star', being an optical double to the sober, one or three to the overindulged. It was a bravura performance.

By the end Oblong felt infinitesimally small, but this was only the introduction.

Bolitho made an expansive gesture. 'Above you spreads the unique celestial geometry of a particular night in England four and a half centuries ago, 1546, to be exact. Astrologers focus on the moment of birth, but it's the moment of conception that fixes our talents. All those stars have their gravitational pull on those miniscule lines of DNA as they mix and match. This rare alignment of the heavens brought the most particular gifts and defects into the world.'

He flicked another switch and the sky vanished. Ordinary lights came up and the skin retracted back into the rim of the dome.

Bolitho suddenly looked frail, and said as much. 'A star near the end of its existence we call an "evolved star". Yes, I am unwell, Jonah. I may not be around much longer. I wanted to give you a glimpse of Rotherweird's origins. As our only historian . . .'

He turned off the lights.

Back in his lodgings Oblong reflected on his unexpected astronomy lesson. He checked the birth dates of his class, but they were scattered, as he would have expected. Then he remembered that Bolitho had talked of Rotherweird centuries ago, and a generation of prodigies connected with her past. The town's extraordinary concentration of scientific talent had to have a rational cause, and an exceptional gene pool from long ago made sense – but why here? And why had they been brought together? An exceptional teacher might be an answer, but that explanation raised questions about the original owner of the Manor and why the town's main building had been closed off for centuries. Oblong felt as if he had the outlying jigsaw pieces only. They provided the background, but left the main story obscure.

Old History

1561. The Rotherweird Valley.

Dusk, early autumn – you can tell from the colours. Master Malise, older now, cheeks lightly stubbled, dark hairs covering his arms, has ventured beyond the Island Field in breach of Sir Henry's instructions. He is pursuing the study of toxins, another breach of the rules. Here on the margin between woodland and meadow grows *Amanita virosa*, the destroying angel, which he prefers to *Amanita muscaria*, the fly agaric, another deadly mushroom found nearby. The agaric is too showy, its bright red-orange cap declaring its danger. This mushroom is all innocence on the outside, all white cap, white gills and white stalk, dressed like a saint. He has already force-fed a paste to mice and studied the convulsions and organ damage that followed.

He hears someone nearby, and then *that* voice: 'Not that clump, Calx – they're spent – go to the left.' A pause. 'Ah, a boy is watching us. If he has manners, he will show himself.'

So Geryon Wynter introduces himself and that famous sixth sense he so likes to display. 'It's one of the wonder children if I'm not mistaken.'

The voice is sibilant, yet penetrating in its unforced quietness. They make an incongruous couple: Wynter, lean of body and aquiline of face, and the corpulent servant. The servant bustles about as Wynter stands motionless, save for the coal-black eyes, which dart from boy to servant to mushrooms to possible paths – a quicksilver mind.

Malise has never felt dominated before. He half resents it, half welcomes it.

More names are exchanged.

'He wonders about our baskets.'

Wynter the mind-reader: Calx Bole, the servant, holds several wicker baskets. From inside them Malise can hear scratching and fluttering. He is indeed curious.

'Shall we tell him? Shall we show him? Such an interest in mushrooms deserves reward. No doubt Sir Henry is learned on propagation and edible fruit, but I teach too. Your little white mushroom attacks the liver, which the ancients list, with the brain and the heart, as one of the three principal organs of the body. Who needs armies when you can strike down rulers with mushrooms? Now tell me – how are your class? Are all ten of you alive and well?'

He is being toyed with. Malise is fascinated, drawn to Wynter and his arcane knowledge, but repelled at the same time. He senses love can be like this. 'There are two peasant children also.'

'Twelve disciples, Calx, locked away in this valley, with no possible future but arid, unapplied study. We could elevate them. We could show you a *real* future, Master Malise.'

Malise does not reply. He already knows he stands before Grassal's polar opposite. Of the Tree of Knowledge of Good and Evil, Grassal knows only half. This man knows the Tree through and through.

'Give him a pot, Calx. Even wonder children must learn to fetch and carry.'

Malise is flattered by the invitation, but resentful of Wynter's knowing assumption that he will comply. Wynter moves for the first time, so light of step that he slithers rather than walks.

On through the woods they go. Malise cannot imagine what the baskets are for, what destiny awaits the creatures inside. After some way he is blindfolded.

When the strip of cloth is removed, they are in a bowl beneath a ring of trees. A square white tablet is set in the ground. A pile of small cages stands nearby, which Wynter leaves to Bole to carry.

'Gateway,' he says, gesturing to his servant, as if inviting a lady to lead off a dance.

Bole stands on the tile and disappears with the cages, and Malise follows without argument. A sense of dislocation is superseded by a strange new world. Bole, a dagger suddenly in hand, crouches, so Malise follows suit. The grass feels alien. A bee with the carapace of a beetle scissors into the air, warbling like a bird. Wynter arrives, and he too crouches, before blowing on a wooden whistle. They wait, heads in the grass. Only the puffs of white cumulus could be called normal, but nothing prepares Malise for the creature that rises from four legs to two in front of him.

'*Sum Ferox*,' says the creature.

He sees the weasel in the man (who could not?) and understands the Latin, but something deeper stirs: a kinship. Malise, the precocious analyst, tries to articulate this attraction. He likes the predatory perfection, how the creature's constituent parts marry so exactly, and the way, despite the loping walk, he carries his makeshift spear with aplomb.

'I teach it English,' says Wynter.

'Let me help him,' says Malise.

'Him', not 'it'; 'help' not 'teach'. Ferox nods to himself. He prefers the boy's English. In return he will teach the boy how to navigate the dangers of this place.

'Whether you do that depends . . . on how your future plays out,' says Wynter before turning to Ferox. '*Labor omnia vincit.*'

Ferox leads and Malise follows obediently in the tracks of the furry feet, Ferox parting the stalks with his spear. The strange fauna of this kingdom appear to respect the weaselman. Distorted creatures fly, burrow or scuttle away.

'Open the baskets!' cries Wynter.

The great tree stands out, not just for its isolation and size, but for its falling leaves, which flap and glide like bodiless bats, the seeds lined along the back like spinal vertebrae.

The servant chooses a particular cage from the pile as Wynter points to a shimmering patch of sky. 'No god, please note, Master Malise, just a physical phenomenon for use by any creature with the wit to understand it.'

Wynter places four stones, each in a notch in a bar of the cage, only one to a side.

'An ancient art, creaturing. The Druids studied it.'

Calx Bole unloads two baskets, places a russet squirrel and a thrush in the cage and slides the bars across.

'Sometimes it reduces, sometimes it enlarges, but it always mixes.'

Into the shimmering patch of sky went the cage; out came the cage. Wynter hit the palm of one hand with the other fist as a misshapen mix of feather and fur, beak and mouth struggled to fly. He kicks it.

'Go on, Bole!'

The servant clumsily tries to kill the monstrosity as it lurches into the air, only to plunge into the long grass. Wynter laughs as Ferox moves with lolloping grace and strikes once. It is enough.

'Better,' says Bole, as Wynter retrieves the stones.

'But not good enough.' Wynter turns to Malise. 'Experiment requires many hands – to note, to cage, to measure, to adjust. If in time we are to advance ourselves as well as the lower orders of life, we need assistants with sharp minds.'

Even Malise is shocked. 'You mean you'd put people in there, mix people with—?'

Ferox looks sideways, oddly distracted, as Wynter continues regardless, 'With hope, in time, we will. Our slippery pocket of air does not distinguish, does she, Calx? She replicates. She does what she's told.'

'But we're all different.'

'Any worthwhile task has the spice of risk. Never fear, you'll soon discover a taste for it.'

After another failure there is success: a small hairless creature with splayed feet and tiny eyes that Wynter calls a rat-mole, despite the presence of stunted wings.

'Keep it,' says Wynter. 'They won't believe you otherwise.' His words have layers of meaning: persuade your fellow children; choose my way, not Grassal's; recruit. 'Feed it mice, worms and small birds, and make sure they're alive. Now, let me show you our best experiment.'

He raises a tiny box, a latticework prison with protruding blades of grass. 'In here we have our shortest-lived insect, the mayfly. After immersion in the mixing-point, still it lives. How long, Bole?'

'Sixty-nine days.'

Malise is quick. 'How old then is Ferox?'

'Past counting,' replies the weaselman.

He comes from an age of Latin, concludes Malise.

They return to the white tile.

'Ferox stays here,' Wynter says.

Malise and Ferox nod to each other.

'May he return,' whispers Ferox in his new language, with a nod towards Malise.

'That is in his hands – he has much work to do.'

The basket judders as Malise carries his trophy home. How he would have their attention now!

At first, all has gone well at Rotherweird Manor. The Seers and the newcomers have discovered their identical ages and the closeness of their birthdays, all within weeks, most within days, of each other, and their diverse gifts from mathematics to alchemy, anatomy to celestial studies. Hieronymus and his sister have introduced their new companions to the richness of the Rotherweird Valley. Only Malise has held aloof, a cruel boy, an experimenter with animals.

Yet he has excelled at whatever subject Sir Henry chooses to teach, save for the more artistic.

But over time the Seers' influence has waned as Malise has made his move for dominance. The girls have sided with him, jealous of Morval's beauty. He has discovered the locals' humble background: the children of swineherds! He calls them 'countrysiders'. Only Throckmorton, an enthusiast for celestial theory, planets and stars, has remained loyal to the Seers. Yet so immersed are they in the natural world and its portrayal, visual and analytical, that they have taken little notice of their exclusion.

Then Malise begins to disappear at night. He asks questions in class unrelated to their curriculum – about poisons, parasites, the study of political power. Then he releases his creature in the dormitory, his 'familiar', as he calls it. The Seers sense its disfigured nature.

Sir Henry notices the change and turns to his first charges for help. 'You'll not wish to talk of friends out of school, but sometimes the young must be saved from themselves. Malise went missing again last night. Do you know where he goes? Whom he sees? He returns well cared for. I would send searchers, but we must preserve our secrecy here. We don't know how the new Queen stands on the matter. Anything you can tell me ... ?'

Sir Henry does not expect an answer: informing would appear vengeful – but Sir Henry has overlooked a different force. The two orphans live by a fierce moral order, with Nature at its centre.

'Malise has another teacher,' says Hieronymus.

'An evil teacher,' adds Morval.

'Why evil?'

'He made Malise a pet.'

'An unnatural creature,' they add together.

'Who is this teacher?'

'Charon or some such ...'

Geryon Wynter, thinks Sir Henry. *Why is Wynter stalking my charges?*

'Show me,' he says, and they do, when Malise is absent – not a rarity these days.

The children advance in a line with sticks. Sir Henry fumbles for and finds the basket under Malise's cot in the great barn. He turns it out. The creature is not of this world: bald, with purple skin, lidless crimson eyes, stunted, half-developed leathery wings, ferocious claws and jagged teeth. Grassal calls for a net as the creature half flies, hissing and snapping, but they do not listen; they are seized by a mixture of fear and the excitement of the hunt. The abomination is beaten to death despite Sir Henry's calls for restraint. Only the Seers and Throckmorton hang back.

Malise has a gift for timing. He appears in the doorway as Sir Henry shakes the body from the net. He picks up his 'familiar', cradles it, and leaves, with a parting glance at Sir Henry of unadulterated hatred.

'The creature is not of this world.'

Two months later. The Tower of Knowledge once more.

Sir Henry has moved on to perspective and optical instruments. It is near midnight, close to the Feast of the Nativity, the golden door is open to the sky's most wondrous gift – the winter constellations – and Sir Henry, face aglow in the candlelight, is speaking of reconciliation. Using a tube with proportional glasses, they come up, one by one, to observe the smudged outline of mountains on the face of a waning moon.

'I don't know how you came by this, or who fashioned it, but what a gift!'

Malise presents the object as a fawning tribute and apology for the monstrous creature. Bought from a merchant in Hoy, he says. Sir Henry holds up the lens with its bulbous, brassy body.

'We fix it here and . . .'

The old man bends to the telescope, pressing his right eye to the rim. There is a *click*. A *whirr*. A terrible scream. He falls, hands streaming blood, as Malise smiles. Arms and legs dance in shock as the poison works behind the eye. There is pandemonium – the Seers try vainly to absorb the tainted blood with cloth; others rush to Sir Henry's library, but they lack a starting point. A physician comes and offers comfort, but no cure. Malise and the eye-piece disappear.

The old man's limbs begin to dance. His mouth leaks blood. He takes a day to die.

Sir Henry, confident in his health for a few years yet and concerned not to jeopardise the progress of his charges until at least their majority, had postponed arrangements for his succession.

Wynter, primed by Malise as to the absence of any apparent heir or successor, appears at Grassal's funeral. He pays tribute and explains how at a lunch Grassal appointed him to be their teacher and life-tenant of the Manor after his death. Think of his age, says

Wynter; he had to make provision. He promises the children that Sir Henry intended for them unimaginable power, the chance to write their names in history.

He does not linger. The next day he takes them to Lost Acre and they stand in awe before Ferox and then the mixing-point. The weaselman escorts them at noon, the safest time in this horribly dangerous place, on a path through the forest to a mere where fish break the surface and fly, snapping their jaws on insects as they pass.

'Why we keep to the plains,' explains Wynter, keen that his charges should understand the perils of the place. Malise skims flat stones along the surface of the water at the fish, and strikes lucky.

That evening there is no more mention of Sir Henry. They are fifteen now, and it is time for change, Wynter tells them. They will have new names, a baptismal moment. His charges may choose one; and Bole will choose the other.

Malise, ever searching for a drug that might induce truth-telling, chooses an unknown word: Veronal. Bole awards him Slickstone, superficially for his prowess with the skimming pebbles at the mere, but Wynter suspects there is intended ambiguity – hard and polished, but somehow slippery too: one to watch, in other words. Only the Seers decline to participate. Wynter makes no move. These are Grassal's children in a way the others are not. Their friend Throckmorton, the student of the heavens, is named Fortemain by Bole, again a play of multiple meanings – a firm hand for the telescope, but perhaps a pointer too to the boy's strength of character, a moral force who might yet cause trouble.

That night they sit at a round table in the Great Hall. Wynter has provided a feast – brown trout from the river, venison from the woods, and plentiful mead. This is the beginning. His once-extravagant ambition takes flight. He has twelve disciples, a route to immortality and the chance to create the kind of monsters from which legends are made. Darker chapters lie ahead, for horror is part of the divine fabric. Gods and their stories are not knitted fireside toys.

By flickering candles he christens himself and his new recruits the Eleusians. In London he has noted the coats of arms that decorate the banners, carriages and fireplaces of the rich and powerful.

'Now you have names and soon, if you work hard enough, you will be the first in the history of Man to have living coats of arms. Morval Seer will record them.'

After Lost Acre not one of them doubts that if they comply, this outlandish prophecy will come to pass.

This scene will come to Sir Veronal as another bubble of memory slips through the tiny hole in the ruptured membrane of his temporal cortex and unloads its cargo of sound and image.

Night after night the bubbles come and break, filling in the detail of his lost youth, chapter by chapter.

MARCH

I

Of Pupils and Paddles

On the first Monday of March, with little left of term, Rodney took his place in Form IV. To Oblong's mild surprise he proved the perfect pupil on his opening day, speaking only when spoken to, and resisting any urge to exploit his father's celebrity.

The show of respect proved to be only an overture. The Rotherweird academic day ended with five minutes in the Form Master's company. Rodney waited for his classmates to disperse.

'Sir.'

'Slickstone.'

'I love my history, sir.'

'That's good to hear.'

'We're both outsiders, right?'

'But outsiders in Rotherweird,' replied Oblong.

'Father requires you to teach me local history: how the town was built, when, by whom, why. I mean, good historians like you are inquisitive, aren't they?'

Oblong noted the familiar slippage from sycophancy to insolence and back, as first experienced at Sir Veronal's party.

'Yes, but when in Rome . . .'

'Just what Sir V said you'd say. They learn our history – we should learn theirs.'

'Sir V' had become Rodney's preferred form of address and reference to his putative father. Sir Veronal had never objected.

'After 1800 elsewhere, Rodney, but here never – rules are rules.'

'Sir V said you'd say that too. Remember, sir, he pays private rates for private lessons.' Rodney offered the bribe with a tell-tale wink.

'I'm sorry to disappoint.'

'Look – if the town bothers you, we'll explore the countryside – Saxons, Druids . . .'

'I'm sorry, Slickstone. It's more than my job's worth.'

The boy turned on his heels and marched out, leaving Oblong ill at ease. The *History Regulations*, once means to the political end of preserving Rotherweird's independence, had probably lost their usefulness long ago. He found himself sympathising with Sir Veronal's stance.

At the School gates Rhombus Smith accosted him. 'Remember your reports, Oblong: make them prompt and pithy.'

'Headmaster, would the *History Regulations* allow a little exploration of our rural sites – burial mounds, forts, stone circles?'

'The deeper you dig, the more you disturb – so, in a word, no.'

Oblong debated these issues with himself so intensely that the Headmaster's initial reminder only registered on his arrival at Artery Lane. *Reports!* Having never before lasted to the end of a term, he had overlooked the teacher's most basic chore.

Aggs arrived to replenish his cupboard with her homemade jam. 'You ain't writing their life histories, yer know,' said Aggs, peering over his shoulder.

'Much as I like Mr Fanguin, I don't go for his one-word approach.'

'And I don't go for your one-volume approach. Anyways, you ought to be out and about, getting fit.'

'For what?'

'The Great Equinox Race, of course.'

'Ah,' said Oblong, who, despite his gangly shape, fancied himself over a middle distance, 'if it's eight hundred yards or so, I'm your man.'

'Who's talking about running?'

'Come on, Aggs, out with it. You're my general person.'

'Avoid a single – they capsize unless you're an expert, which you ain't. He be a turner and a twister, Old Man Rother.'

'I'm losing you.'

'The pub is the place to find a partner – people always chop and change. It's about the weight – two-ers and three-ers need just the right— Blimey, Mr Oblong, you never look, do yer? Right now through them trees . . .'

Through his study window and the sweeps of willow breaking leaf, he glimpsed what looked like a half-walnut shell, and then another, in which figures paddled and poled for dear life. 'What are they, Aggs?'

'And you the historian! They're coracles, the finest of vessels, to them what understand 'em! Willow and hide!'

They looked impossible to control. Oblong's swimming stroke had once been charitably described as puppy-paddle. As for rowing, his legs were too long and his right arm stronger than his left. He shook his head with an apologetic smile.

Aggs smiled back. 'I'll send a costume round. I know just the thing.'

'Costume?'

Aggs had a look for closing a subject. She would jut her jaw and grimace while the right eyebrow rose very slowly. She did so now and Oblong obligingly took the cue.

Aggs returned to the reports. 'Why d'yer think Mr Fanguin kept 'em short? There's someone reads all the reports, ain't there?'

'Like whom?'

'Like His Snorkelship.'

The jaw jutted, the eyebrow rose like a tyre inflating, the grimace came and went.

When Aggs left, Oblong remembered Fanguin's reference to Snorkel's ability to control. Getting to grips with the true pulse of Rotherweird was like peeling an onion – a process, he recalled, that usually ended in tears. He rewrote the reports, Fanguin-style.

*

An aggressive tuition programme with the best teachers money could buy had hurried Rodney to competence in most subjects, and the lure of the Slickstone inheritance ensured dedication, but he still lagged far behind in Rotherweird's specialties, the sciences and mathematics. Briefed by Rhombus Smith, the teachers made allowances, but nonetheless resentment simmered in Rodney, especially in algebra classes, where the cow-faced countrysider Gwen Ferdy, seated one desk to his left, fielded every question the rest could not answer with matchless speed and accuracy.

The teacher, Miss Sine, a feisty middle-aged spinster, never put a question to Rodney. 'Is xy a monomial, Collier?'

Collier, the class's slowest intellect, gaped.

'Ferdy?'

'It is.'

'Correct. What happens if you multiply monomials?'

Rodney felt it time to make a mark. 'You get a polynomial, *of course*.'

'Wrong. Ferdy?'

'You get another monomial.'

'Correct.'

'Why do you always ask her? I thought algebra was about balancing things.' Rodney's tone was surly, bordering on the aggressive.

'Sorry you're feeling out of it, Slickstone. Easily remedied – is 2x+5 a monomial or a polynomial?'

'It's eleven if x is 3.'

The class tittered. Sine did not make concessions in matters of discipline. 'We're not in the nursery now, Slickstone. Do the work to catch up.'

In the break Gwen Ferdy for once miscalculated. She approached Rodney in the Quad. 'All this must seem very strange. I can help you—'

'Where I come from, *you* give *me* respect.' Rodney jabbed her hard, just below the throat, to make the point. 'You countrysiders are the ones with learning to do.'

Ned Guley came to the rescue. 'Ease off,' he said.

The punch took Guley entirely by surprise, winding him. Slickstone strutted off to join Collier, a triumphant smirk on his face.

Sir Veronal rebuked Rodney for such a crude display of aggression, promising a reckoning with the countrysiders when he took over governance of Rotherweird, but not before.

Reluctantly, Rodney agreed to bide his time, but honour demanded revenge.

Roy Roc, Orelia's great-grandfather, had won the 1894 Great Equinox Race single-handed. This year she felt a whimsical urge to emulate him. Behind a jumble of boxes, crates, unsold items and newspapers in the basement of *Baubles & Relics*, she found his coracle. It was a single, made of willow and tarred hide, as all Rotherweird coracles had to be. The skin remained sound, and so were the paddle and pole. In keeping with her life to date, she would be going it alone. She embarked on a haphazard programme of training and physical exercise, brave in the Spartan conditions of early spring, which turned more methodical as a mild flirtation with an idea became a dedicated goal. She watched others and proved a quick learner.

To her surprise her aunt agreed to her participation without a quibble. Since the party she had been uncharacteristically subdued, forever muttering about its shameful conclusion. Orelia could not square Mrs Banter's intense distress in the alley on the night of the party or this lingering malaise with their only apparent cause, Valourhand's ill-mannered performance. She judged it best not to delve deeper, and Mrs Banter offered no detail.

Valourhand did not do communal events, and even less so now. She had sought celebrity, only to find herself cold-shouldered outside School society. She immersed herself in work and avoided Strimmer, their fragile intimacy finally ended by her demonstration, a defiant rebuttal of Strimmer's desire for control. She knew that Gorhambury had been dismissed for a venal offence and wondered why Sir Veronal had adopted such a forgiving approach to her. She looked to the Lord of the Manor for the next move. The lightning still nagged away at her. In her rooms she tried to construct lightning machines, but with little success. Every Rotherweird pupil knew how to generate sparks and static electricity with a balloon and a spoon, but a full-scale lightning bolt?

She did not like, or believe in, insoluble problems.

Oblong enjoyed a weekly drink at *The Journeyman's Gist* with Fanguin. On this particular evening they were discussing possible subjects for the next term's history curriculum when Fanguin polished his glasses, so heralding an announcement of moment.

'I've reached a decision,' he boomed, thumping the table. 'This year, *you*, Jonah Oblong, are crewing my coracle!'

Half the pub heard the news as the rosy colour that goes with Sturdy beer drained from Oblong's cheeks.

'It'll be a riot. I've a new method – we can't have Strimmer winning a third time. Up Form IV!'

'Strimmer?'

'Cocky bastard!' Fanguin lowered his voice to a conspiratorial whisper. 'But they haven't reckoned with the "Fanguin rotator".'

'I'm useless in a boat – I go round in circles.'

'You sit in the stern, admire my technique and bale like a loony – piece of cake.'

'Bale?'

'What else are buckets for? Just remember, the long scoop beats the quick dip every time.' Fanguin's blue-grey eyes had the glint of a fanatic as he delivered a dramatic monologue on the Great Equinox Race, its rules, the thrills and spills, the dress code (only requirement: bizarre) and his own near-misses with the winner's podium.

Oblong felt a sense of impending doom, deepened by Aggs'

delivery of a grasshopper costume – green tails, a green and yellow top hat complete with antennae, green and yellow striped trousers supported by black braces and a pair of ancient plimsolls painted – no surprise here – green and yellow.

Had Oblong been more observant, he would have been less astonished. Rotherweird's most *outré* clothes shop, *Ragamuffin* in Grove Lane, had for a month been plying a roaring trade in finished costumes for the well-off and in do-it-yourself components for the mean or impoverished, including feathers, ribbons, plastic wings, false noses and beaks and foam-rubber claws.

Orelia Roc invested in feathers and wings to mimic her namesake.

Strimmer declined to expand his wardrobe, settling for the guise of a wasp, as in his winning performance of the previous year.

Gregorius Jones entrusted his costume to his class; he found their choice pleasingly exotic, and the *fashionistas* of Form VIb did not disappoint in its execution. He would be hard to miss from the towpath.

Miss Trimble's Viking dress, based on a Victorian novel from *Baubles & Relics*, boasted a horned helmet and silver *lamé* chainmail.

Oblong agreed to meet Fanguin in *The Journeyman's Gist* for a final briefing on strategy. The pub heaved with patrons discussing how the Rother would behave this year; whether better to draw the western or eastern circuit; the betting; new technology, and, inevitably, the weather.

Oblong found two stools in the garden and waited. To his dismay Strimmer arrived first.

'Stool,' barked Strimmer, pointing at the spare seat.

'I'm keeping it for a friend.'

'I don't care who you're keeping it for. I'm here; and he's not. *And* I'm from this town and you're an outsider.'

Fanguin arrived in the nick of time. 'Ah, Strimmer, having a history lesson? Or is it manners?'

'He's hogging the seats.'

'Not any more.'

Fanguin placed his ample behind on the stool.

'I hear you two are in the same boat,' smirked Strimmer, 'up the creek without a paddle.'

'Youth and Beauty,' said Fanguin pleasantly.

'You're all wind and no trousers,' said Strimmer, 'and your crew looks ready to wet himself.' He guffawed at his own joke before moving to the bar.

'*Right* – strategy lesson!' The crazed glint had returned. Fanguin took out a chart. 'Here is the start – at dawn.' He pointed north of the town. 'Every entrant draws east or west and has to follow his drawn direction when the river divides. The finish is here.' He pointed two hundred yards below the southern bridge. 'But here's the catch: Rotherweird has a bore, and I don't mean Gorhambury – it's an underground tidal freak that delivers a surge, always at dawn at the Spring Equinox. It can knock out half the field. That's where craftsmanship comes in.'

'Don't we practise?'

Fanguin slumped in mock outrage. 'Practise? We're amateurs, Oblong – Olympians, the last of a dying breed! Now, attend to your Skipper. Poles propel, but also attack. They have squidgy balls on the end—'

Oblong had an instant vision of Strimmer tilting him overboard.

'Cheer up! You try poling people in a coracle – fraught with peril. Now look at this . . .' Fanguin's voice sunk to a conspiratorial whisper as he flourished a piece of paper crisscrossed with sums, formulae and diagrams. 'The "Fanguin rotator"! Spin like a beetle, sting like a bee.' He downed his pint of Sturdy before adding, 'Uniform – I trust you have suitably exotic plumage?'

'Idiotic.'

'That's the spirit,' said Fanguin, heading off for his early bed.

Jovial banter with the landlord was standard fare at *The*

Journeyman's Gist, so customers assumed there must be good cause for Bill Ferdy's silence over the last two weeks and respected it. Ferdy had placed the Town Hall's letter under the lip of the bar in the hope it would disappear. Tonight, on the eve of one of the pub's busiest days, the aftermath of the *Great Equinox Race*, the notice period expired, and Slickstone had retaliated with perfect timing.

With an hour to closing time Bill Ferdy rang the old sailor's bell, with which he had called 'time' for decades, and announced that drinks were on the house. The more sensitive present detected a troubling air of finality in the gesture.

2

A Most Unexpected Result

Oblong and Orelia greeted the morning of the Spring Equinox in contrasting moods. Oblong was not one of Nature's early risers; Orelia was. He peered in horror at the mirror; she looked with amusement in hers, looking absurd with ill-matched plumes in unexpected places and a bright orange cardboard beak. Oblong barely made it out of the door; Orelia bounded down the steps.

Meanwhile, Gorhambury arrived in the courtyard of *The Polk Land & Water Company*. Facing him stood the Polks' house, five-sixths occupied by Bert and his ever-growing family; a vertical sliver by bachelor Boris. On every side sprawled outhouses and sheds storing various vehicles and workshops. The charabanc had already left, laden with coracle repair materials, as well as the Polks' bizarre costume, but his own vehicle, the Umpire's chair, had been left for him, the brass stair rail polished to a shine, the telescope fixed to the left of the single elevated seat, the lectern to the right for the Rulebooks. Snorkel had forgotten to cancel an appointment that had, as tradition dictated, been awarded to the incumbent Town Clerk at the beginning of the year, and Gorhambury had no intention of surrendering this privilege.

He pressed the starting piston, clambered up the steps of the tallest vehicle in town, switched on the fog-lamps and set off for the towpath. The early mist promised a fine morning. His last Equinox Race would, he hoped, be special.

*

On the towpath at quarter to five in the morning chill steamed the breath of competitors under a clear, lightening sky. Cheered to discover that others were dressed in costumes no less ludicrous than his own, Oblong's step lightened. Spectators headed north to the start, south to the finish, or to a betting tent.

He could make out many school staff, none of whom had made any effort to preserve their self-respect. An attractive if dishevelled parrot came alongside, spinning a single coracle with aplomb.

'It's our resident historian,' she said.

'Oblong.'

'We met – remember?'

Oblong remembered his inept response to her cheerful welcome at the party. He mustered a nervous grin.

'Nice costume – suits you. Double or single?'

'I'm in a double with Mr Fanguin.'

'So you seek the rapids and the crocodile!'

Oblong gulped.

'Good God!' giggled Orelia.

A dodo strode towards them with a familiar bouncing gait, paddle, pole and a small bucket in one hand, a coracle bowling along under the other.

'Fanguin!' cheered Orelia. 'I thought you were extinct!'

'Only a question of time,' replied Fanguin, turning like a model on a catwalk, the effect marred by an over-mobile beak.

'Where's my—? Ah, Oblong, me ol' hearty . . . Crew, take the accessories!'

Mr Oblong was thrown the pole with its squidgy boxing glove at the end, and, ominously, the bucket.

'Perfect conditions,' added Fanguin, looking skywards. The mad glint in his eye was back.

Behind an arras of willows a cryptic conversation unfolded in whispers. On the ground a tan-coloured costume lay open, two foam-rubber protuberances on the back. Beside it stood a coracle with four shoes fixed to the floor.

'Gyroscopes connect to the soles – they tilt as the river tilts, so compensating for our limited vision. They come with a foolproof guarantee!'

'In this suit, Boris?'

'Bert, we are pioneers.'

Encouraged by their own rhetoric, the twins clambered into their single costume.

At the start a menagerie of lost species milled around the towpath – birds, insects, exotic animals, even the occasional dinosaur. Between a wooden rostrum on either bank hung a golden ribbon. Between the start and the walls of the town, the water meadows teemed with spectators and bicycles.

'You get the pole-flag, Oblong, and let's hope for beginner's luck!'

'Pole-flag?'

'Over there, over there!'

The Headmaster's wife, Silvia Smith, a pleasant-looking lady with well-groomed chestnut hair, stood by the rostrum dispensing large envelopes, each containing sets of four cards, marked W for west or E for east, and a unique number. The cards had adhesive sides and, once drawn, were attached to the coracle pole, the side of the vessel and the costumes of the crew. Oblong drew W4 and an encouraging smile from the Headmaster's wife.

Strimmer passed by, twirling his pole with the flag E7. The black and yellow stripes gave him an air of menace. Even the diaphanous wings looked more in keeping than absurd.

'Damn,' said Fanguin on hearing the news, 'he's on the other side. We won't know what he's up to. Worse, nor will Gorhambury. The Umpire always takes the western station.' He pointed to the Umpire's chair.

Gorhambury sat aloft, dressed in an ill-fitting blazer and baggy cream-coloured flannel trousers, attention forever shifting from his megaphone to the Rulebook. From his vantage point Gorhambury felt uncomfortable. Everyone knew of his dismissal, and he had garnered few of the usual greetings. He suppressed the urge to explain so as not to expose Mrs Banter, but as the frenzy of gathering racers and supporters intensified, the melodrama of the event dispelled his *angst*. He had too many rules to apply to be distracted by his personal tragedy.

The parrot waved and waggled her orange beak. 'Have a whale of a time, Jonah.'

'Watch out for the Rocs,' retaliated Oblong.

'Stop chatting up the opposition,' yelled Fanguin.

A peacock in full plumage strutted past, spinning a single with the tips of his fingers, the vigour of the stride a give-away. Gregorius Jones had drawn E33. His tail sporadically fanned and contracted, obeying a device fixed to the small of Jones' back by the *fashionistas* of Form VIB.

Fanguin was unimpressed. 'He always leads, but never wins. Only question is, who's the lucky damsel this year?'

Spectators waved poles with puppet-style mascots on the end, imitating in miniature the costume worn by the entrant they supported. Oblong spotted Bomber, waving a cutout Dodo, and Aggs, brandishing a grasshopper. W4 had at least two supporters.

Betting tents on either shore listed the current odds on large blackboards with costume names and real identities in parenthesis: Dodo/Grasshopper (Fanguin/Oblong).

Loudspeakers would provide a running – and falling – commentary. Betting slips bore the words: *The Rotherweird Betting Company: Proprietor: S. Snorkel*. Near the finish, south of the town, close to the riverbank, *The Polk Land & Water Company* had a large tent emblazoned with the legend *Coracle Casualties*. The untenanted charabanc stood on the towpath ready to transport damaged coracles from higher up the course to their place of surgery. Of the Polk brothers there was no sign.

Angela Trimble, who'd drawn E37, stood motionless, a Viking, pole held upright like a spear, her flaxen hair platted down her back. Maroon ribbons crisscrossed her legs from knee to ankle. She shut out the human sound and concentrated on the river. Somewhere upstream, deep and out of sight, the swell would be building.

From the Umpire's chair Gorhambury's reedy voice delivered a stream of reminders to the gathering fleet: '*Downed oarsmen may return to their own coracles, but nobody else's* – Rule 16(4)(b). *A double coracle may finish with a single crewman* – Rule 17.'

'Wake up!' yelled Fanguin.

Chastened, Oblong leapt into the coracle and almost fell out the opposite end. It was so *light*.

'In the back,' screamed Fanguin, getting more and more excited.

Oblong held the view that an open circular boat had no such thing. 'Where's the back?'

'I'm the front, idiot.'

The coracle rocked alarmingly as Oblong installed himself behind Fanguin.

'Tactic number one – we go back to go forward.'

This further confused Oblong, until he noted that the Umpire's chair and a good third of the flotilla – about forty coracles – were heading gently upstream away from the start, before heading back to the line.

'Hit the road running,' explained Fanguin. 'First up, you paddle and I pole. I shall ward off pirates.'

As they turned, the deep cobalt blue to the east turned silver. Nearby, Gorhambury issued his final warning: '*Rule 13(c) – All coracles must be within twenty yards of the starting ribbon at the start. Penalty – disqualification.*'

Then several happenings converged: a gurgling subterranean grumble slowly grew to a growl and then a roar; the water began to seethe as if coming to the boil; the sun's rim emerged from the eastern hills and cannon boomed from the northern and southern gatehouses, belching out plumes of green smoke to mark the advent of spring.

Orelia decided to pole, keeping the paddle for emergencies. You had to be careful to keep your weight central, she'd quickly learned, or the coracle went one way and you the other.

Strimmer eyed the field and found little to trouble him. Jones would do the usual. Trimble he could deal with. Fanguin, surely too old to be a threat, would be further handicapped by the imbecile historian. Roc had pedigree, but no experience.

'No dirty work, Strimmer!' Trimble wagged a finger as she passed. 'Now would I ever—?'

'How about last year?' added Miss Trimble fiercely.

Fanguin harboured similar thoughts to Strimmer about the value of his deputy. Oblong was not concentrating as a mariner should, being transfixed by the movement within the upper reaches of Miss Trimble's Viking costume.

'What are you gazing at?' yelled Fanguin. 'We're being passed by the School Porter – how humiliating is that? – keep her at bay, man . . .'

Fanguin flung off his dodo beak as it clacked against his pole for the umpteenth time. Slowly but surely they picked up speed. As the boats turned back for the start, the water, silver as a fish's back a moment earlier, shone like burnished copper.

'Middle of the field,' boomed Fanguin, 'just where we want to be.'

Oblong kept terror at bay by musing on the origins of this tradition. Had Rotherweird been invaded by coracle, escaped by coracle, invented the coracle – or had some traveller arrived by coracle and set a fashion? Unravelling such mysteries was the historian's task. He let his imagination roam as Fanguin, bent over with a hand on each side of the coracle, whispered, 'She's a-coming, boy, a-coming . . .'

Most had experienced the surge before, but it always differed in shape and timing – high left and low right, or vice versa, or high in the middle with curling sides. This year the river excelled itself, running high right *and* left, with a diminishing low point in the middle, which sucked all the coracles into a heaving mass before dispersing them one way or the other. In addition to achieving survival, competitors had to keep right or left of the town in accordance with their flag.

As the surge struck, Gorhambury cut the golden tape marking the start and chaos ensued. Everyone started yelling and gesticulating as their vessels spun and collided, rose and fell. A few unfortunate debutants put poles through the floors of their coracles; others toppled in with little chance of reboarding until the main fleet had moved on. Onlookers cheered and jeered; mariners cursed and encouraged, and Gorhambury noted all infractions, consulting, whenever necessary, his Rulebook.

Whether by luck or timing, the ribbon parted as Orelia swept through, giving her the privilege of an early lead. She felt the great-grand-paternal spirit in her veins as she ducked a side-swipe from Strimmer's pole like a veteran. She crouched to make her centre of gravity low.

Many W numbers were pushed to the east and E numbers to the west, creating a scrum in mid-stream, even after the surge had passed. Several more tipped over. The Polk gyroscopes could not manage so much contradictory data and the fixed shoes hurled Boris to the left and Bert to the right. With a sound of tearing Velcro, the camel suit disgorged the Polk twins. On the floor of the coracle the shoes still twitched as if inhabited by ghosts.

The brothers hauled themselves ashore.

'It just needs minor adjustments – so close,' declared Boris.

'If you kept the accounts, you'd not be worrying about minor adjustments!' replied Bert.

Boris' creativity contributed as much to the family business as

'. . . which sucked all the coracles into a heaving mass before dispersing them one way or the other.'

Bert's repairing and accountancy skills, but Boris accepted the hint of rebuke. After all, this looked to be a bumper Race for business.

Strimmer, meantime, was inflicting almost as much damage as the wave. He caught the poleman of a short-odds crew, a pair of frogs, flush on the head. Every successful bump and strike was greeted with a self-congratulatory cry. Leaving empty coracles in his wake, the wasp entered the eastern Rother with only Miss Trimble in front of him.

Fanguin kept low as Oblong shut his eyes: this was the worst of fairground rides. The coracle lurched to meet the sky, slid up one side of the bow wave, wobbled on the crest, then skidded down the back of the surge as it passed. Oblong's stomach suffered as much as his balance. Fanguin looked unconcerned by being in the middle of the field.

Orelia trusted to instinct and rode the wave, the pole across her like a tightrope walker. Whether by luck or inherited judgement, she narrowly maintained her lead.

Despite the big talk, Fanguin allowed their coracle to drift towards the back of the pack of surviving W numbers. Having found space and plotted a route, he announced, arms akimbo, 'Ladies and gents – the "Fanguin rotator"!' The dodo planted his pole and with a curious swivelling, dancing motion spun the coracle several times and then released, achieving a skimming forward lurch. Jeering and hilarity moved to admiration as in five minutes W4, now passing under the town's western walls, overtook the parrot and edged ahead of the field on the eastern station.

'Learned from the Bolivian waterbeetle!' shouted the dodo-biologist.

Many rushed to bet on Fanguin-Oblong and the cashiers happily took the money. Fanguin had a record of colourful near-misses in the Great Equinox Race – but they shortened his odds, just in case.

As the Rother split, taking W numbers one side of the town and E numbers the other, more committed supporters of the latter poured over the north bridge and on to Grove Gardens to keep them in view.

No mariner caught the eye like Gregorius Jones, who added his own chivalric code to the Rulebook, attacking only those who attacked him and shouting out warnings to anyone he judged vulnerable to sneaky attacks by the likes of Strimmer. Above all, he practised elegance with a twirl of the pole and a shimmer of the body after every manoeuvre, his resplendent tail opening and shutting all the while. From the bank and then the railings of Grove Gardens, peacock feathers waved as Form VIB cheered on their hero.

Miss Trimble held the lead on the eastern station in determined mood, staring fixedly ahead, until a cry from Jones and a glance behind confirmed that action was called for. Strimmer was closing, his pole shouldered like a lance, the squidgy ball bobbing nearer and nearer the small of her back. She feigned tiredness and then, with Strimmer poised to strike, she abruptly changed tack. Strimmer jabbed so hard at thin air that he lost balance and fell, just managing to stay aboard despite a painful blow to the shins.

In her exhilaration she did not see the recumbent Strimmer raise his pole and take careful aim. With a hiss of compressed air, the pole extended by a third of its length and caught Miss Trimble full on the left shoulder. With a large splash she fell overboard, to a groan from the betting tent. She had been fancied as a dark horse. The extension retracted so quickly that everyone assumed Miss Trimble had lost her footing. The wasp forged ahead to meet his rivals on the eastern side, confident that downing Trimble would deal a double blow.

Strimmer was right: as in previous years, the sight of a woman in the water proved fatal to Gregorius Jones.

'Jones to the rescue!' he boomed and plunged overboard.

Miss Trimble was in no mood to be rescued. 'Go away, you silly man,' she spluttered, bosom heaving with rage.

'It's all right, young woman, I teach river-rescue—'

'Sod off!'

After further exchanges and a swipe from Miss Trimble's paddle, Jones gave up. Both were out of the race as potential winners, although Miss Trimble, now helmetless, righted her upturned coracle, hauled herself aboard and resumed. Jones, sitting disconsolate on a mudflat as detached peacock feathers swam away on the current to bring the news to his supporters south of the town, felt a tremor of desire. Angela Trimble had reboarded. She had shown pluck. She knew the code.

To Strimmer's consternation, three W numbers had reached the confluence of the Rother before him and were only two hundred yards from the finishing line.

At this critical juncture a problem emerged with the rotator technique. After Fanguin's sustained burst, advancing years and his new retirement diet of Sturdy and risotto were taking their toll. Speechless with exhaustion, Fanguin handed over to Oblong, who had not devoted hours to mimicking the movement of the Bolivian waterbeetle. Like a demented dancer without elegance or rhythm, the coracle jerked round and round the pole with no forward movement. Fanguin put his head in his hands and moaned as the crowd jeered or went silent (depending on their betting choices).

Orelia Roc had both rhythm and elegance. Her slight craft skimmed past Fanguin's double. Her thighs and calves ached, but she was enjoying herself. To her left she could see Strimmer raising the pace. It would be close.

'Passed by an antique dealer!' snorted Fanguin.

Damp and humiliated, Oblong made a final effort. He ran two paces, planted the pole as hard as he could and pushed with his feet. By a miracle of timing the coracle shot forward. Fanguin, amazed, disappeared out of the back and Oblong found himself high in the air. The coracle skimmed on. From his privileged vantage point he surveyed the crowd, all of them laughing.

Oblong glanced down and a simple idea took root. He was a grasshopper. He landed in Roc's coracle, accidentally tipping her into the Rother to join Fanguin, replanted his pole and flew high into the air once more. Strimmer surged on, left fist raised as victory beckoned.

As if by a miracle, ahead of him, Oblong's empty coracle, the right way up, skimmed along. Adopting Fanguin's surfing pose, he freakishly landed like a born gymnast. Impelled by his momentum the coracle accelerated alongside the wasp. They broke the finishing ribbon together. Snorkel, busy calculating his profits, broke his pencil in disbelief. A tie meant two winners, and well-backed winners at that. Roc had finished second (third in view of the tie) and Miss Trimble fifth after a pair of bats.

Gorhambury, peering through his telescope, could only agree.

'Cheat!' Strimmer screamed. 'Stewards' Enquiry!'

In the winners' enclosure a scrum surrounded Strimmer and Oblong. A dripping Fanguin belatedly joined them.

'He's an outsider,' protested Strimmer. 'He can't count, not alone.'

Oblong meanwhile was more concerned to apologise to Orelia.

'Never apologise for a smart move,' she said.

The Umpire's chair drew up. Gorhambury savoured one of those moments where the Rule of Law struts in plain view on the popular stage. He spoke solemnly, a judge giving judgment: 'Rule 37 says: *The winning coracleer or coracleers hoists or hoist the summer flag on Rotherweird Church Tower at noon on the day of the Spring Equinox.* There's an asterisk to which is appended a footnote in the 1675 edition.'

'Get on with it, Bore-em-very!' shouted a wag in the crowd.

Gorhambury produced a worn diary-sized leather volume from under the lectern and turned up the relevant page. '*In the improbable event of a tie, the first mariner to pass the line in each winning coracle shall race the other to the top of the Church Tower. The first to touch the flagpole shall have the honour and privilege of raising the Equinox flag* . . . So it's Mr Strimmer versus Mr Oblong.'

'Don't worry, ladies and gentlemen,' Strimmer crowed grandly to the crowd, 'he doesn't know the way and he hasn't a prayer.'

The betting tents reopened, though not for long. Nobody would bet against Strimmer, although Oblong did receive a winding slap on the back from a soaked Miss Trimble. 'Legendary leap,' she said, 'quite legendary.'

A press of spectators and competitors in their bedraggled costumes followed Gorhambury and the two winners up the Golden Mean to the church. Even the Polks abandoned their work to watch the first tie-break in the Great Equinox Race in living memory. Municipal workers swiftly erected a tape to keep the crowd back.

'Nervous?' said Strimmer. 'You should be.'

Gorhambury replaced his megaphone with a starting pistol and declared the rules of the tie-breaker. 'The flag is, unsurprisingly, where the flagpole is. First there raises it – and wins. Play fair, gentlemen. We don't want accidents.'

Oblong could see no scope for accidents. Strimmer knew his way round the church and he did not. It would be over very quickly.

'On your marks . . . keep to your lane . . . go!'

Oblong jumped as the pistol went off, much to the pleasure of the crowd. Strimmer ran to the front of the church, ignored the door and started to climb stone rungs set in the outside wall.

Oblong went to the door. Locked. More hilarity.

'Lane!' shouted Rhombus Smith in his direction. '*West!*'

Oblong blushed. He had not the slightest clue what was going on.

Then Fanguin's voice boomed over the hubbub, 'Climb, man, *climb!*'

He could see Strimmer walking along the spine of the roof over the nave towards the tower and the penny dropped. Strimmer was an E number – so he started at the front. He was a W number, so he must start at the rear, and not go through the church, but up a sheer wall.

Oblong jumped over the cemetery wall and located two parallel rows of stone rungs near the northern corner of the church's rear wall. They rose to the parapet of the tower high above him.

The crowd, scenting that Oblong would provide richer entertainment, surged through the gravestones after him.

Cocooned in concentration Oblong looked only at the green-grey stone in front of him, climbing up and up until he reached the join of the nave to the tower, marked by a lip and a small gulley, a gap he had to cross to reach the next run of footholds. Wooden slatted windows just above marked the belfry.

Clambering over the ledge broke the spell as Oblong unwisely glanced down and then up. Sky and building spun. A clammy sensation gripped the small of his back. Frozen by vertigo, he used a tiny red spider to restore focus. He placed his right foot on the next rung and began to climb again.

The morning had been calm and the gust of wind caught him unprepared. His gangly legs flailed like a sheet in a gale and his right hand came away. Miraculously, he was thrown across, into and through the shutters. He clambered to his feet to see two large bells hanging beside four smaller ones – but they were nothing compared to the extraordinary frescoes. They were beautiful and, to judge from the colour and relative naïveté, very early.

The west wall illustrated husbandry – cornfields, harvesters, men with sickles, horses, cottages, fishermen, birds; an early version of Rotherweird with no gatehouses and no towers.

The south wall showed the Rother teeming with coracles, crewed by men and women, their urgency explained by a column of armoured soldiers closing on the island. Romans. He could make out the standard bearing the letters SPQR – *Senatus Populusque Romanus*.

The north wall resembled a doom painting – a soldier being ushered through a cloudy door, to emerge with snout and whiskers like a weaselman, while a second waited behind. Legionary prisoners, it appeared – but why dress the first in an animal mask? Oblong feared some ritual execution, a victory celebration.

The base of the east wall showed a single plant with spreading green stalks and one flower bud. Beside the plant a peculiar tree spread its arms, laden with blossom. In the opposite top corner, pipers played and dancers danced against a background of flowering plants and berries, an incongruous scene set against the others. The central section had been obscured by damp, reacting with the fresco's paint to produce an explosion of purple, in which disconcertingly, due perhaps to a peculiarity of the particular pigment, isolated arms and legs survived. Below there appeared the letters MXVII.

A thick carpet of dust recorded his footprints. Nobody had been here in years.

A cheer from the crowd declared Strimmer's victory. Oblong could not face descending the outside wall again. He found a trap-door, bolted on his side, leading down to another room with bare walls where a proper staircase delivered him to an alcove behind the choir. His luck had changed. The church door had been unlocked.

Outside, the crowd engulfed Strimmer, throwing him into the air. Strimmer grimaced, unamused by the vulgarity of it all, as Oblong ambled past, suffering no abuse, merely ignored. The spectators began to drift home. Oblong sensed a popular unease, not with the result, but with the aftermath, which he could not place.

'Bravo, Oblong!' The ever-loyal Boris Polk approached. 'I assume Gregorius messed up again. Who was the lucky lady this year?'

'Miss Trimble.'

'He doesn't understand that women wish to be impressed, not rescued. Sorry, gotta go – Bert's overwhelmed, it's a bumper year for repairs.'

Oblong walked to *The Journeyman's Gist* to find a notice nailed to the door: *Closed pending new management – By Order of the Licensing Committee*. Now he understood: Rotherweirders must have been discussing the ins and outs of the Great Equinox Race over Ferdy beer in *The Journeyman's Gist* for centuries. This year they were forced to drink homebrew in the churchyard.

He noted a telling clue: Snorkel's name was missing – never court unnecessary unpopularity. Oblong peered inside. Men carried cabling, and on the bar stood a toolbox with the name *SLICKSTONE ELECTRICS* in red. He felt shocked that such a conservative town could bear such a change without protest.

Two notes awaited him on the front door mat.

Dear Honourable Second,

Support appreciated, performance adequate plus.

 Yours in adventure,

 The Skipper.

PS Shocking news about the JG.

The second was barely literate.

Dere Sir,

You did you gennerel person prowd, you did. A.'

Oblong felt he had earned a siesta, and yet sleep would not come. The belfry's frescoes danced in his head. Saxon peasantry, going about their seasonal tasks – the scene did not fit the town's current hostility to 'countrysiders', so where had that come from? Then there was the peculiar image of the cloudy door and the emerging human-animal clones, and the letters MXVII. He instinctively translated the Roman numerals to 1017 – and with a start, sprang from his bed and rushed to his sock drawer to retrieve Robert Flask's notebook.

STOLE CAR ASC 1017.

Oblong cursed his stupidity at missing the glaring connection between MXVII and 1017. The date, and the image in the frescoes of the harvesters in their primitive smocks, provoked a flash of inspiration: ASC referred to the *Anglo-Saxon Chronicle*.

By happy coincidence Oblong's old university notes included a printed summary of the *Chronicle*'s coverage after 1000. The brief entry for 1017 did not make happy reading: Danes had ravaged their way from Cambridge to Northampton to Bedford, and then into Wessex, a time of unrelieved misery. Nothing connected to Rotherweird, but Oblong remained convinced he was right.

King Alfred had founded the *Chronicle*. None of the nine surviving versions were the same, and the original no longer existed. Copies had been distributed to various monasteries, where they had been updated by local scribes. The oldest survivor resided in Winchester. Seven of the nine were in the British Library. His notes cited papers by an expert in early English manuscripts at the British Museum, a Dr Pendle.

Despite the fact that he was following in Flask's footsteps and breaching his contract by raking over the past, he reassured himself that a historian's duty demanded no less. The following morning he took the charabanc to Hoy and found a telephone box. After a relay through various switchboards, he reached his target.

'Donald Pendle.' More croak than speech, the voice was dry as dust.

Notebook at the ready, he introduced himself. 'Oblong, Jonah Oblong.'

'I trust you live up to your name – *oblongus*, meaning rather long.'

Oblong ignored him. 'I'm ringing from Rotherweird School.'

'How strange. You're the second in six months. As I said to your colleague, weird comes from the Saxon for 'come to pass' – your fate, in other words. If you're ringing about the *Chronicle*, your Mr Flask can explain.'

'I'm afraid he's left us.'

'This is unpaid time, Mr Oblong.'

'I'm sorry—'

'There are only two entries, both for 1017, and similar. They end with a savage winter, but it's summer that's interesting.' Oblong heard the rustling of papers. Flask must have asked the self-same question. He was definitely on the trail. Pendle croaked on, 'Here is Worcester: "*In these days a monster came to the Rotherweird Midsummer Fayre to wed. The place was saved by the Green Man and the Hammer.*" And Winchester: "*Strange reports from the village of Rotherweird. A Druid priest tells that a monster came to their Midsummer Fair with the midsummer flower. All were saved by the Green Man and the Hammer.*"'

Oblong recalled the curious flowering plant in the fresco. 'Can you help on the midsummer flower?'

'Rest assured there's no such thing. I've read *Beowulf*, *Sir Gawain* and the *Flora Britannica*. I've checked the Library's works on herbology. And don't ask about Norse myths, I've read them too. As for the Hammer, he sounds like the sort of Dane you wouldn't want marrying your daughter, but there's no trace of him either. The Green Man is a universal among vegetative deities and a symbol of rebirth. Find him in churches, pagan sites and hanging outside an excellent pub near Reading. I blame the monks – they were partial to psychedelic mushrooms.'

'I'm mighty grateful.'

'Yes, well, it's time for old Pendle to keep the wolf from the door. And just remember: the Saxon language has seven vowels and six diphthongs, but still informs hundreds of our words. Including goodbye.' With that *envoi*, Pendle hung up.

Oblong felt a ghost at his shoulder. Flask had been there before him, but he had not been prompted by the frescoes. He wondered whether Flask's note ASC 1017 had come before or after his conversation with Dr Pendle. Moreover, how could such apparent gibberish matter?

How more knowledge can deepen a mystery, he reflected ruefully.

Elsewhere the Great Equinox Race was judged exceptional – the first dead heat in a century, and the outsider shown up, the grudging respect for his coraclemanship quickly displaced by his farcical failure to ascend the tower. To the universal revelry, there was but one exception.

Gorhambury traipsed home, his last formal duty done. He could not raise the rent for April. A mind tuned to toil would fall into disuse, coils of once-hyperactive cabling gathering dust, a recipe for deep depression.

3

A Dangerous Play

The actress' research into the Sir Veronal's character stalled as soon as it began – there was nothing of note in his bedroom or library, or indeed, anywhere else. Only the ground floor study held hope, but it was always locked and Sir Veronal had the only key – until by a cunning sleight of hand, she managed to steal an impression in a bar of soap. Getting it to a locksmith on Aether's Way would be the next challenge. She had been housebound since their arrival.

Stereotypically, a woman in her position in a comic play would find a stratagem, but she felt the role of Lady Slickstone worked better as a truth-teller. She also doubted that comedy was the right genre.

'I've been asked by a Mrs Banter to tea. May I go?'

Sir Veronal's forehead twitched. 'Yes, please do – and investigate a purchase of mine. Your wretched hostess owns *Baubles & Relics* where I bought some stones – find out where they came from, all she knows. Bargain if you have to.'

Her interest in him had sharpened since the party. Initially Rotherweird had induced uncertainty, but recently he had changed, acquiring an intensity which, in her experience, his business activities had never provoked. Some grail still eluded him, but she suspected he was closing in.

'Anything I should know about these stones?'

'Only that their provenance is a mystery worth solving.'

The actress knew better than to probe further. 'I'll report back,' she said.

With the actress out of the room, Sir Veronal summoned Rodney. 'I have a task for you. You may reconnect briefly with your former self.'

He gave his instructions, emphasising the need for caution and noting with pleasure the boy's increasing deference, to him at least. He then adjourned to his study to record the previous night's revelations. Frustratingly, he could not summon these lost memories of his own volition. They came only in sleep and, with few exceptions, the earliest and deepest first. His notes remained fragmentary. He recalled his parents' disbelief at his precocious talents, his mother's suffocating affection and his father's suspicious distance. The memory was as much intellectual as visual. He recalled how his desire for change had been satisfied by his removal to the great castle in London, and his mixed feelings at having to share with children similarly blessed, nine to be exact. But unlike them he understood that force of intellect is nothing without force of spirit. The mysterious journey, the change from one cart to another and his arrival at Rotherweird Manor – these images had returned. He recalled even the teaching regime and Grassal's library.

Yet they must be preliminaries: somehow, somewhere, by some dark miracle he had acquired the gift of lightning. Every night he blew out the candle in anxious expectation.

The actress enjoyed her walk, politely acknowledged more than ignored. Modernist productions favoured free movement among your audience.

Her chosen locksmith on Aether's Way made no comment on the bar of soap and promised to have a perfect key by six. He insisted on no charge by way of thanks for the party. Valourhand's speech did not appear to have had an adverse effect.

Mrs Banter greeted her at the door in a cashmere jersey, a smart skirt and elegant shoes. 'It's so gracious of you to come, Lady Slickstone.'

A well-to-do sitting room suggestive of moderate wealth, social ambition and a sound but unimaginative taste would have been the appropriate stage direction. Mrs Banter came across at first as a farce stereotype, the shallow and pushy socialite. She served china tea with a sponge cake, all the social niceties observed.

'I do so like Lapsang,' said the actress, setting a ladylike tone for the first twenty minutes. Mrs Banter advised on hairdressers, the only nail parlour worthy of the name, and Snorkel soirées. She dropped a few names and cut the cake. Flour spangled her lower lip.

Her opening move in the real game was surprisingly direct. 'I fear I have offended your husband.'

The actress responded in kind. 'I fear you have.'

'Do you know how?'

'He described you as greedy.'

Mrs Banter changed gear. 'I have been ostracised, Lady Slickstone, for my business acumen.' She produced Snorkel's letter. 'Your husband purchased some beads from my shop. I ensured a fair price, as no doubt he would have done in my position.'

The actress wondered what the script required. She felt the sense of power that improvisation brings. You act as you write – *her* script. Should she lie, or tell the truth? If the former, how should she present it? She decided that the scene needed more tension. 'Is that all?'

'I assumed I was excluded from the party by mistake. It seems I was wrong.'

'Talk me through it.'

Mrs Banter gave a subtly edited version of her intervention in the sale before hinting at the solution to her predicament. 'The problem with the likes of Sir Veronal and Mr Snorkel is *reaching* them. I need someone of influence to intercede.'

The actress did not rise. She asked for a description of the stones.

'Like beads without holes – but good colour, and unusual.'

'Worth what he paid?'

Mrs Banter arched her back. 'For every odd object, there is a collector willing to pay. Sir Veronal understands that, *surely*.'

'Where did they come from?'

Mrs Banter's eyes narrowed. 'One good turn deserves another.'

'I have little influence.'

Mrs Banter tutted. 'All wives have influence. They know so much.' She delivered a cold smile, and the actress felt a prickle of dislike. 'I like secrets too, which is why I excel at *observing* when *unobserved*. I know, for example, that this is the second time you've been out of the Manor on foot.'

'*Second* time?'

'People regard between two and three in the morning as the safest hour to wander the streets undetected, but I have long sight and a commanding view. I knew Sir Veronal would come that morning to buy because I'd seen him and his young friend the night before, huddled round my shop like a couple of carol singers. That's why I dropped in, just at the right time.' Mrs Banter paused to let the implications sink in. 'But of course, you followed that night, no doubt intrigued by such a strange outing. You weren't with them because you weren't asked, and you weren't asked because you weren't wanted.'

The actress revised her view. She was not sharing the stage with a farce stereotype. Mrs Banter was an altogether deeper and darker character.

Mrs Banter's voice upped a semitone. 'He wouldn't tell you the whys and the wherefores, now would he? He's that kind of man – the sort who does *not* like to be followed – and you're expected to be that kind of wife.' Mrs Banter paused. From her bag she produced a leatherbound notebook. On its spine the actress saw the initials Sa-Sl. Mrs Banter patted the book with a proprietorial air. 'You left the Manor at two-thirteen in the morning.'

The actress allowed herself a half-smile at this intriguing turn of events. Mrs Banter might not be what she seemed – but then, nor was she.

The actress countered neatly, 'He may require an apology. He may even want to recruit you. He's like that.'

Recruitment! Mrs Banter's hatred dissipated. To join the retinue of a knight of the realm! The hard edge to her voice softened. 'Help me, Lady Slickstone – I never forget a favour.'

'Then tell me where the stones came from.'

'When I'm reinstated to my proper station, I shall do so with pleasure.'

By way of reply the actress summoned a nuanced facial expression, implying an understanding between women.

The key she collected on the way back. Hopefully, she now had the wherewithal to hoist her part to new levels.

True to her interpretation of Lady Slickstone as a risk-taking truth-teller, she revealed to Sir Veronal that Mrs Banter snooped on her fellow citizens. Surprisingly, Sir Veronal seemed more interested in this news than Mrs Banter's refusal to assist on the provenance of the stones before her restoration to high society.

'Let her stew,' he said, 'then we'll see.'

Three words of dismissal, three words pregnant with some unspoken plan for the future – annoyingly, Sir Veronal still had all the lines.

Old History

1570. The Rotherweird Valley.

'Hieronymus says autumn starts the day after the last full moon in August. He says you can tell from the dew and the spiders.' Morval Seer holds up her paintbrush. She sits beside a tangle of hawthorn by the river. Her hair is plaited, thick, fine and golden.

'Pig's bristle,' whispers Slickstone, his breath catching her neck. *You're a swineherd's daughter*, he implies, *count yourself lucky to have my attention.* Her skin tightens as he runs his finger from her shoulder to her elbow. She shrugs him off.

'Who do you think you are to say no to me?'

'There is ugliness – and ugliness,' she replies.

She enrages him, speaking back, accusing him of ugliness of spirit. God, he wants her. 'The other women – I have had all three. You'll find me expert.'

'You think it a science, do you?'

'How would you know? Or are you and that brother of yours bedfellows?'

She hits him with the back of her hand – not hard, a gesture.

He smiles. 'He shows no respect. He will be punished.'

'Hieronymus is Hieronymus.'

Yet he catches the quaver in her voice – the hostage, the oldest card in the pack. 'You'll need a special friend, or his punishment will be harsh.'

He will not win this particular game, he knows that. She will draw and colour for the Eleusians to save her brother, but that only – and Wynter will protect her so long as she does. He leaves her by the river, trying to catch the tumbling water in paint.

Her own words sow the idea: *you can tell from the spiders*. He will bide his time, and then, when her painting is done, she will learn not to fence with him.

There is ugliness and ugliness.

1571. *Rotherweird Manor*.

Ten years pass from Wynter's usurpation, the course set from the beginning of his rule – experiment, experiment, experiment. They spend three days a week in Lost Acre, the remainder in record-keeping and analysis. Fortemain is excused, as Wynter shares his obsessive interest with celestial movement and the dynamics of force. Fortemain knows that orthodox theory, with its structure of crystalline spheres, is wrong. There are moving bodies in the heavens that would smash them to smithereens. From time to time Wynter insists on access to his notes, where Fortemain is exploring the interrelationship between the Rotherweird Valley and Lost Acre.

Hieronymus Seer absents himself, pursuing the life he led under Sir Henry, studying unsullied Nature in the confines of the Rother-weird Valley. He justifies his inertia on the pusillanimous ground that Nature will win through in the end, but in truth, he has left his sister to languish and prostitute her gifts. She illustrates the successful experiments (if they can be so described) in *The Roman Recipe Book* – 'Roman' being a childish anagram for 'Manor'. She does so only to spare her brother, but she knows their time is running out. As in a fairy-tale, where death comes with the last leaf's fall, the book tells her fate. Now there is but one leaf left to fill. Her beauty, she feels, is wasted. She loves Fortemain, but does not dare risk the consequences. The others envy her beauty, all the more for her celibacy.

The experiments have long ago moved beyond the mixture of mere animal and bird or fish and insect. Slickstone gathers children from the valley's peasant families and, when they run out, the slums of London. These constructs mostly fail. Secretly she keeps a second book with Fortemain's help, of these half-viable failures and the stones' positioning. Maybe one day the process can be reversed and they can be restored to their former selves.

Then comes the strike: Hieronymus Seer disappears. She hears malevolent talk about a visit to the mixing-point and then the mere in the forest. Fortemain has vanished too. That night Wynter comes and makes her fill the final page. This time there is no creature, just the stones in allotted positions and human silhouettes of no consequence – a soldier, a jester and the like.

Bole lingers in the doorway, lengths of rope over his arm, a lopsided cat twined round one knee.

Wynter speaks portentously. 'I am betrayed. My time is nearly come – you must seek death to find resurrection.'

So this is Wynter's madness, Morval realises, *a craving for divinity*.

He smiles, and Bole does too. 'Gods have their monstrous guardians,' he adds, 'and the best need angels and demons.' He adds, as if it were a gift, 'You will have long life.'

The sky in Lost Acre is dark as pitch. The Eleusians stand away from the tree for safety as the storm gathers. They usually jeer and cheer, but not today. They are rapt.

Slickstone's cage is of iron, not wood, and in touching distance of the mixing-point, only the thinnest of threads holding it back. He is dicing with death. The other men have been weak, choosing to create familiars rather than go in themselves. The bizarre creatures sit on their shoulders or flutter around their heads. He does not think to ask what Wynter has done with the women; women are there to serve, after all.

Only Slickstone seeks to take power to himself.

The sky crackles. The bolt strikes. Slickstone screams as the cage careers into the mixing-point, sparking as it goes.

They wait. Seconds seem like hours. Then the cage swings out and Slickstone bellows. He is Zeus, a god: he feels the power deep in his being, there to be summoned, but for the moment he holds it in check. Let them wait.

A second cage waits, this time made of wood. Morval Seer stands beside it in a white shift like a classical sacrifice. Nearby, Calx Bole holds the Recipe Book in which she has made her last entry.

Wynter is strangely subdued. Slickstone wonders, *Is he weakening?* It is too late now for mawkishness – sentence has been passed.

She is placed in the cage, and on each side a stone is fixed to its allotted place in its allotted bar. He does not want her dead, he wants her monstrous. Into the wooden prison she goes with her eight-legged friend, a huge, misshapen creature from Lost Acre's forest, trapped at his request by his good friend the weaselman. The cage swings into the mixing-point. He notes the greedy looks on the women's faces. They have lived too long with her beauty and innocence.

The chain judders and Slickstone knows the moment it re-emerges that he has achieved vengeance beyond measure. Even the Eleusians recoil, even the women. Now is the time. He will make the spiderwoman dance all the way to the forest, and there Morval can hide her shame.

Blue light plays across his fingers.

APRIL

A Most Peculiar Business

The actress decided that although Lady Slickstone should be a person of honesty, she must not be played as a dull, straight heroine. She made no attempt to use the key until Sir Veronal was drawn to London on business.

That night she descended at Mrs Banter's witching hour, two in the morning, with a single candle, having first noted that Mrs Banter's tower was neither close nor high enough to observe the Manor's ground floor.

The modest square windowless room had wall-to-wall shelves stocked with identical leatherbound books, suggesting more a room of records than a study. The numbers on the spines ran into the middle hundreds. High on a side wall she spotted a volume with *Index* embossed at the base of the spine.

She climbed the polished oak stepladder, retrieved it and sat down on the only chair at the only table. After a few pages she realised that the *Index* held a historical summary of a financial empire of enormous reach and antiquity, the volumes divided by title into time, place and sometimes trading partners. For example, it listed *Volume 1* as *Trade with the Dutch West India Company 1623–4: salt and tobacco*. Within ten years this mysterious business recorded trade with the Honourable East India Company, and by the 1700s with China. Over the years the merchandise expanded into mineral resources, slaves and gold. At intermittent intervals the trading name changed from Slickstone, but always with 'stone' in it – Waterstone, Barstone, Firestone, Meldstone.

She ran her torch over the shelves again – unsurprisingly, the later volumes were thicker, despite being bound with finer paper. She returned to the *Index* to find several volumes summarising political donations, apparently to any party of note in every country of note, and then, every fifty years or so, there was a volume headed *Black Book*, of which there were eight in all. She picked one at random, covering the period 1800–1867. It featured – under the name Garstone – corruption trials, business scandals, murders of investigators, including a judge and a newspaper editor, alongside records of bribes, blackmail victims and the fruits of extortion. She noted that the *Index* listed the next *Black Book*, 1867–1923, under a different trading name: Turnstone.

The recurrence of such unusual names, all with a 'stone' suffix, could hardly be coincidence. She wondered how any criminal dynasty could sustain its efforts for so long. The geographical pattern was peculiar too, a steady expansion to new countries while always maintaining a presence in the old. England featured late in proceedings. How could one family guard and expand such an empire without exposure? How could the heirs always match their forbears? How had so many generations ridden the fickle tides of historical change?

She drew but one conclusion: Sir Veronal had inherited vast wealth from a criminal dynasty founded long ago by a foreign ancestor. The *Index* ended in the 1950s. The name 'Slickstone' did not feature again, leaving it unclear whether Sir Veronal had continued the tradition. She saw difficulties ahead. How to enquire without looking suspicious? At least her part had acquired a new dimension. The audience would be watching her progress in the play with renewed interest.

And what kind of play was it now? A history-tragi-comedy, all rolled into one?

*

The boy sat on his haunches and laughed – what better place for a criminal than a town without crime, police or even rudimentary precautions. The hearth of *Baubles & Relics* still glowed. Outside, the shop sign squeaked as it swung in a light wind. The door had succumbed to a strip of plastic, but he had not been casual, knowing that for Sir V the worst crime was being caught.

The ledger lay conveniently on the desk. He took out his note of the date and found the entry with ease – *Rotherweird Comfort Stones – forty guineas – Hayman Salt*. He relocked the door and slipped back down the Golden Mean. He found it strangely satisfying. All his life he had stolen objects, but he had moved up in the world. Now he stole information.

The following evening Sir Veronal returned. His character had evolved again, still the frustration, but exuberance with it. The actress could not fathom the cause and doubted the audience would, unless she could reveal it, but his first interest lay with the boy. They sat in the library around a blazing fire.

'Wine, Rodney,' he said, 'first the colour, then the nose, and last the taste.' The boy imitated Sir Veronal's treatment of his glass – up to the light, under the nostrils and then tilted back. Abruptly Sir Veronal changed tack. 'You have a report?'

'Hayman Salt, Sir V. He's a Town Hall Gardener. He sold them for forty guineas.'

'Where did he get them?'

'The book didn't say.'

Disappointment registered on the old man's face. He turned to the actress. 'This Mrs Banter: you said she observes the late-night movements of Rotherweird's citizens?'

'So she said, with some pride.'

'Why?'

'"Knowledge of people is power over people" were her exact words.'

Sir Veronal smiled – Mrs Banter was indeed right.

'She records them in notebooks.' The actress trimmed in the cause of credibility. Even a truth-teller would not confess that her own nocturnal ramble featured in one of them.

'She told you that?'

'She wished to impress. She wants your favour.'

Sir Veronal dropped one of those offhand mysterious remarks that had become an increasing feature of his conversation since their arrival in Rotherweird.

'I dislike the name Banter.' He sniffed the air and turned back to Rodney. 'Let me tell you, Rodney: among the most pleasing things in life is killing *three* birds with one stone.'

That night Sir Veronal checked his study, a traditional part of his security review in any home where the records of his empire were kept. His infrared lamp danced across the shelves. The spray had been of his own devising, leaving the finest film on the spines of the books, invisible, but sensitive to human skin.

Smudges shone in the gloom like footprints in sand. The interloper had been selective – the *Index*, an early volume or two and, disturbingly, one of the *Black Books*.

Sir Veronal held the only duplicate key in London. He had taken the actress's fingerprints from the very first glass she had held in his employment. He speedily convicted her, but deferred sentence – she could make no move while confined to the Manor; the records did not come close to the whole truth and he had backstories in abundance should anyone penetrate the complexities of the corporate veil. Also, he had more pressing concerns, first and foremost locating the white tile.

He did take the precaution of adding a second lock.

He retired early. In his bedroom he opened a square wooden box with ventilation holes on his dressing table and lay on his four-poster opposite, head propped up on the pillows.

The creatures rose, shadows dancing in the light of the single candle on his bedroom mantelpiece. Sir Veronal lay on his back, eyes closed, listening for the flap of the moth and the buzz of the flies, slow and fast, different flight patterns, different targets. In the old days he had made it an art form – ten fingers, a filigree of electricity, joining and arcing.

Take it slowly, he said to himself, *draw on the buried memory*.

By the early hours he could throw a crackling line from a single finger and sustain it. Tiny bodies lay strewn across the floor.

2

A Commission

Two days before the commencement of term, Aggs delivered a note from the Headmaster.

'Them's rare in the holidays,' she said. 'Either he's got a special task or you're in the doghouse.'

Oblong, anxious about his reports, was relieved to discover that the note fell in the former category:

Oblong — too much time on hands — unsatisfactory. Have task so talent will out. Report 6ish. RS [H/M]

At six o'clock precisely Oblong knocked on the Headmaster's door.

'Come in,' replied the door wearily.

Spring it might be, but the easterly breeze had a cutting edge. Oblong found himself addressing the Headmaster's backside as Rhombus Smith addressed the hearth. 'When life and the burdens of office get you down, light a fire – ancient Smith family saying.'

There followed a flicker of flame, a violent blowing noise, an oath and then nothing. As many books littered the floor as the shelves, interspersed with School messages, spent like paper darts.

'Allow me.'

Rhombus Smith had many gifts, but apparently igniting firewood was not one of them, despite the family motto. He had balled the paper too tight, pressed down the twigs too hard and mixed green wood with the dead and dry.

Oblong began to dismantle.

'Good man!' Enthusiasm, whether in cheering a boundary or complimenting his staff, was the Headmaster's trademark virtue. He talked as Oblong re-laid the fire.

'History has been pruned next term – sorry about that, but Mr Snorkel was most insistent. I take it to be a reaction to Miss Val-ourhand dabbling in old history – which his Worship put down to your predecessor.' He paused. 'Anyway, Midsummer Day fea-tures the most dismal act in the academic calendar: Prizegiving, an exercise that puffs up the already conceited and depresses everybody else – and I include the parents. There's a Fair of sorts in the evening, but nowadays it's little more than coconut shies, candyfloss and palm-readers. The best bit is – or at least *should* be – the School theatrical show that follows the prizes. Every year it's a different form, and I thought you might do the honours this year. On these lines . . .'

Mr Smith handed over two pieces of paper, both written in the same hand, the first a letter:

Dear Headmaster,

Midsummer Show

I attach an excerpt from the Anglo-Saxon Chronicle, which I commend as a theme for the Midsummer show. It appears to have all the ingredients - hero, monster, damsel, and local connection.

An Admirer.

and the second an attachment with an instant familiarity:

Strange reports from the village of Rotherweird. A Druid priest tells that a monster came to their Midsummer Fair with the midsummer flower. All were saved by the Green Man and the Hammer. [ASC 1017]

Oblong's left hand flew to his mouth. The writing of ASC 1017 bore an uncanny resemblance to the identical entry in Robert Flask's notebook.

'May I ask, sir, when you got this?'

'Does it matter?'

'I just wondered.'

'It came a few months ago, anonymous, bizarrely – but the point is, Oblong, would you organise it?' He saw Oblong wavering. 'My dear boy, it's meant to be a privilege.'

'What about the *History Regulations*?'

'I didn't say *research the past* – I said organise a show. It's utter bunk, but isn't that how good theatre works? You've all the staple ingredients – local theme, goody, baddy, damsel up the creek without the proverbial. And why not in verse, so it rollicks along. A pacey ballad about Old Rotherweird.'

'All right,' stammered Oblong, remembering Fanguin's recommendation of the ballad form for a juvenile audience, 'why not!'

'*Splendido*,' cried Smith as the reassembled fire burst into life, 'and how's young Slickstone doing?'

'He seems a model pupil.'

'A form's dynamic is a delicate animal,' replied Smith cryptically before showing Oblong out.

Oblong left in part downcast, the ballad not being his preferred form, and in part uplifted, a chance to shine. Pacing the Quad, deeper questions surfaced on Flask, frescoes and fairs. Flask must be a sentimentalist, still striving to connect Rotherweird to her history despite his dismissal. Re-enacting the *Chronicle* legend was nonetheless an inspired choice, the legend so outlandish that surely nobody could invoke the *History Regulations*.

But was it gibberish? He recalled the white flower in the church wall fresco, which must be eleventh century at the latest. His rational side could only agree with Dr Pendle: the monks had been at the mushrooms.

Instinct, however, delivered an inexplicable unease.

Oblong rehearsed in front of his bathroom mirror the presentation of his new commission. He must inspire. 'Class, the Prizegiving play has been awarded to us this year. You act it; I write it and your parents make the costumes.'

Rodney sniffed an opportunity for his overdue vengeance on the countrysiders. 'Plot?' he asked.

'Cast?' added Collier.

Oblong read out the entry from the *Anglo-Saxon Chronicle*. When he reached the monster, Collier, Slickstone's neighbour and lieutenant, shrieked, 'Guley's dad!'

'Thank you, Collier. In short: a monster tries it on with a village girl, but she's rescued by a local knight known as the Hammer.'

Slickstone intervened again. 'It's a Form IV effort?'

'Of course,' said Oblong. 'We have ten weeks to produce a masterpiece.'

'Then you'd better get writing . . . sir.' The voice sounded new, stripped of any pretence of deference. 'And if it's a form effort, the form should surely decide the cast.'

'Hear, hear,' said the front three rows, Rodney's placemen.

'I suggest two for the monster, sir – like a pantomime horse.'

'All right, all right,' added Oblong, with the same queasy feeling that had dogged him at Wyvern Lane. He was not in control. Those in front of him were.

'Show of hands!' declared Slickstone.

The resulting cast was predictable:

Knight: Rodney Slickstone.
Squire: Sam Collier.
Damsel: To be decided.
Monster rear: Ned Guley.
Monster front: Gwen Ferdy.

Oblong rightly attributed Rodney's adjournment of the damsel's part to his desire for longer to survey the field, but he could not explain the transformation in the boy, nor the fervour of his hatred for countrysiders. He felt weak for having succumbed to it – that was the trouble with taking hospitality from the very rich.

Rodney could not wait for the day when Sir Veronal took over the town, as surely he would. Only his ambition to be heir apparent moderated his behaviour. He knew Sir Veronal would purge the countrysiders when the time came, but he had to make his own demonstration, and Rotherweird's rituals had gifted him the opportunity.

The following evening he asked Collier round to the Manor. 'Ordinary knights have swords,' he said.

'I do metal-work. Only prize I ever won.'

'But I'm the Hammer, so I need a special weapon. Can you make me a special hammer, with teeth that go round?' The image of a chainsaw appealed to Rodney.

'Sure – but I'd need a furnace – and the parts.'

'Come with me,' replied Rodney. In the basement he showed Collier a furnace as good as any the School could offer. 'Forge a weapon to be remembered. I don't want some common mace.' He pointed at the circular saw on a nearby table, metal teeth gleaming.

Collier put the glee in his new friend's face down to show, or, rather, he decided that his own interests required him to give the heir to the Manor the benefit of the doubt.

*

In April Hayman Salt plaited spent daffodil leaves like a Martian hairdresser. In Grove Gardens the early shrubs were in bloom. The rich scent of azaleas induced visitors to sit and muse on nothing in particular. *Hayman's Galanthi* held their yellow-white heads aloft.

Salt brought science and observation to his gardening. Take snails: Salt knew from observation how they hibernated, their nocturnal habits and impressive lifespan (beyond twenty years for some whose shells Salt had spotted with paint as a young man). He knew from Fanguin that snails could see and hear, and mated to breed despite being hermaphrodites. By night Salt collected from the municipal beds the four harmful species of slug for transportation to the outer reaches of the Island Field, leaving the other twenty species to continue their good work.

Slugs are snails without shells. Thoughts about evolution constantly brought Lost Acre to mind.

He made regular nocturnal pilgrimages to the white tile, but the surface remained dead to the touch. The weaselman had believed in the possibility of a rescuer, but how, with the portal closed and Ferensen, the one man who might know, so aloof? The old man swung between favouring Lost Acre's destruction and anxiety over an unspecified consequence of such an outcome.

He supported a snowdrop on the tip of his little finger: bloom, slumber, rebirth.

Saeculum.

Oblong wrote out his chosen title, *The Ballad of the Midsummer Fair*, repeatedly, in varying boldness and script, but still he could not get launched. His opening verses sounded trite and undramatic. He worried that teaching worked the safer channels of the brain and neglected more offbeat paths where inspiration lurked. Mindful of the example of Thomas de Quincey, he caught Miss Trimble at a rare moment when the Porter's Lodge was traffic-free.

'How is Professor Bolitho?'

'He's in a night owl phase. Nobody sees him.'

'I'd like to see him. I could do with one of his specials.'

'Many of us could, but when he's fishing the heavens, he's a different person. I take him food and the rudiments, but he barely registers; it's that kind of work.' She gave Oblong a firm look. 'I see endless teachers with hardly an explorer among them. He's a man to be treasured.'

The answer loosened Oblong's previous two-dimensional assessment of Miss Trimble. 'I don't need long, and my diary has spaces.'

In truth Oblong's dairy was all spaces.

'If you want to see him, go to his lecture in School Hall. It's a Professorship commitment. You'd best get there early.'

Oblong did not regret taking Miss Trimble's advice. Every faculty had turned out, and every form, packing the largest chamber in Rotherweird School. A surprised murmur greeted Valourhand's appearance – an unprecedented visit by a North Tower scientist to a South Tower lecture.

Bolitho turned the lights out and announced in his sing-song voice through speakers, hidden high in the hammer-beam roof, 'A time before time . . .'

White particles darted about the ceiling.

'The proton . . . the electron . . . the neutron . . .'

Dark particles suddenly emerged and pursued them.

'The antiproton, the antineutron and the antielectron – they have the same mass as their positive twins but an opposing electrical charge. Put them together and they mutually self-destruct. Let us imagine this primitive duel.'

A big bang – or rather *the* big bang – detonated under Bolitho's lectern. Proton and antiproton disappeared, only for a new-formed galaxy to spin over the heads of a startled audience, a hologram of Bolitho's devising.

'Early theory,' continued Bolitho, 'had matter and antimatter in equal quantities – a boneheaded view, as they would have cancelled each other out, leaving no room for anything. Next up, the boffins suggest that matter had the advantage by one – meaning that the miniscule early universe was – what, Symes?'

Every Bolitho performance featured ambush questions. They prevented drift.

'Asymmetrical, sir,' stuttered the sixth-former.

'Not as bright as Symes. We assume matter won the day – but did it?' He slid briefly into complex physics before abruptly changing the subject to astronomy. 'I turn to the question of comets. Clear the floor, boys and girls. It's time to fashion a solar system in which I shall play the forces of Nature.'

With a long cane Bolitho selected a mix of pupils of both sexes to play the Sun and the planets, acting with the decisiveness Oblong's casting of Form IV's play had lacked. The exercise had apparently been done before. In minutes a central space became a human astrolabe, planets rotating as they orbited a central Sun.

'For the uninitiated, their order is . . . ?'

The older pupils intoned Bolitho's unusual mnemonic for the order of the planets: '*My versifying elephant mixes jolly strong uplifting negritas pensively.*'

Mercury, Venus, Earth, Mars . . .

Oblong joined the applause, only to find Bolitho's wand pointing directly at him.

'Mr Oblong will be our system's resident outsider: a ball of dirty ice and cosmic dust. Step forward, man! You are at aphelion, the furthest point from Dawson minor, alias the Sun. You have a tail a million miles long. On Planet Earth, Egyptians struggle with the basics of astronomy, and our island is a swamp for paddling primitives. Imagine what forces Comet Oblong might unleash?'

Oblong caught a wave of half-suppressed laughter from his audience as he walked slowly towards the Sun. Bolitho cast two girls and a boy to follow him as fragments of his tail, spinning them into the Earth as meteors.

'Suppose Oblong were made of dark matter? What then?'

More giggling as Oblong reached Earth.

'By now Saxon battles Dane – and Englishmen can write!' announced Bolitho.

So the lecture played out, a fusillade of facts, theory, performance art and stand-up, which left the audience as exhausted as the speaker.

'Next term I shall educate you about the differences between matter, antimatter, dark matter and negative matter,' concluded Bolitho.

Valourhand hung back at the end, as did Oblong. She ignored the historian and only offered Bolitho a question – no thanks or compliments. 'I assume antimatter requires an antiperiodic table?'

Bolitho had the wit to realise that his usual small talk would cut no ice with Valourhand. 'Surely, and antimatter can bind together just as matter does.'

She flicked her head back to Bolitho as she moved through the doorway, too casually not to be rehearsed. 'Another time perhaps,' she said.

Bolitho tapped her shoulder gently in response. On one level diplomatic relations had been opened, but Oblong sensed a deeper engagement, from Bolitho particularly, which he could not decipher.

He seized his moment. 'Terrific, Professor – I dare say you need a sharpener after that.'

'I've a new creation – the *Sloe Burner* – but she has to wait. It's the fishing season, you see.'

Miss Trimble materialised and steered Oblong away. 'Night work, he means – you won't be seeing him for weeks.'

Falling prey to that siren voice which says that what you do not have is what you need, Oblong headed home in a gloom. The *Sloe Burner* would surely have dissolved his writer's block as a candle melts wax.

3

Sir Veronal Makes a Move

The message appeared in Strimmer's pigeonhole in the Porter's Lodge. The watermark of a weasel's head on the envelope was as good as a signature. The note inside came straight to the point:

13 Old Ley Lane. First floor, neutral territory, only you and me. 12 noon. No strings, no conditions, no recriminations, no second chance. The North Tower interests me.
  Kind regards,
  Sir Veronal Slickstone

Strimmer smiled at the words 'kind regards'. This man did not deal in kindness. The letter contained no mention of a reply. Sir Veronal knew he would come. He would, however, tread carefully.

He faced a second dilemma. The quality of Sir Veronal's collection of old books had filtered through via Oblong and those children who had been invited by the young Slickstone to the Manor. Sir Veronal might pay well for *The Roman Recipe Book*. If not, he might at least enlighten him about its subject matter. The last sentence of the message carried ambiguity. He recalled Sir Veronal's interest in Flask. Was the newcomer interested in the North Tower's current work, or its history – or indeed both? *Nothing ventured, nothing gained*, Strimmer decided. He felt an urge not to disappoint.

*

Strimmer found the door of 13 Old Ley Lane unlocked. The walls, though bare, were tastefully painted and the floors swept. In Rotherweird's crowded streets the ability to command an empty house spoke eloquently of Sir Veronal's power and Snorkel's subservience.

His host's affection for candles persisted: creamy yellow beeswax on giltwood torchères in the hallway and on the landing above. Light from another illuminated the single large room on the first floor.

Two chairs faced each other across a round table, on which stood a fine period cut-glass decanter and two tumblers of the same design. The decanter held iced water with slices of lime. 'Neutral ground' was the message.

Sir Veronal emerged from the shadows to greet him. 'Shall we sit down?'

They did so. Strimmer approved – no flannel.

Sir Veronal filled the glasses. 'I propose some rules. We tell no lies – but may decline to answer any question or any part of a question. We ask alternately. Your involvement in your colleague's pitiful stunt at my party is an irrelevance. I'm interested in what you have to say, and I'm not hostile. I assume your position is the same.' He paused before adding, 'The fact of this meeting and our exchanges are confidential on pain of death.' Sir Veronal spoke in a matter-of-fact tone.

Strimmer nodded acceptance.

'I'm the host – you go first.'

'Why buy the Manor?'

'In search of my past, which lies here somewhere. I believe it was erased by some cataclysmic event – which, *ex hypothesi*, I cannot remember.' Sir Veronal told the truth about his arrival in Rotherweird. He just ignored what his dreams had revealed since.

Surprisingly open, thought Strimmer, *save that nobody had ever suggested that Sir Veronal had been to Rotherweird before. Another damned mystery.*

It was Sir Veronal's turn. 'Have you fully explored the North Tower?'

'There's an old classroom above my study, long sealed off.'

Strimmer decided to be more forthcoming – nothing ventured, nothing gained. 'It was an observatory, but the telescope is gone.'

Sir Veronal smiled appreciatively.

Strimmer took the plunge. 'What do you make of this?' he said, placing the slim leatherbound volume on the table.

Sir Veronal's eyes narrowed. He picked the book up, sniffed it, rubbed the spine with his index finger and weighed the whole in his hand. It was an act – the moment he saw the title – *The Roman Recipe Book* – he knew, for now his memory had blossomed, making connections rather than merely retrieving moments at random. More locked doors opened as he struggled to suppress his excitement. With a small gold magnifying glass he squinted at the covers and the inside pages, one by one. He held the spine with its mysterious title up to the candle. He took considerable time over the frontispiece of the seated devil above a monogram.

'Remarkable,' muttered Sir Veronal. 'Quite remarkable.' He hesitated. For such rich fruit to fall so obligingly into his lap might be accident (wealth and celebrity attracted good fortune more often than not) or malevolent design – a false facsimile, perhaps? He turned back to the front, and there was the inscription, if fainter than he remembered it:

I

Was

Bound

Bearing

Mysterious

Recipes

The writing he recognised, and the hidden message he already knew. He held the genuine article, beyond the slightest doubt.

I have the book and the stones.

Fearing that his sense of triumph might come across, Sir Veronal launched a distraction, opening a page with a dog and bat in silhouette above the usual diagram and a fearsome mix of the two on their right.

'Not a Recipe Book for pets,' he said, as his mind continued to work out the consequences of this outrageous stroke of luck. All he needed now was the location of the white tile. Still, he must give Mr Strimmer a little more to secure his trust.

He closed the book and placed his right hand on the cover, as if taking the oath. 'Elizabethan, 1571. The numerical letters MDLXXI are spread about, in order, buried close to the spine. You need my glass to see them. But the monogram repays special attention.'

'It's a place, not a person,' he explained. As is the way with monograms the answer, once revealed, appeared blindingly obvious. Sir Veronal ran his fingers along the lines – an 'O', a 'Y', and an 'H'. 'Hoy. The town had several presses. This one ceased to be active in about this time. The title is obscure, but it must be rare indeed to merit binding of this quality. My turn, I think – where did you find it?'

Strimmer described the small recess in the floor of the Observatory Room at the top of the North Tower. There had been no room for a companion volume, he said, adding that Valourhand knew nothing of the book. He did not mention Robert Flask as the man who had tipped him off about the unusual profile of the North Tower's roof. The book, after all, had been *his* discovery.

Sir Veronal found the explanation amusing. Wynter had chosen the hiding place for his most precious artefact well, no doubt foreseeing that in the event of his fall, the authorities would close the observatory as a mark of 'respect' to Grassal.

Strimmer saw a question he should have asked at the beginning. 'You say you came in search of your past – but what told you your past was here?'

'A letter.'

'That's not very informative.'

'Your Mayor said he was prompted to write by a Paul Marl, but the man does not exist. I assume Mr Snorkel was after my money. If so, he succeeded. The letter used the term "outsider". It struck a chord, but I've yet to learn why.'

There are hidden layers here, thought Strimmer. *How did Snorkel know to ask Sir Veronal?*

'Does anyone else know of your tower room?'

'Nobody.' The answer was prompted by vanity. After all he had discovered the room. Flask had merely encouraged him to look, indirectly.

'Valourhand – why does she oppose me?'

'She's a perverse exhibitionist. Don't waste your time on her.'

'Her performance required courage.'

'If that's what you call a reckless search for limelight.'

Sir Veronal nodded and stood up, the questioning phase apparently over. 'I have two requests. I shall reward you for both. First, I wish to borrow your book, and I do mean *borrow*. Second, I would like you to watch Valourhand. What she gets up to, whom she sees.'

'What reward exactly—?'

'You may choose certain money now, or a chance of power later.'

Strimmer sensed a test – two caskets, one banal, the other transforming. 'I can wait.'

Sir Veronal nodded approvingly.

Strimmer could not explain his decision rationally. He knew Sir Veronal was ruthless, and yet he felt a nascent trust between them.

Sir Veronal appeared to read his thoughts. 'I've travelled the world a long time. Kindred spirits are hard to come by. I have a final question, which you needn't answer. Your age?'

'Thirty-two – and you?'

A coldness flitted by, incongruous after their mutual openness on far more intrusive questions. 'As the older man, I decline to answer that one.'

On the tiny balcony a misshapen cat wobbled precariously. As Sir Veronal craned his neck, it arched its back, spat and leapt into the street.

'I'd drown such things at birth,' said Strimmer.

'An experiment gone wrong, perhaps,' replied Sir Veronal.

Strimmer, no stranger to dark humour, found the inflection in the remark odd.

Strimmer left the meeting with mixed feelings. He believed that Sir Veronal had observed the rules of the game and told no lies, which meant that *The Roman Recipe Book* had use beyond its rarity value. As to his own prospects, he felt he had passed a preliminary interview, but tougher tests lay ahead. Money was power, and Sir Veronal had the wherewithal to displace Snorkel. His coattails were well worth hanging on to.

'An experiment gone wrong, perhaps.'

4

Oblong in Search of his Muse

Keats' nightingale, which

> *In some melodious plot*
> *Of beechen green, and shadows numberless,*
> *Singest of summer in full-throated ease.*

had infected Oblong with an interest in ornithology in the hope that he might produce a work of similar permanence. With acquaintance the interest deepened, despite the absence of any artistic by-product, although his fieldwork suffered from an inability to remember defining features – leg colour, eyepatch, tail shape.

Woken by a territorial wren in the ivy beneath his bedroom window, he felt a surge of ambition. If fine poetry could flow at dusk in a country churchyard, why not during the dawn chorus in Grove Gardens? From April the gates stayed open, and at this early hour on a Saturday he would be untroubled by human company.

Thunder had crackled in the night, but cloud and humidity had cleared. Notebook in pocket, Oblong hurried through the streets. Shadows still prevailed, but bars and pools of light were beginning to appear and spread. The cobbles glistened. Words came and went – half lines, titles, adventurous rhymes. Once in the Gardens, he settled on a stone bench near the edge of the cliff. The birds sang with gusto, but his Muse stayed away. Thoughts refused to knit together. He decided to probe the gardens' darker corners.

Grove Gardens took its name from the life-size statue of a Druid, leaning forward in an attitude of defiance, his staff levelled eastwards across the river. Frost damage repaired with modern materials lent the old priest an unflattering blotchy complexion. Salt's design fitted the garden to the name, and the Druid to the garden. Slender trees, mostly silver birch, suggested a grove, and the rock benches resembled fallen megaliths. Swathes of *Hayman's Muscari*, multicoloured white and blue, hung over the paths, whose elliptical route fostered an illusion of space with sporadic open views of the river. Dead tree stumps supported wild roses and clematis, in bud but not yet in flower.

At the path's end a lantern hung on an ornate iron frame swathed in honeysuckle that created a bower-like effect: scene of many a Rotherweird marriage proposal. A bird trilled – warning or welcome? The ambiguity held literary promise, but was it a visiting warbler or a resident chaffinch? He moved to get closer, and tripped.

He looked down and managed only a curdled cry. Two stockinged legs protruded unmoving from the foliage, toes pointing upwards.

He did not want to see the face. He did not want to touch anything. He retreated a few steps, and then ran, mouthing like a fish the single syllable 'help'. Half glancing back, he collided with the ample frame of Hayman Salt.

'Bitten by something?' asked Salt.

'There's . . . there's—'

Salt took Oblong by both shoulders and shook him twice, firmly. 'There's what?'

'L – l – legs by the lantern . . .' stuttered Oblong.

'Show me.'

Shame gripped Oblong as Salt showed the calm head he had so conspicuously lacked. The gardener instructed him to keep back and took a roundabout route so as not to disturb any clue. He crawled into the undergrowth and checked for any sign of life, then clambered back and pointed out to Oblong the blistered paintwork on the lantern and the melted wires.

Emotion registered in Salt's face and voice, but with restraint. 'Horrible,' he said. 'I knew her.'

'Was she—?'

'A lightning strike, but not without . . . its oddities.'

Salt watched Oblong, mouth still agape, and decided against allowing him to go, lest he blurt out the news before the next of kin had been told. 'Come with me,' he added.

'Where?'

'*Baubles & Relics*,' replied Salt.

Ever level-headed, Salt locked the gates as they left.

Orelia, the early riser, greeted them, mug of coffee in hand.

'The historian and the gardener – what can I do for you?' An astute reader of body language, her tone changed in an instant. 'What's happened – to whom?'

Salt recited the facts without embroidery, adding comfort only at the end. 'I'm so sorry.'

Orelia stood up. 'I need to see the body,' she said, her numbed state of mind giving way to an urge to be positive.

'It isn't pretty.'

Nothing more was said. Oblong felt an urge to speak, but Salt gave him a deterrent look. The first countrysiders' stalls passed them on the Golden Mean, and the newspaper boys were out. In the gardens the magical early light had given way to morning as the birdsong subsided. Salt unlocked and then locked the gates behind them and stood back with Oblong as Orelia crawled into the tangle of leaves. She did not emerge quickly. Salt stood downcast, as if in meditation. The gesture seemed right, and Oblong followed suit.

Orelia rubbed earth from her face. She held Mrs Banter's handbag. 'Her personal effects – I don't want anyone going through them.'

'Of course,' said Oblong lamely.

'It must have been instant,' added Orelia.

'Yes,' said Salt.

'Of course,' chipped in Oblong.

'Thank you for finding her early. I couldn't bear the thought of a crowd. She liked her dignity.'

Oblong blushed.

'I'll get the arrangements done,' said Salt.

'You mentioned oddities, and you were right. She's dressed to the nines, and her watch is frozen at ten past midnight.' Orelia bit her lip as she spoke. The bare words might be those of a detective, but she did not sound like one.

Scarily self-possessed, thought Oblong, and Salt appeared to agree.

'You really want to discuss this now?' Salt asked.

'Very much – it's our discussion to have.'

'There's something odd about the shoes. They look new.'

'They are new.'

'There are scuff-marks on the heels, as if she'd been dragged. Lightning would throw you, I think. Unfortunately, we can't be sure, because the path is disturbed.' Salt did not mention Oblong's clumsiness.

'There was thunder in the night,' added Oblong, desperate to contribute, but Orelia continued her dialogue with Salt.

'The oddest thing of all is why she came here so late – to meet whom? And why did he or she take no action?'

'*He*, surely – those shoes, that dress.' When she nodded, he continued, 'We've had another freak lightning strike in recent weeks, remember?'

'What possible motive could Slickstone have?' Orelia's final observation came on impulse: 'They'll cover this up. Don't tell the Town Hall I was here, or Oblong. *You* found the body.'

Not for the first time, Oblong felt relegated to the periphery of events.

They left the gardens. Salt arranged for the undertaker to remove the body, Oblong returned home and Orelia entered Mrs Banter's house with the keys from her bag. The house looked undisturbed. An array of dresses draped across the bed testified to a desire to impress – yet hitherto, Mrs Banter had shown no interest in finding a replacement for Mr Banter.

Orelia climbed up to the tower rooms and stumbled on a side of her aunt that she had never even guessed at. The two powerful telescopes on their tripods were bizarre enough, but the rows of notebooks in alphabetical order, all crammed with observations, spoke of a voyeuristic obsession with the lives of her fellow citizens. Orelia shuddered. She knew their purpose: social leverage.

Prurience is an insinuating vice. Orelia could not resist perusing a few selected volumes. Mrs Banter's pungent notes yielded no joy and much sadness, as with the disheartening number of visits by Fanguin 'without his wife' to *The Journeyman's Gist* since his dismissal – 'a broken man' was her aunt's note. To her irritation, her aunt had detailed her own nocturnal movements with wounding accuracy – 'goes to a party, returns alone again'. Not everyone's movements were so conventional – Vixen Valourhand apparently vaulted the rooftops at night.

She dithered. Revealing such a library to the authorities would tarnish her aunt's memory, but their retention would be a serious breach of the *History Regulations*.

When in doubt, buy time.

She returned the books and dismantled the telescopes – and only then did she notice that the Sa-Sl volume was missing. S for Slickstone? Surely her aunt had not been foolish to enough to attempt to blackmail Sir Veronal – but if so, what with? He hardly ever ventured beyond the Manor.

She turned her attention to Mrs Banter's desk diary, a tale of bridge evenings and cocktail parties, which stalled at the end of February, nothing thereafter but blank pages, save for a tea-time visit from Lady Slickstone. She remembered her aunt's distressed state after the party and sensed a missing chapter.

Then the shell of rational analysis dissolved. The drab tidiness of her aunt's life, guilt at the lack of warmth between them and the thought that she might have prevented this tragedy, had she known more, assailed her. She knelt by the bed and wept.

When she eventually returned to *Baubles & Relics*, she found a Town Hall messenger on the doorstep, where he delivered a predictably sanitised version of a most unhappy death.

Rotherweird had no police service, so all deaths were investigated by Mors Valett, the town undertaker – himself an *habitué* of Snorkel's *soirées*.

The bizarre circumstances of Mrs Banter's demise alarmed the Mayor.

'It's odd,' said Valett. 'Her date scarpered, or didn't show.'

'Do you blame him?'

Valett persevered, 'You'll recall, your Worship, an electrical incident at a recent party. Coincidence, maybe – but some might wonder—'

'A is for Accident,' Snorkel said firmly. 'Don't complicate. A lantern incinerates and a woman dies. Bad luck, but it happens. As for this date of yours, he doesn't turn up, or if he does, he misses the body in the dark. Who's the next of kin?'

'Orelia Roc, *Baubles & Relics*.'

'Arty type, isn't she? They're the worst. Close it down, Valett, close it down.'

Valett thought of his grace and favour residence and the plush upholstery in his grace and favour rickshaw. Rocking boats was rarely wise. He wrote the word 'Accident' on the front of the shiny new file headed *Mrs Deirdre Banter (deceased)*.

*

The ensuing notice in the Rotherweird Chronicle had a predictable blandness, with an undertone of tastelessness to the few who knew the true facts. It mirrored the way Mors Valett had delivered the news to Orelia:

> Deirdre Banter, widow of the well-known architect, was found dead yesterday after a sudden heart attack suffered in the vicinity of Grove Gardens, which will be closed for a week as a sign of respect. The Mayor complimented her contribution to Rotherweird society and offered his condolences to Miss Orelia Roc, her niece, who has promised 'business as usual' for the family antique shop *Baubles & Relics*.

Closed out of respect! Workmen would be in the Gardens at this very moment, rewiring, repainting and raking over the unexplained drag-marks in the gravel. Mrs Banter's dress and shoes had been returned, but not the watch.

BANTER, Deirdre: widow of Bartholomew Banter (architect), died without issue on . . .

Marmion Finch's quill scratched in the date, reducing another life to a statistic in the great Register where in alphabetical order arrivals rubbed shoulders with departees in respectively green and red ink.

She had been a friend, or rather, rival, of Mrs Finch, with their common interest in social advancement and the Rotherweird Riparians, until her recent and unexplained ostracism. Finch distrusted the Town Hall when it dismissed troubling events with bland explanations. 'A picture of rude health,' Mrs Banter's doctor had confided in Finch earlier that day. 'She must have been overcome by the blossom.'

The word 'architect' tripped a memory. Finch rarely visited the heavy folios that held the original designs for the town's oldest buildings; their historical voice was too rich, even for him. Now he opened the plans for Escutcheon Place – one man's vision realised in bricks, beams and mortar. The designer's name: Peregrine Banter.

The Manor reopens. A descendant, in name at least, of a founding father dies in rude health.

The gold key round his neck weighed more heavily with every passing day.

5

Last Rites

Attendance at Mrs Banter's funeral service was modest. Mrs Snorkel represented the Mayor, and stayed no longer than the decent minimum. Salt sat near the front and sang heartily. Oblong, at the back, mumbled along. Outside, Salt had patted him on the back and Orelia awarded him the faintest of smiles.

A sprinkling of shop owners made up the numbers. A young priest spoke well, less about God and more about the existence of dimensions of which Man knew nothing.

At the end of the service a woman with a black mantilla over her face wafted up to Orelia and whispered, 'I cannot say how sorry I am. I do hope your fortunes change.' Orelia did not know the voice, but it had elegance.

Orelia would have followed her, but the undertaker approached with a small jet-black urn. 'Such a tragic accident,' he said, almost apologetically.

Anxious to complete the last rites, she cajoled Salt into joining her. Beyond the finishing line for the Great Equinox Race, the banks narrowed and the river flowed faster and deeper. She emptied the ash into the Rother and as the thin grey film passed out of sight, she shed a tear or two. 'I should have been kinder to my aunt,' she mumbled.

'We are how we are, and there's nowt so strange as folk,' replied Salt, not one of Nature's grief counsellors.

'Can a man throw lightning?'

'No,' said Salt. 'You're upset.'

'There's much electricity in the human body.'

'No. Anyway, why would Slickstone kill your aunt? Think of the risks.'

Kill her for driving a hard bargain? Orelia could only agree it made no sense. Even the removal of the 'S' volume from Mrs Banter's secret library required theft, not murder.

'And if he did kill her,' continued Salt, 'why did Lady Slickstone come to the service?'

'You mentioned a threat to Lost Acre. Suppose that's what connects?'

'Lost Acre is gone for all I know,' grumbled Salt.

They parted on the riverbank, Salt leaving to check the Island Field colonies of the Rotherweird eglantine for blossom.

Among Rotherweird's more peculiar legal instruments were the *Inheritance Supervision Orders*, issued by the Town Hall on the death of anyone over the age of eighteen. The policy was, as ever, to discourage any interest in history: the nearest relative of sound mind had to weed out from the deceased's effects any material more than twenty years old, including letters, diaries and photographs, which were later collected by the Town Hall's scrutineer for destruction.

Orelia returned to her aunt's house and rifled through her papers with little return. Business aside, Mrs Banter had not been given to writing or receiving letters, still less taking personal photographs. On her return to *Baubles & Relics*, she checked through the attic storeroom. In a hatbox, among invoices for the original refurbishment of the shop, two nondescript black sheets of paper enfolded a mounted sepia photograph of her great-grandfather, Roy Roc, the owner of the coracle and an amateur photographer and naturalist. He stood at the foot of a woodland bank with a large butterfly on the flat of his open hand. Above him sat an incongruous figure on his haunches, holding a parasol. A manuscript caption read:

RR and the Purple Emperor
Rotherweird Westwood
1893

Orelia remembered the family story: Roy Roc had sought the purple emperor since childhood, the most elusive of woodland butterflies, which fed on aphid honeydew high in the canopy, descending only briefly to lay their eggs or to feed on less rarefied substances.

One summer day far from town, in a shawl of ancient oak trees, an elderly man had appeared with a parasol. He had asked a simple question: 'Do you have a killing jar?'

'I wish only to watch them.' Roy Roc had confirmed his pacifist intentions by pointing to his notebook, tripod and camera.

'What are you missing?'

'*Apatura iris*,' replied Roy, to test the stranger.

'Follow me,' he replied. As they walked, the old man, his parasol still up despite the woodland shade, had explained how the lower slopes had once been entirely wooded. He had shown Roy Roc a cluster of purple emperors feeding on a salt lick. The old man never gave a name, and later proved untraceable. Generations of Rocs nicknamed him Quirk, after the Latin for oak, but he had never been seen again.

The photograph confirmed the old story, but much more besides. Despite the dappled light, the seated figure was unmistakable: Ferensen, or a double of Ferensen. It made no sense – how could he have been there then?

This unsettling feeler from the past prompted another thought. On the white wall of her bedroom she projected the photographs taken in the Manor's attic on the night of the party. Two-thirds of the way across the tapestry's mythical narrative appeared a man in a cage. She had taken the golden threads descending towards him to be a blessing, but now she had doubts. Lightning? She stood up close. Something about the cage caught her eye: tiny dots of colour, the colour of the stones.

Making many things of living things.

In other cages there were monsters, mixes of man and animal or animal and bird. She went up to the screen and shuddered. Again on some of the bars – but never more than once to a side, and never on the same bar in the same place – appeared a tiny dot of colour, red, blue, white or brown.

Orelia suddenly felt afraid. This wasn't myth at all, but *history*, real history, reaching out across the years. She mulled over where to take her suspicions. Salt had hidden private agendas. She didn't know Ferensen well enough, and there was truth in Salt's complaint that he garnered more information than he gave. She sensed a flaw in Ferensen too, which she couldn't place, for all his apparent wisdom.

A thought came to her and she began to write, holding nothing back. In disregard of Salt's instruction she mentioned Ferensen and the photograph. She explained the sale of the stones, her aunt's observations, the library of notebooks, the missing volume and her theory about her aunt's untimely death in Grove Gardens.

On the envelope she wrote,

> *Strictly Private and Confidential*
> *Marmion Finch Esquire,*
> *Escutcheon Place*

She delivered it by hand herself, early the following morning.

On her return she set about the shop, hustling between the basement and the ground floor, giving abandoned unsold stock a second chance and relegating selected present failures. The old ruler had passed away, the state funeral had been held and now the new regime could show its style. Within days the hippopotamus head, subject of so many of Mrs Banter's spiky barbs, had sold. The suffocating fog of bereavement began to lift.

6

Gorhambury Finds a Mission

As the victim of various improvement notices under the *Tenancy Regulations*, Gorhambury's landlord took an unforgiving view of the erstwhile Town Clerk's failure to pay his rent. He refused any extension.

The civic sense of community was strong in Rotherweird, and vagrancy almost unknown. Anyone losing a job could expect replacement employment – unless blighted by Mayoral disapproval. Like Fanguin before him, Gorhambury could not overcome this handicap.

After two nights sleeping in doorways, Gorhambury decided that self-help had its limits. He signed into *The Shambles*, Rotherweird's refuge for homeless unfortunates – though the lodging's seven rooms were more often than not unoccupied – tucked into the town's north wall. Bo Tavish, who ran *The Shambles* and had a burning desire to do good, greeted Gorhambury as a long-lost friend.

He found the registration process humbling. After entering his name, date of birth and resident number, Gorhambury recorded the reason for his homelessness as 'unfair dismissal' – a minute step, but the child's rebuke 'unfair' marked his first adult challenge to authority. Gorhambury had embarked on a new journey without yet knowing it.

Bo expounded a simple regime: 'Dinner at eight, no booze on the premises, lock up at midnight, rent is bargain basement at seven guineas a week, to be earned by labour. No liability on the management for theft, flood, libel, slander or illness of any kind. I likes a chat; my husband don't. Breakfast at eight; lunch is your affair; dinner is mine – wholesome tucker, nothing fancy.'

She developed an intrusive habit of pinching Gorhambury's cheeks – 'Colour, Mr Gorhambury, give us colour!' before sending him out every morning at nine. 'Chin up, chin up!'

Gorhambury felt embarrassed walking the streets. Some gave him the brush-off, others a fleeting expression of sympathy; a few offered money, which Gorhambury, twice shy, always declined. Time sat heavy on his shoulder; every minute crawled. In the evening he sewed tapestries, his choice under the *Rotherweird Poorhouse Work-to-Reside Regulations*, which he himself had drafted. Though adept at *petit point*, his idling brain, overworked for so long, protested. He developed headaches, and depression set in, Bo's cloying kindness paradoxically deepening his gloom.

Salvation came by a circuitous route.

'You look a practical man, Mr Gorhambury,' said Bo, wagging a finger at the leaking downpipe beside the front door of *The Shambles* and the blocked drain below. With a coat hanger, plunger and a bucket of boiling water Gorhambury unblocked drain and pipe, but permanent repairs exceeded his expertise. However, pipe and drain carried a unique municipal number, and several nearby pipes, gutters and drains looked in no better condition. A sense of mission took hold, and he retrieved from his suitcase the leather ledger from his old office and the municipal keys.

On the frontispiece of the book he wrote

GRAND SURVEY of ROTHERWEIRD

Her Exterior Fittings

By Reginald Gorhambury

To his surprise, Bo Tavish embraced the plan. Gorhambury's hours reversed, breakfast becoming supper, and supper breakfast.

He fitted in his *petit point* between six and eight in the evening, shortly after getting up.

In this new nocturnal world, quiet and study dispelled the shroud of despair, as his notebook began to fill. Sometimes he glimpsed others at work or play in the darkness – most strikingly Hayman Salt hunting gastropods in the municipal flower tubs and a mysterious rooftop vaulter. Gorhambury shrugged off the latter's disinterest in the *Highwire Safety Regulations*. They were no longer his concern.

7

Finch Makes a Decision

'Shot ... gun ... barrel ... organ ... pipe ... smoke ...' Finch sat at the round table in the middle of the *archivoire, his* room. No one else came in here; he alone swept the floor, cleaned the windows and maintained the ancient books (using the Finch patent mixture of cedar oil, beeswax and lanolin), just as his Finch forbears had done before him.

On the table lay Orelia Roc's letter – extraordinarily candid, a serial breach of the *History Regulations* and therefore to be taken seriously.

Problem one: he, Marmion Finch, archivist of Rotherweird's citizens, living and dead, had never heard of any Ferensen and could find no reference to such a family since the commencement of records in 1581 – no birth, no death and no request for arms or carvings.

Problem two: if Orelia Roc were to be believed, a photograph showed Ferensen in the company of her great-grandfather in an outlying oak wood well over a century ago.

'Sauce ... pan ... fried ... egg ... white ... knight ...' *Blink, scratch.*

Finch turned to the crux of the issue: his inheritance, the other unopened letter. He read again the prohibition on the front:

To the heirs and afsigns of Hubert Finch – only to be opened on fufferance of death, when the direſt peril from the other place ſtalks the fief of Rotherweird.

Orelia Roc had talked of a secret place known only to Salt and Ferensen. Mrs Banter had died in mysterious circumstances.

Finch made his decision. He would suggest a meeting with the enigmatic Ferensen, but for the moment the Great Seal of State would remain unbroken. He followed Orelia's suggestion that he use Hayman Salt for the message out, and Bill Ferdy for any reply. Salt could be trusted only so far, apparently. But her selection made sense: Salt was the townsman closest to the countrysiders, and Ferdy the countrysider closest to the town. Everything seemed to link.

Knight . . . time . . . past . . . memories . . . lost . . .

8

Valourhand Makes a Discovery

Every massacre has its survivor and every secret a confidant ready to pass it on. The morgue assistant saw the ashy residue of Mrs Banter's right arm and shared the shocking image – in strictest confidence – with her sister, who told her best friend, also in strictest confidence. Twenty links down the line, the news reached Valourhand, and with it came another thread: Roc, Oblong and Hayman Salt had been seen close to Grove Gardens in the early hours.

Valourhand doubted very much that Mrs Banter had been killed by conventional lightning or by faulty cabling. The image of Sir Veronal Slickstone cupping his hands before the bolt lanced towards her had lodged deep. She needed more information, but she dared not risk Sir Veronal. She could see only one other potential source.

Oblong was fine-tuning the props for Form IV's production for the Midsummer Play when there was a knock at the door. Expecting Fanguin, he opened it with a flourish.

'Jonah Oblong?'

He stared at the young woman in front of him holding a bundle of books tied up with a strap. Her build was slight, her features gamine, her hair short but frizzy, her dress gipsy in style. For Oblong first impressions were cultural as well as physical: he was in the presence of an enlightened Bohemian.

'Meet the one-woman Rotherweird Travelling Library.' The voice had a pleasingly musical timbre.

'Miss . . . Mrs . . . ?'

'Sheridan, Cecily Sheridan, *Miss* Cecily Sheridan.'

'Do come in.'

With one lissom movement Cecily became the first woman other than Aggs to cross Oblong's threshold. She had pronounced eyelashes and a warm complexion. Oblong was finding it hard to concentrate.

'Of course,' she said, putting down the books, 'home visits are entirely pot luck.'

'I can imagine!'

'I find a drink a good start.'

'I've only got . . .' *What have I got?* thought Oblong. *Get a grip. Be in control. 'Old Ferdy's Feisty Peculiar?'*

Cecily gave a staccato nod of approval and sat down as if sitting were an art form.

As nervous men sometimes do, Oblong turned parrot. 'The Rotherweird Travelling Library!'

She extracted one of the books from the strap. 'Montaigne – it's frightful. Half the town hasn't heard of him.'

'Shocking,' echoed Oblong, struggling to summon the little he knew about the great Renaissance essayist.

'"Am I playing with the dog or is the dog playing with me?" Of course, Montaigne wrote that of a cat, but I prefer dogs.'

Oblong watched in astonishment as the slightly built Cecily took her third gulp of *Feisty Peculiar* in as many minutes.

'What's it cost?'

'What does what cost?'

'Membership of the Rotherweird Travelling Library.'

'This'll do.' She stretched out her legs and held her glass to the light, tilting it slightly. The pose was delightfully decadent.

He opened a second bottle.

'Do you know any connoisseurs?' She rolled the French word like a jazz singer. 'I need patrons with money to spare.'

Oblong was keen to please. 'Sir Veronal Slickstone has the best collection I've ever seen. His library is packed with first editions – early, early.'

'He showed you. How exciting.'

'He has pretty well everything. What he wanted was a book on old Rotherweird.'

'There aren't any books on old Rotherweird – they're not allowed.'

'I thought it damned odd: why buy a Manor with no idea of the town?'

'You had nothing to tell him?'

The question was throwaway, but Oblong caught a change in tone. *Am I playing with the cat or is the cat playing with me?* He was beginning to wonder.

She appeared to catch his hesitation. 'But you're our historian – you must know something.'

'I didn't tell him anything.'

'I'm sure you didn't. But you could tell me.' Cecily removed her right shoe and began caressing her instep.

The need to impress was becoming more acute. 'There are the frescoes.'

'Ah, yes.' Cecily seemed most engaged. She even put her glass down before her next question. 'What do you think they mean?'

'I haven't an idea.'

'Bearing in mind where they are?'

'I assume some religious significance.'

'Because . . . ?'

'Well, being in the church tower.'

Cecily rewarded him with a smile. 'I have just the book for you, a novel by our best young satirist – *Gullible's Travels*. I'll drop it in as soon as it's returned.' She drained her glass like a Russian. 'You know my favourite Montaigne saying? "A wise man sees as much as he ought, not as much as he can".' With this statement, she abruptly gathered her books, shook Oblong's hand and opened the door.

Oblong tried desperately to prolong matters. 'How do I return a book, where, when—?'

'When and where I feel like it,' she said. 'I'm that kind of librarian.'

Oblong gazed after her as the door closed. He had been so smitten by Cecily Sheridan that he had forgotten the deep dust on the floor of the belfry. The frescoes had been unseen for decades.

Outside in the street Valourhand placed a scarf over her head and slipped into the shadows. Cecily Sheridan would not withstand local scrutiny for long.

In recent months she had had increasing recourse to her nocturnal world. The gaps between Rotherweird's roofs, their pitch, the grappling points, the best for a view, the best for concealment, the linking bridges – she knew them all like the back of her hand. In this starlit universe she was sole ruler and single subject. As a matter of pride, she never touched the street. Her flexible balance doubled as a vaulting pole as she revelled in the exercise and the solitude.

Even as a child, Valourhand had hunted out hidey-holes in the town's jumbled roofscape, mapping and naming them. She called a favourite space close to Oblong's lodgings in a narrow cul-de-sac known as Palindrome Cut 'The Undercroft'. Two buildings joined at ground level, but separated about ten feet up before the left building leaned back over, providing shelter to anyone standing in the space below. Conveniently, a disused lantern brace provided a climbing aid for access. She had installed a primitive floor and here she kept her climbing aids, a sleeping bag and her crystal light.

After shaking the latter, she removed Miss Sheridan's more distinctive features – the eyelashes, the tinted contact lenses, the wig and the complexion. Then she lay down and reflected. She had visited Oblong hoping for information about Mrs Banter; instead, she had made a far more significant discovery. Flask, who was more prepared to talk about the past than anyone else in town, had never mentioned frescoes.

She waited until midnight before shinning up the church tower. The wooden shutters yielded easily. She crouched on the sill and shook her crystal light gently. Oblong had told the truth: his were the only footprints crisscrossing the floor. She placed her own smaller feet within his, although so fierce was her independent spirit, she found even this exercise in shadow dancing embarrassingly intimate. She shook the tube harder and the room flared into life. For someone strictly rationed on images of the past, the frescoes were a revelation.

Valourhand had never seen a representation of life so long ago. Some images connected with the present and were explicable; the sight of unarmed Saxons fleeing a Roman army in coracles explained the Great Equinox Race. Others were humdrum – the workers in the fields, the husbandry, the seasons.

The documentary nature of these scenes made the more obscure north and east walls baffling. She noted the silver door through which a Roman soldier mutated into a weaselman, and on the east wall, the spreading white flower and the extraordinary tree with a similar blossom, its trunk and boughs shaped to form an almost human aspect – a Druid god, perhaps – but why in a Christian church? And why had this literal artist suddenly turned imaginary? She wondered what images the dampness on the east wall had expunged. The fragments of branch and human limbs amid the purple discolouration were tantalising.

The frescoes must be early, for she saw only an island with sarsen stones and a Druid community. Valourhand left more puzzled than enlightened.

9

Epiphany

Back in his library, *The Roman Recipe Book* acted as a memory prompt for Sir Veronal, bringing long-forgotten creaturing days to life. Only the significance of the final page, with its ordinary figures in the margin and no hint of the monstrous, eluded him. He worked away at it, his mind now able to dredge deeply buried images back to the surface, even though the process was haphazard. Some permanent damage had been done to his abilities of recall.

When the solution did come, past and present fused in a moment of glorious revelation, and he clenched his fists and cried out. He was looking at Wynter's last experiment, the most ambitious of all, and only he now knew what it did. He had the stones and the book. He needed only the white tile and the mixing-point to open the way to omniscience. He read again through the notebook containing Mrs Banter's nocturnal observations of Hayman Salt, the finder of the stones – a sequence of night-time journeys on foot to the woods to the south of the Island Field. Surely the tile would be easy to find.

What of human obstacles? He had Snorkel on a silver lead, and Strimmer onside. He considered Valourhand too ignorant to pose any serious threat. The actress puzzled him. She had read one of the *Black Books*, which had, surprisingly, prompted not discretion, but an uncharacteristic display of independence, which he could hardly miss. Why else attend the wretched Mrs Banter's funeral? He anticipated a demand for more money. Disposal presented a problem – he could not afford another death in Rotherweird, nor could he risk sending her back to the outside world. He would find a way.

He moved to the next task. With a ruler and squared paper he began to copy the last page of *The Roman Recipe Book*. He added dimensions before calling his most trusted retainer.

'Get this to the foundry and keep it secret. The specifications must be exact, and the material light. Use titanium.'

The man, now in his sixties, peered at the page and blinked, and Sir Veronal could not resist sharing his moment of triumph, however obscurely. 'It's nothing – only a cage with special attributes,' he added.

'For?' mouthed the servant, fearful some monstrous pet would be joining the household.

'A remarkable illusory trick,' replied Sir Veronal.

10

Inertia

April ended well, the skies clear, the breeze light. When rain came, it was fresh, and mostly at night. Swallows arrived early, swooping above and below Aether's Way, taking insects on the wing. The bakers' crumbs they left to the common sparrow.

Only Ferensen did not relish the change of weather. His skin felt dry; his eyes puckered in open sunlight. He would rise early to continue his search for the black tile in the shade of a parasol. There was system in the way the hedgerows radiated from the town, in the location of ancient barrows and beech clumps, the latter's roots binding the ceilings of the tombs below. Ferensen drew diagrams and pursued possibilities, like Professor Bolitho hunting an undiscovered planet, working on a mix of data and hunch. Yet Rotherweird stubbornly refused to yield her secrets, and he began to fear that the entrance might be in town, out of his reach.

Deeper down, Ferensen knew he was marking time, all too keen to obey his own advice to play the waiting game, such were the ambiguities of his position. He had long shut out memories of the old times, the images too horrific, too painful. But Veronal's return had left him no choice but to face his buried demons. And if Salt was right, Lost Acre was facing destruction. Ferensen considered the place depraved, a distortion of the natural order, creatures jumbled together by the mixing-point to make grotesque parodies of their original selves. Salt, in thrall to diversity, thought differently, but Salt had not witnessed how the mixing-point could be abused.

So Lost Acre's apocalypse had to be a blessing, and all the more so with Veronal closing in – but for one desperate qualification: he loved his sister, and she remained marooned there, imprisoned in such a cruel and ingenious way that he alone could never rescue her. Veronal might know how – if he recovered his memory – but that was the last thing to be desired on every other ground.

Ferensen's uncertainty had been aggravated by Mrs Banter's death. Boris had passed on via Panjan the rumours about a lightning strike. He knew freak bolts occurred, but not in the prevailing atmosphere of that particular evening, which he could recall like a book. Veronal's powers appeared to be returning, another bad omen.

Ferensen walked to the maze he had constructed long ago in the woods beside his tower. At first sight it appeared conventional, with the oak-beech hedge turning this way and that; only inside did the wooden gates reveal themselves, each one locking another as it opened; and bridges that rose and descended over streams: a challenge of almost limitless permutations – the closest Ferensen came to training, should the Eleusians return.

An oak chair like a small throne greeted anyone clever enough to reach the heart of the maze. Here Ferensen opened the letter from Rotherweird Town, its existence alone a matter of concern. He went straight to the name at the end – Marmion Finch. Finch – the surname of the first governor, left behind by Robert Oxenbridge to oversee the orderly transition to independence.

The text's businesslike tone reassured Ferensen.

Dear Ferensen,

As Rotherweird's hereditary Herald, I reside in Escutcheon Place, an unusual house with an unusual history. I hold a letter, closed with the Great Seal of State, which is to be opened only in time of 'direst peril'. Might this be such a time? I have reason to believe you may know, although I have no inkling how. I have undertaken to keep your presence secret.

If you were interested in meeting, I would reciprocate. In the interests of openness I

enclose also a letter to me from Miss Roc. I believe you know her.

  Yours very sincerely,

  Marmion Finch.

According to Salt and Bill Ferdy, Finch did no more than super-vise grants of arms and carvings in public places, but Elizabeth I's advisors had not been fools. Granting Rotherweird her independ-ence and banning the study of history had been a solution of genius – but suppose this defence failed, there would need to be a record to warn the world of what lurked in Lost Acre. Where else to keep it than in Escutcheon Place? Outsiders' England would not do; it leaked like a sieve. The Finches must still be the custodians.

At first he fretted over Orelia's breach of confidence: towns did not understand secrecy. They lacked the iron loyalties of the country-side. But he calmed down. Finch's ancestor had been a decent man. Orelia Roc had lost her aunt and action was needed – but to prevent *what*? He hesitated over Finch's proposal of a meeting in town, which felt premature. Only the pawns had moved; don't move your big pieces out too early. Finch hinted at secrets hidden in Escutcheon Place. *Best guard them for the present*, he decided.

He therefore penned a qualified response, hoping Finch would understand:

You were right to inform me. But to re-open the past in Rotherweird may have consequences beyond imagining. As to good cause for a meeting or breaking the Great Seal of State, dire peril is not here yet. We will know if, God forbid, it comes. In the meantime you might care to check your records for The Dark Devices.

As he wrote, the germ of an idea took root. He might need a company, an alliance of town and country, as in the old days. He wrote down some names in ink, the certainties:

Bill Ferdy.
Boris Polk.
Orelia Roc.
Marmion Finch.

The questionable followed in pencil:

Oblong – the new historian and a decent, if naïve, man according to Boris. A single question mark.

Bert Polk – less original than Boris but more level-headed; in practice you could not recruit one without the other. Ferensen promoted him to the first list.

Vixen Valourhand – an ambiguous figure; the name, the protest – and yet a North Tower scientist. *What an irony*, he reflected, *that the North Tower ended up this way.* He awarded her a double question mark.

Ferensen handed the letter to Ferdy with evident nervousness. He was on the brink of changing the habit of a lifetime. The town beckoned with all its buried memories.

A Strange Encounter

They came like ghosts, miniature whirlwinds raising dust, leaves or water before subsiding. In the atmosphere, cloud similarly misbehaved, forming and dispersing with bewildering speed, just as they had in 1017 – *Saeculum*. The forest creatures no longer ventured onto open ground. They knew, and Ferox knew, cataclysm was but weeks away.

What had saved their world then? Would the saviour, whether process or person, come again? Ferox did not know. He had pinned his hopes on a visitor from the white tile, but then the portal had failed after the plantsman's fleeting visit. There had been the cat's strange reappearance, and the shudder as the black tile opened, but nobody would survive entering Lost Acre that way.

He maintained his vigil by the white tile, crouched over his spear, near-invisible in the ever-taller grass. So many centuries had passed since his immersion in the mixing-point that he could summon only disconnected images of his human childhood – cornfields, roads straight as a rule, a kinder light and a kinder climate – and of his army days, marching in step on sandalled feet into ever harsher extremes of cold and damp. A civilising empire required an iron fist and he had been brutal and merciless – perhaps why the *barbari* had chosen a weasel to share his cage after his capture. His Latin had survived the transformation, but little else. Of his fellow prisoner, the legion's scout, his *speculator*, he had seen neither hide nor hair.

Much later he had befriended one of the untouched humans who occasionally came through the tile, Master Malise, who later changed his name to Veronal Slickstone, a kindred predator. From him and Wynter he had learned English, and with it the pleasing discovery that his Roman tribe had impregnated their vassals with words in perpetuity, like a mile, or *mille passuum*.

He had not seen Malise for more than four hundred years, but he had been in the mixing-point too, so he could, like him, live for ever. He believed in his return because he had to. He could not escape in this form – he would be nothing more than a freak for a circus or laboratory. The stones had made him; only the stones could unmake him. He had smelled their presence near the white tile, and latterly, on the plantsman. That gave him hope too.

Strange things happen as cycles approach their zenith, and so it proved today with yet another unfamiliar visitor who this time came not from the white tile, now apparently closed, but from the forest – so how, and from where exactly? First the cat and now this human appeared to have passed by the guardian, survived the un-survivable.

Ferox's snout twitched: again the prickle of the stones, although, as with the plantsman, a trace only. Ferox was supremely self-confident as a rule, but he felt uneasy. It was not a physical threat – the man's build was stunted and his gait shambling – but something else.

He downed his spear. If the intruder turned difficult, bare hands would do; for now, best not to frighten him away. Saviours can come in strange forms.

When the man saw him, Ferox's hopes soared as paradoxically his unease deepened.

The man did not retreat, or even flinch. He stood still, opened his arms and smiled.

Old History

1571.

Sir Robert Oxenbridge is not retained as Constable of the Tower on the new Queen's accession. Thirteen years have passed, and his life is closer now in style to Sir Henry Grassal's, tending his fruit trees and devising games for his grandchildren. He has heard nothing from his old friend; a secretary replies whenever he writes. The children have realised their potential, and his efforts will forever be remembered. He would have been more suspicious of this blandness had he not treasured the memory of so many children saved – a talisman against his more disturbing memories of siege and casual slaughter.

It is an autumn evening when a message arrives, forwarded by his successor in London. It has, he is told, been delivered to the Tower by a bird whose like the Warden of the Ravens has never seen before. The wax seal on the tiny canister has not been broken. He uncurls a miniature scroll. The language is direct:

We are ensnared in the Rotherweird Valley. Your friend is long dead and his charges have been put to ill use. You will need to bring men of discretion who are hardened to horror. Help us, please.

Long dead . . . the truth sinks in. The false Grassal, the masquerading secretary, had a cultured hand. There is devilry here. Surely Mary Tudor could not have been right? He recalled the cold face of Master Malise and the words of the Yeoman Warder all those years ago: 'One serpent in the Garden is enough'. Chivalry, a friendship from childhood and curiosity engage. He will raise a troop of old companions, but only the unmarried men. He has had enough of orphans.

He strides to his hall, unaware of the new vigour in his step. He unsheathes his sword and begins to scrape away the rust.

MAY

I

Mayday

Rivers never repeat themselves.

On early Mayday morning not a breath of wind ruffled the water, which lacked a single cloud to reflect. Gone was the foaming flood of the Equinox; the Rother slept, still as glass. This was a morning to throw open your windows and inhale deeply; this was the day of the Mayday Fair.

In town, two concerns animated every household: picnic and dress. Some cared deeply about picnic presentation (wicker hampers, polished silver, linen napkins and cut glass); others cared not a jot, happy with plastic and paper. On the matter of dress, however, there was unanimity: the everyday would not do for opening the gateway to summer. Dresses, jackets and hats must be adventurous in both design and colour.

The southern portcullis rose soon after dawn to disgorge a shuffling queue with parasols, boxes and collapsible chairs, all in party best, with the Scrutineer leading the way in full regalia.

Performers followed, each grasping a permit quantifying the space allotted to their activity, but not stipulating where. By the *Mayday Fair Regulations*, performance spaces were awarded on a first-come, first-served basis. Many had queued through the night for a prime position.

The performers dispersed to mark their plots and raise their flags, their skills declared by pennants on tall poles. The most common motif was the hand – palm up (fortune-teller), in silhouette (shadow-players), cards between the fingers (tricks and other *legerde-main*), on a glass (glass music-makers), with coloured balls (jugglers), with paper (origami) and finger to mouth (mummers). One of each skill only had been allowed through, earlier elimination rounds having sorted through the multiple entries.

After the performers came the craftsmen from Aether's Way, bearing their wares, from model aeroplanes to fantastical clocks and astrolabes.

At the Scrutineer's signal, tents, awnings and pennants went up. From afar the Island Field resembled a mediaeval encampment.

Snorkel drew his damask curtains and assessed the view from a political perspective. His offshore trust accounts had never been so healthy, but the benefits of Sir Veronal's presence were now looking distinctly fragile. He had counted on the restoration of the Manor as a mark of his regime's progressive outlook. However, while the outsider's largesse might yet make the new pub a success, his interest in Rotherweird had been disturbingly intense of late, and his attitude to the Town Hall increasingly dismissive. Gorhambury had proved impossible to replace, and administrative efficiency had suffered.

While generations of Snorkels had avoided democratic process, an election year loomed. You could never be sure. At least good weather equalled good spirits, which could only assist the present incumbent.

The portcullis rose again at ten o'clock, and this time the Mayor and his wife took the lead, followed by a succession of dignitaries in traditional order followed by the Guilds, each with a distinctive standard and costume. The Apothecaries came first, an incongruous exception to the dress code in their puritan black and white. At the rear came a single figure in a multi-coloured uniform embroidered with stars and zigzag lightning motifs. Even his face was covered: the anonymous Master of the Guild of Fireworkers. Behind them came the rank and file with hampers, baskets and backpacks in all shapes and sizes. At the entrance bridge to the Island Field rickshaws awaited the elderly and the Scrutineer turned his attention from performers to the public, exercising quality control over pets, golf clubs, extravagant cleavages and the noisier musical instruments.

Entertainments prospered. Rotherweird was at peace with itself.

The performers halted at noon, in accordance with the *Mayday Fair Regulations*. The Rother cooled bottles and feet while offering her banks as benches and her trees as shade; the crowd attacked their hampers, while three criers, tolling hand-bells, recited the municipal achievements of the previous year.

Snorkel basked as citizens inclined their heads or raised a hand on passing his magnificent tented pavilion where he was entertaining Rotherweird's movers and shakers. Only countrysiders offered no salute.

Then Snorkel's world turned sour: over the Island Field bridge sauntered Sir Veronal and Lady Slickstone with their son. In dress and manner they exuded an easy elegance.

Sir Veronal left money for free coracle rides, overpaid craftsmen and tipped the performers. Worse, contrary to what his eavesmen had reported, Sir Veronal drew greetings and smiles like a magnet. Snorkel had no difficulty recognising his own stock-in-trade: glad-handing and patronage. A new political heavyweight had entered the ring.

'How low is that,' he hissed to his wife, 'canvassing at the Fair!'

'Let's go and see the fire-eaters,' replied his wife, wings ever beating against the bars of her gilded cage.

'You do your job here,' hissed Snorkel, before sliding away in the hope of easing his angst in the fortune-teller's tent.

Compliments swarmed about Sir Veronal – the party, Rodney, the restoration, the anticipated reopening of *The Journeyman's Gist*. Sir Veronal felt ordained as Wynter's successor: the Rotherweird Valley was his to claim.

By contrast, the actress felt more sidelined than ever. She bobbed and smiled and mouthed sweet platitudes, a study in blandness, how not to be noticed.

Just short of the southern end of the Island Field, where the picnics and stalls ceased, Sir Veronal raised a lordly hand. 'I wish to be alone,' he announced, and walked on. Time had twisted the stream's contour, reshaped the profile of the trees and obscured the old paths. The very lie of the land appeared to have altered, like a body moving in sleep.

Sir Veronal cursed. Where was the tile? Yet another search confronted him.

Oblong had assumed that the Fair would feature an appearance by Rotherweird's only travelling librarian, but Cecily Sheridan did not show. He vainly sought Bolitho in the hope of finding solace in a cocktail, but the astronomer too had kept away.

In the late afternoon he found a secluded promontory close to where the tributary surrounding the Island Field met the Rother. He dabbled his toes in the chill water. On a fresh page in his notebook he wrote, yet again, *The Ballad of the Midsummer Fair by Jonah Oblong.* He listed the cast: Knight, Knight's equerry, damsel, monster – hardly King Lear, but he would show them. Painfully, a mirror to his present mood, some opening lines at last began to shape:

> *Beyond Civilisation's cultured reach*
> *In a cavernous lair of moss and stone,*
> *Uncomforted by laughter, love or speech,*
> *A dark eyed monster sits – and broods – alone.*

Strimmer returned to his rooms in a rage. Sir Veronal had shaken his hand as if he were a stranger. He attributed this offhand behaviour to his failure to find anything of interest so far in Valourhand's movements.

The North Tower's work included surveillance. The following day he fixed a tracking device in the sole of the heavily studded, highly unfashionable shoes that his colleague inexplicably wore for evening wear.

With the School emptied, Valourhand progressed her experiments, the flashes at her study windows unseen and the explosions unheard. Soot peppered the ceiling; the fall-out from her various lightning machines and magnifying transmitters.

She strutted about the room dressed like a surgeon in gumboots and rubber gloves for safety. She did manage to create the occasional bolt, but try as she might, she could not direct it, or even envisage how that might be done. She studied the experiments of earlier pioneers, but none had attempted to channel lightning in any particular direction.

Sir Veronal must have a most peculiar contraption.

She prowled. She talked to herself. 'So if that is how he creates the charge, how—? Think, Vixen, *think*.'

She knew this self-enforced solitude was harmful. Never socialise, and you cannot break the circle. She had lost what little self-confidence she had. Strimmer's predatory eye had moved on to a former pupil in the linguistics department, who was relishing the attention. Her protest at the Slickstone party had not earned her fame or infamy, merely the cold shoulder, and she had barely any acquaintances, let alone friends, inspiring affection only when acting out of character as Cecily Sheridan, and then in someone she despised.

True to his new regime and mission, Gorhambury slept through the entire Fair.

2

A Monstrous Meeting

Valourhand abandoned her lightning contraptions the day after the Fair to fret over a different puzzle with these pieces discovered so far: Sir Veronal's reopening of the Manor (how did he come to buy the house?), the bolt at the party, the death of Mrs Banter, the Church frescoes, Flask's disappearance and Strimmer's sudden change of attitude, which had brought an unhealthy interest in her movements out of School hours. The first three had potential connections, but instinct told her the others mattered too.

Literature for Valourhand meant scientific text. She had never probed the origins of the town, how its independence came about, or who had built its oldest buildings, or why. She had not even thought to query the origins of the unusual tower in which she worked. Curiosity diminishes the closer you are to home.

Now her perspective changed: the Manor and the church felt highly significant. She had been to the belfry; now she needed to understand its coded messages. The night of the Fair would be too dangerous, with revellers loose on the streets, but the night after always witnessed a lull for hangover recovery time.

She went to the Undercroft at eleven or so, earlier than usual. She hauled herself up to the roofline, a moment that never failed to excite – the slate-grey roofs like a pitching sea, and above them the towers, some lit, some not, the masts of a fleet at anchor. Little did she know that her every step was being recorded by the tiny tracking device in the sole of her right shoe.

Her destination lay on the other side of the Golden Mean. She worked her way to the North Gatehouse, glimpsing only one pedestrian on her journey – a lone figure, bent over a street drain, drunk, presumably. She did not give him a second thought.

Sculptures of men and women reading in various attitudes adorned the wooden columns of the entrance portico to Rotherweird Library. An island in the centre of the main reading room allowed Reception a good view of their visitors. Four spiral staircases led to twelve alcoves on the first floor, also open to view from below. The more recondite sciences lurked in small basement rooms off a single rectangular passage, their doorways adorned in gold lettering with alliterative flair – *Quarks, Quasars and Quantum M*; *Fiction Furious and Fantastical*, and so on.

Valourhand came only at night. Under the eaves a row of sky-lights looked over racks of reserve second copies and outdated early editions. Alarms protected the more valuable books, but not here. Once in, Valourhand would vault from the ground to the first floor, planting the balance beside the central island. She would jump from side to side without stopping until she had landed in every alcove, one to twelve: a gymnast's clock patience.

Tonight, though, she had come in the hope that the library's more arcane rooms might bring coherence to the fragments of her puzzle. She descended to the basement and wandered along the rectangular passage. Her eerie green tube-light made the silent warren of the lower rooms feel like catacombs. After a fruitless twenty minutes in *Architecture* she removed her shoes and settled in *Astronomy, Asteroids & Astrophysics*, having been unexpectedly engaged by a recent lecture on antimatter from Professor Bolitho. Only then did she feel a tingling in the soles of her feet.

She walked towards the right-hand shelves and the sensation strengthened. She walked the other way and it weakened. She followed the pulse into the next room, *Gems & Geology*, where the signal intensified slightly. She shook her tube-light and titles came into view, some devoted to precious stones, others to less rarefied rock types and volcanoes. She paced the room slowly, moving the small desk and two chairs aside to expose the hot spot, just off centre, beneath a small, nondescript rug. She rolled up the rug and sat on her haunches. She could see no discolouration or other sign of activity.

It took an hour of painstaking work to extract the wooden nails and prise up the floorboards without causing damage. A cavernous space opened up below. She tied her light to the rope and lowered it, illuminating a jumble of huge slabs of stone – sarsens, judging from their size and rough-hewn surfaces.

She retrieved her shoes before squeezing her slight frame through.

The chamber had no obvious entry or exit. On the only patch of bare ground, a single jet-black square tile had been set in the floor. The refined craftsmanship of the flower etched into its surface contrasted with the brutishness of the huge stones. She rested the flat of her hand on the tile: the energy was palpable. Around the stone, strange luminous plants flourished, tiny white skeletons littering their fleshy leaves. They were carnivorous – she had never seen their like before.

She left her pole on the ground and, with her light in her right hand, stood on the tile. Her head rushed to her feet and her feet to her head. Instinctively she raised her arms and shut her eyes as the tile sucked her in. Unbeknown to her, the process destroyed the tracker beneath her right foot.

Although underground and still beside a black tile, Valourhand quickly realised that she had exchanged the underground chamber for a circular end to a winding passageway. Huge stones set in the walls supported the roof. Duckboards paved the way ahead, lit by luminous purple-yellow rocks. Above her head the dome of the ceiling boasted a mosaic: a young man with an intelligent face animated by a quizzical expression – an intimate portrait. Relaxed by its humanity, she nonetheless advanced slowly, and on tiptoe.

Racks were attached to the walls with handwritten labels: pickled girolles, blackberry coulis and dried bird blood. One shelf contained a row of ancient cookery books whose spines were stained with smudged, earthy fingerprints.

Where was she?

On turning the first corner, the smell of damp receded in favour of a refined fragrance. Valourhand lived off ready-made meals and had not the slightest interest in fine food, but the irresistible piquancy of this aroma, a tang of citrus with a dash of chocolate, drew her on. The passage ended in a hallway with intricately painted doors on each side and another ahead. She followed her nose through the right-hand door into an extraordinary kitchen.

Embers glowed in a huge hearth, above which hung pots of various sizes on an array of iron grills and hooks, some with ladles; some not. Pulleys controlled floating shelves, crammed with jars and various cuts of dried meat. On a large rectangular oak table Valourhand counted six chopping boards with as many knives. A stained leather apron hung over the back of a chair.

In front of the chair a place had been laid for one with a disconcertingly large number of knives and forks, a plate made of wood and a horn goblet. On either side of the fire, four double oven gloves hung over a bare iron fender. Vixen savoured the steam billowing from the various pots. She was about to pick up a ladle when she heard movement behind her.

For nights to come, she struggled to exorcise the horror of the creature standing in the doorway. The face had vestiges of humanity, but like the jointed arms and legs, was predominantly arachnid. The creature currently stood on three legs and held in its hands a jar, a bowl and three knives. The eight eyes had human features, including eyebrows and coloured irises, but were suspended on stalks rather than set in the skull. They blinked and swivelled. Between its teeth a dark purple tongue darted this way and that.

Valourhand froze. *What was this abomination?*

'Young meat must come to me,' hissed the creature, dropping the bowl and sharpening one knife against another.

The unexpected voice and the equally unwelcome invitation brought Valourhand to her senses. She played for time. 'I'm sorry to trespass like this. I didn't intend—'

'Of course, you didn't. Nobody intends to come here.' The voice was feminine.

'I do like your books.'

'Then you'll enjoy being pickled.'

'I could get you more.'

'You won't come back.' Again the eyes joggled. 'No, forget pickle – you'd be better raw – *tartare*.' Flecks of green foam bubbled in the spiderwoman's mouth as the creature's body swayed in a disconcerting way. Valourhand twirled her bolas as she edged towards the table, eying the longest knife. She snatched for it, but the spider was quicker. With uncanny accuracy a thread of silk arched through the air and snared the knife. With one hand the spider yanked it back and whipped it forwards again. The blade passed just over Valourhand's shoulder as she ducked. Deciding defence was the best means of attack, she tried to push the table into the spider's body, but the oak was too heavy to shift.

'Fresh, so fresh,' muttered the creature, passing the three knives in her hand through the poison bubbling in her mouth, greening the blades.

Valourhand ducked again, but the knives were not aimed at her upper body. They were thrown from under the table. Quick though she was, she could not evade all three, and one sliced through her left leg. Clutching the wound, she arched back and hurled the sticky contents of the nearest pot at the spiderwoman's eyes.

'Spirited girl means lots of blood,' snarled the creature.

Valourhand felt her leg stiffen. Worse, the spiderwoman had seized a long iron rod with a sharpened end and effortlessly pushed the table aside with a shrug of her bulbous body. A new line of thread wrapped round her shoulder, reeling her in towards the point of the spear. She flayed at the silky string, only to snag her arm too. She had no weapons now; she was out of reach of the fire and too close for the bolas.

A new voice intervened, male and prissy, hardly that of a born rescuer. 'Now look here,' it said, 'haven't you heard of the *Library Regulations*—?'

The voice cut off in mid-sentence. Valourhand could not see its owner with the spider in the way, but nor could the spider. A multiplicity of arms and legs had many advantages, but one weakness: turning round. As the spider lurched about, the levelled spear moving away with her, Valourhand took her chance. Seizing a broom with her free hand, she severed the silken threads and darted through a narrow gap between the creature and the wall, almost knocking down the new arrival. She screamed in agony as her wounded leg took the weight. The newcomer, a vaguely familiar middle-aged man in a crumpled suit, stood stock-still, gawping like a fish taking air, as the monstrous creature turned to face him.

'Two for the price of one,' hissed the spiderwoman.

Valourhand grabbed the man's shoulder. 'Run, you idiot!'

And they did.

The spiderwoman, taken aback by the appearance of her former quarry alongside the new, hesitated long enough to allow them to get back down the passage.

To Valourhand's amazement, the man stopped just before the tile. 'Library books – this really won't do . . .'

But before he could retrieve them, she pushed him onto the tile and he disappeared – but when she tried to follow, the tile did not respond. *It needs time to recharge*, she reasoned, and adopted a defensive posture, a lopsided crouch to compensate for her wounded leg. Above the din of falling bottles and disturbed shelves around the corner of the passage ahead, she heard two syllables – still the spiderwoman's voice, but in intonation and message very different: 'Let be.'

The creature appeared to be in turmoil, responding brutally to its own suggestion, 'Such meat!'

'Let be,' repeated the gentler voice.

As the bulbous shape lumbered round the corner towards her, she backed onto the tile.

This time it worked and she found herself back in the rock chamber beneath the library, dishevelled, breathless. Gorhambury moved towards her, relief evident on his face, lit only by the eerie glow of her lantern.

'You bloody idiot.' Valourhand fell to her knees.

'*Library Regulations* Rule 3 (4): *Unless extended, all books must be returned in three weeks.* Books in that passage have been there for—'

'Do I know you?'

'Gorhambury. There was a Reginald, but it got lost. Everyone calls me—'

'Gorhambury, next time a giant spiderwoman is closing in, forget your fucking library books.'

Gorhambury winced at both the language and the message. She crawled to the tile. The energy had dissipated. The gateway was, for the moment, closed.

'Might it yet come through?' asked Gorhambury.

She glanced at the earth of the chamber – no sign of disturbance by any eight-legged creature, or indeed, anything sizeable.

'It never has.'

She peered at her pallid rescuer. Mentally cleaning up his features, she recognised in the crumpled suit and cadaverous looks the former Town Clerk. 'Why are you following me?'

Offended by what he took to be an accusation of stalking, Gorhambury explained – he had been dismissed thanks in part to her protest at Sir Veronal Slickstone's party; he had been conducting a survey into a disturbing decline in the town's fabric, and he had seen her enter the library roof. He produced his set of Town Hall keys by way of indirect corroboration.

Valourhand believed him; such a pedant would be incapable of embellishment, let alone a lie. She softened. 'Well, I suppose, without you, I'd be—'

'—*tartare.*'

She grasped her leg and grimaced. An angry green discolouration had already spread well out from the wound.

Gorhambury turned solicitous. 'You're going to the doctor.'

'I don't do doctors.'

'Always a first time, Miss Valourhand. I'm going to carry you.'

'You're bloody not.' Valourhand picked up the vaulting pole, but it was no use. Her injured leg would bear no weight at all. 'Bring it,' was all she could say.

The girl's condition had deteriorated by the time they reached the street. As Gorhambury fretted over the quickest route to the nearest doctor, out of the shadows, snail and slug bag in hand, sauntered Rotherweird's troublesome botanist.

'Salt?'

'Odd time to be browsing for books,' replied Salt with an odd look in his eye.

'Odd time to be walking the streets,' retaliated Gorhambury.

'Odd time to be carrying . . .' Salt broke off on seeing the injury. 'Good . . . God.' Before Gorhambury could stop him, he sniffed the wound. 'Where have you been? Where did she get this?' His tone was accusing.

'You wouldn't believe me.'

'Oh yes I would. How long ago – how *long?*'

'Ten – fifteen minutes—'

'We're going to the Ferdys – *now!*' Salt placed the flat of his hand on the girl's cheek. 'There's only one man who can deal with this.' He ripped the bottom half of his sleeve from his shirt and tied a tourniquet above the wound. 'I'll take the front, you take the back – and we run.'

'Why should I trust you?' Gorhambury remembered Salt's pollution of Grove Gardens with *Snorkel's Petunia* the previous spring.

Salt bared his left arm – a long ugly scar ran from the elbow to the hand. 'I was lucky,' he said.

'Are you saying that's the same?'

'It's the same all right: eight legs, or are they hands? She still visits me in my nightmares.' Even Salt realised now was not the time to ask how this incongruous couple had found a way into Lost Acre. It might be the burning question, but saving the girl came first. He added, 'If it's a bite, there's not much hope; if it's one of her knives . . .'

It felt like an eternity before they reached *The Polk Land & Water Company*. The girl was now cold, her colour ghostly.

The Polks and Gregorius Jones were playing cards. Salt took Boris aside and cut the courtesies. 'Boris – we must get her . . .' he paused, then said firmly, 'to the Rainmaker.'

'I'll run,' offered Gregorius, as ever inspired by a lady in distress.

'You won't, you're pedalling,' replied Boris.

Gorhambury offered to stay behind so as not to slow the charabanc.

'No, we need you. For a start, have we any keys to the North Gate?'

'Yes, but I'm not permitted to use them,' replied Gorhambury.

'You'll use them!'

'If you're not back, I'll use the reserve charabanc for the morning run,' said Bert, subdued at missing out on yet another adventure.

Boris placed a consoling arm on his twin's shoulder. One of them had to play by the rules.

Salt joined Valourhand under a blanket as Gorhambury fooled the gatekeeper with an outrageous lie and the straightest of faces. After a *frisson* of self-disgust, he found to his surprise that he had rather enjoyed the experience.

Boris and Jones pedalled like fanatics, the pistons and drums whistling and wheezing. Gorhambury barely knew the rural roads beyond the main highway to Hoy, but the novelty of this journey into the wild unknown did not dispel his conservatism. He was appalled that the town's long-distance transport had been entrusted to such a reckless driver. Despite the gravity of the girl's condition, Boris Polk yelled '*Yahoo!*' and '*Bazoom!*' as they cut corners at speeds Gorhambury would have thought impossible.

When well away from the town, Salt emptied his bag of slugs onto the verge, as Gregorius Jones, ever the mediaeval knight, produced a stream of enquiries about the patient: 'Look to the lady! Mop the brow, Gorhambury! Hang on, dear girl, cling to the rope!'

They were quick. The roads were clear and the weather dry, and in half an hour, they were at the Ferdys' farm. Ferdy took in Boris and Jones as Salt carried Valourhand to Ferensen's tower. Gorhambury trailed behind, unclear as to which group to join.

'Follow me, man, follow me,' Salt instructed him.

At the door of the tower an old man with a lively face and a firm handshake greeted them. Ferensen and Gorhambury were hurriedly introduced. The formers expression changed when he saw the wound. 'Here,' he said, 'by the fire.'

It was the same piece of furniture on which a frozen Salt had been revived some months earlier. This evening the battle between life and death was closer.

The old man cleared a table. 'Crush these!' He handed Gorhambury a mortar and pestle while mixing the contents of two small phials. The herbs smelled pungent and exotic.

Gorhambury's attention was caught by the volume of objects and books on view, as well as the single room's remarkable shape. He had always assumed countrysiders to be hardworking men with limited intellect, if honest values.

Ferensen cut off the girl's jeans below the knee, removed the tourniquet and applied a steaming poultice. He gave her a tetanus injection and applied a sweet-smelling ointment below her nostrils before turning his attention to the wound. He moved quickly and silently.

'The neurotoxins of this particular creature are not to be treated lightly,' he observed by way of commentary. 'Another half an hour and our patient would be in serious trouble. As it is, I'm hopeful she'll have nothing more than a war wound to show her children. Fit young lady, I'd say.'

'Miss Valourhand is a rooftop vaulter as well as a scientist,' said Gorhambury.

'Is she indeed . . . and you?' asked Ferensen.

'Gorhambury.'

'He's our former Town Clerk,' chipped in Salt.

'And who might you be?' countered Gorhambury.

'Who indeed?' came the unhelpful response as Ferensen ambled over to his drinks rack. 'Arrack with ginger enlivens the vocabulary. A useful side-effect when describing the unusual.'

Salt poured as Gorhambury explained the night's events. 'We were in the library.'

Salt raised an eyebrow.

'It's a long story. I'm homeless but I kept a set of town keys. As security . . .' Gorhambury was protesting too much, a fault of the innocent as much as the guilty.

'Keep going,' encouraged Ferensen.

'I heard footsteps downstairs and went to investigate. There's a small room in the basement – *Gems & Geology*. The boards had been raised. I squeezed through. There was a long pole on the ground, and a black tile.'

Ferensen and Salt exchanged glances. The black tile was in the town itself.

'And you stood on it!' murmured Salt to himself.

'The tile sucks you in and spits you out – I arrived to find this monstrous spider creature – look, please don't think I'm mad – in the kitchen of an underground house and, I regret to say, full of purloined library books.'

Ferensen dabbed Valourhand's forehead with a sponge. 'Did the spider have any humanity?'

'It spoke English for a start – and yes,' Gorhambury seemed lost for words, 'plenty of human bits,' he added, 'but all horribly muddled.'

'Female?'

Gorhambury considered. 'Bristly hair like a man, but voice and eyelashes of a woman.'

Salt watched Ferensen, who had put the same questions to him years ago, when he had staggered to Ferensen's tower, wounded by the same creature. His last question was particularly strange.

Gorhambury thought so too. He did not know this countrysider; the mere fact he had a way with medicine did not make him trustworthy. 'Isn't this a matter for the Town Hall?'

Ferensen stood away from Valourhand. His voice acquired such a tone of authority that Gorhambury took a pace backwards. 'Like it or not, Mr Gorhambury, the Town Hall is corrupt. If you can't see that when you yourself worked there, then you're blind, deaf and dumb. Worse, you don't know what you'd be giving away if you reported this. I do.'

'How?'

'Why do you think we suppress our history? Why does the rest of England keep us at bay? Why was there a prohibited quarter? Why are we blessed with so many gifted scientists? Why do we never pursue the answers to these obvious questions?'

Gorhambury hesitated. He read deep pain in the old man's face.

Salt interrupted, 'Is your black tile a metre square with a flower incised on it?'

Gorhambury nodded as Ferensen resumed, 'It's not so much a door as a portal to a different plane. Isn't that right, Salt?'

The botanist did not reply. Every new recruit diluted his great secret.

Gorhambury reflected: Salt's own scar and his instant decision to take the girl to Ferensen suggested an understanding of where they had been and what they had encountered. Ferensen had now given him sufficient facts to make it clear that he too was well-informed. They seemed to be decent people – and he had no wish to share his nocturnal adventure with the Mayor.

Ferensen refilled their glasses. Valourhand heard the tinkle as the decanter met the edge of the glass. Warmth and feeling were returning, but she kept her eyes shut. She would learn more that way.

'Anything else you can tell me?' Gorhambury asked Ferensen.

'There's another door marked by a white tile – it too has a flower incised on its surface – but you arrive in a different part of the same place.'

Salt clenched his fists. Secrets diminished by sharing, the more so with a narrow-minded civil servant.

'Is this world all underground?' asked Gorhambury.

'Hardly. It's a world not unlike ours was, long ago, but with special and dangerous properties. The white tile opens in a meadow.' Again Salt winced, and again Ferensen took no notice. 'There are probably other ways in too.'

'And that abomination – where did that come from?'

The old man's voice trembled, hinting at a suppressed emotional pain. 'She was not always like that,' he said, before abruptly changing tack. 'We three must make some decisions—'

'We four,' interrupted Vixen Valourhand, swinging her feet round and sitting up normally. 'I've questions of my own.'

'After thanking Mr Ferensen,' said Gorhambury primly. 'You were at death's door half an hour ago. And Mr Salt too.' Ever the unthanked worker, he did not think to include himself.

Valourhand managed a nod, but Ferensen ignored the exchange.

A meeting must be held and a company formed. The black tile had to be kept from Slickstone and guarded.

Valourhand had taken in Ferensen and his tower with no more than mild curiosity. Had she been born a countrysider, she would have lived like this. Yet now he did astonish her. As he bent over to bandage her leg, she caught in his weatherbeaten features an unmistakable glimpse of a much younger man, his face captured in the mosaic on the underground passageway's ceiling. So he had been there – but when? Why had he been commemorated rather than attacked? Before she could fashion a cunning question, a deep, sonorous note invaded the room. Twenty seconds, and the mournful voice of Doom's Tocsin tolled again.

Seconds later Bill Ferdy burst in, pointing back through the open door and crying, 'Look – come look! *Quick!*'

Ferdy ran out, and though still in pain, Valourhand followed. Boris Polk and Gregorius Jones, already halfway up the hill, had stopped and were staring at the valley below. Rotherweird, ordinarily no more than a cluster of lights on the floor of the valley, flickered in and out of view, exposed by a fierce orange glow. For a town of timber, the worst nightmare had come: fire, the great devourer.

The others hurried to the summit of the hill. The spectacle held them briefly, but before Ferensen could digest the implications, Boris had bellowed a call to arms with the single word, 'Hydra!' and rushed downhill to the charabanc, Gregorius Jones following at a sprint. Action was his kind of language.

Ferensen watched them go before taking control. He appeared to see more danger in what lay behind the fire than the fire itself. 'The odds do not favour accident, believe me. Get the beer-cart, Ferdy, we're going in.' He turned to Salt. 'We're calling a meeting – tonight.' He gave Ferdy a knowing wink. 'I suspect you know somewhere safe and hidden.'

'No problem,' replied Ferdy with his own knowing wink.

'I want you, Boris, Orelia Roc.' He paused. 'Oh yes, and bring our new friends, Mr Gorhambury and the indomitable Jones, also the current modern historian. Bert, of course, but above all, I want Mr Finch.'

'Above all, you want me,' interrupted Valourhand.

'Yes, yes,' agreed Ferensen.

Ferdy returned to the issue of Finch. 'You'll have a job luring him from his lair.'

'I doubt it,' replied Ferensen. 'Gather as soon as the fire is under control.'

Gorhambury thought of the possible causes. The *Safety from Fire Regulations* were comprehensive and generally well observed, but of late there had been too much casual smoking in town, a matter he had raised with the Mayor on several occasions.

Ferensen's poultice had remarkably restorative properties. Vixen Valourhand thought not of her wound or people or buildings, only of fire, which she loved for its beauty, fierceness and uncomplicated warmth. She must be up close.

The fire took hold so fast that the town discovered it only minutes before the countrysiders. Frantic knocking at the window of *Baubles & Relics* brought Orelia downstairs. Outside, Fanguin, in overcoat and a faintly ludicrous woollen hat, was gesturing extravagantly.

'Your house is burning,' he blurted as she opened the door. Orelia looked blank. 'Your *other* house,' he added.

Orelia rushed outside: from the far end of town smoke shot through with sparks was pouring across the sky. Other inhabitants of the Golden Mean were emerging from their homes, many with buckets.

'What next?' Orelia cried in despair. She pulled on jeans and boots, a jersey and a long overcoat over her pyjamas.

Two vehicles left the Ferdys' farm that night. The charabanc, with Boris and Jones, travelled at breakneck speed; and some ten minutes later the beer-cart followed at a statelier pace with a crate of pint glasses, a barrel of beer, Bill Ferdy, Ferensen, Valourhand and Gorhambury.

Boris Polk cursed his impulsiveness on finding the portcullis up but the South Gate shut – the keys were still with Gorhambury. But his luck was in: from a small door cut into the great nail-studded oak gate emerged a young guard wearing an overcoat over his pyjamas. 'Nobody's allowed in – order of the Mayor!' he declared, squinting into the headlights of the charabanc. He paused. 'Is that you, B Polk or B Polk?'

Boris stepped out of the vehicle with a flourish, goggles perched above his eyebrows. 'It is B Polk – B for Boris – and you have a choice. Prize prat or superhero!'

'What are you up to?' the guard enquired suspiciously.

'Let me in and you'll find out,' was the riposte. The guard, too distracted to enquire further into what Polk and Jones were doing outside the gates at such an hour, succumbed. 'Where's the fire?'

'The late Mrs Banter's house – she's burning like a torch. It's serious.'

Boris' pace scarcely slowed despite the narrowness of the streets, and in no time he and Jones were hurrying into the yard of *The Polk Land & Water Company*, where Bert stood like a sentry on duty.

'Hydra!' bellowed Boris.

'Shed's open,' replied Bert, 'but have you done your final "minor adjustments"?'

'No time for that – this is the moment she was born for,' answered Boris as he sprinted off with Jones.

3

Fire and Water

It takes a disaster to sharpen any emergency service; and Rotherweird had not endured a fire on this scale in living memory. For a town that prided itself on scientific expertise and logic, the response was chaotic. The compound with the solitary fire engine was locked, and in the absence of Gorhambury, the key could not be found. Once tracked down, the key to the fire engine proved equally elusive. Its route, once mobile, was blocked by a rickshaw in the Golden Mean whose owner could not be found. The Mayor's office rang Gorhambury, only to be tersely informed by his erstwhile landlord that he had been evicted two months earlier for non-payment of rent and had left no forwarding address.

Faced with this abject failure by the municipal authorities, Rotherweird's citizens turned to self-help. Ladders of all sizes were retrieved from unlikely places, metal buckets likewise, and a human chain began swinging pails from hand to hand to Pagan Lane from the pump on the Church Green.

Despite their efforts, the situation remained critical: embers were smouldering on neighbouring roofs as the temperature grew so intense that dousing the flames from ladders became too perilous. Mercifully, Aether's Way did not abut Mrs Banter's tower.

Snorkel arrived with a retinue of Council employees. A large striped drum, designed for traffic duty on market days, served as his rostrum. Snorkel seized a megaphone and climbed onto the drum. 'Don't panic!' he screamed. The Head of Emergency Services ambled towards him.

Snorkel leaned down, forgetting to turn off the megaphone, and cried, 'This is a bloody shambles!'

Together they restored a semblance of order, clearing Pagan Lane of onlookers and diplomatically substituting the more elderly helpers. Ladders close to the fire were recovered, and the main effort shifted its focus to neighbouring gardens and roofs – better to lose one tower than the whole town.

Snorkel then made a mistake by suggesting that anyone with homes at risk should close their windows – as everyone felt exposed in a town of wood, many abandoned the human chain and the supply of water slowed, leaving the fate of the town in the balance. Smoke began to rise from the timbers of two adjoining towers and the embers snagged in neighbouring beams began to flicker with flame. A huge spiral of sparks soared into the sky as the top section of Deirdre Banter's tower collapsed with a roar.

Valourhand worked her way to a convenient viewpoint and gazed into the inferno, her pupils dilating with excitement. She thought of the forges of myth, toiling to produce legendary weapons – the work that the North Tower now performed. She imagined a different crucible where strands of DNA coiled and merged, blueprints for sensory organs and cerebral structures.

Orelia felt near-suicidal. She suspected that her aunt's notebooks had provided not only the tinder but an arsonist's motive – the fire was working *down* the tower towards the ground floor, not the other way. She caught a murmur in the crowd and followed their pointing arms to see a large cat on the first-floor roof, turning this way and that, trapped.

Driven as much by despair at her family's misfortune as by sympathy, she seized a ladder, ran forward and climbed to the hip of the roof before anyone could stop her. The soles of her shoes stuck to the hot slates.

Move fast and on tiptoe, she advised herself, *and you are less likely to burn*. She almost danced her way towards the cat, which had its back to her. Only when it turned did she realise something was wrong: parts of the misshapen face and body, including the eyes and blotches of pink skin between tufts of hair, suggested a half-human creature. The cat arched its neck and spat.

Then to her horror it reared up on its hind legs and spoke. 'Do you have the book? Where—?'

Orelia looked blank, betraying her lack of a useful answer. The creature sprang, its face contorted by a mix of hatred and suffering, claws extended like knives. She ducked instinctively as the cat passed over her lowered head. Fire played around its feet.

'Die, child,' added the creature as it leapt from the roof and disappeared.

Orelia could barely move her feet. Her soles had all but melted through, and more and more flames flickered from holes in the roof as the slates cracked in the heat, split and tumbled to the ground. The smoke closed her eyes.

The crowd below groaned, as horrified as they were transfixed.

At that moment, as if by divine intervention, an extraordinary vehicle lurched into Pagan Lane: long and thin, pillar-box red, with large iron wheels and a forest of multicoloured wires coated in Polk-patented fire-retardant paint. Pedals on each side were manned by Jones and Bert Polk, and Boris steered. On the chassis four white hoses lay coiled around a thicker hose. Pistons rose and fell as if in a demented sewing machine.

'What the hell is that?' bellowed Snorkel, megaphone back in hand. 'It's not licensed, it's not registered, it's not—'

'But suppose it works,' whispered the Head of Emergency Services.

While Bert secured a signature, guaranteeing reasonable remuneration if the Hydra worked, Jones unwound the thicker white hose from the centre of the vehicle and connected it to the nearest hydrant.

'Not that bloody man Fanguin!' complained the Mayor, but too late: Boris had already recruited his crew of four and was busy distributing small boxes with sticks and switches. He gave a one-minute crash course – 'Up, down, left, right, nozzle wide, nozzle tight ... squirt. Awake the Hydra!'

Like cobras responding to a charmer's call, the hoses uncoiled and rose higher and higher, before dipping their heads to spray water.

Snorkel changed tune with alacrity, bellowing encouragement through his megaphone. 'Capital work, Polk! Keep going!'

The Hydra transformed a fiery scene that illuminated everyone into one of steam, where few could see anything. Blinded and drenched, Orelia lost all sense of place.

'Up there!' screamed the crowd, gesticulating at the swaying figure on the roof.

Jones' primal chivalric urge resurfaced with a rush of adrenalin.

'There's a young lady!' he bellowed, jumping up and down like a child deprived of a favourite toy. Boris produced a further set of controls of a different colour covered in sticky labels marked *Do not use – untested*.

'You are sure?' queried Bert.

'Do it!' bellowed Jones.

From a drum in the middle of the Hydra a wire ladder rose.

'Hold on!' yelled Boris, but the intrepid gymnast needed no invitation; he was already in position, clasping the top rung. Boris flicked the switch upwards.

'Eeee–aaaagh—!' shrieked Jones as he disappeared into a roiling mix of smoke and steam.

The ladder did not share the hoses' elegance of movement but shot upwards at breakneck speed. Boris moved the plastic control stick to the right, prompting a further expletive from the clouds of steam through which Jones was intermittently appearing. The

'Awake the Hydra!'

crowd, quietened by the anti-climax that follows the death of a fire, revived.

Orelia sank to a crouch. She was slipping slowly down the roof in a treacherous mix of ash and water, lines of black rubber trailing from her melted soles. Jones swooped from behind and swept her high into the air before being reeled back to earth, to the tumultuous ecstasy of the crowd.

With a flamboyant sweep of the hand Jones waved away the applause. 'Look to the lady!'

A believer in traditional remedies passed a phial of smelling salts across Orelia's nostrils, with instantaneous effect.

The steam cleared, and so did the crowd. From high above the town, charred fragments of the private lives of her inhabitants, as recorded by Mrs Banter, floated down like funeral confetti.

4

Of Towers and Tunnels

Ferensen made his dispositions during the journey, entrusting to Bill Ferdy and Gorhambury the task of gathering his meeting. He accepted Ferdy's choice of rendezvous.

Unlike the charabanc, the beer-cart went to the South Gate and remained outside. Gorhambury apprehensively let them in, but he need not have worried: by the time of their arrival the fire had drawn even the solitary guard to the north end of town. Ferdy and Gorhambury hurried off, carrying a barrel under a blanket.

Ferensen wrapped his cloak around him, pulled down a wide-brimmed hat and headed towards the School. He had watched the town develop over the centuries from afar. Now, inside, close up, the density of the place, the forest of towers, the affluence of the shop-window displays and the sense of a vibrant community enchanted him. He understood now why they tolerated Snorkel: he ran a town that worked.

He recalled a very different Rotherweird: a single wooden bridge, no perimeter walls, no gateways, and stabling and a smithy where Market Square now stood. The School had been nothing more than a tithe barn, and the adjacent Tower of Knowledge, as Sir Henry Grassal liked to call it, was now the North Tower. Other than those buildings, the church and the Manor, Rotherweird Island had been orchard and meadow, with a few scattered standing stones, and enclosures for pigs and sheep. Cereal crops had been grown on the Island Field, the large but flat and less conspicuous island southwest of the town bounded mostly by a tributary of the main river.

Ferensen moved on, a journey motivated as much by pilgrimage as reconnaissance. He opened the School's front gate with a key borrowed from Gorhambury; there was no porter on duty, and no sign of life. He felt himself once again the local country boy.

Using another of Gorhambury's invaluable keys, he entered the North Tower enclosure, only to be halted by a growling mastiff. Ferensen stared at the dog and whistled, low, then high, with an occasional trill. The dog unbared his teeth, smiled quizzically, rolled on his side and fell asleep.

Gorhambury, ever efficient, had taped the combination to the compound key. As a boy and a young man Ferensen had climbed these oak stairs daily. He found studies, gaining in size and grandeur as he ascended, noting the names on the doors, which culminated in *H Strimmer*. He quickly found the ceiling panel and opened it with a short, sharp shove. He pulled his Polk-designed phosphorescent tube-light out of a pocket, shook it and hauled himself up into the gloom above.

The twelve hinged seats were intact, although only three retained their initials – the Seers, and Fortemain. Intact too were the golden door and the painted ceiling. Even the wheel that turned the floor was still there.

It was here that Sir Henry had opened their eyes to the wonders of the universe. And here Slickstone, in his true name of Master Malise, had taken his terrible revenge.

Ferensen explored the remainder of the floor. A loose board close to the trapdoor had recently been lifted to expose a rectangular recess, now empty. The hiding place looked designed for a specific object. Ferensen's magnifying glass revealed a few dusty brown particles, the tell-tale spoor of old leather. A book had been placed there.

Not that *book*, he prayed.

Elsewhere in Rotherweird the past was breaking through.

Finch watched from his window: the burning tower, the sixteenth trump in the sixteenth-century tarot pack, symbol of the powerful brought low. It could hardly be coincidence. Mrs Banter's tower, the *late* Mrs Banter – an inexplicable death, and now an inexplicable fire. He recalled the plans of the Master Builder Peregrine Banter and sensed unseen dangerous connections. Sparks drifted past his window like molten snow.

Dire peril indeed – it was time. So as not to deface the Great Seal, Finch opened his ancestor's letter with a paper knife to find a disappointingly cryptic message:

The key is in the dragon's mouth.

He had expected more enlightenment on this threat from the past. The *archivoire* contained not only a register of every public carving, it was liberally blessed with examples itself – animals natural and fantastic covered the woodwork of the shelves and columns, several dragons among them.

None held any clue until he reached the rearmost bay, which stored the two contrasting collections of sixteenth-century books taken from the Manor, the one bound in beige leather and the one in black. Examining the vertical partition, he found a dragon's face at the very top. Precariously perched on his library steps, Finch peered in and spotted a tiny keyhole, and instantly understood: the architect had devised a triple security system. You needed the letter, the tiny key attached to the chain round his neck (a family heirloom), and access to the *archivoire* to progress.

Only a Finch, thought Finch.

He inserted the key and turned. No sound, no change. *Blink, scratch.* As a last resort he tried swivelling the scaly snout, which turned full circle, triggering a sequence of muffled clicks around the room like a plague of deathwatch beetle.

Finch took some minutes to discover that two panels had opened high up in the central bays, and another at the back of the room. Each of the former revealed a book – one large and thin, bound in black; one small, bound in ordinary leather, with further loose pages behind. The third cavity was disturbingly empty.

The title of the black volume had been removed, leaving only the year 1571 in Roman numerals; the spine of the other read: *The Trial of Geryon Wynter*.

After ten minutes of study Finch felt reassured that he had made the right decision.

Gorhambury relished having a task with human contact. He planned to use each person found on his list as an additional searcher, while keeping for himself the most testing invitee.

Orelia sat on her haunches in what remained of her aunt's tiny back garden, a ruinous landscape of charred stems protruding from pools of dark water. Her unseen torturer clearly revelled in his work, delivering a wound, allowing a measure of recovery and then striking again to rip the bandages away.

The Emergency Services staff respected her privacy. The loss of an ancestral building was a bereavement any Rotherweirder could relate to.

Her shock had an added source. She had been appalled by the attack of the cat with fiery feet, not to mention its gift of speech and declaration of interest in an unspecified book. She remembered the missing 'S' volume from her aunt's notebooks of the nocturnal movements of her fellow citizens. The lack of reference points tormented her. Her aunt's murder and the fire both appeared to be Slickstone's doing, but if the cat were his ally, how and where had he acquired it? And what book were they pursuing?

'Miss Roc?' She looked up to see Gorhambury. 'I'm sorry,' he said, 'I know this is poor timing, but there's a countrysider who wants to speak to you.'

She looked at him, eyes suddenly alert. 'Name?' Mindful of security he gave a description instead.

'He lives in a tower.'

'How convenient – I very much want to speak to him.'

It was Gorhambury's turn to be surprised. 'We have others to find.'

'Place? Time?'

Gorhambury whispered, before adding in his polite municipal voice, 'Would you be so kind as to find Mr Oblong?'

'Leave it to me.' She moved away, shaken from the torpor of despair.

Gorhambury felt he had helped by providing a distraction. Bill Ferdy would be gathering the rest, leaving him to recruit the incorruptible hermit Marmion Finch.

Lights shone from the ground-floor windows of Escutcheon Place. Gorhambury rang the bell, then knocked, and when no reply came, he bent down and shouted through the letter-box, 'Gorhambury here – a countrysider wishes to meet, now, tonight.'

'What on earth took him so long?'

Another unexpected reply. The mysterious countrysider commanded respect in the oddest places.

In minutes the great door of Escutcheon Place disgorged its owner. Finch looked raffish, more bandit than Herald, in leather boots, a long leather coat with a sheepskin collar, an astrakhan hat and a staff with a carved bone bird at the top – a finch, presumably.

His welcome was cryptic. 'We cannot have the Town Herald in the company of a former Town Clerk at dead of night – villainy, sir – villainy, corruption and preference. So – you may not see me, but I shall see you. Raise your hand sinister when you reach where we're going. Look back, and you've had your lot.'

Gorhambury worked through the Finch-speak. 'Lot' must refer to Lot's wife, turned to salt for disobeying the orders of the angels of deliverance when fleeing the city of Sodom. If he looked back at Finch, the expedition was off. The hand sinister meant the left hand. He left the house and started walking without looking back. It had been a most peculiar evening – what next?

The Hydra remained beside the ruined house. Its operators had left. Orelia found Oblong in the Golden Mean, and then chance took a hand. On a roundabout route to the rendezvous, they stumbled on Valourhand, lounging against a wall. She looked exhausted, but paradoxically also wore an expression close to ecstasy. The girl with the golden bolas obviously liked special effects, whatever their cause, purpose or destructiveness. Nonetheless, Orelia made an impromptu decision based on Valourhand's protest at Sir Veronal's party. Any enemy of Sir Veronal was a friend of hers.

'You're coming with me. We've a meeting to attend.'

The evening delivered yet another surprise. 'I know – with a countrysider who lives in a tower.'

The grate, in a tiny alley off a small one, lifted easily. Gorhambury raised his left hand without looking back and descended the iron rungs beneath. The tunnel felt as cold as a prison cell. He headed for the voices, magnified by a cavernous echo, to find a vaulted crypt supported by rocks of great age, lit by candles in spent bottles scattered about on trestle tables. The floor was paved, but not in a modern, orderly way. Barrels lay stacked on the walls, a few chairs in front of them. Above the barrels hung a freshly painted sign bearing the painted legend *The Journeyman's Gist Underground*.

Before Gorhambury could remonstrate about the vices of trading after midnight in flagrant breach of the *Licensing Regulations*, he received a ribald welcome from Boris ('it's old Bor'emvery'), a pint of Sturdy, a seat, a warm handshake from Ferensen and a pat on the back from Finch with the words, 'Ale met by moonlight.'

Finch's expression turned grave on seeing Orelia. 'Condolences,' he said, 'and time for us both to open up.'

She nodded, remembering their exchange at Slickstone's party.

Ferensen surveyed his polyglot company: the known quantities – Boris and Bert, Bill Ferdy and Hayman Salt; the recently met: Gregorius Jones, Vixen Valourhand, Gorhambury and Orelia Roc, and the unknown: Marmion Finch and the fresh-faced historian Jonah Oblong.

He opened proceedings. 'To the few who do not know me, I am Ferensen, a countrysider with the town's interests at heart. If I am to be effective, my presence in the valley must remain a secret. You will in time discover why.' He paused. He was asking them to take much on trust. He hurried on, 'Rotherweird has suffered the closure of its only pub, a suspicious death, an attack by lightning, the arrival of a man of unparalleled wealth and power – and now a fire.'

Salt noted that Ferensen had omitted to mention Sir Veronal's status as an outsider – the most telling point against him, surely.

'You might think that enough, but tonight two of our company have had a most unexpected journey.' He let the words hang, before pointing at Valourhand and Gorhambury. Two more unlikely companions it was hard to imagine. Ferensen, despite the suspicion, had won his audience's attention with a minimum of effort.

'These are symptoms of a danger whose potency you cannot begin to guess at. I have called you here to pool experience and to decide on a strategy. We must do the first before the second. Nobody knows all there is to know, but everyone knows *something*. We need whatever you have – and especially anything odd, however trivial.'

He gestured gently at the former Town Clerk. 'Mr Gorhambury.'

Accustomed to marshalling facts for committee meetings,

Gorhambury came over as concise and clear. 'I am the former Town Clerk, disgraced because I gave my party invitation to the late Mrs Banter.' Gorhambury speaking with *feeling*? The audience was intrigued. 'Sir Veronal bypassed *every* regulation. Every permit went on the nod. The closure of *The Journeyman's Gist* was his doing too. He is obsessed with the past.'

Ferensen intervened. 'Before we get to tonight's events, any questions for Mr Gorhambury so far?'

'Why let that bastard nick my pub?'

Ferensen saw a need to focus where it mattered. 'What brought Slickstone here?' he asked.

'The Mayor wrote to him after someone wrote to the Mayor.'

'Who?' asked Valourhand, revived by the beer.

'Marl,' Gorhambury replied, 'Paul Marl.'

'Never heard of him,' grumbled Salt.

Nor had anyone else.

Ferensen wrote the name down. This mattered, he sensed, but he could not see why. Finch sensed trouble too. He had never encountered a well-intentioned anonymous letter, and here, with past and present so horribly entangled, he feared the worst.

Gorhambury moved on to his visit to the library, the effect of the magical tile and the fight with the spiderwoman, modestly portraying Valourhand as the heroine.

Boris Polk was incredulous. 'A spiderwoman!'

Jones giggled.

Valourhand sprang to her feet, wincing as she did so, and yanked up what was left of her jeans leg. 'Where do they think I got this? Ice skating?' She raised her leg.

'It's true,' repeated Gorhambury.

'Of course, it's true,' growled Valourhand, her perspective on the world too self-centred to appreciate quite how bizarre their adventure must sound.

Ever sensitive to those he had rescued, Gregorius Jones restored order. 'You have our apologies, Miss Valourhand. We will not be ribald again.'

Even she could not reject such a retraction. With a petulant, 'You'd better not!' she sat down. The feline way she did so electrified Oblong. What was it about her? *What was it?*

Ferensen turned to Orelia who stood and surveyed the company. They hardly inspired confidence. Countrysiders and townsfolk were unnatural allies – the Valourhand woman was unduly aggressive, whatever the truth of the bizarre story about the spider. Boris Polk might be a lovable maverick and a brilliant inventor, but reliable? Jones belonged to some mediaeval order in which physical fitness and damsel-rescue passed as the Holy Grail; Oblong should be in a class, not teaching one; Salt had the selfishness of the self-appointed loner; Gorhambury's world was hemmed in by rules and regulations, and, she thought, *I'm no better*. She drew little comfort from the fact that Finch, the macabre-looking Herald, probably rated as the sanest there.

Go for broke, she decided. 'I believe my aunt was not killed by a malfunctioning garden lantern. I believe Sir Veronal did to her what he tried to do to Valourhand. As for the fire, I'm afraid my aunt had an inquisitive side. She tracked our movements from her tower – at all hours – with telescopes. She kept notebooks. They're not very savoury. When I went there on the day of her death, the first S volume was missing. And another thing. Sir Veronal bought four stones from *Baubles & Relics*. We got them from Salt.' Salt did not react; he continued to stare glumly into his beer. 'Sir Veronal thought them important, without knowing their purpose. My aunt impolitely upped the price. As to what they do, I'm hoping someone here might help. You see—' She looked at Ferensen who did not immediately respond. Orelia disliked being kept from the truth.

'—our Chairman might know, the indestructible Ferensen, who hunted butterflies with my grandfather in Rotherweird Westwood – in 1893.' She ignored the uproar and laughter. 'When he didn't look a day younger then than he does now.' She noticed Ferensen was not laughing. Nor was Marmion Finch.

'Truly, seriously,' she added. With those two words Orelia sat down.

Bill Ferdy could not accept such a seismic shock to family tradition. 'Lookalikes,' he said. 'Ferensens are always coming and going.'

'Salt – help us on the stones,' said Ferensen, almost too hastily.

'I ain't telling much, seeing it's none of your business.'

Orelia glared at him. Salt always played the idiot gardener when he wished to be obstructive.

He shrugged. 'Only, that the place Gorhambury says he's been to – it exists. It's called Lost Acre, and I'm her guardian. You don't play games with Lost Acre or you'll end up like them two: facing a monster you don't understand.'

If only you understood, thought Ferensen, but he said nothing.

'I dunno about the stones, except they're creepy. They were just there in Lost Acre, as if waiting to ambush me. Why I sold 'em dirt-cheap . . .'

And on the sly, thought Ferensen privately. *If only you'd told me first – this is the root cause of all our trouble.*

'I don't know what this meeting is designed to achieve, but . . .' He repeated his mantra, 'Just leave it to me. I know the place.'

Orelia felt like pointing out that Salt had no better prospect of passing the spiderwoman than Gorhambury or Valourhand, but Ferensen intervened. 'Tell them how Lost Acre is *now*,' he prompted.

This time Salt did respond. 'All right – everything over ground is dying or hiding.' Unaware of it himself, Salt turned emotional. 'This wonderful, dangerous, extraordinary place is about to implode or explode, while we sit and drink beer.' He crashed his glass on the table.

Boris added an enigmatic contribution. 'On behalf of *The Polk Land & Water Company*, and consumers of Ferdy beer in all its multi-marvellous forms, I offer my latest invention, once the prototypes are tested.'

'What invention?' asked Ferensen.

'Bubbles,' said Boris. Pressed, he would only say that *The Polk Land & Water Company* would soon have to change its name.

Oblong felt an urge to contribute. 'I can add something. My predecessor, Robert Flask, disappeared.'

'Dismissed, then disappeared,' muttered Gorhambury.

'Sacked for meddling, as I heard,' interrupted Salt, now keen to break up the meeting, 'and anyway, that's old hat.'

'I have his notebook, which was given to me by Fanguin.' He explained how the sole surviving entry, *STOLE CAR*, had turned out to be an anagram for Lost Acre. Most had forgotten Rotherweird's previous historian – he was just another outsider, after all – but the linkage of Flask with Lost Acre did engage their interest.

Salt stood up, red in the face. 'If you've told Fanguin about Lost Acre, young man, the whole bloody town will know.'

Oblong made little effort to defend Fanguin. 'No, I haven't. He's a good friend, but . . . mercurial.'

Nods all round. The epithet was well-chosen.

'Let him tell his tale,' boomed Finch.

'The other entry was ASC 1017.' Oblong explained the Chronicle's bizarre entry about the Midsummer Fair, the frescoes in the Church Tower with their strange flowering tree and his correspondence with Dr Pendle. 'All this leads to a puzzle: our special Midsummer spectacle this year is to be a re-enactment by my form of that very event – thanks to an anonymous letter to the Headmaster.'

'Who from?' asked Jones.

'Anonymous – stupid,' whispered Boris.

'It looked like Flask's writing,' said Oblong. 'Uncommonly like.'

Ferensen again had the uncomfortable feeling he was missing something, but Valourhand offered an insight. 'Flask played the fool when he wasn't. He was a proper historian – which is why he found out more in a few months than the rest of us have in years.'

The intervention prompted Ferensen to give Valourhand the

floor. Apart from her class, this was the closest she had come to addressing a group of people since the Slickstone party. She did not do small talk – no introduction, no words of welcome, no thanks for her rescue – but instead she delivered a blunt report on the meeting's scant progress to date. Even Salt responded to her directness by sitting up and putting down his glass.

'There's no use in data without analysis. Let's start with the spiderwoman. The thorax was complete without sutures or joins. So too were the eyes, feet and other visible parts. So this is no Frankenstein, nor, I think we may safely assume, the product of a passionate encounter between a giant arachnid and a human. Nor could any creature evolve into a spiderwoman who speaks English and has an interest in French cuisine. Conclusion: the creature resulted from a process that only Lost Acre offers. Such a devilish potential for playing with Nature would explain why Rotherweird is kept both from the rest of England and its own past.'

The reason of her argument held the floor as the blizzard of strange facts began to cohere. There was more to come. Without knowing it, Valourhand revealed a sensitive side. 'As we were escaping, the creature could have caught and killed me, but it didn't. There was a moment of divided personality, a fight between violence and restraint – indeed, I would say a fight between the bestial and the human.'

Ferensen felt a mix of horror and relief: if the human side could still fight, there might yet be hope.

'The animal I tried to rescue showed no restraint, but also had a command of English,' Orelia added, before explaining her near-fatal encounter with the cat with fiery feet, its vain enquiry about an unspecified book, its English speech – and its desire to kill her. 'A spiderwoman and a catboy appear to be products of the same process. What is interesting,' she added, 'is that the cat called me *child*, which clearly I am not.'

Ferensen clenched the table. Interest in the book suggested

someone who already knew about the experiments, the mixing-point and what it could do – and aspired to start again. Sir Veronal? Or might it be another player, as yet unknown?

'The spiderwoman called me "girl",' added Valourhand.

'It didn't call me anything,' muttered Gorhambury glumly into his beer.

Valourhand found herself enjoying her interchanges with these strangers. They had a common cause, which she was only beginning to grasp, but it felt like a *good* cause.

'If we're so young, these creatures must be bloody ancient – like Ferensen!' added Jones.

Valourhand wondered whether the gymnast was quite as slow as she had previously thought. There were hidden layers there too. She resumed her analysis. 'I come to the curious question of the doors into Lost Acre. There are two, which apparently do not work at the same time. The white has been open for years. Suddenly it closes in favour of the black, where any visitors must pass a formidable guardian. So who – or *what* – closed the white door? And why?'

'Nature closed it,' grumbled Salt. 'As I said – *if* you were listening – Lost Acre is under threat.'

'You mean the underground door is an escape-hatch for monsters,' said Gregorius Jones, puffing his chest with excitement.

Boris brought a more political perspective. 'It's not monsters we should be worried about, it's what follows them. With that kind of trouble there'd be outsiders all over us.'

There followed a string of Rotherweird pet hates, all beginning with P:

'Politicians—'

'Press—'

'Police—'

'Pundits—'

'And we can say goodbye to independence.'

'High stakes indeed,' added Ferensen.

'The stones must have a role in all of this,' interjected Valourhand, but Oblong was no longer listening. He had solved the Valourhand puzzle: the more he looked and listened, the more striking the resemblance to Cecily Sheridan became. He assumed they must be contrary twins, one literary and warm, the other cold and scientific, and both with a sense of adventure.

Orelia watched Oblong watching Valourhand. It was most peculiar: he looked besotted and puzzled at the same time. She decided to play her last card. No time for secrets, no time to play like Salt. 'I think so too. A tapestry hung in the Manor before Sir Veronal moved in – I've seen it. There was a good man in the Manor who was killed, which would explain why the house was sealed off. There's a section with monsters in cages, mixes of man and animal. The cages have dots of colour on their sides. Perhaps the stones helped create these monstrosities.'

'Are you saying the mixing-point can be controlled?' asked Salt.

'What's the mixing-point?' asked Valourhand.

Ferensen made his first substantive contribution. 'It's a place in Lost Acre where species mix and match. A slippery patch of sky, which can be reached and could in theory be used . . . and abused.'

Marmion Finch stood up, scratched his ear, polished his nose with the outside of his little finger and cleared his throat. 'Point of order, Mr Ferensen. You discuss the present, but you cannot begin to grasp it, and the future it holds, without reliving the past.' He took a rolled-up piece of paper from his pocket. 'This is the section of the *Rotherweird Statute* that binds me—'

'Mr Finch!' spluttered Gorhambury, appalled, and he was not alone: everyone knew their exemption from national government had been enshrined in an old and secret law, which it was a grave offence to discuss.

'Back in your box, Mr Gorhambury, history must out. The *Rotherweird Statute* has a preamble: "*Records shall be kept of all matters pertaining to Lost Acre, lest, should its secret ever emerge again, the evils can be understood, proven and scotched. Their Keeper shall be a single Herald sworn to secrecy on pain of death.*" And from Section 3: "*Any display or use or manufacture of The Dark Devices as hitherto fashioned and designed in the Manor of Rotherweird is forbidden on pain of death. On like penalty the creatures there depicted shall not be used on any crest, shield or other heraldic device by any person within Her Majesty's dominions*".'

'What creatures?' asked Bert.

'Which Majesty?' asked Boris.

'Elizabeth I of England,' replied Finch.

Vixen Valourhand asked a more chilling question. 'Creatures like a cat with fiery feet? Or a spiderwoman?'

The Herald did not answer directly. His audience were beginning to realise he rarely answered any question directly. 'I hold a record of these forbidden animals. I would like to show you, but only on your oath of absolute secrecy – hands?'

Orelia raised a hand. One by one the others followed, Gorhambury last. Unanimity.

'Follow your Herald!' cried Finch, and brandishing a Polk-tube, he disappeared behind the barrel through an archway between a row of rough-hewn columns.

With Ferensen and Valourhand, who produced their own tubes, at front and rear, the company set off in pursuit, through archway after archway.

5

Escutcheon Place

Sometimes the road ran straight and all three lights could be seen; at other times it twisted so deviously that those in the middle found themselves immersed in darkness. Ferensen had never known this subterranean Rotherweird; now, a student of mazes, he admired how often the wrong way looked inviting and the true way insignificant. He picked up the tiny carvings of flowers that marked the Herald's route – Druids' work, surely.

Gorhambury kept to the rear, his mind awash with the reams of legal provisions they were breaching – the *History Regulations*, the *Subterranean Tunnel Regulations*, the *Escutcheon Place Regulations*, the *Countrysider in Town Regulations*, to name but a few. He did not doubt their essential wisdom, but clearly the legislature needed to fashion an exemption for actions in the public interest. At the same time he worried about the scope for abuse of such a provision. He worried even more about where this particular appeal to the public interest was leading them.

In front of him a whispered conversation struck up. Oblong sidled up to Vixen Valourhand. 'I say, do you have a twin sister?'

'I hope you're not referring to the immensely tedious do-gooder Cecily.'

'She's awfully well read.'

'She's a pain in the butt.'

Gregorius Jones, fearless of heights, suffered in subterranean darkness. 'This is all a bit constricted,' he stammered. 'And stop crab-walking, Polk.'

'Think of it as an adventure,' replied Boris breezily, 'good for the CV and impressing the fair sex.'

Gregorius cheered up. 'Finch had better right that stoop or he'll be a wizened dwarf in five years. He should take up Pilates.'

Orelia kept her peace. She wanted vengeance for her aunt's death, and understanding. Both required the production of hard evidence, and if that meant unravelling the secrets of Escutcheon Place, so be it.

Seething with resentment, Salt also spoke to nobody. All these nonentities were discussing *his* world as if it were their own. He had to find a way to save Lost Acre and then close it to all but himself. The party had focused on abuse of the mixing-point long ago, but the rescue of Lost Acre *now* was the true priority. Oblong's bizarre reference to the *Anglo-Saxon Chronicle*'s entry of 1017 surely mattered: *All were saved by the Green Man and the Hammer.* Salvation – that was the goal. The weaselman had said that someone must come when the time is right – or ripe. That someone had to be *him*. Salt the gardener could surely play the Green Man.

After some forty minutes Finch stopped and pushed up a flagstone in the ceiling. They climbed into a cellar and then followed Finch up and across a landing, down two passages, up a further shorter flight of stairs and into the magnificent *archivoire*.

Here slow candles were burning. Off a central aisle six open bays with bookshelves rising from waist-height to the ceiling had cavernous cupboards beneath. Wooden busts of Rotherweird notables from long ago looked down. Books, the majority of great age, ranged from the monumentally large to the ridiculously small.

Overawed, the company stared round in silence until Finch summoned them to a table in the centre of the room, on which lay a large volume, strikingly bound in black, entitled *The Dark Devices*. Despite the size, there were few pages. The title had been removed despite the beautiful spine. The letters MDLXXI appeared at the bottom. Finch opened the front cover, blank save for the following in small, faded writing:

This book contains The Dark Devices as designed by Geryon Wynter and his disciples. It was fashioned at Rotherweird and found at the Manor there. Its use or distribution is prohibited by law, and preserved only to ensure that this law is observed and its justification understood.

Sir Robert Oxenbridge

An intricate armorial miscellany held within a circle filled the next page – feet, talons, fantastic heads, hairy legs, winged bodies, armoured beaks, eyes and leathery wings. The colours shone, untouched by time. Inspired draftsmanship brought out the different textures and every detail.

Over the circle curled the single word *ELEUSIANS* in red and gold. The four corners of the page also held a single circle, coloured but empty – one red, one blue, one white, one brown.

'They look like the stones,' said Orelia.

'Who or what were the Eleusians?' asked Gorhambury.

Oblong had barely said a word. Here surely was his chance to impress. He put on his most authoritative voice. 'The Eleusinian Mysteries were ancient Greek initiation ceremonies, practised by the cult of Demeter and Persephone. The name of the town, Eleusis, probably derives from Elysium or Paradise.'

The majority looked at Oblong as if he were mad – only an outsider could harbour the notion that the Ancient Greeks, faraway history before 1800, could possibly help.

Ferensen interrupted gently, 'They were in fact ten children of brilliance who found their way here. Wynter gave them this name to foster the sense of a secret society.' He paused. 'It's likely that their genes live on in Rotherweird.'

Finch nodded in tacit agreement.

'When did they come?' asked Jones, as ever, puzzled.

'1558. There was the Manor and the North Tower then – a church, a great barn, a few cottages and orchards, a single wooden bridge.'

Orelia focused on the mysterious countrysider. Ferensen had never come to town – yet he and the Herald had formed an instant and deep understanding. They appeared to know about each other. The source of Finch's knowledge would be the records, but Ferensen's?

'Keep going, Finchy,' cried Boris.

Finch turned the page again, and they craned over the table as he rotated the book. At the top of the page the word *Magister* curved over a single quartered shield, larger than the rest. In one quarter stood three creatures, each clasping a grey shawl about its face. In the centre of the shield were the familiar four circles from the previous page, within a larger, brown circle.

'The arms of Geryon Wynter,' announced Finch.

'Who's he?' asked Gregorius Jones.

'He's the man who set up this dark order of chivalry.'

'And who's below him?' inquired Boris.

'I don't know – the names have been removed with acid, so there's no trace.'

Twelve smaller shields followed on the next page, nine decorated and three at the end blank. There had been names, but only the three below the empty shields survived – Hieronymus Seer, Morval Seer and Thibo Fortemain. Nobody said anything, but everyone (except Gregorius Jones, who had no knowledge of French) cast a surreptitious look at Valourhand.

'Okay, I get it: Fortemain and Valourhand. So one of my forbears joined with this criminal Wynter. No surprise there; I always knew I had bad blood.'

'Told you!' cried Salt triumphantly. 'You're dabbling in what you don't understand.' Ferensen tapped the table.

'Actually it's you who doesn't understand. The blank shields belong to the three who resisted Wynter: he refused them arms because they refused to use the mixing-point. Miss Roc was right. You lift your ingredients in a cage into the mixing-point, and out again. Your stones, Hayman Salt, controlled the outcome. Each fixed on one side of a cage; different positions produced different results.' Ferensen, usually a model of moderation and fairness, for once uttered a rebuke: Salt had been too surly for too long. 'You should have told me of their return – *before*, not after the sale.'

Salt felt sick. He had as good as handed the stones to Slickstone on a plate.

'There were, I'm afraid, many preliminary experiments, often with terrible results, mostly inflicted on orphan children gathered first from outlying villages, later from London.'

Again Finch turned the book round so all could see that each shield held a creature – a grotesque mix of animal and animal, or animal and bird, or animal and insect. Only one shield departed from this rule: the first on the second page, an armoured fist holding bolts of lightning, with a tiny weasel on the knuckle.

'Oh God,' muttered Valourhand. She saw a caged man in a thunderstorm, iron bars drawing the lightning, though she did not articulate the thought.

'You can't mean Slickstone inherited lightning hands?' asked Boris.

'No, not *inherited*. He chose to be his own monster. He acquired lightning in the mixing-point.'

Orelia thought she now understood: the mixing-point conferred longevity, which explained Ferensen's presence in Rotherweird Westwood in 1893 and his intimate knowledge of these events, as well as Slickstone's survival.

Valourhand saw another angle. 'You said there were ten brilliant children. There are twelve small shields.'

'There were two locals, conceived at the same time as the others,' replied Ferensen.

Orelia did not ask the obvious question because she no longer needed to; she now knew beyond doubt who Ferensen was. So, she suspected, did Finch.

Finch turned over the final page to reveal a small, single shield boasting a cat with fiery feet, prompting a general intake of breath round the table. Past and present were fast converging.

'That isn't a likeness, that's exact,' said Orelia. 'It's the very creature I met an hour and a half ago.'

'Creatures from the mixing-point must live on ... and on,' chipped in Valourhand.

Orelia watched Valourhand, whom she barely knew, watching Ferensen. *Clever girl,* she thought, *she's on to him too.*

'But whose creature is it?' asked Boris. 'Whose shield is it?'

Here too the owner's name had been erased.

'I wish I knew,' replied Ferensen.

However much Ferensen had been editing his contribution in his own interests as well as theirs, she took this answer to be entirely truthful.

'What did the cat say again?' asked Oblong, feeling left out.

'"Do you have the book?" followed by, "Die, child" when I didn't answer. Not a nice cat.'

Valourhand intervened. 'You don't conduct experiments – at least successful ones – without recording them. There must be a record or a book or—'

'Yes,' said Ferensen, 'there was a book. I saw it only once. It's called *The Roman Recipe Book.*'

'You're having us on,' giggled Boris Polk.

'I'm afraid I'm not. For "Roman" read "Manor".' He had suppressed his memories for too long, and opening them up was causing him all manner of unexpected pain. He had seen this book once, when it was almost complete, and he had the chance to destroy it, but had wavered. The consequences seemed too uncertain. Now another memory surfaced, as disturbing as the rest. 'Long ago I was shown this inscription: I was bound bearing mysterious recipes. It's in

Wynter's writing. Wynter liked anagrams, you see.' He scribbled down the words *bearing mysterious recipes* and rearranged the letters, one by one, crossing them out as he did so. A new title emerged: *Geryon's Precise Bestiarium*. Silence descended. 'This book does indeed contain the successful experiments,' Ferensen confirmed at last.

Orelia watched Ferensen draw back into the shadow, close to emotional collapse.

Finch came to the rescue by bringing over a second, much smaller book. 'This is the end game: a record of the trial of Geryon Wynter, mostly written in a code I cannot decipher. But we get good old English for an account of verdict and sentence.' The Herald read from the closing pages, '*We find you guilty, Geryon Wynter, of offences against Nature and against God. You have treated children and animals as the stuff of experiment. You will be taken to this lost country of yours, be hoist in one of your own cages, with the stones arranged to ensure your own vanishing. Justice will do to you what you have done to others. Then all records of the gate's location will be destroyed. Laws will be passed to keep Rotherweird's secret safe from the world so Man may never be tempted again.*

'*The accused sought no pity from the Court. He said he would be back, and that vengeance would be his. He said another would come to pave the way. Yet his countenance lacked the usual arrogance. Sentence was duly carried out. The other accused, all Eleusians, were sentenced to tabula rasa et exsilium—*'

'*Tabula* . . . what?' asked Gregorius Jones.

Ferensen returned, still pale, but answered, '*Tabula rasa* is Latin for another effect Wynter discovered the mixing-point could have: place the stones in a particular place and you can wipe the mind. So the authorities turned it on the Eleusians, and then added exile for good measure. The defendants were left with the empty brains of a newborn baby, as good as a sentence of death, or so they believed.'

Valourhand jumped up and down with excitement. 'That explains everything – why Slickstone held a party, why he pumped Oblong with questions about history. He wants information to revive his memory!'

'Why he stole my pub,' interjected Ferdy.

An image came to Orelia from late in the narrative in the Manor tapestry: a man in a cage with his head leaking coloured birds. She shivered. *Tabula rasa*: they had wiped his mind clean.

Valourhand continued, 'There must be some vestigial memory, or he wouldn't have bought the stones. He plans to take over where Wynter left off – reacquire his book and start again.'

'I fear the book was hidden in the North Tower,' said Ferensen, 'but I know it's not there now.'

Strimmer, thought Valourhand instantly, *that bastard Strimmer – Flask told him and he never told me*. She edited her suspicions before declaring them to the company. 'The North Tower roof is above a colleague's rooms – you all know him, Hengest Strimmer. He's fascinated by Sir Veronal. I fear the worst.'

A gloomy silence descended. Slickstone appeared to hold all the cards. They drifted back to the shields, discussing the creatures on view and their constituent parts.

Ferensen took Finch to one side to ask why the Herald had taken such a risk.

'Your letter mentioned Wynter's book of arms – *The Dark Devices*. Nobody else knows of it – nor did I until the book revealed itself. So how could you? Then there's your name. In my job you can smell an anagram a mile off, even a German one. Ferensen. Add an H for Hieronymus, jumble the letters and you get *fernsehen*, meaning to see into the future, which is what a seer does.' Finch added in a whisper, 'Good evening, Hieronymus Seer.'

He asked how Ferensen had kept his secret, and the answer was simple: he ensured that his visits were spread decades apart, splitting Ferdy generations. He would present himself as the son or nephew of a previous Ferensen – the Ferdys had the pragmatic good sense not to pry, and the *History Regulations* did the rest.

Ferensen asked the next question. 'Is there anything else in those papers?'

'Prison records, a strange assault on Wynter in prison, distressing statements about the experiments – I've not had time to study them all, but you're on the list of victims.'

'Does it say what they did to me?'

Finch shook his head apologetically. *What this man must have been through* . . .

Ferensen remembered nothing of the Lost Acre part of his ordeal; recall began with his return, hauling himself from the river to the north of the town, naked, his body cut with tearing wounds. From one he had removed a small hook; others had the appearance of teeth-marks. For fear of being recognised and taken back, he had crawled through the water meadows and up the slope to the woodland beyond. There he had been nursed back to something approaching health by a brewing family called Ferdy. He had never returned to town; he kept away when Wynter and his followers were arrested and gave no evidence at the trial. As the years passed and his relative immortality emerged, he travelled, wherever wheel, tide or wind took him, always returning to the Ferdy estate. There he built his tower and made his only home.

The Finch and Ferensen discussion continued. 'That's my sister's workmanship.' He pointed at the figures hunched over the exquisite paintings of *The Dark Devices*. 'They forced her to draw and paint for them. And when Fortemain eventually got word to London, they punished us all. Slickstone told me what he would do to her – he kept his promise.'

The old man again was close to breakdown.

Finch changed the subject. 'They're flagging. They need biccies and brew for the brain,' he boomed, and from one of the cavernous cupboards he hauled up three dusty bottles, a miscellany of glasses and a large biscuit tin with a picture of Doom's Tocsin painted on the lid. As the company enjoyed his hospitality, Finch hesitated. He had in mind one more disclosure – but should he cause pain in the interests of truth?

His character assessment of Orelia decided the answer. He beckoned her and Ferensen into one of the bays. 'Boris suggested hiking the price of the stones could not have cost Mrs Banter her life. He was right.' The Herald shuffled through the trial papers. 'The trial record lists the execution party: a "Peregrine Banter (Master Builder)" was one of them. He guarded Slickstone on that last journey to the mixing-point. Slickstone is a cruel man – what prettier revenge, generations later?'

Orelia felt a deep wound. 'He killed my aunt for that?'

'Never forgive, never forget,' contributed Ferensen.

Finch turned the page over, and another name caught the eye: Benedict Roc (Master Carver).

'What became of him?'

'He designed this room. Hubert Finch records his death. They found his body by the island stream on the twentieth anniversary of Wynter's execution – to the day. He'd been strangled.'

'Does he say why?' asked Orelia.

Finch shook his head. 'He does say his ghost called at Escutcheon Place within hours of his death – here, the very house where he had plied his trade for years. They were superstitious then.'

'Wouldn't you be?' whispered Orelia before asking the obvious question. 'Calling for what?'

'To check the mechanisms in this very room – which I now know has three secret compartments. One held the trial record, another *The Dark Devices*. The third was empty.'

'No doubt it held the stones,' added Ferensen.

Orelia recalled Sir Veronal's Breughel and visualised the scene as that artist might have done: Rotherweird's gabled houses in the background, plumes of smoke rising straight, a foraging dog, the ground iron-hard under a leaden sky, ice fringing the river, the master carver face downwards in the snow and his incorporeal twin setting off townwards for a haunting. She felt very alone.

'I'm sorry,' said Finch.

'Enough is enough,' added Ferensen gently.

With the company's capacity for attention revived by Finch's wine, Ferensen closed the meeting. 'You have all contributed, and we are the wiser for it. But we have made errors too. First and foremost, we must not help Slickstone in our efforts to hinder him. However, we can all do a little.' He pointed at the company, one by one. 'Miss Valourhand will sound out Strimmer with her usual lightness of touch. Gorhambury, being temporarily unemployed and a night bird, will be our sentry in *Gems & Geology*. In any event, he has to return there now to repair the floor. We will have a roster to keep him fed and watered. We must watch the Manor like hawks. Jones – you're in charge of surveillance. Your running habits free you of suspicion. We communicate via Boris Polk's remarkable parrot-pigeon, Panjan, who reaches me quickest. Never trust the post. We must not forget the *Anglo-Saxon Chronicle*. As the entry has a rustic feel, Ferdy and Salt can follow up the Green Man.'

Ferdy nodded, and Salt muttered inaudibly in grudging acceptance of the one task he found acceptable.

Ferensen continued, 'Boris will perfect his invention. Orelia and Oblong will keep an eye on the Midsummer Fair. The *Chronicle* suggests it may have a part to play. Finch will go where his mind takes him.'

They left, one by one, through Finch's front door.

Ferensen held Orelia back. 'Do you have anything for me?' Orelia gave him a penetrating look. Nothing got past Ferensen. 'I'll look after it,' he added.

She dipped into her bag and handed over the camera. He might find some clue in the tapestry that she could not. 'Promise to talk me through it one day?'

'Promise,' replied Ferensen.

'Who made it?'

'I never came back to the Manor. Rumour says the three female Eleusians made them for Oxenbridge as a penance, to escape punishment.'

Ferensen watched his makeshift company disperse. He sensed a change in them: they, Rotherweirders, had a chance to right an ancient wrong. A new land with limitless potential had been abused by Man – and Wynter and Slickstone had both in origin been outsiders.

Orelia looked round her shop before going to bed – all objects in transit, without owners, sentimental flotsam until reclaimed, their old past buried now – the boy who had ridden the rocking horse, the amateur explorer in his snowshoes, the scientist peering through the outdated microscope. The stones were different, forever seeking repossession by their former owners, still propelled by the malignant impetus of their past. Would an executioner's axe do the same?

She felt like the rest of her stock, adrift without an animating presence.

She wondered how much Sir Veronal's wife knew of her husband's past and present actions.

The next morning she suggested to Gregorius Jones that he keep an eye out for Lady Slickstone. She might be in danger. His eyes lit up.

On his return home Ferensen cleared a wall and projected the tapestry, and tears came to his eyes at the all-too-fine rendering of Sir Henry's last years, the hunting of Slickstone's creature and the murder. Something about the portrayal made him uneasy – apology might be there, but he read defiance too.

His attention turned to the two wagons and the substitution of the urchins for the crop of brilliant banished children. He climbed his library steps and retrieved a slim volume by the polymath John Dee, a set of aphorisms about the special capacities of Nature, addressed to his friend, the Flemish geographer Gerardus Mercator. Ferensen quickly found the one he was looking for, number XXI. Here Dee asserted that the qualities given at birth *unfolded in the way in which the nature of the place of the conceiver and the surrounding heaven work and conspire together.*

Next he took down his version of the *Anglo-Saxon Chronicle* as translated by the Reverend James Ingram in 1823 – a special edition prepared for his fellow antiquaries. The entry for 1017 read: *Strange reports from the village of Rotherweird. A Druid priest tells that a monster came to their Midsummer Fair with the midsummer flower. All were saved by the Green Man and the Hammer . . .*

Oblong had referred to a strange flowering tree in the frescoes in the Church tower. The entry did not seem to connect with the stones or the mixing-point. The Green Man was a staple of European rural mythology, but had no obvious connection with Lost Acre. As for the Hammer . . . He sensed an older mystery here.

He thought lastly of his drunkard of a father and the beatings they had endured. He remembered his mother's brave efforts to shield them and her early death, stretched out on the earth floor of their hovel. Last, but not least, he recalled his sister's astounding gifts. She could capture not only the appearance of things, but their very soul.

He went outside to peer at the stars, which were dimming as dawn approached.

His regime had been designed to keep the past at bay: all fitness and the courtesies, avoiding intimacy lest it brought interest in his origins. Exercise kept his sleep untroubled.

Despite the evening's revelations, his defences against old history had by and large held. Awake and in sleep he would dismiss unwanted images – here a line of infantry, there a coracle, a stone altar spattered with blood . . .

Only the letters could not be banished. They came as if chiselled on stone: his letters, his language.

Druidus.

Exercitus.

Ferox.

And, yes . . . *Gregorius.*

Oblong clambered into bed with a sense of vindication, although less for himself than his subject. History had her claws in the present and, he did not doubt, in what was yet to come.

6

The Morning After

Dawn brought a dispiriting mood despite the fine weather. In centuries the town had never lost a tower. The charred beams seared the consciousness of her citizens. Soot blackened nearby roofs and walls like canker.

Snorkel showed his better side: by breakfast scaffolders were swarming up and down ladders, clad in red safety hats and green coats and looking like beetles on twigs. By mid-morning tarpaulins shrouded the wreckage.

And still he felt outflanked: Sir Veronal had offered financial help to affected homeowners without consulting him; this new arrogance in his manner only reinforced Snorkel's fears about the new Lord of the Manor's political ambitions. The man owned yachts, houses and aeroplanes – and now he desired to add a town to the portfolio. Snorkel no longer believed in the anonymous letter that had prompted him to ask Sir Veronal to Rotherweird; indeed, he suspected Sir Veronal of fabricating it himself, with an insider's help. After all, as Snorkel himself knew, most had their price.

He felt exposed by the one political process he could not abolish: the five-yearly municipal elections, due the following winter. His dynasty had successfully avoided elections for decades, but Sir Veronal would not hang back. After a year's residence he would be entitled to stand as well as to vote. Snorkel would be outgunned.

He needed to fight back.

*

Gorhambury remained in *Gems & Geology*, managing three hours' sleep, before the library opened. To his surprise his first morning visitor was Strimmer.

'Mr Gorhambury. Rock around the clock?'

'Sorry?'

'Joke – *Gems & Geology*.'

'Ah.'

'Is this a secondment?'

'I'm unemployed, in case you hadn't heard. So, it's back to learning – geology day.'

Strimmer gave Gorhambury a suspicious smile and left. The scientist's failure to show interest in a single book had not gone unnoticed.

Orelia dropped in with a take-away coffee and a large pastry. Boris came later with more substantial supplies. None could explain Strimmer's presence in the library basement. Just before closing time, Gorhambury tidily stacked his books and wrote a request to the librarian to let them be. He then secreted himself in the broom cupboard just before the library closed.

As time passed and his vigil lengthened, to his surprise and comfort, Gorhambury developed a genuine interest in the beauty and permanence of rocks.

Valourhand had no difficulty with the concept of Lost Acre, a hidden world with isolated points of access and new physical laws. Her world had only recently discovered that electrons could freely appear in one place and then in another without visibly moving between them. Why should there not be similar phenomena to these rules of quantum mechanics operating on an even grander scale? As cells join and separate at will, the mixing-point sounded equally credible.

She ranked as more disturbing the disappearance of the all-important book from the attic room above Strimmer's study, rebuking herself for not having noticed the peculiar pitch of the roof before. Challenging Strimmer directly seemed daunting in the cold light of day; but in the event she was spared.

As her red pen danced over exam papers about the six different types of quarks, curiously known as flavours, Strimmer sidled in. Uncharacteristically, he held a noonday cup of coffee for her as well as himself. 'Where were you last night?'

'Up and about, lighting a fire.'

Strimmer ignored the facetiousness. 'Returning overdue books perhaps?'

Valourhand stared at Strimmer. How on earth could he know? Yet in his interest lay possible advantage. 'If you know, why ask?'

'I know you were there. I don't know what you were after.'

Valourhand gambled. 'Your attic room begged questions. I wanted to know more.'

Strimmer's eyes narrowed. 'How do you know about that?'

'Flask told me.' She told the lie with bravado, and Strimmer rose to the bait.

'Well, you missed something.'

'Did I?'

'My secret.'

'Not if you mean *The Roman Recipe Book.*'

Strimmer went pale – surely *he* had found the book? There had been no sign of disturbance in the thick dust. Maybe Flask had known all along.

'What did you make of it?' Valourhand added quickly.

'Lines and coloured circles – pointless,' replied Strimmer.

'Obviously not in a binding of that quality – try harder.'

'There are four squares to a page, each with four interior lines, running top to bottom, six if you include the edges, and in each square just one small circle on one of the interior lines. The circles come in four colours. Each colour appears once on each page, but the positions are always different between pages.'

He has thought long and hard about this, reflected Valourhand, *with the kind of driven logic that once attracted me.*

'Just as I remember it.'

'There are creatures in silhouette on the left – and always a composite on the right, always grotesque – except for the last page, which has no creatures at all, just ordinary people on both pages – a jester, a soldier, a bishop, a nun. Maybe it's a primitive musical notation? A cycle of songs about mythical beasts, with a homely last verse?' Not that he believed this, but he felt the need to say something.

'Why don't we take a closer look together?' Valourhand said cheerily.

Strimmer hesitated, fatally, and Valourhand pounced. 'You haven't got it any more.'

'Who says?'

'Where is it then?'

'I loaned it.'

'To whom?'

'An expert in old books.'

They exchanged glances. Strimmer knew she knew.

'You've been to the Manor. Whatever he paid you, you don't know whom you're dealing with. You shouldn't give a Rotherweird book to an outsider.' Suddenly she felt uncomfortable; Strimmer looked too smug. 'Let me help you get it back.'

'No need,' he replied.

She changed tack. 'Who put you on to the observatory?'

'Flask said there must be a room in the eaves of the roof, so I looked.'

Valourhand cast her mind back. Flask had told them both about the scientist who first lived in the Manor, and how Snorkel was desecrating his memory by handing over the place to a multi-millionaire to line his own pockets. This titbit he had saved for Strimmer alone.

'People never tell you everything they know,' added Strimmer with a grin.

His egotistical smugness disgusted her. 'You're a selfish bastard,' she said.

As she turned back to her work, Strimmer thrust his hands into the waistband of her jeans and yanked her into his groin. 'You know you miss it,' he whispered in her ear.

She elbowed him in the stomach, but Strimmer was ready, abdomen clenched for the blow. Hands still down the back of her trousers, he kicked her feet away and she hung there, flailing, before he dropped her on the floor like a bag of refuse, an act of dominion.

'*Valour* . . . hand . . .' he sneered, before leaving.

Had she had a knife, she would have used it.

Bruised in body and spirit, she contrasted Strimmer's values with the eccentric chivalry of her new companions. Weak and unfocused they might be, but she could not fault their decency. It was decision time – Strimmer must have no dominion.

She went late to the premises of *The Polk Land & Water Company*. A sequence of explosions from the top floor of Boris' lodgings echoed around the courtyard. Valourhand rang the bell of his front door, wondering why the inventor should conduct such dangerous experiments in his living quarters rather than one of the numerous outhouses. The upper windows were covered in canvas, presumably destroyed by an earlier blast.

Boris eventually appeared, face smeared with oil and soot. 'The bubbles are bubbled,' he said.

'And I've a message for that pigeon of yours,' she replied.

7

Of Stones and Tiles

Two nights after the Escutcheon Place meeting, Oblong suffered a crisis of morale. He cursed himself for not having asked Valourhand how to contact her sister. In cold blood he found the physicist unapproachable, not least because she resolutely avoided him. Only art could muster relief, and he needed something deeper to earth his grief than *The Ballad of the Midsummer Fair*. His search for a muse in Grove Gardens had delivered only a dead body.

A nocturnal ramble along the Rother could hardly do worse. The gates did not close until midnight. He passed through at half past ten, crossed the bridge and followed the river as it skirted the Island Field. The usual metaphors assailed him: *time's flow, the river's inexorable progress to the sea, men as flotsam and jetsam;* and similes equally worn: *reeds like spears, rocks like knuckles.* His struggle for original insight lasted until the furthest corner of the Island Field.

'It's Obbers!'

The welcome – or was it a warning? – drifted round the bend of the river. Oblong gingerly crossed the raised stepping-stones over the Island Field stream. From close to the far bank, under an over-hanging willow, splashing alternated with silence and suppressed laughter. A man had called, but he could hear a woman too.

Oblong scrambled down the bank as a dark shape detached itself from the curtain of the tree and headed towards him, underwater. Cries of 'no' and 'don't' from the shadows could only have encour-aged the swimmer, such was the giggling in between.

Gregorius Jones broke the surface like a porpoise and with enough vigour to reveal that he had not a stitch on. He strode out of the river. Mud stained his thighs, which he instantly slapped.

'Togs off, Oblong,' he cried, 'this is the time, this is the place – one to remember in the old rocking chair!'

From beneath the trail of the willow, Miss Trimble's head appeared. She swam towards them before veering upstream, close enough for Oblong to glimpse a back view worthy of Rubens. She too was naked.

'For God's sake,' added Jones, 'the crayfish won't mind.'

The spontaneous warmth of the invitation conquered Oblong's considerable inhibitions. He backtracked to a large bush, undressed and coyly threw himself into the pool from which Jones had emerged.

Jones followed. 'Follow our Leda,' he yelled, a classical pun that Trimble caught, despite a vigorous crawl. Such a bewildering man – the closet classicist – and, though drawn to her, he always held back, though not, she felt, out of shyness. Perhaps he had fled from a shrew of a wife when going native in Rotherweird Westwood? She determined to break down the barriers, however long it took, and however bizarre Jones' idea of an evening out.

The chill of the water eased with the effort of swimming. No weed snagged the feet and the bottom had fine gravel, easy on the toes. Oblong had never done this before and felt invigorated.

'Ladies first and eyes left,' Jones shouted over his shoulder as Miss Trimble strode ashore. Jones followed, and Oblong glimpsed an ugly zigzag scar from his left shoulder to the base of the spine, white as old wounds are. Jones threw Oblong a towel and a cross between a judo jacket and a dressing grown.

Here, beyond the Island Field, Jones and Trimble had established a primitive camp – no tent, only groundsheets and blankets, with a simple iron grate, food and a frying pan. Jones set the fire going without matches.

'How a gentleman ignites,' he announced, 'a flint, charred cotton in which we place dried wool for tinder, and a firesteel.' Jones held up a C-shaped ring like a knuckleduster.

'The flint strikes off a sliver of steel and the friction heats it. High carbon steel works best and stainless steel doesn't work at all,' added Trimble. 'Yes, Mr Oblong, I went to school too. Jones is the only primitive here.'

Only Trimble and Gorhambury still called him *Mr* Oblong.

Jones cooked straightforward fare; his conversation had a similar simplicity. He explained how you should always sleep out on a south-facing slope, and talked of navigation by the stars. Miss Trimble deduced that Jones had led an itinerant life.

Oblong's concentration drifted until Jones suddenly sprung into life. 'Miss Trimble, an hour to midnight – time for our naughty lecture. We'd better take Obbers.' He giggled inanely, but gave no further clue as they tramped across the Island Field and into the meadows beyond. Mist scarfed their feet, but the starfields shone brilliantly above. Dark shapes emerged – megaliths. Inside the stone circle stood a familiar figure beside a tripod, wrapped in a scarf – Vesey Bolitho, the School astronomer, had finally emerged from his South Tower observatory.

He spoke of the ancient people who had built these structures, of their astronomy and their engineering skills. He spoke of a mysterious priesthood and seasonal renewal, and Oblong finally understood the naughtiness: Bolitho's lecture was pure, unadulterated *history*. He talked about other circles hidden away in Rotherweird Westwood, explaining how each circle had a central stone, and how they all pointed to the same celestial point. He claimed that other stones were aligned, not to indicate the solstice as in wider England, but Midsummer Day.

'Did they wear clothes?' asked Miss Trimble.

'Wolf pelts in winter,' replied Bolitho, leaving their summer attire unaddressed.

Miss Trimble glowed.

Oblong decided that a more searching question was called for. He followed the line of the jagged stone into the heavens. 'The North Star perhaps?'

'No – no star. Why this point in empty space matters is a mystery lost in time.'

Bolitho's talk lasted the best part of an hour. At the end he packed up his telescope, shook hands and headed back to town. 'Secret way through the boathouse,' he murmured to Oblong as he left.

They trudged back to their camp, where Jones gave Oblong a rug and lay down a respectable distance from Miss Trimble.

Much later, Miss Trimble, cocooned in her blanket, rolled towards Oblong. 'Are you cold under there?' she whispered.

'Middling to all right, thank you,' replied Oblong.

'My toes need warming up,' replied Miss Trimble, raising herself onto her elbows and revealing a glimpse of a magnificent billowing bosom.

Odd that only her toes are cold, reflected Oblong.

Miss Trimble flicked a swathe of flaxen hair away from her cheek. She looked more than ever like a Viking, and not the kind who stays at home. 'I'll tell you the trouble: Jones is ever so friendly, but he doesn't *engage* fully. He seems nervous of me.' At that moment, to his amazement, Trimble leaned over and kissed him on the cheek. 'I like gangly men,' she whispered.

'But ... I ... I am bespoken.'

'You're a tailor too?' she giggled.

'No, but it's early stages—'

'Imagine we're in one of those circles, and it's Midsummer Night ...'

'I really mustn't ...' babbled Oblong.

'Oh, men!' exclaimed Miss Trimble, and with an air of distinct disappointment she rolled back the way she had come, leaving the historian in dismayed confusion.

He had sacrificed much for Miss Cecily Sheridan.

Throughout the exchange Jones lay as dead to the world as a stone. When you rest, you rest: that was always the soldier's rule.

Miss Trimble woke Oblong at dawn – Jones had disappeared. Oblong felt mildly offended that she was more concerned about Jones than making a further bid for his affections.

'He talks in his sleep, you know,' she said, sounding worried. 'Something like "malaria" and "Vic's tricks". I think he may be mad.'

Sir Veronal strode across the Island Field with the actress stumbling to keep up.

Unsettled by the absence of any complaint about her attendance at Mrs Banter's funeral, the actress found the trip, which lacked any explained purpose, and her inclusion in it, deeply puzzling. Under a hazy but unthreatening sky, the riverbanks untenanted at such an early hour, they crossed the small footbridge by a yew tree at the southwestern corner. From time to time Sir Veronal sniffed the air. They tried various meadows and copses before stumbling on a sunken way, choked with undergrowth. The actress noticed broken stems and trampled grass: someone else had been this way.

She felt Sir Veronal's confidence grow as they pushed through, and an old road opened up.

'They say charcoal-burners lived here,' declared Sir Veronal, following the sunken road to emerge in a bowl with an apron of trees high above them. He prowled the ground, sniffing more intently now, and extending his hands. He paused in the middle and scuffed away the topsoil, exposing a white tablet with a single flower finely incised in the centre.

'Ah-ha!' he exclaimed, 'a Druid stone. They are said to bring great luck.' The actress watched his face – it looked transformed, almost youthful.

In fact, on the very threshold of Lost Acre, he felt a sudden nervousness. The landscape had changed; might not the tile have changed too? *Reconnaissance is needed*, he decided, *but not by me.*

'Ladies first,' he added.

The actress looked up. The beeches peered down as from the Royal Circle. Sir Veronal's face had changed again: a trapper, now, hardly the expression of a bestower of good fortune.

But with no prospect of escape, she could only play the game. 'Of course,' she replied gracefully. She stepped on the tile and opened her arms dramatically. Nothing happened.

Sir Veronal's mask of self-satisfied triumph slipped, and he pushed her roughly aside.

The audience must be gripped. She had turned the tables and stolen the scene.

'This isn't possible.' He stood on the tile himself, again with no visible effect, and kicked the ground violently.

'Get on there again,' he barked, pushing her back, 'and take your boots off.'

The aggression gave her something to work with. 'I'm touched you wish to bless me with luck,' she said, a strong line, defining her character, not his – defiant but polite. She had control of the scene, but feared it would die, unclear as to how the tension could be sustained. She need not have worried.

A strange apparition in white shorts and running shoes, naked from the waist up, descended the steep slope, half-skidding, half-jogging.

'Glorious morning,' said the apparition with an easy heartiness.

'Who the hell are you?' growled Sir Veronal, scraping the earth back over the tile.

'Gregorius Jones, Head of PE at Rotherweird School,' replied Jones, bowing faintly. 'You all right, your Ladyship?'

She bit back the words 'narrow escape' and smiled: a handsome man, although perhaps more likely to shine on film than stage.

'Of course she's all right.'

'These are ancient woods,' replied Jones. 'Take nothing for granted, including the way out.'

'Home,' barked Sir Veronal, his mind in turmoil at this unexpected setback. He could not believe his ill luck. The tile had *failed*. He had recovered his past – but to what purpose, if the prize it had revealed remained forever beyond his reach?

At the bridge, the actress rested a hand on the yew's gnarled trunk and opened her face to the sun, seeking to convey what she felt – reprieve from a danger she could only guess at.

Buoyed by his night in the open air and Miss Trimble's unexpected offer, Oblong returned a little regretful that he had declined her invitation. During the mid-morning break he hurried to the Town Hall Information Desk, whose middle-aged occupant evidently disliked outsiders.

'*What?*' she responded to Oblong's innocuous request.

'Miss Cecily Sheridan. Her address is not in the book.'

'It's not in the book for a very good reason.' Oblong imagined a harsh injustice he would shortly remedy. 'She doesn't exist.'

The remark did not register. 'I only want to make contact.'

'You deaf?'

'She's Miss Valourhand's sister.'

'Miss Valourhand has no sisters.'

'She looks like her.'

The woman looked at Oblong as if he were mad. 'Frankly, nobody looks like Miss Valourhand.'

'She runs a travelling library,' he added.

'How interesting: a woman who doesn't exist runs a library that would be illegal.'

Oblong gasped for air. She was right. Rotherweird would *never* allow a trade in old books. He thought back: Cecily had inveigled him into telling her about the frescoes. How could he have been so naïve! First a snowball, then fancy dress – he had served as target practice for the girl with the golden bolas.

'Sorry to bother you,' he replied limply. 'Must be the heat.'

By lunch the receptionist had told her colleagues, and by tea-time Oblong's infatuation with a woman who did not exist had become the talk of the town. Snorkel greeted the news with merriment and satisfaction – Oblong could hardly be bettered as Flask's replacement.

After his single afternoon lesson, Oblong rushed home, drew the curtains and lay on his bed. He had turned down Miss Trimble for *this*. Another detail deepened his humiliation – the book Cecily had promised him – *Gullible's Travels*! He contemplated winning her over by confrontation, a flawed plan as Cecily did not exist. He then raged at Valourhand for treating his kindness with such insouciance.

Slowly he admitted a truer voice to the debate: to be made a fool of requires of the victim more than a grain of foolishness.

Late afternoon was losing out to dusk when a knock at the door brought further embarrassment. He had forgotten an appointment to visit *Baubles & Relics* to discuss the Midsummer Fair. Orelia Roc entered, not in a forgiving mood. 'Fable tells us grasshoppers have short memories where work is concerned. Always summer, never winter.

'Sorry.'

Orelia dropped, rather than placed, a bottle of red wine on the table. 'Corkscrew?'

'I can do a screw-top.'

'Thought as much.' Orelia produced a corkscrew and uncorked the bottle. 'Would glasses be stretching hospitality?'

Oblong shuffled to the kitchen and back. Why did people always bring drink to his flat? Was he such poor company?

She poured two glasses and toasted him. 'Here's to your celebrity!'

Mindlessly Oblong took a cheery swig before absorbing the import of the toast. '*Celebrity?*'

'You fancy Valourhand dressed up as a travelling librarian – we're not used to that kind of thing in Rotherweird.'

'It was the way she ... the way she ...'

'The way she what?'

'Well – played the librarian.'

'Really?' Orelia plucked a random book from Oblong's shelf and then put on a seductive pout and a mock intellectual accent. '*En attendant, Monsieur Oblong ...*'

Oblong physically wobbled. How could women turn on the sex appeal like this? Orelia looked and sounded gorgeous. His weak response to Miss Trimble made him determined to be more positive: he craved a ringing romantic line – he was a poet after all – but nothing came, only words so humdrum they would demean her.

Then his frustrations, failures and desires combined in an irrational explosion of energy. 'Oh Orelia!'

He lunged, missed, tripped and disappeared over the back of the sofa.

'You're the silliest man I've ever met,' giggled Orelia, hauling him up into her arms.

Only a monk would have described the ensuing hour as a passionate encounter, more a mix of tussle, fumble (mainly Oblong), warm embrace (mainly Orelia), and occasional laughter. Yet both emerged the better, having discovered a mutual point of suffering in their reservoirs of unspent affection.

Old History

1572.

Wynter sits at the head of the table, his right hand resting on *The Roman Recipe Book*. Slickstone, the cold man of reason, for once sounds close to panic. 'There are horsemen on the road, armed horsemen.'

'Are there?' says Wynter nonchalantly.

'Witchcraft is a capital offence. We must go.'

'They think science is witchcraft and witchcraft is science. Poor souls.'

'I'm going to the other place – there's nowhere else.'

Wynter merely smiles. 'They will first secure the tile. Fortemain will have told them. You have no time.'

'Fortemain is a traitor.'

'No, he is a sentimental fool, which is different. He has always acted consistently with his idiotic beliefs. Traitors disown their loyalties.' Wynter taps the book. 'I have done the last experiment. I have glimpsed a power that only the gods enjoy.'

The last experiment: Wynter has spoken to him of this most subtle of all powers, so potent and yet so hedged with risk. Slickstone craves it for himself.

'What use is it if you're hanging from a rope. You talked of tunnels under here – why don't we use them to escape?'

'I've no wish to escape. I shall be in the garden. Join me.'

'Give me the stones and the book. Let me try the experiment.'

Wynter ignores the request and passes the *Recipe Book* to Calx

Bole. 'Secrete it in our chosen place, then leave me alone in the garden with my closest friend, Veronal Slickstone.'

Slickstone shivers. Wynter is half mad. He is planning his own godlike Passion, from the agony in the garden to his execution. Now he understands: Wynter must be as great as the Messiah himself, and so he must play Judas to feed the story.

He needs no prompting. *Jack be nimble, Jack be quick.* A new game starts: Wynter is now his enemy, the armed horsemen are his friends. He feels a surge of liberation. He has been dominated too long. His submissive love for Wynter turns to hatred. The power of Wynter's last experiment should be his.

He hangs back, watching Wynter slide in that weightless way of his among the lawns and fading lavender, apparently reconciled to what awaits him. He hears hooves, the hiss of drawn swords and feet running through the manor house.

The men are led by a tall, familiar figure: Sir Robert Oxenbridge is back.

He hurries towards him and points. 'If you want the devil, he is there.'

In the gloom of the makeshift court the white ruffs shine – as if necks matter most – on prosecutor, judge, usher, even the guards on either side of the dock. Collarless, with a clean-shaven head, the defendant looks a different species.

Species – the word has run through the trial like a poisonous thread.

'Geryon Wynter, I find you guilty of foul experiment, of merging children with animals, insects and birds and deforming natural species to your own end.'

Sir Robert Oxenbridge pauses. The words tinkle, trite, beside the reality of the creatures they have found and destroyed 'in the other place', as the indictment so gently puts it. Such horror is beyond the language of the courtroom. He should have hired a poet to close the case. The second charge sounds merely quaint.

'I find you guilty of taking an unknown land for your own rule and not in the name of your Sovereign, Queen Elizabeth.'

Wynter smiles as if to say, *What are temporal rulers to me?*

'Have you anything to add before sentence?'

It has been a contest of voices – Sir Robert, deep and strong, the soldier-statesman; Wynter, quiet and sibilant, the snake in the garden. No wonder they have draped the windows and locked the doors.

'I have done what I am accused of – *and so much more*,' Wynter opens. 'Who else has enhanced Man's powers as I have? Who else has fashioned such creatures? Who else has travelled to a stranger place? And where is progress without failed experiment? Do what you will; I shall have revenge on my betrayer. And I will return, when another has paved my way.'

They no longer react. Wynter always uses the language of the semi-divine.

'Read the list of victims, Mr Finch.'

Hubert Finch, the prosecutor, does so, though most are as nameless as their gravestones: 'Orphan boy from London', 'Waif from Hoy', page after page of them.

Wynter interrupts only once, when two names join the roll-call of anonymous dead: 'Hieronymus and Morval Seer, twin brother and sister, local inhabitants—'

'Error – they were not experiments, they were punished.'

'Are you saying they're *alive*?'

'Let's hope so – that was part of the punishment.'

Sir Robert has questioned all the witnesses himself. Many locals have mentioned the Seers with reverence – humble beginnings, as brilliant as the outsiders, and of the same age, and alone with the courage to resist Wynter. Within days of each other they had been sighted, hands bound, with Wynter and his retinue in attendance, crossing the fields towards the entrance to the other place.

He shudders to think what Wynter's notion of punishment would be, if worse than the horror of his failed experiments. Maybe they have been among those put out of their misery, barely viable as living creatures.

Finch hurries through the rest, and Sir Robert passes sentence. 'You, Geryon Wynter, will be taken to "the other place", where you will be caged and "disappeared", the very disintegration you practised on your first victims. Your younger and less responsible conspirators will endure another effect your early experiments played with, *tabula rasa* – the wiping of the mind. Then they will be exiled as far from here as her Majesty's ships may manage. Take him away.'

The usher drags open the damask curtains, admitting the dazzle of a clear winter's day, as the soldiers escort a compliant Wynter from the room. Eager to escape his lingering presence, Oxenbridge ushers Finch into the adjoining library. A plume of smoke rises from a neglected fire. He attempts to lighten the mood.

'Well, Mr Finch, how does it feel to have a hereditary title? Herald of Rotherweird – her governor in all but name.'

'But I have only a few peasants to work with,' mutters Finch nervously, overawed by the task ahead.

Sir Robert places a consoling hand on his shoulder. 'Places grow and change. Houses become outposts become towns. The Inner Council has passed a law to guard Rotherweird's dark secret. This valley alone will not be answerable to her Majesty or Parliament. *Your* writ runs here – just remember always to act as if Wynter, his disciples and the other place never existed.'

'Why give me freedom from government?'

'Isolation is the price your subjects must pay for their freedom. Here, alone in England, the study of history will be forbidden.'

'Why so?'

'Let them study the past and they'll find the way to the other place. Rotherweird must live in the present, and keep itself to itself.

Let nobody in, let nobody out. We will build you a new house, suitably imposing for a governor, where you must keep hidden the trial record and Wynter's more demonic possessions – including that very particular book.'

Sir Robert judges it time to lighten the mood yet further. 'What shall we call this new house of yours?'

Hubert Finch thought of his title, Herald of Rotherweird, and the need to create new orders to replace Wynter's sect. 'Escutcheon Place?'

Sir Robert nods approval, but reads the continuing uncertainty in Finch's voice. Finch doubts his ability to build an imposing house with such slender resources, let alone a settlement.

'I leave behind all my men – they know too much. They include a master craftsman, Mr Banter; he was working at the Palace of Whitehall, but succumbed to the lure of designing an entire town—' Sir Robert moves to the desk and unfurls Mr Banter's plan: bridges, walkways, a sewage system, a central square.

Finch gapes in admiration. He can even make out the shape of his house-to-be. As for the present Manor, where they now stand, a wall without an opening encloses it. Sir Robert explains, 'The Manor we shut from view. Who knows what Wynter hid here?'

'I'm impressed,' stammers Finch.

'Your town will need substance to hold its people. One last matter – we found this.' Sir Robert placed a single page on the table. 'Meaning Wynter wanted us to find it.'

'*Strange reports from the village of Rotherweird. A Druid priest tells that a monster came to their Midsummer Fair with the midsummer flower. All were saved by the Green Man and the Hammer.*'

'Gibberish,' comments Finch, a man long on practicality and short on imagination, the very qualities for which the Council has selected him.

'Were it not from Wynter's pen . . . You've not been to the other place. I have.' Sir Robert peers through the window. Sarsens poke through the meadow grass like old teeth. Here Druids and monsters would not be so outlandish.

The fire shakes off its slumber, ash logs suddenly ablaze, and he nods as if acknowledging an omen. 'That's the past for you, buried for centuries and then ... *pffft* ... she awakes! I have no fears for you, Mr Finch, or your sons or grandsons. I fear for the remote future, when all is forgotten and the guard is down. So we'd best leave the barest minimum.' Sir Robert casts Wynter's Delphic note into the fire. 'And best destroy anything Wynter would have us keep. Now, Mr Finch, we have wine to celebrate the closing of this wicked business.'

Now Finch glances out of the window. He sees fertile soil, fresh water, abundant timber and only one road in. If Mr Banter proves true to his designs, the Rotherweird Valley will surely grow and prosper under his rule. She will shed her past as a snake would its skin, to renew.

JUNE

I

Gawgy Rises

Gwen Ferdy and Ned Guley had caught the rumour that Slickstone and Collier were planning an unpleasant surprise for the play. Mrs Ferdy had taken precautions: one fine summer's evening in early June, she presented her handiwork.

'Meet Gawgy!'

Across the roof of the Ferdy kitchen-dining room snaked a twelve-foot-long green-red dragon, a construct of wire, linen and *papier-mâché*.

'That has no chance if Slickstone's hammer is what they say it is,' stammered Gwen.

'Trust me, our inventor friend has given Gawgy an unusual defence.'

Megan lowered the costume, lifting the skirt below its torso to reveal a wire frame.

'Gawgy the Shocker!' announced Ned Guley.

Boris Polk entered, tankard in hand. He explained the remote control, which fitted easily in the palm of the hand.

Megan counselled restraint. 'Slickstone should be a cultivated boy, and we only have rumours. So it's a reserve, only to be used in need.'

The remote control looked similar to that which had twisted the Hydra's heads this way and that. Outside in the warm sunshine Bill Ferdy used a steel rake for attack, and Gawgy wove through the fruit trees with increasing fluency. Guley, upright as the head, soon acclimatised to Gwen bent low as the body, her hands clasping his hips.

Boris tested the controls on low power, mildly electrocuting Guley, then Gwen and finally himself. After half an hour of minor adjustments he handed over to Megan, and after an hour, Gawgy had perfected movement and defensive timing, the rake spinning from Ferdy's hands in a shower of sparks whenever he struck.

After Boris' departure, Ferdy was still nursing a burning desire to make a more substantial contribution to the campaign. His assignment from Ferensen had been the Green Man, and he had repeatedly read the *Anglo-Saxon Chronicle* entry, although he could see no sense in it. Now he called Gwen and Guley over.

'You're acting this strange *Chronicle* story – what do you make of it?'

Gwen spoke first. 'The Green Man sounds like you – a country-sider making country cider.'

Ferdy smiled. Gwen could shuffle words like numbers.

'And what about the Hammer? Ned?'

'Isn't that what you do in pubs – get hammered?'

Gwen chuckled, but the remark struck a chord; Ferdy played with an idea and found it bizarrely plausible. 'Want to be guinea pigs?' he asked the children.

'For what?'

'A very special tasting.'

'Sure thing!'

'Then get me a thimble.'

Armed with the tiny silver cup, the children followed Ferdy into the main barn. He tossed aside a pile of hay bales to expose a small door fastened with a rusty padlock. Stooping low, he oiled the lock and opened it with an equally rusty key. The tiny room beyond hid in the gloom a single barrel, grey-green with age and marked with a barely visible 'H'. *H for Heavy*, thought Gwen, *why we only get a thimbleful.*

Ferdy flicked the tap. He held up the thimble like a chalice as a scent of autumn and earth pervaded the room.

'Who brewed that?' asked Gwen in admiration.

'Not me, not my father, nor his father. It's an heirloom from the mists of time.' He handed her the thimble with sacramental seriousness.

Gwen tilted it back, then Guley followed, and in seconds the suspected hangover symptoms were confirmed: their afternoon lessons and the journey home had vanished from memory. His reading of old history just might be right. Exhilaration seized the brewer, the joy of unravelling riddles, and at last contributing to the company more than just beer and a rake.

Ferdy ran uphill to share his idea with Ferensen.

'We need to inoculate the company, or some of them,' the old man promptly responded. 'Have you any tiny bottles or test tubes?'

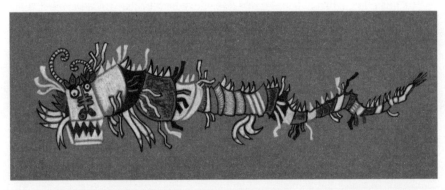

'. . . after an hour, Gawgy had perfected movement and defensive timing.'

2

Strimmer Takes Sides

Strimmer could not believe his luck. He hurried through the side streets and took up position by the most remote of the Manor's security cameras to attract attention without being seen. Within fifteen minutes he and Sir Veronal were sitting opposite each other in the library. Strimmer looked round. How could *The Roman Recipe Book* rival these priceless volumes? Sir Veronal appeared restless and unengaged.

'I have endured a dispiriting day. This had better be worthwhile.'

'I was to keep an eye on Valourhand. On the night of the fire—'

'Her antics do not interest me.'

'Not breaking into Rotherweird Library after hours?' Strimmer noted with satisfaction a striking change in Sir Veronal's expression. 'She gets into the library late, at five to eleven. At half past eleven she disappears.'

Sir Veronal leapt from his seat. '*Disappears?* How do you know?'

'I fixed a tracking device in her shoe. She disappears for eighteen minutes, then the device fails – but I saw her later near the fire. She appeared to be limping.'

Sir Veronal pulled a thick gold and purple rope and spoke into a small tube beside it. 'Bring me a *Trockenbeerenauslese*, the best, two glasses, and flavourless biscuits.' He paced the room, weighing the implications: one tile closes, another opens. To every action there is an equal and opposite reaction.

A servant entered, the bottle in a silver cooler inscribed with a weasel's head. The biscuits lay in a white linen napkin, lined up like poker chips. The servant poured a fingerful into a glass. Sir Veronal examined the colour, swilled the wine round the glass, passed it under his nostrils and nodded. The servant filled Sir Veronal's glass and handed another to Strimmer.

Sir Veronal dismissed the servant with a flick of the hand. 'And what happens after the fire?'

'Much later Valourhand is seen coming out of Escutcheon Place, where Finch hangs out. She's noticed because it's forbidden, and Finch is a stickler. Oblong was with her, and Roc.'

'Have you any idea where in the Library she disappeared?'

Strimmer produced his map, marking *Gems & Geology*.

'Your device is that precise?'

'I have supporting evidence. I checked *Gems & Geology* out the following morning. It's a basement room. I found Gorhambury at the very spot where she vanished. He gave a passable impression of a nervous sentry.'

Sir Veronal recalled the name: the petty bureaucrat who had sold his invitation to the wretched Mrs Banter. 'How amusing,' said Sir Veronal, 'as if I would be so vulgar as to go through a library floor.'

Wynter had often talked of the tunnels under the town. The Manor had had its own entrance; the tile would be easy enough to find. All had fallen into place: they had handed him the stones, the book and now a replacement tile, one that worked.

Strimmer watched his host's mood rise from sullen to ecstatic; he refilled their glasses and started pacing the room.

Strimmer took the offensive. Candour had not disadvantaged him at their previous meeting in Old Ley Lane. 'Is this connected with my book?'

'Think of it as neither yours nor mine. Think of it as a power, handed down to whosoever has the wherewithal to exploit it. I shall shortly be embarking on a dangerous journey.' He sprang to his feet. 'To the new dispensation,' he said, raising his glass.

Strimmer's glass followed, and not without eagerness. Despite the strange hue of his skin, the old man cut a figure of intellect and vitality.

As if sensing Strimmer's admiration, Sir Veronal turned. 'You should know, Mr Strimmer, I do not have an heir. The boy is merely a convenience, and you have not disappointed me.'

That night the actress had a nightmare she could not dispel: Sir Veronal picking the clothes from a wooden doll and then plucking off the limbs before tossing it on a fire: a fire grown tall on the ash of his other discarded toys.

3

Fanguin Finds an Interest

Fanguin had taken up the Headmaster's suggestion of extra-curricular classes, advertising in the *Rotherweird Chronicle* and on the School noticeboards, with Rhombus Smith's support. Children would have come, but their parents would not let them; that awkward maverick Flask had encouraged the biologist to breach their most basic taboo. The desks in Fanguin's upstairs study, bought for the purpose, remained untenanted. Fanguin declined to recognise the incipient tremor in his right hand and the ever redder rims beneath his eyes or to acknowledge that the niggling tickle in his throat now had a more insistent edge.

In his clearer moments he resented that fact that Oblong had slipped off with Orelia Roc on the night of the fire, and he had seen the unemployed Gorhambury heading in the same direction. Like others, he had made the connection between the lightning strike at the party and Mrs Banter's death. Unlike others, he had provided Oblong with Flask's notebook and introduced him to the excitements of the Great Equinox Race – but the new historian had not reciprocated with any intelligence of his own. Indeed, he had not seen him in weeks. He felt betrayed and excluded.

Bomber put her arm round his shoulder as he sat vacantly at a window, waiting only, she knew, for his first drink. 'You must *find* an interest.'

'Must I?'

'You're slowly destroying yourself, and it isn't pretty to watch.'

Fanguin let his head drop. An interest required enthusiasm for life, and his, once abundant, had seeped away.

'However peculiar,' she added.

The word 'peculiar' did it, conjuring an image of Flask, with his flexible face, the mild limp, one shoulder lower than the other. Flask's disappearance, and his fatal speech to Form IV, had always struck Fanguin as odd, the former unexplained and the latter out of character. Flask did nothing without calculation, which was in part why he complemented Fanguin's impetuous personality. An idea germinated and blossomed. 'Yes,' he said, 'you're right. I need something – or someone – to research.'

He gave her a hug.

'As to *something*, how about the effects of abstention on the once-addicted,' added Bomber.

His investigation showed early promise. Flask had once confided in him an undeclared gift for compiling crosswords, which the *Rotherweird Chronicle* published from time to time under the name *Shapeshifter*.

Fanguin visited the library and wrestled with one or two. They were rich in anagrams and classical references; some even showed wit. For example: *Old horses far away, but only half the way from here to Rome* (11).

After two black coffees from his thermos Fanguin got there – *Equidistant*.

With Aggs' help he tried Flask's last lodgings, in the highly insalubrious Box Street, but found no clues other than a bicycle rental slip. He had never seen Flask ride a bicycle, nor did Flask's unimposing physique suggest hire for pleasure. Flask was tight with his money, so he must have used it – but when, and where? The bicycle shop had written it off as unreturned, a dead end.

Fanguin was not blind to his shortcomings. He knew he had hit the buffers, and that his long-suffering wife deserved better. He sat on a kitchen chair and engaged with a bottle stamped *VSOP* on its side: *Very Special Old Pale*.

Vitality Spent Obsolete Person.

Vintage Superannuated Off Peak.

Inspiration came courtesy of this rambling sequence of discon-nected thoughts as under the brandy's influence he toyed with ever-more-bizarre four-word phrases or sentences, limited to the first letters VSOP. One creative combination slipped through: *Velo Seen On Platform.*

That must be where Flask had gone. He could produce no alter-native solution – and Hoy Station did have a bicycle compound. He was up and running again.

He drank a tumbler of water and climbed gingerly to bed.

To Bomber's astonishment, Fanguin leapt up the following morning like a man possessed, cooked breakfast for them both, gave her a kiss and left on his bicycle, unused since his dismissal – much to the relief of pedestrians. The weather had turned cloudy, but it remained warm.

He reached Hoy at lunchtime, and found Flask's bike in the compound, splattered in mud, the hire number barely legible.

'Been in a sauna?' asked the stationmaster, before answering Fanguin's question. 'Only the stoppers take bikes.'

'Ever know a Robert Flask?'

'This is a railway station, not a hotel bar.'

'Short, peculiar face, slightly lopsided – he would have had a bicycle—' Fanguin produced a grimy photograph from his pocket, hoping that Flask's distinctive appearance might register longer than most.

'Maybe I do, maybe I don't.'

Ten pounds revealed that he did. The man always went one stop to Hirstoak, and always carried a backpack.

At Hirstoak the stationmaster was no sunnier, but at least charged rural prices: five pounds revealed that Flask left on the lane back towards Hoy. A shrug of the shoulders implied a route leading nowhere.

Fanguin quickly agreed: up, down, twist, turn, potholes and then a sign declaring a dead end in two miles. Half a mile further on, an enclosure ran alongside the road, shielded by a high, dense hedge of holly, yew and *leylandii* – a barrier fortified by razor-wire. A sign marked *Contaminated Ground* only stimulated Fanguin's curiosity.

Fanguin left his bicycle and followed the hedge round, to find on the opposite side a modest entrance cut through wire and hedge. At the expense of a tear to the seat of his trousers, he crawled through.

'Contaminated' implied bare earth, not a one-time Eden abandoned by its gardeners. Amid a riot of brambles, convolvulus and dog-rose, Fanguin found more rarefied plants, terraces with their walls breached and a finely carved water trough drowned in ivy. Little survived of the house – ceilings and stairs had all fallen in – but remnants of the panelling showed fine carving, and on the ground floor he found the collapsed shelves of a one-time library. An outbuilding provided another find: broad oak beams set in the floor with huge bolt-holes. He rejected the idea of a fruit press, there being no sign of the other essentials, including an orchard.

Outside, a huge tree dominated the garden, different branches displaying different shaped leaves, some almost round, others spear-shaped. He could see no trace of a graft. Contaminated ground?

Intent on the tree, he almost missed the tent. The poles sagged, the brown tarpaulin merging with the undergrowth. He peered through the flaps: a hurricane lamp, a rolled-up sleeping bag and a piece of paper, squared off in black and white. He squeezed his way in for a closer look. Though stained by damp, the pencil faded, he could just make out a single clue – 1 down: *Troupes with bad posture* (7). Fanguin smiled. 'Troupes' was an anagram of 'posture' and vice versa – a nonsensical clue, but he had stumbled on a crossword in the making, and that meant Flask.

Fanguin took stock. Flask had discovered a significant connection between this house and Rotherweird's forbidden past – but why would he make a base here?

On impulse he lifted the groundsheet, and uncovered a large animal skull that flummoxed Fanguin, the expert biologist. Skulls protect the brain and sensory organs. Complex, three-dimensional objects, they are as distinctive between species as an individual signature. Fanguin would expect to be able to identify class, then order, then family, then species – but this skull defeated him. A mix between weasel and human, he fancifully decided in the end.

First the tree and now the skull. Fanguin was feeling unsettled. He had an impulse to escape. Outside the tent the late afternoon light had turned milky. 'Contaminated,' whispered the garden. He imagined weasels the height of a human, rising from the ground, baring their teeth. This creature lived here once; perhaps its relatives still did. Clasping the skull, he broke into a run and then a breathless sprint. He rushed back to his bicycle and pedalled furiously.

On his return, he declared his fears for Flask's safety to Bomber – he had discovered more than was safe.

Bomber struck a less pessimistic note. 'Who knows? He went cycling, he found what you found – then he got the sack and abandoned the project. I always thought him indestructible – but at least he's given you a task worth doing.'

Fanguin looked blank.

'I mean the skull. First you draw it – which takes a steady hand.'

Her code for not drinking, thought Fanguin. 'No, no – *first*, you name it,' he countered.

'Like what?'

'*Mustella ampullae.*'

'Meaning?'

'Flask's weasel.'

Fanguin sat down with pad and pencil, the skull and a glass of tapwater. He added ice, pretending the frozen cubes were as wicked as alcohol. As he applied pencil to paper, he saw that his hand held still. Thanks to Robert Flask or his ghost, recovery beckoned.

4

An Opening and a Closing

The opening of *The Slickstone Arms* lacked the preliminaries of the Manor-warming party – no formal invitations, no issues on costume or when to arrive, just a bare summons on cheap paper fliers: *Slickstone Arms opens: June 18th: 7 p.m. to midnight: food and beverage free*. The allure lay in the last syllable. Add natural curiosity, and few doubted attendance would be high.

Fanguin reluctantly kept away. Bomber not only forcibly pointed out that it would be the end of his new diet of elderflower cordial and sparkling water, but also that he must choose between the demon drink and her.

Oddly, he was feeling more isolated since his discovery of the weaselman's skull. He wanted to share it, but he felt that the others – whoever they were – should come to him. But no one did – Oblong, Orelia Roc, Salt, all kept their distance. Perhaps they viewed his former closeness to Flask as a handicap? The dryness in his throat tortured him. Ice could masquerade as alcohol only for so long. His wife did not begin to understand the challenge of abstinence.

Orelia determined not to go out of loyalty to Bill Ferdy, only to change her mind for the sake of the company. Free drink would loosen the tongues of the Polks and Gregorius Jones, so they needed watching. She resented this role, policing middle-aged unreliables, but who else was there? Orelia had thought hard about her hour of teenage playfulness with Oblong. She had laughed for the first time in weeks, but the emotion felt like fondness only. She wanted *passion*, the kind that cannot be taught, and she somehow knew Oblong was not that type.

Oblong went for a variety of reasons. He had to face his friends after the Cecily Sheridan affair and this seemed as good a place as any. He judged (rightly) that Valourhand would not show. There was also the question of Orelia. He admired her and he found her attractive. But his progress with the fair sex had moved up the gears dramatically in the last two days, and a mild conceit set in. He felt uncomfortable with the notion of being 'the silliest man Orelia had ever met', preferring Miss Trimble's more admiring approach. He felt like indulging in the luxury of choice. A waiting game felt like the right strategy, and easier to play if their next encounter were in the public domain.

The Slickstone Arms emerged as a spring-cleaned *Journeyman's Gist*, tables and chairs repaired or replaced and lavatories upgraded, but no more; the new owner gave every appearance of having lost interest in the enterprise. The lager could not compete with Ferdy beer in taste, colour or texture.

Sir Veronal, however, did turn up. In a light tweed suit, a touch loud in its spit-new condition, he sat in the garden, the very picture of relaxation – gone the cold autocrat of the Manor party; he welcomed all within range.

Orelia positioned herself near the main entrance. Gregorius Jones arrived wearing a tracksuit and an idiotic grin. 'I can't wait to see Obbers.'

Despite her reservations, she had no difficulty defending him. 'You be kind.'

‐'If he took more exercise, he wouldn't make such a crass mistake.' Jones suddenly turned serious, ushering Orelia to one side and recounting how he had followed Sir Veronal to the bowl of beeches beyond the Island Field. 'Lady Slickstone is in danger. Believe me.'

'What was Slickstone doing there?'

'I— I don't know, but he was furious – with her, with the place, with me. He was pushing her.'

Then Orelia remembered her aunt's entry about Hayman Salt's lamp disappearing over the island stream footbridge and into the woodland beyond. The white tile must be nearby. A horrifying thought came to her: Sir Veronal wanted rid of Lady Slickstone – perhaps she had been closing in on the truth? And what better place to send her than Lost Acre? Orelia found one crumb of comfort: Sir Veronal had expected the white tile to work, suggesting ignorance of the black tile's location.

'I believe you, but what can we do?'

'Warn Gorhambury,' replied Jones. 'He's next in the line of fire.'

'I meant Lady Slickstone. Surely he can't risk another death here – and he can't send her back to the outside world. If he finds the black tile, she's doomed.'

The penny belatedly dropped. 'Oh, you mean he'll use the black tile – but he doesn't know where it is.'

'Strimmer visited Gorhambury in *Gems & Geology* the morning after the fire. I fear if Strimmer knows, Sir Veronal knows.'

Gregorius Jones pulled a most peculiar face, shoulders back, all humour gone, and ran off.

The mood lightened with Oblong's arrival. When Orelia kissed him on the cheek, he blushed, but he rode the Cecily Sheridan banter. Nothing was said of Escutcheon Place. Oblong's own goal had proved a useful diversion.

'Pint of weasel-piss,' said Bert Polk peering into the pallid beer.

'Where's Boris?' asked Orelia.

'Bubbles,' replied Bert.

Sir Veronal nonchalantly looked on as a bartender served him white wine from his private bottle nestling in a silver wine cooler. VIP remained the message. Snorkel's lieutenants paid court, unaware of the shift in the Town Hall's allegiance.

As Oblong and Orelia passed, he beckoned them over with a languid wave of the left hand. 'Miss Roc . . . Mr Oblong . . .'

Sir Veronal had changed, nervous anxiety replaced by confident energy. He gestured. They pulled up a small bench.

'Best not mix your – whatever it is – with this.' He raised his glass. 'How does my son?'

'He has a starring role at the Midsummer Fair,' replied Oblong.

Sir Veronal changed tack. 'So – what do they say behind my back?'

'You're a catalyst for change in a place that never changes,' chirped Oblong.

God, Oblong has changed too, thought Orelia.

'Change for the good I mean,' Oblong added hastily.

'I wonder. Wouldn't that be the ultimate gift – to move among your self-styled friends and discover if they really are? Pascal was right – if everyone knew what others say behind their backs, there wouldn't be four friends in the world.'

Orelia shivered. Sir Veronal would relish exposing false friends and punishing them. Wealth had made him suspicious of deference; he craved admiration but would eradicate dissent. She thought of her aunt, punished for another's offence centuries earlier. *Calm*, she cautioned herself.

Oblong sailed on, 'You asked me once why I came to Rotherweird – might I return the question?'

'A town built on a secret – what could be more tantalising? But where does one look, with all these rules and regulations?' Sir Veronal took a sip. 'Escutcheon Place, perhaps?'

The remark betrayed a weakness. Sir Veronal liked to toy with his prey. Oblong surprised her. 'Strange you should mention Escutcheon Place. After the fire, old Winch—'

'—Finch,' interrupted Orelia.

'He asked us back there.'

What *was* Oblong doing?

'Escutcheon Palace is forbidden territory,' observed Sir Veronal, 'why let you in?'

'We had an argument about some carving or other. He wanted to prove his case.'

Sir Veronal smiled and stood up. 'I always try, Mr Oblong, to be a catalyst for change. I hope Rotherweird will be no exception. Do enjoy your evening. I must circulate, or they'll think me an absentee landlord.'

So at ease, Orelia thought. *This man knows who he is and where he is going.* Distracted by Sir Veronal, Orelia had missed the most striking absentee: Snorkel, whose presence could normally be guaranteed wherever a scintilla of glory might be had. He had been all over Sir Veronal at the Manor, yet tonight there was no sign of him.

Around the piano, a trio of the better voices were well into a local ballad – 'The Man Who Tried to Drink Moonlight' – accompanied by the School's Head of Music.

'Do look,' said the pianist, 'a wee mouse.' A white member of the species posed on the piano top, red-eyed, apparently enjoying the music. Several screamed and glasses smashed as horror and hilarity shared the stage and mice romped everywhere.

Orelia instantly suspected the absent Snorkel, remembering the Mayor's pained expression at the Mayday Fair – but what a powder-puff blow! He had no idea what he was up against, and like them, he had reacted far too late.

'Well, go on,' shrieked Miss Trimble, a closet musophobe, to Oblong. Not especially keen on picking up small rodents, he hung back, making futile grabbing motions. 'Useless man,' grumbled Miss Trimble, her mood further darkened by Jones' disappearance.

Orelia caught Sir Veronal's expression of unsurprised amusement. *The Slickstone Arms* must indeed be surplus to requirements. He must know and have all he needed – the tile's location, the book, the stones. How were they going to stop him?

5

Valourhand Goes Prospecting

Following the meeting in Escutcheon Place, Valourhand lapsed into an agony of indecision. Jones the jogger spy had reported Strimmer's visit to the Manor. Strimmer had clearly joined forces with Sir Veronal. She had received no reply from Ferensen to her report about *The Roman Recipe Book.* Though desperate to examine the mixing-point and to analyse its treatment of matter, she dared not face the spiderwoman again. She had no clear allies and no plan. Only the implication that Fortemain was an ancestor, the one man who had had the wit and fortitude to challenge Slickstone and Wynter, brought a modicum of comfort.

Every thread seemed to return to Flask. She felt sure he had been on an important trail when he disappeared. He had known about Slickstone's imminent arrival. He had known about the tower's attic room. He had communicated with Pendle about the *Anglo-Saxon Chronicle*.

She had one lead, a decision by Flask that nobody had understood at the time and whose potential significance everybody had overlooked. He had left stylish lodgings in the School for Rotherweird's least salubrious alley. Why?

Valourhand tried the Porter's Lodge, but Miss Trimble was obdurate. 'The Box Street annexe is closed, and I'm down to one key.'

Valourhand had an idea: one witness, one chance.

*

Tucked between the School and the eastern wall huddled a cluster of sad towers. Each was just one room and a stairwell wide, and each blocked the others' light. Subsidence, worm and damp had twisted them to all angles. Halfway up one lived Aggs in a single room with her mostly single possessions – one bed, one stove, one table, one cuckoo clock, one chair, one cupboard, one cushion, one bookshelf, one pot plant and one mechanical singing caged bird. Aggs would have liked a live version of the latter, but feared it would languish during her long working hours. Despite the gloom, Aggs' quarters had a pleasing cosiness.

Aggs could tell that her visitor hailed from a more affluent neighbourhood from the ascent – two steps at a time. Menial labourers did not rush in their recreation time.

She opened the door to a slight young woman with an alert expression, whom she knew by reputation.

'Is it Aggs?'

'It is, and you're Miss Valourhand, what likes dressing up.'

Valourhand glanced up and down the dilapidated stairs. Aggs, recipient of many a confidence, got the message. This was not a social visit. 'Come in.'

'Nice place.'

'Don't sound surprised, love, I'm a professional. But my list is full. The dusting arm ain't what it was. But I does a mean coffee.'

As Aggs put the kettle on, Valourhand seized her chance. 'You looked after Robert Flask?'

Aggs pursed lips and brow. 'I did and I didn't. But I don't shop customers, even if they are dodgy and disappeared.'

'Dodgy?'

Aggs' pained expression deepened, and Valourhand understood. Flask had abandoned not only his prestigious rooms in the Main Quad, but also Aggs' tender care – without due thanks. The rest of her clientele had no doubt been more appreciative. She noted the pot plant – *Hayman's Silver Pothos.*

'Not even a note – and then he goes to Box Street – makes this place look like the Town Hall.'

'Those are the rooms I want to see.'

'Room.'

'*One* room – how do you know that?'

Caught out, Aggs' chin jutted and her eyebrows pumped. 'Cos . . . cos . . .' Valourhand waited. 'Cos someone wanted to check. So I snaffled the key from the Lodge, didn't I. You wouldn't tell, Miss Valourhand, would you?'

'Not if you don't want me to.'

Aggs relaxed. She could tell Valourhand had her complexities, but this at least sounded like a genuine promise.

Valourhand pressed on, 'Who wanted to check?'

'His friend.'

'Strimmer?'

'Oh no, not him.' Sensing a free spirit, Aggs warmed to Valourhand, having expected not to. 'Mr Fanguin.'

Valourhand kept her surprise to herself. 'I don't mind Fanguin.' In Valourhand's lexicon of compliments, 'don't mind' came near the top.

'Some of 'is personal habits are *vix satis*,' commented Aggs, who liked deploying fancy phrases picked up from her teacher clients, 'like odd socks and all that, but he's all right at heart.'

'You wouldn't still have the key?'

'I might . . .'

'I'll return it to the Lodge – *discreetly* – no worry.'

'If you promise not to trick young Mr Oblong again – 'e's a laughing stock, Miss Valourhand. It ain't good for him.'

'Promise,' replied Valourhand, amused at the triviality of the condition.

Aggs handed over the key. 'Number seven, and you watch them stairs. Fanguin fell down them – and by the way, he found nowt when he got up.'

From what she knew of Fanguin, he had difficulty finding his own pockets. For no logical reason she found his blank return encouraging.

Had Box Street been a living thing, it would have been old, blind, stooped and asthmatic. The tall thin houses bowed across the street to each other, their upper floors almost touching, leaving the thin strip of road below in gloom and the air dank.

The narrow staircase lacked several banisters and suffered from loose boards, explaining Fanguin's mishap. Rusty nails protruded from the handrail. Dust from untreated beams and damaged plaster polluted every surface with a yellowy greyness.

Flask's attic bedsitting room offered no relief. Net curtains flapped over a grimy double window. A sheet of polythene protected a bare mattress. Any surviving possessions had been cleared away. In one corner a single plank, bowed in the middle, leaned against the wall, top almost reaching the ceiling. The small kneehole desk, the mantelpiece and the solitary table yielded nothing of interest.

She lay down on the mattress, resting her head where Flask would have done. The hairs on the nape of her neck prickled. Hatred, dark and malignant, not of her, but of someone or something else, lingered in the room. 'Look, look, look,' she chided herself as she flung open the window. A few feet away the window in the equivalent room opposite stood slightly ajar. *The plank!*

Excited now, she ran the plank through Flask's window and eased open the window opposite. A veteran of the high wire, she had no difficulty crossing to the storeroom that doubled as Flask's study.

If in search of seclusion, he had chosen well. Dilapidated filing cabinets and broken chairs blocked the door. On a table stood an array of pens, fine-haired paintbrushes, small pots of ink and tubes of paint. She explored the rest of the room, finding nothing until she reached the fireplace. Raking through the ash, she found a fragment of charred paper – or was it parchment? On it, in black

'Had Box Street been a living thing, it would have been old,
blind, stooped and asthmatic.'

silhouette, she could just make out two figures – one a jester, the other a soldier. She remembered Strimmer's description of the book in the North Tower. This was the last page. It could hardly be coincidence.

She wrestled with the chronology: Flask arrives. Flask directs Strimmer to the North Tower room where the book is found. Flask warns Strimmer about Slickstone. Flask disappears. Strimmer shows Slickstone the book. The book disappears.

Flask appeared to have copied the book, or parts of it, at or about the time that he had encouraged Strimmer to explore the North Tower roof space. The book had been there when Strimmer discovered the old observatory – so when had Flask first tracked down Wynter's record of his successful experiments? How and why had it found its way to the observatory? That Flask knew about Lost Acre was clear from the notebook Fanguin had given Oblong.

She articulated a theory: Flask, a resourceful historian, is fascinated by Rotherweird. Somehow, somewhere, he finds the book and discovers the truth about Wynter's trial (maybe through records in London?) and the existence of Lost Acre. The book clearly concerns the mixing of species, a disturbing science. He obtains the post of modern historian at Rotherweird School to continue his investigations. Flask somehow discovers Slickstone's interest in the Manor well before he arrives – a leak from the Town Hall, perhaps. He suspects him of knowing about the book and wishing to use its powers. He sets up Strimmer and herself as opposition to Slickstone, hoping to flush out more of Slickstone's intentions after his arrival. Flask copies the book in case Slickstone reacquires it. Slickstone gets wind of Flask's unhealthy interest and disposes of him.

But three flaws confronted this working hypothesis: the virulent hatred she sensed in Flask's room did not readily fit, although Slickstone and Flask might have met before they came to Rotherweird. Nor could she see why Flask would lead Slickstone to the book. Maybe he wanted to use Strimmer to confirm Slickstone's identity, or maybe Strimmer had indeed discovered it himself. Third, would Flask have acted so far ahead of Slickstone's physical arrival in town? And how had Slickstone unmasked Flask as an enemy so early in the story?

She pocketed the fragment of paper and locked up, kicking herself for not having shown a closer interest in Oblong's predecessor. They had so little time.

Midsummer's Eve was only two days away.

6

Orelia Goes Prospecting

Orelia sank her frustrations into the shop. Aided by her revamp and the removal of Mrs Banter's censorious eye, custom increased and she shifted obstinate stock by lowering the price and attaching more honest labels. The ledger reminded her of Salt's visit in the fog, as did *Hayman's Croci*. Their flowers, though long spent, had been unlike any known example of the species, both in colour and time of arrival. She fumed over Salt's egotistical performance on the night of the fire and decided to beard the gardener in his den.

It was the day before Midsummer Eve, when Rotherweird garlanded every street – tower to tower, balcony to balcony, window to window. Traditionally roses and white jasmine dominated, with the more exotic blooms strung along the front of the Town Hall. To Snorkel's irritation Salt had failed this year to produce anything novel. As Orelia hurried along, municipal workers were busy with ladders, ropes and carts of flowers brought in by the countrysiders.

Conveniently placed in a pleasant square not so far away, Salt's house, though narrow, had a low extension that snaked behind a neighbour's garden. Her knock went unanswered, but Salt had left his front window ajar. True to her new spirit of adventure, she clambered in.

Up a trellis nailed to the end wall of the entrance hall climbed a plant with pale green leaves, thorns and a profusion of small crimson flowers. On the pot hung a copper label – *Hayman's Darkness*

Rose. Unlike any rose she knew, it had grown away from the light and into shadow. She turned right into Salt's living room.

She could barely see the walls, so close-hung were the botanical paintings and prints – some in section, some suspended with their roots bare, others as imagined in nature. A faint fragrance hung in the air, as if exhaled by this sumptuous gallery.

Orelia was puzzled. The oil paintings, the botanical books with gilt spines and the eighteenth-century prints would surely challenge the salary of a municipal gardener.

She opened the baize door at the back of the room to find a heavier door behind. She undid the bolts and pushed. Along the side of a passage ran a trestle table with knives and scalpels laid out as on a surgeon's trolley. The shelf above held plastic bottles in differing shapes and sizes, sealed and labelled with floral names in Latin. Many had the prefix H – H for *Hayman's* she assumed. A bin beneath the table contained creamy yellow slices of the discarded remnants of corms and bulbs. On a peg by the table hung a pair of overalls, which extended like a beekeeper's to cover face and hands.

Sharp right, another bolted door led to the extension. A row of plugs at wainscot level, each with a red eye, glowed in the gloom. Orelia drew the bolts and stepped in warily, only for the door to slam behind her. The low blue-purple light conjured a moonlit jungle. Six oak beams rose from ground to ceiling, so swathed in foliage that she could only glimpse the ropes and platforms they supported. Variegated ivy covered the ground, and through it wandered daisy-like plants. Higher up, other species clung, climbed and trailed, unfamiliar variations of familiar types, including a white honeysuckle with black leaves and a thorned clematis. Just visible among them hung a clock with transparent sides. Wires protruded from the rear before disappearing into the canopy of vegetation.

Orelia breathed in the cloying tropical atmosphere for some minutes. The clock made a whirring noise, the light lowered further and unseen sprinklers released a fine spray, dampening her face and hair. Flowers closed, but she sensed an awakening too, and instinctively retreated. At ground level the foliage twitched, tugging at her shoes. Like a dancer on points she leapt towards the door. Unseen tendrils beneath the ground cover tore at her shoes and strove to bind her feet. *The protective suit!* She cursed her stupidity.

But she was quick and light enough on her feet to make the door. Slamming it behind her, she sank to her knees. Shoes and trousers were badly torn and crimson weals pockmarked her ankles and lower legs.

Back in the sitting room she went through the desk to find invoices for substantial sums to various Rotherweird worthies, so explaining the quality of his pictures and books. She also found letters of complaint at the failure of his plants to propagate or to last into a second year. No wonder the *Hayman* varieties in Rotherweird's public beds were replaced every season.

Salt stood in the hallway and watched Orelia flicking through the book. Lost Acre had taught him the art of stealth. 'Miss Roc?'

'How could you? Digging them up! Selling them!' She flourished the ledger.

'Guilty,' admitted Salt, 'although you too dig up old things and sell them.'

Orelia flung herself into a chair and swung her legs over the arm. 'All right. Explain yourself.'

Salt made a decision. He needed an ally. He had two tasks ahead and could only do one of them. Of all the company he trusted Orelia most. 'On recent visits everything – flowers, trees, grasses – has been throwing seed.'

'So you said.'

'They're under threat. Believe me, they *know*.'

'So you bring them back to sell.'

Salt told the truth. 'I'm afraid this is not so recent. I needed money for my nursery.'

'But they don't breed.'

'Worse, they don't last either. Which means . . . it's Lost Acre itself we have to save.'

'From what?'

'I've no idea. But it's happened before – Oblong told us, didn't he: 1017. "*All are saved by the Green Man and the Hammer.*" Surely "all" means Lost Acre. The millennial recurrence can't be coincidence. I'm convinced its fragile existence tires. Suns consume energy, become gross and expire.'

Salt sounded too certain for the little she knew. She peered deep into his face and saw evasion. 'Do you think I'm a fool?'

'Less of one than the others.'

Orelia all but lost her temper. 'You were holding back the other night, and you are now. You want help, you share.'

Salt relented, marginally. 'On my last visit to Lost Acre, I met a weaselman. *Seriously . . .*' Salt paused.

'I believe you.' *Talk about getting blood from a stone.*

'He said someone must come at the "right" or "ripe" time, if Lost Acre is to be saved.'

'You, presumably.'

Salt did not catch the mild sarcasm in her voice. 'There remains Sir Veronal.'

'Right, I get it: you play the Messiah while I take on the harmless Slickstone.'

'He murdered your aunt. I rather assumed . . .'

Orelia changed tack. 'Have you any idea what to do when you get there?'

'Nope.'

'Or how to get there?'

'Nope.'

Impasse.

They sat in sombre silence until Orelia glimpsed a familiar figure loping towards Salt's front door.

'Oh God, he does have this gift for cropping up!'

'Who bloody does?' Salt stumped to the door and flung it open with a graceless greeting. 'What do you want?'

Orelia offered a reassuring wave. 'He's a historian – he ransacks the past for clues. We best hear him out.'

Oblong sat, or rather sprawled, in Salt's last unoccupied chair. Salt smiled, unexpectedly charmed by Oblong's clumsiness. A ludicrous image came to him: Oblong rooted in Grove Gardens, a human climbing frame festooned with clematis. The Green Man?

Orelia summarised their discussion to date.

'It's a race to get in,' said Oblong. 'Sir Veronal knows the white tile is closed. He'll go after the black tile now. He must know roughly where it is. The spiderwoman was surely put there to guard it.'

'How would Sir Veronal get past her?' asked Orelia.

'He made her – he promises release. He threatens her with lightning hands. He'll find a way.'

Orelia stated the obvious. 'We have no such advantages.'

Salt raised his left sleeve, revealing an ugly scar, but Oblong continued, 'I think there's another way in – an aerial gate.'

Salt looked urgently at Orelia as Oblong explained Bolitho's lecture, how the central stones pointed on the same axis to a hole in space, how the circles were aligned to Midsummer Day.

'*The ripe time*,' muttered Salt.

'And how do we launch ourselves into this millennial aperture?'

'*The Polk Land, Water & Air Company*,' replied Oblong.

'Bubbles!' cried Salt and Orelia in unison.

'I've come from the church,' added Oblong mysteriously.

'A wing and a prayer – just what we need,' said Salt, but without the grumble. Oblong had delivered a smidgen of opportunity.

'The priest is happy to show you his bell tower.'

They left at intervals to avoid suspicion.

The priest was welcoming; he lifted the trapdoor and helped them up. He pointed at the footprints in the dust. 'We might be suddenly fashionable, but do keep this to yourself. Human interest – and indeed, human breath – are not always for the best.' With this, he left them alone.

Different minds see different things.

Oblong had focused on the coracles and the mysterious mirror where men and animals appeared to merge. Salt's horticultural eye went straight to the clumps of Rotherweird eglantine dotted between the dancing men and women, and then the mysterious flowering tree and the very different plant beside it. The latter's leaves resembled no earthly species, but he recalled a strikingly similar upland plant in Lost Acre, discovered before he appreciated the dangers of the place. The quality was high, the details carefully rendered.

By contrast Orelia was drawn to the Saxon figures, feasting and dancing on the same east wall as the flowering tree. She noted the date, 1017 as in Flask's notebook, and remembered the words of the *Chronicle*. She turned to Oblong. 'Your play matters. I don't know why, but it does. The Midsummer Fair is part of this.'

'So I stay behind?'

Orelia placed a consoling arm on his shoulder.

The priest rejoined them.

'Pity about the damp,' said Salt, waving an arm at the purple explosion disfiguring the central section of the east wall, close to the flowering tree.

The priest shook his head. 'My tower is dry as a biscuit and always has been – two courses thick, and built to last.'

The vision of Oblong as the Green Man danced in his head, and with it, and some basic biology, came a bizarre notion.

'True,' Salt replied to the priest, 'very, very true.'

*

Oblong returned to his new role as writer-director with brio. He worried about entrusting Orelia's fate to Boris' prototypes, but he felt that the Lost Acre part of any solution belonged to Rotherweirders rather than him. Salt had been there before and Orelia had a score to settle, whether you termed it justice or revenge.

With Rhombus Smith's permission he enlisted Marmion Finch as a narrator – no child would carry the necessary gravitas. The role of damsel went to a simpering girl with ferrety good looks, Angie Bevins, the vote fixed by Rodney Slickstone.

An artistically creative parent designed and made a huge cave on wheels, as if cut into volcanic rock, with a dark horseshoe entrance topped with tussocks of grass.

His first onstage rehearsal, lacking props, passed without serious hitch, save that Finch absented himself, dismissing rehearsals as for the unprepared. Classroom tensions gave edge to the production, Slickstone and Collier addressing the monster with venom. By contrast Gwen Ferdy and Ned Guley brought charm to their part. He looked forward to their costumes.

His mind occupied, he noticed only at the end of rehearsals that towards Rotherweird Westwood, but still on the Island Field, a new and substantial rectangular tent had been erected, flaps closed and padlocked.

He ambled over to find a rolled-up banner behind it in the grass. He unfurled it. Ornate gold-green letters declared: *By the Courtesy and Clemency of the Mayor: THE JOURNEYMAN'S GIST revived.*

Oblong felt yet again that all was not as it looked. Would Bill Ferdy indulge Snorkel quite so readily after his earlier treatment?

He returned to his lodgings to find a parcel containing a tiny glass phial of golden liquid with a short letter:

Via Panjan and Boris Polk

Dear Mr Oblong,

We barely know each other, but your role in this matter may be of the essence. To understand it, please drink the enclosed, soon and when alone, and mark its effects. In the course of your play please expect surprises and be sure to afford and assist all exits and entrances. Use your historian's imagination.

Yours in strictest confidence

F

Meanwhile, Miss Trimble accosted Fanguin in the Golden Mean. She looked uncharacteristically flustered. 'Gregorius Jones has vanished.'

7

Sir Veronal Goes Prospecting

The actress' dual nature, the player and the real life person, felt more riven than ever. Her part was growing richer as the threat intensified. Sir Veronal's savage reaction when the tile failed to live up to his expectations had been disturbing. She could not imagine what ill effects the tile achieved when active, but felt sure they connected to the Manor's past.

The Rotherweird play had veered into gothic darkness, more Webster than Shakespeare.

When Sir Veronal asked her to search the cellars for an entrance to yet lower chambers, she undertook the task as would a prisoner instructed to dig her own grave. Her brief scenes of defiance had passed. Now she must play the victim.

Honeycombed with rooms of various sizes, the cellar housed brick alcoves for wine bottles. Ancient barrels rested on wooden trestles. She tapped the barrels and probed their interiors with torchlight. She pushed at the walls, examined the pointing and tugged at old iron candle fittings, but nothing untoward emerged.

Then she noticed that the wide stone steps up to the ground floor had wood-panelled sides, which bowed, suggesting open space in between. Loyalty to her part and the play compelled her to push the action on. She cut a way in with minimal damage. Inside, a stone landing led to another flight of steps down into the dark.

Sir Veronal soon joined her and delivered a rare compliment. 'Well done, Lady Slickstone. You have opened the way.'

'Where to?'

'We leave in an hour.'

'What do I dress for?'

'A long journey.'

The actress went to her bedroom with a sense of foreboding. Would she be garrotted like the Duchess of Malfi? Buried alive? She dressed in white and filled a pocket with purple bath salts. As in legend, she would leave a trail behind her in the labyrinth.

Back in the cellar, she found Sir Veronal in thick winter clothes carrying a powerful torch in one hand and three gates of identical size, four feet square, in the other. Each side had a flange. They must join to make a barred cube, she deduced. As if to confirm, he gave her another three. They were extraordinarily light.

'Is that for me?' asked the actress, pointing at the unassembled cage.

Sir Veronal smiled. 'Oh no, my dear, it's for me, and me alone.'

With that *envoi*, he plunged into the dark. As her part demanded, she followed.

It was Midsummer's Eve.

From time to time Sir Veronal produced an unusual instrument, part compass, part echo-sounder, to map the tunnels ahead, but he did not halt until they stood on the threshold of a cavern, its features part obscured by shadows thrown by a jumble of huge rocks. After a cursory examination with his torch, Sir Veronal gestured the actress to wait and tiptoed in.

He returned quickly with a finger to his lips and led her into the rock chamber. He pointed out the black tile incised with a flower. The actress' heart missed a beat.

'You said the white tile brings good fortune. What does the black tile bring?' she asked.

'New worlds,' replied Sir Veronal, 'new powers.'

'My contract relates to this world,' replied the actress firmly.

Before Sir Veronal could conjure a suitably commanding reply, chaos struck: a track-suited Gregorius Jones charged into the chamber, waving his tube-light and yelling, 'Flee, m'lady, flee!' as he wrestled Sir Veronal to the ground. The old man showed remarkable strength and dexterity, but his resistance was waning when a roaring noise, bellows-like, brought the action to a standstill.

At the mouth of the chamber a cat stood on its haunches, ribs glowing orange-red, fire licking at its open mouth. Jones disengaged, jumped to his feet and cried, 'Run!' at the actress, and this time she did, dropping the gates at her feet. Judging the cat to be the more dangerous enemy, Jones followed to cover her back. The creature sent a spout of flame after them, but did not follow. Its flanks reverted to bone and fur.

Sir Veronal clambered to his feet and dusted himself down. 'I remember you,' he said to the cat as the fire in its flanks died away. 'Such immaculate timing.'

'You best hurry,' replied the creature.

Sir Veronal hesitated. 'Why are you here?'

By way of response the cat rubbed its body against his legs, crackling more than purring.

'Is there trouble in Lost Acre?'

'It is a difficult time, but you look well prepared. Your mission matters to us all. I'll see you're not disturbed.'

Sir Veronal nodded. In the old days the creature had been a good servant to the Eleusians. He wondered whether any others survived in Lost Acre other than the spiderwoman.

He picked up the six gates, stepped on the tile and disappeared.

Gregorius Jones caught up with the actress, following the sound of her running feet. 'Quiet,' he said; 'the sound may help it.'

But the cat had slunk away from the chamber in a different direction, its task now done.

'Mr Jones, you have a gift for unexpected entrances.'

'I'm not so good at exits.'

'Find the purple grains. There'll be one by each arch we went through.'

Jones' light just held, and the aroma of the bath salts helped as they crawled from arch to arch. After a painstaking reconstruction, they re-emerged in the cellar.

'What now?' asked the actress.

Jones glanced at his watch. 'The North Gate closes in twenty minutes. You must go, and never come back.'

Yes, thought the actress, *I am played out*. Yet she retained an interest in the final act. 'Where does the black tile take him?'

'The end of the world,' replied Jones before adding hastily, 'you don't want to know.'

The actress danced up the stairs, crammed everything she valued into an overnight bag and joined Jones in the garden. 'Here's the Manor's front gate key. Wait there, and I'll show you how to write a stylish exit.'

The Rolls Royce Silver Phantom eased up beside Jones. The streets and squares beyond were deserted, such was the call of the Midsummer Fair.

'Always surprise at the end,' she said, getting out of the car to give him a kiss any man would remember. She knew his best role, the straight leading man, the kind who allows others to shine. 'You can join me, if you like.'

Jones rested a hand on her shoulder as he shook his head. 'Alas, m'lady, I have commitments here. Promise you'll tell nobody what you've seen and heard.'

His expression carried an unexpected intensity, but his refusal enriched her departure: a worthwhile audience would dislike over-simple happy endings.

By way of agreement she placed a finger to her lips. The car purred forward, and with a wave she was gone.

Jones closed the gate, locking it from the outside. Then he did what he always did when emotion threatened: he set off at a run, to nowhere in particular.

On the rim of the valley the actress stopped. A sprinkling of lights marked Rotherweird Town. She got out of the car and bowed to them – her finale, her curtain call.

Above the black tile, Gorhambury had heard the sound of muffled voices and a strange roaring sound. By the time he had lifted the boards, the cavern below stood empty. A trail of soot marked the floor.

Sir Veronal must be in.

8

Parallel Journeys

Salt and Orelia delayed their visit to the Polks for fear of attracting attention. With directions from Bert, they quickly found their way to the Eureka Room, the top floor that housed Boris' most secret (and precarious) inventions. The noise behind it suggested a mechanical polisher: Boris was still at work.

No one acquainted with Boris Polk would expect tidiness, but this chaos was special. Dozens of inventions littered every work surface and the floor – some in draft, yet to progress to physical existence, some in crude model form, and a few in the prototype stage. Orelia kept her fluorescent tube low. They could not make out Boris in the gloom.

'Hello?' asked Orelia.

'Bubbles!' exclaimed Salt.

The two transparent spheres hung like giant Christmas decorations, each large enough to accommodate a crouching adult. From one emerged Boris, even more tousled than usual.

'Finishing touches,' he announced, gesturing flamboyantly to the bubble's entrance as if inviting guests into a stately home. The bubble was bare, save for arches in the floor and sides for hands and feet to grip, and a tiny microphone dead centre. The propulsion source appeared to be a ring at the top, which glowed golden yellow, like a halo. The skin gave slightly when pressed. Access was through a circular porthole, near invisible but for two small hooks on the inside and the outside for leverage.

Boris needed no plea to allow them the luxury of the maiden flight. Invention stood apart as the purest and most valuable creative art – the first wheel, the first pump, the first camera, the first flying bubble. Wynter, Slickstone and their Eleusians had disfigured the ethic of scientific experiment and Boris still burned with rage – hoisting children in cages to merge them with insects and birds? He wanted his bubbles to fight against *that*.

'Now?'

'Now,' replied Orelia.

'We think there's an aerial route into Lost Acre,' added Salt.

Boris gave a crash course in the bubbles' controls, entirely based on refined movement of the handholds and footrests, and capabilities with the *brio* of an enthusiastic schoolboy, his language infectious, even to Salt who found himself asking, 'Suppose there's a prang?'

'Prangs put the PR in progress,' declared Boris. 'Just ask the Wright brothers. If you crash-land, aim for the Guleys or the Ferdys. Lambing is over.'

Salt felt a flicker of doubt and asked the question usually posed by Bert. 'Have you tested them, Boris?'

'My friend, they're faultless.' He paused. 'Conceptually.'

'But have you?'

Boris, the inventor, knew the dangers of excitement, how basics were sometimes overlooked. Yet he knew too, some risks had to be taken.

Belatedly Salt feared for Orelia, up against Sir Veronal. Only one potential ally came to mind. He scribbled a map on a piece of paper and gave it to Boris. 'In case Ferensen chooses to risk the black tile, I've a coracle hidden *here* – he'll find a hidden door in the town's outer wall *there*.'

Boris pocketed the map and cleared the surrounding debris, piling models, paper, tools and unused materials on top of each other.

'This way I know where everything is,' he declared.

The two pioneers clambered into their craft. Once hermetically sealed, they could not hear Boris, even as they discovered the perils of imprisonment in a freewheeling sphere. Salt lurched to the horizontal as Orelia, more intuitive, tried out the intercom system.

'Salt?'

Her microphone appeared to transmit and receive.

'Aaargh.'

'Lean into one knee, like a skater,' suggested Orelia.

Salt's bubble careered across the room, inflicting a triple cartwheel on the pilot, as Boris, with a combination of wheels, latches and pulleys, raised the canvas covering the windows and opened the entire front wall.

'*Avanti!*' cried Boris.

The inventor waved one arm like a traffic policeman and flourished in the other a piece of paper on which he had scrawled: 'PRESS Z!'

They found the button, and obeyed. The bubbles began to hum, and then the room turned purple as the rings changed colour. Stately in their progress, the two spheres floated out and up into the night sky. Boris gave them a wave and set about restoring the Eureka Room to its chaotic normality.

Twenty minutes later, another knock interrupted him.

Gorhambury looked stressed. 'Bad news,' he spluttered, 'fool that I am.'

Five minutes later Panjan was yet again winging his way to Ferensen's tower, this time with a map as well as a message.

The spheres' transparent skin fostered the illusion of suspension in space held by no more than floating footholds and armholds. *How an angel must look from the ground*, thought Salt. The rings above their respective heads glowed a golden yellow once more, like halos.

Salt steered his way to the library, exploring the sky above from all angles. Stars stared back – nothing. His second choice, the sky over the white tile, he wished to keep from Orelia.

'Just a quick sweep,' he said casually, slipping away over the Island Field. Salt paused above the clearing with the white tile – stars above and branches below – but again, nothing.

He was about to wheel away when a mild tremor jolted the sphere, which suddenly acquired a life of its own. 'Boris!' he hissed under his breath as he began to rise in a slow lazy arc, like a bird in a thermal. 'Over here!' he shouted to Orelia.

Salt quickly realised that neither Boris nor the controls were at fault. He sensed a pending return to Lost Acre. The freewheeling sphere imparted a sense that his fate was not in his own hands, and this mix of freedom and helplessness instilled a freshness of thought.

He systematically ran through the evidence: one, *the midsummer flower*: during an early visit, when he had been foolhardy enough to venture far from the tile, he had discovered one plant in Lost Acre that might qualify, judging from the image in the church wall fresco, although it had not then been in flower. It grew high on bare rocky ground on Lost Acre's rim. His study had been curtailed by an attack by flocks of predatory birds. He did not relish the thought of a return visit, but it was there he had to start.

Two, the *Anglo-Saxon Chronicle*: he had first read the Winchester entry in the *Rotherweird Chronicle*'s announcement of the Midsummer Play. Oblong had mentioned another version from Worcester that talked of a monster coming to the Midsummer Fayre to '*wed*'. Everyone assumed a Rotherweird damsel under threat of abduction, but he believed they were wrong. The Green Man held the key.

Three, *the mixing-point*: might Lost Acre's most dangerous property be its sustaining force? If so, he might require its assistance. Thanks to Ferensen, he knew where to find it.

Four, *Ferensen*: nobody was saying out loud what some knew and all suspected. Ferensen and Slickstone were old adversaries; Ferensen had lived through Wynter's rule, trial and death. Ferensen must have entered the mixing-point to live so long – but what other peculiar properties had he acquired? Ferensen's areas of ignorance also struck him as significant. He could answer questions about the stones and their misuse, but he had been as flummoxed by the midsummer flower as they were, suggesting that Lost Acre had not been under threat in Wynter's time, or since – indeed, probably not since 1017. So: a millennial threat to be met by a plant that flowered every thousand years?

Five, *the frescoes*: He recalled the east wall and its explosion of purple, and the disengaged limbs and branches. The priest had dismissed his assumption that the discolouration had been caused by damp. Reflecting now, he recalled that the surface of this part of the wall had been no different. *Suppose* ... His theory fitted every strand, but defied belief. He reminded himself of the Universe's inherent strangeness – the pelican and the climbing rose had emerged from a single cosmic explosion. He *had* to believe.

He ran through his list with Orelia, whose bubble flew far below him, trapped in the same parabola, omitting nothing but his final theory. 'Anything to add?'

'You're very high, Hayman. You sure this is safe?'

'Damn safety – I want your thoughts.'

'I'm convinced the Midsummer Fair is part of this – the place, the timing, the distractions it brings?'

As she spoke, he placed another piece of the jigsaw, as logical and outlandish as the rest.

Orelia changed the subject. 'To stop Slickstone I need to know what he's after.'

'He craves a particular power from the Recipe Book.'

'But what power? What's better than lightning? Zeus had lightning.'

Silence. Both realised their lives might be the price of any success.

A brief recital from *Paradise Lost* stuttered into Orelia's bubble:

Immortal amaranth, a flower which once
In Paradise, fast by the Tree of Life,
Began to bloom —

—only to be cut off by a crackle of static. Anxiously craning forward she watched Salt's bubble accelerate, a speck of dirt drawn to a plughole. The analogy proved good. In seconds it had vanished.

Ferensen sat outside his tower with only a hurricane lamp for company. Puzzles bred only puzzles. Midsummer's Eve, and time was running out.

What was Wynter's last experiment? On whom had he practised it?

How could he save his sister? He had assumed her dead until Salt had arrived some years back with a hideous wound, inflicted in Lost Acre by a monstrous spiderwoman with the gift of language. He had always hoped the stones might separate what they had joined, but Slickstone had the stones and the book. Should he face his sister in her disfigured state? How would she react? What would the spider part of her make-up do?

Last, and perhaps least, what had Wynter and Slickstone placed in the cage with him? All these centuries on, he still did not know.

He felt guilty as well as powerless. He had released the past into the lives of his friends. What chance could they have against Slickstone? He had endangered them, to no purpose.

His musings were interrupted by Panjan alighting on the grass beside him. He released the small tube, which contained a laconic note in Boris' childlike writing:

Slickstone in, via tile under Gems & Geology, two bubbles launched in search of possible aerial gate.

With the note came the key to Rotherweird Library, courtesy of Gorhambury, and Salt's tiny map.

Ferensen's mind cleared. He had to return and take on the old enemy. His first thought was 'one last time', but that was untrue; until now he had always ducked the contest – but no more. Morval and his friends deserved no less.

As the redoubtable Panjan headed back with a new message, Ferensen went inside to prepare. He wondered what the bubbles were up to, and where in Lost Acre an aerial gate might open.

9

Old Friends

Sir Veronal arrived in Lost Acre flushed with excitement, finding himself in an underground passage, the walls part earth and part rock. Shelves with bottles and books added a peculiarly domestic touch.

'Fascinating,' said Sir Veronal to himself, finding in the books stamps from Rotherweird School and Rotherweird Library on works as diverse as mining, mosaics and cookery and, unexpectedly, a price list from *Alizarin & Flake*, the artists' shop in Market Square.

A long-buried pain also surfaced, the keen edge of unrequited love. He had stooped to offer his hand to a peasant girl, or at least, to the talent she possessed, only to be rejected. He had made her pay, but not enough. He scoffed at the mosaic on the ceiling, the finely rendered face of a young man – her brother. If only they knew he was more than a man – so much more.

The scent-sensitive hairs on the spiderwoman's legs smelled Slickstone as soon as he entered. She also sensed the stones, and remembered Slickstone's lightning hands.

Run? Talk? Hide? Faced with a plethora of choices, the spiderwoman froze where she felt most comfortable – in her kitchen. Slickstone had little grasp of the debilitating damage he had done to Morval Seer. He expected her to hate him, and hoped for a fight. Electrocuting the creature would be amusing.

He entered the kitchen. Faint traces of her beauty survived in the eyes and human remnants in her leathery face, but the bulbous body and spread-eagled legs were as hideous as he remembered them. He smiled at her orderly kitchen and her diet of blood and skin – Morval Seer, the nature lover!

The spiderwoman's eight eyes blinked. Part of her did not know the intruder, but part of her did; within her divided being the spider deferred for the moment to Morval Seer. Slickstone had aged, but the eyes, the set of the jaw, the bloom of the skin and the high brow were unmistakably him. She assumed his cruelty, cleverness and powers were undiminished.

Slickstone gestured at the bottles and jars. 'Fine work.'

'Keep away,' hissed the spiderwoman.

'My dear Morval, when you've waited so long?'

Somewhere in her tangled being Morval Seer felt proud of rejecting him. 'Keep away!' The monster cowered, almost pitiful.

Then a faint tremor puffed earth from the ceiling like smoke. Pots and pans played a percussive tune.

'What's that?'

'Turbulence – deeper and older than you can imagine, Veronal Slickstone.'

'You'd better explain.' The menace was palpable.

The spiderwoman's eight eyes registered different emotions, appropriate to the complexities of her make-up. Her voice sounded more vulnerable; the hiss of the animal softened by a human intonation. The effort appeared painful. 'There is technology and there is Nature. Some activities require an understanding of both – painting, for example. But your stones are bare technology. They can deform Nature, but Nature wins in the end. Lost Acre faces apocalypse – and your stones cannot save her.'

Slickstone's temper frayed. 'What are you blathering about?' He removed his gloves. A faint spark of lightning played over his fingers.

'In every millennium Lost Acre faces extinction. Her sustaining forces tire and need renewal. That demands *respect* for Nature, not abuse.'

The creature's mind had distinct compartments. Most of the time, Morval's delicate sensibilities could not match the spider's brutality. Even the gift of speech had been brutalised. However, a small part of its brain remained unpolluted. Here she cherished memories of the countryside, Sir Henry and her brother, and guarded her humanity like a candle. Meanwhile, the spider plotted ridding herself of this hateful human companion.

By a supreme effort, and because the spider had no knowledge of Slickstone, Morval had dominated the initial conversation, but now the spider asserted control. Morval's decency disappeared. The voice turned sibilant and cunning. 'Listen, Veronal Slickstone, all is not lost. You have a cage. I want rid of the woman. Release me – and I'll help you. It is dangerous out there. You'll need Ferox.'

So Ferox lived! The weaselman had lived in Lost Acre for centuries before them; he had become Slickstone's guardian and guide in Lost Acre. Subliminally, Ferox had never left him. He stood guard on Slickstone's chimneys, his weathervanes, the bonnet of his Rolls Royce, on his slippers and cufflinks, on the arms of his chairs, and many other places besides.

'Where is he?'

'Ferox will find you.'

'How?'

'As he always did. Ferox is Ferox.'

'That was a long time ago.'

'He will feel the pull of the stones. They made us what we are.'

Slickstone paused. 'Guard the way in. Kill whoever comes. We have common interests, you and I.'

The spiderwoman blinked. As he left, she considered a strike at the unprotected back – but the spider did not know how to place the stones. Ferox had promised assistance. Nobody trusted Ferox, but a hope was better than nothing. Then there was the other visitor with his promises who had yet to return. She decided on a waiting game.

Sir Veronal had attributed the oppressive atmosphere to the spiderwoman's kitchen, but when he opened the outer door in the face of a steep bank, he understood the creature's reference to apocalypse.

Ribbons of light zigzagged through a sky of the deepest grey. The spiderwoman's house was set into the bank at the forest edge. With the static, the webs around her lair came alive, glimmering like ghosts. Signs of trouble were no less ominous in the meadowland beyond. The grass hung unusually limp, heavy with seed. This was no ordinary storm.

He set out across the sloping meadow. A garish orange light washed the grass and a wind began to blow, increasing in force and veering from one direction to another. He paused to wipe his forehead with a silk handkerchief. Bullying the meadow this way and that, the wind created a shimmering effect – light to shadow, shadow to light. Then he caught something else disturbing the grass: a dark line, heading towards him, sleek and direct. He stood stock-still and waited.

Ferox did not stand up until he reached Sir Veronal. The weasel in him was unmistakable – the face pinched, the snout sharp, the eyes red and the sallow skin blotched with patches of red-brown fur – as indeed was the human in the extended nose, earlobes, fingernails, eyelashes and speaking voice. His face was covered with a scarf, his clothes fashioned from patches of leather.

Ferox bowed to Sir Veronal. 'Master,' he said, 'your visit is well-timed.'

The earth shook, a stronger tremor; they had no time for small talk about their Elizabethan days. A flicker of doubt crossed Slickstone's mind – how curious that his return to Rotherweird should coincide with Lost Acre's hour of need. If someone thought he would be Lost Acre's rescuer, they were wrong – he would plunder the mixing-point for this particular superlative gift and then let the place implode. That way, he would have no rivals.

'You have a cage. What will you put in it?' enquired Ferox.

'Mr Wynter's last experiment.'

'Then you have the stones and the book?'

'I have all that I need.'

'Then this last experiment worked?'

'If it's in the book, it worked.'

'What does it do?'

'Get me there and you'll find out.'

The crown of a tree not far below exploded into flame.

'We best find shelter until morning,' said Ferox.

'I want to go now.'

'Use the mixing-point in darkness – and a thunderstorm? Again?'

Another fork jagged from horizon to horizon. 'First light then,' conceded Slickstone.

'Master,' said Ferox with a shallow bow, ending the conversation as he had begun it.

As the light began to fail, it did not feel like Midsummer's Eve.

By the time they reached the soaring rock face with the cave at its foot, more trees had ignited, the impression of candles enhanced by the descending darkness. Inside the cave, a low fire, skins on the floor and a battered cauldron provided a welcome harbour from the storm. Ferox seasoned a rich stew, which they ate with horn forks. Slickstone did not enquire about the origins of the meat, which he found spicy but wholesome to taste. A twist in the short entrance tunnel muffled the thunder and obscured the lightning. The cave was almost homely.

'Have you ever seen such a storm before?' asked Sir Veronal.

'Once,' replied Ferox, 'long ago. We will have different challenges tomorrow.' He declined to be drawn on what those challenges might be. He watched as Slickstone slipped quickly into deep sleep, throwing the remains of the seasoning onto the fire with mint to mask the dose of Lost Acre's potently soporific valerian. Long fingers extended like a pickpocket, he lifted the stones with ease. Gathering his spear, he loped off into the dark.

10

Metamorphosis

Salt's bubble hurtled through a vortex for several hours, a spinning darkness with streaks of ambient light. This gate had none of the instant transportation effects of the tiles. Salt was beginning to fear his journey would never end when, in a blinding change of colour, the bubble lurched into very real weather.

In sepulchral gloom, clouds more black than grey cohered, divided and ran amok, as if every contrary wind was vying for supremacy. Treetops blazed in crazy lines, marking the path of lightning strikes. Thunder growled like distant artillery. Watercourses steamed like broth.

As the bubble plunged, static dancing across its skin, Salt thought of his beloved plants, their leaves scorched, sap dried out and roots starved. *There is always seed awaiting rebirth*, he reminded himself.

His hectic descent stalled in a corridor of calmer air – Lost Acre's birdlife had found it too. Thousands of birds, large and small, feathered and leather-winged, the brilliantly coloured and the drab, glided and hovered to avoid the turbulence above and below. Two large predators with clawed wings and eyes like fish peered into the bubble and tapped its exterior with their scissored beaks before losing interest.

By luck or design, this passageway of calm air kissed the summit of Lost Acre's craggy uplands, Salt's intended destination. An eerie blood-red, more suited to heralding dusk than dawn, stained the eastern horizon. Even inside the bubble Salt sensed a change of

'Lost Acre's birdlife had found it too.'

atmosphere: no lightning, no thunder, stillness and silence. The birds vanished too, now preferring to risk shelter in the wreckage of the landscape below.

'Orelia?' Salt enquired, belatedly remembering his companion, but there was no reply. To his relief, the rolling peak of Lost Acre's mountainous rim was still carpeted with the extraordinary plant which he had come to find. He manoeuvred the bubble into a long gentle trajectory and a perfect landing.

Salt had never seen the plant so luxuriant. The leaves had acquired an unexpected leathery texture, perhaps in anticipation of the extreme conditions. He could see no sign of a flower.

On hands and knees, Salt established that the spreading growth belonged to a single specimen, rooted in the shelter of two flat rocks that abutted each other close to the summit. He lay across the higher and peered into the gap between. The leaves and stems below were larger. He felt the air on his face cooling fast, despite the imminence of dawn. Salt rolled up his right sleeve and thrust his arm in, gently probing with his fingers for the casing of a bud or the petals of a flower. The leaves and stems were soft to the touch and without irritants. At the base of the rock he made contact with what felt like a thicker stem, having the unnerving sensation that it was also searching for him. The stem touched his finger and began to twine itself around it.

For half an hour he lay there as the stem unfolded itself and climbed his arm. He dared not move for fear of disturbing this mysterious process, an ordeal in the conditions as snow began to fall, shrouding the back of his body. The rock turned icy-cold, his shoulders ached, his outstretched arm went numb.

At last the plant released him. Gingerly Salt lifted his arm from the crevice. From wrist to well above the elbow the stem wound round, ending in a single bud, its sepals closed tight, the colour of the flower still hidden. Salt stood up. He could see no further than ten paces ahead in the snow. Planning a route was impossible.

Keeping stem and bud from damage, he clambered back in the bubble. Even assuming he had to replicate the events of 1017, there remained the question of timing: the window of opportunity must be small. He had no idea how to return to Rotherweird with the white tile closed; still less did he know, even if he managed that feat, what he would look like and how he would be received. Times were different now – people dismissed old myths as ignorant fancy. The Saxon precedent suggested he should arrive with the Fair in full swing. Deciding that he had a little time, Salt conserved his energy and slept.

Orelia's bubble careered through a much faster wormhole and arrived in Hell itself: deep night with burning trees on one side and rocky uplands on the other, sporadically illuminated by silvery-blue lightning. Lashing rain came and went in perplexingly short intervals. As her craft lurched up and down and side to side, she searched, dangerously close to the ground, for a suitable landing. Only the meadowland made practical sense. The lush vegetation brought the bubble to an almost instant halt, nearly costing Orelia her front teeth. She jumped into grass up to her neck and the wind blew her forward, then back. New phenomena bombarded eyes and ears – the atmospherics, the extraordinary trees, even the grass, with its octagonal seed. To keep focus, she kept muttering, 'Stop Sir Veronal!' to herself.

But how? She had no map and (foolishly) not even a compass.

In the event, the decision was made for her. Some way on, a head rose clear of the grass, a feral head, all pointed snout and scrawny neck, flicking left and right, sniffing the air. A spear rose with it. Flames from the nearby forest bathed it in an orange glow, and she could not be sure the russet impression was natural. The head and the spear dipped back, grass furrowing as the creature barrowed along – a Lost Acre hybrid. She followed, lightening her tread to lessen her own wake. Her quarry held a line, which slowly took them away from the forest. Despite the conditions, the creature had a mission.

She followed for a good half-hour before the grass dwindled in thickness and height. The arms of a great tree spread-eagled the sky; vines or ropes hung from an outer branch. In the air nearby, all tricksy, like moonlight on fish-scales, she saw the mixing-point. The creature stood up, and again she glimpsed that characteristic flick of the head. Closer, on more open ground, the mix was clear: he was half weasel, half man, with a striking resemblance to Slickstone's shield and ubiquitous mascot.

Below and to the left, she caught more movement in the grass. She'd been expecting Sir Veronal to emerge, but instead the spiderwoman lumbered out of the sward. Even in near-darkness the horrifying marriage of animal and human disgusted her, much aggravated by the fact that it had been deliberately contrived. Her respect for Valourhand blossomed into admiration. To have survived a close encounter with this creature with such equanimity suggested enormous reserves of courage and spirit. Likewise, her loathing for Sir Veronal deepened – to inflict *this* on a fellow human being . . .

The two creatures stood beside the tree. She could not hear their conversation, but the exchanges had the appearance of negotiation, with the weaselman in control.

The spiderwoman manoeuvred her bulk into a wooden cage beside the tree, legs slipping in and out of the bars. The weaselman walked round, stooping at each side. Questions clamoured for answers. The weaselman must have the stones – but Sir Veronal would hardly release them, unless perhaps he and the weaselman were one and the same, or the weaselman was a trusted servant. When had the cage been built? How did the weaselman know where to place the stones? What were they creating?

She could not make out the detail of the apparatus, but the weaselman hoisted the cage to just below the branch, where it swung crazily in the wind, before a yank on another rope sent the cage into the mixing-point where it disappeared.

The weaselman lounged on his spear, the devil-may-care pose

suggesting he had used the mixing-point before, or seen others use it. The boom swung back out. At first she saw no change – the cage and the giant spider remained intact. But then she noticed that the spider's eyes were lower in the head, the legs more even, the thorax more as Nature had intended. And now, behind the spider, she made out two pale arms, *human* arms, protruding from the bars and gripping them.

A naked body slipped out, lithe, pale, and visibly feminine. With balletic grace the young woman slipped from the cage to a rope to a branch to the ground and disappeared into the darkness.

The spider, reviving more slowly, thrashed against the bars, buckling them. The weaselman waited, his demeanour now more alert. *He wishes to spare the girl*, thought Orelia. He walked round the cage, stooping at each side, keeping the spider at bay with his spear – re-gathering the stones, no doubt. Then he released the spider, which stumbled out, turning full circle, flexing its legs, settling back into its old self. Orelia felt a flicker of pride that her own species had been quicker to adjust. Disconcertingly, the spider did not run off; it leapt high into the dark and disappeared downhill towards the forest.

Who was the woman? How had she been lured into this monstrous partnership? She recalled the books, the mosaic of the young Ferensen and the cookery, and it dawned on her that she must be Ferensen's sister, Morval Seer, painter for the Eleusians. But what had been her crime? And why was the weaselman aiding her release? Orelia had a burning desire to help her, but felt obliged to stay. The weaselman must hold the key to Sir Veronal's location.

The digression had distracted her – the weaselman had vanished. She zigzagged through the grass, pausing every fifty yards or so to check for pursuit. At the third stop she eased herself up for a longer look. The blow from behind struck the side of her neck. She dropped unconscious at Ferox's feet.

Hostilities Resumed

Ferensen had followed Salt's route in before dawn, taking the gardener's tiny coracle across to the concealed gate. Gorhambury's key gave access to the library. As he entered, he detected another human presence – he could do that in enclosed spaces; warm blood affected the atmospherics.

His fellow intruder awaited him in the basement. 'Miss Valour-hand.'

She was almost as unseasonally dressed as he was, and they both carried sticks, although his held a long concealed blade.

'Gorhambury has gone to the Fair. Down here, he was beginning to turn yellow.' She paused, before adding the truer explanation. 'I thought you would come.'

Ferensen smiled. In the set of her eyes and her refreshing direct-ness he caught a glimpse of Fortemain. 'Let me guess. You're a physicist, and witnessing a world at the end of its natural cycle is not an opportunity to miss. And then there's the mixing-point . . .'

'There's nothing comparable here.'

'But you haven't gone in. You're brave but not foolish. One meeting with the spiderwoman is enough.'

'I'd take the risk if you were there.'

'You would provoke its darker half, and that will reduce my slight chances to nothing.'

Valourhand recalled the words 'fresh meat', the spider's brutal rejection of its gentler half's call for restraint. Ferensen was right. 'I'll guard your back then.'

Ferensen nodded. She had not fully declared her intentions but he had no time, and moral lectures about the perilous temptations of Lost Acre would cut no ice with Valourhand.

They shook hands, and on impulse Valourhand gave him a secret. 'Perhaps you should see this. It's from Flask's rooms in Box Street. He appears to have copied the *Recipe Book.*'

Ferensen glanced at the charred fragment. In the margin a silhouetted jester danced with pointed shoes, a simple soldier and other harmless human caricatures beside him. He felt uneasy. The former historian and outsider Robert Flask appeared to have come close to a great many secrets. He recalled the empty alcove in Escutcheon Place. Finch had not suggested any recent theft. The book had been removed long ago.

'Let's discuss this on my return,' he said with a wink.

'*Bon voyage,*' she replied as he stepped on the tile and vanished.

Ferensen did not at first register the books, the smudged footprints or even the passageway. He stood transfixed by the image of his younger self in the domed ceiling above the entry point. The tiny coloured chips of stone had caught him body and soul – a tribute, but also an anchor for his sister to cling to.

His skin took over. So much contrary data – heat in the earth, electrical energy nearby, and, his palms told him, extreme cold fast approaching: all the seasons in quick succession – autumn blown out, now only winter to go, the final transition from high fever to death. The image galvanised him. Within a few paces he knew the spiderwoman had left – twins reach out; twins know. In the kitchen the hearth still glowed, illuminating shelf upon shelf of blood and offal. Morval's predicament screamed from those bottles – creatures poisoned, strangled in webs, sucked dry. He opened the front door a fraction – a scene from his namesake, Hieronymus

Bosch, fire and devastation, only without the monsters, at least for the moment. They would be out there somewhere.

The observation troubled Ferensen. Any creature with any sense of self-preservation would be underground. Here the spiderwoman had walls of rock, food, insulation from extreme heat and cold and potential access to the only way out. So why leave? He dampened his right palm and pressed it on the floor, catching mostly streaks of fur and tiny feathers, prey presumably. He tried again and retrieved a single long tapered russet hair with a fleck of white at the tip. A nearby footprint confirmed Ferensen's suspicions: Ferox, Slickstone's kindred spirit from Lost Acre, had been here – and recently, to judge from the freshness of the spoor. The odds on success lengthened – nobody knew Lost Acre like Ferox. But what had the three of them discussed?

Back in the kitchen he spotted two tell-tale muddy lines on the floorboards, with bare human footprints between them. Sir Veronal had brought a cage – unsurprising, as the mixing-point must be his destination. But all questions returned to the same conundrum: what power did Wynter's last experiment confer?

He released the blade on his stick and ventured outside. The cut of the ground below suggested a wider river, its course now much reduced. Debris from the forest, including a few dead bird-insects, littered the ground. Coils of sundered gossamer hung from the trees.

Even now the past intruded. He and Morval had quickly worked out that the forest held more dangerous inhabitants than the meadowland; he saw no reason to change that opinion now.

Wynter had been clever in introducing his charges to Lost Acre, allowing them to wander before introducing the mixing-point as a crude phenomenon, lacking the refinement only they could provide. Design was the key. Paint without pattern, he had said, to prepare them for the trial and error of mixing. They progressed from small birds and insects to children. The Eleusians acclimatised to failures with horrifying speed, focusing on the triumphs, all carefully recorded in *The Roman Recipe Book*. Nobody asked Wynter how he had discovered the stones' ability to shape.

Ferensen, still mulling over the past, reached the meadowland before the change struck him. He had suppressed these memories because they brought to mind his sister's fractured essence, not as a memory but a present reality, communicated by a twin's sixth sense. Yet now that connection had gone. He still felt her presence, but *unpolluted* – how had this happened? Where was she now? He cried out her name without success, but his conviction of her release fortified him for the fight ahead.

He strode through the meadow, surprised, weather conditions apart, how little the landscape had changed. Even the tree by the mixing-point was familiar. He assumed it too had been fashioned there, and shared with him unusual longevity.

Ferensen took a position close to the tree. Planting his stick, he stood and half-slept – another trick, this gift for shutting down while maintaining balance. The cold was closer. Frost and blizzard would envelope him in hours.

I 2

Nemesis

The sun rose sluggishly, a bloated deep crimson, quickly disappearing into a wall of deep grey. The lightning had passed; the wind too, and the temperature began to plummet.

Sir Veronal's uneasy sleep gave way to instant anxiety. His hands flew to his pockets. The stones were gone: *the stones*. Ferox appeared at the mouth of the cave and slung Orelia down by the fire. Gagged and bound, she could only groan.

'You had a visitor,' said Ferox, returning the stones to Slickstone's anxious hand. 'A most stealthy visitor.'

'How dare you take the stones?'

'I judged them safer with me. As you see, there are thieves abroad.'

Orelia frantically tried to unravel the weaselman's words: he was presenting her as a thief – but why? She could not speak, but she could shake her head. She decided against; the weaselman might yet be a force for good. He had rescued Morval Seer from the spider, after all.

Her thoughts were interrupted as Sir Veronal brutally kicked her body round to see her face. 'Banter's niece – kill her.'

'Don't you want her to watch?' suggested Ferox.

Sir Veronal reflected and succumbed again to that temptation to toy with his prey. 'Maybe I would.'

'It's harsh out there – all the seasons in no time,' added Ferox.

'Let's get on with it then,' barked Slickstone, noting how well Ferox's English had held up since his absence.

Here and there trees smoked like snuffed candles, their trunks split, their branches blackened. Beneath their hurrying feet, the soil, soft the night before, was hardening. Then snow began to fall, soon turning heavy, and the landscape's distinguishing features dissolved into isolated smudges and lines marking the undersides of branches and rocks. Sir Veronal kept close as Orelia stumbled along beside Ferox, tied to him by a rope. Ferox's step and direction never wavered.

Even in this white-out, memories flooded back to Sir Veronal, as he succumbed to the excitement of changing the very *nature* of things. He recalled his own immersion in the mixing-point, the punishment of the Seers, and his final ordeal, *tabula rasa et exsilium*.

One particular thought stirred him. Always before, he had gone to the mixing-point with Wynter who, as master of the Eleusians, made the choices and gave the orders. It was he who had delivered the children to Wynter, but his shield in *The Dark Devices* had no more prominence than the others. Only his lightning hands confirmed his supremacy. The other men, even Wynter, chose pets, lacking the courage to enter the mixing-point themselves. Now he alone would enjoy the mixing-point's ultimate power.

'There!' he cried, sighting the upper limbs of the tree, the distinctive silhouette little changed, and soon the mixing-point too was visible. In daylight Orelia found the patch of slippery sky no less unsettling.

'Ferox!' shouted Slickstone, gesturing ahead. At first sight the figure by the tree resembled a snowman or marble statue, set in guardian pose, leaning forward, peering down at its spear, but in a flurry of snow and flailing arms it came alive.

'Welcome, Veronal Slickstone.'

Ferensen! But Orelia wished he had not come – he could have no chance against Sir Veronal and Ferox.

Sir Veronal instantly regained his composure. 'If it isn't Master Seer, the teacher's pet!'

Identities slipped, and at last Orelia saw Hieronymus Seer, not Ferensen. She struggled to break free, but Ferox held firm.

Slickstone looked more amused than unnerved at the encounter. 'Remember Hieronymus Seer, Ferox? Always happy to watch, always afraid to act.'

'My mistake was in not acting sooner,' replied Ferensen.

'Let me deal with him,' said Ferox, closing in.

'Take pity,' sneered Sir Veronal, 'he doesn't even know *what* he is.'

Ferensen played his only card. He turned to Ferox. 'You think he'll let you escape – but why should he? You know too much – and you wouldn't last a minute where we come from. He won't take you back.'

Ferox laughed. 'What do you know?'

Ferensen turned back to Slickstone and tried a different tack. 'Are you sure Wynter's last experiment works? Are you sure about what it does?'

'Wynter bequeathed that power to me. He was ready to die, but I was not.'

Ferox lowered his spear. There was urgency in the weaselman's voice. 'Let me kill him, we must get on,' he said.

'That would be too crude at this particular moment,' Sir Veronal said grandly. 'He must witness this first.'

Ferensen took his chance, charging straight at Slickstone, quick for one so old – but not quick enough.

Sir Veronal raised his hands.

The lightning did not strike Ferensen, it *encased* him. Sir Veronal had perfected the technique long ago, and revived the skill with hours of practice at the Manor. Now he moved his fingers to create fine lines of crackling electricity that shaped together like a birdcage. One touch would mean instant death, as Ferensen knew.

'Now, dance like your sister did!' cried Sir Veronal, rotating the cage and so turning Ferensen to face the mixing-point.

The taunting continued. 'Pretty, aren't they?' He flourished the stones as Ferox assembled the cage. The snow had stopped, but above their heads the sky began to change again, veins appearing in the clouds. Such was the urgency that Sir Veronal quite overlooked the broken wooden cage lying in the grass.

Ferox bound Orelia's ankles and tightened her gag. Something about his expression alarmed Orelia; she could not weave the threads together. The weaselman's ambiguous behaviour, the release of Ferensen's sister – something had gone right, but she sensed something was also *wrong*. She shook her head and made such noise as she could.

The blow from Ferox, delivered hard with the flat of his hand, caught her flush on the temple. This time she stayed down, barely conscious, but aware that Ferox could have killed her and had chosen not to.

Assembly of the cage took a matter of minutes. Sir Veronal clambered in and Ferox fastened the final section behind him. Crouching, his eyes alight with excitement, Sir Veronal passed the stones to Ferox, instructing him as to which stone fitted which receptacle. They could now see the hinged boom that would take the cage into the mixing-point.

A high singing note chimed in the distance, as if ice were threatening to crack.

'On! On!' cried Sir Veronal.

Ferox tugged at the weathered rope. The pulley held the cage stationary after every upward movement. Sir Veronal prowled about as it ascended, peering always at the mixing-point, reaching through the bars as if pleading for its power.

Ferox went up and down like a bell-ringer, rising from his haunches to upright and back, keeping the rhythm. Orelia caught something more in the weaselman's face than physical strain: a look of triumph, as if a long-awaited moment had arrived.

Somehow Ferensen had managed to keep still enough to avoid

electrocution, and he, like Orelia, watched the proceedings with horrified fascination. In the eerie silence Orelia felt extraneous, redeemed of any further obligation to intervene. The cage was in place and the boom swung towards the mixing-point as if drawn by the magnetic pull of the stones. Seconds before the cage disappeared, Sir Veronal flung wide his arms and roared.

Then silence. The chain juddered and went slack. Nobody moved. Even the cataclysmic sky seemed peripheral.

Minutes later the boom swung out again of its own accord, as if the mixing-point knew its work was done. The cage was intact and Sir Veronal apparently untouched.

'Down!' he shouted. 'Down! It's done. I felt it! Down! *Down!* Then you'll see—'

Ferox yanked the rope and let the cage descend a few yards before yanking again. Despite Sir Veronal's impatience, an air of anti-climax prevailed: nothing had ostensibly changed.

Then, halfway down, Ferox abruptly halted the descent. Ferensen and Orelia could do no more than gape as the slit of Sir Veronal's mouth turned into a vertical O. With a strangled cry of 'What's happening?', his ears and nose retracted into his face and his fingers merged, one with the other. As his clothes burst away from his body, other features dissolved and mutated: fur changed to hide to scales – and then, as quickly, he returned to normal, screaming at Ferox, only for the process to resume: tusks, teeth, beaks, legs, wings and talons came and went at extraordinary speed.

Soon he had no recognisable body, only a heaving mass of different parts, fleetingly conjoined. As the monstrosity grew, the cage swung crazily from side to side. The titanium bars started buckling and twisting before the cage fell apart, and the ever-changing mass that was Sir Veronal Slickstone fell too.

At the last mutation Sir Veronal briefly reappeared, diminished and naked, on all fours. 'But Wynter—' he hissed, '—how?'

Then he slid into nothing but gore and gristle.

Nobody had moved. The horrific process had been too swift and too savage.

Ferox's face wore a chilling smirk, as if he had known all along how the frantic sequence of transformations would end. He retrieved the stones from the remnants of the cage. Orelia sensed a malignant hand from the past, and some deeper mystery, but she could not work out who or how or why.

Ferox suddenly made an extraordinary keening noise, an animal cry of victory, before bounding away across the snow, sometimes upright, sometimes dipping to all fours.

The lightning round Ferensen flickered and died. He went to Orelia and released her. 'Are you all right, dear girl?'

'What *was* that?'

'I don't know – everything here is in flux.'

'But Ferox – did you see Ferox?'

'I fear nothing is quite what it seems. We will have to unravel.' He paused, his face sliding into panic. 'But first I have business to attend to. Avoid the forest, whatever you do. There was a cave at the end of the meadowland – look for that.'

Ferensen was looking distracted, as if Sir Veronal's death were an irrelevance.

'But what happened?'

'I don't know ... later ... *later*.' Ignoring his own instruction, Ferensen ran off towards the forest and was soon swallowed up by the snow-covered grass.

Orelia had dreamed of an epic battle: her youth against Slick-stone's lightning, revenge for the death of her aunt. Instead, she had been a mere onlooker. She did not relish staying near the mixing-point, but equally she had no intention of returning to Ferox's cave. Fine silvery lines were crisscrossing the sky like veins on a pottery glaze.

She was marooned in a world on the edge of self-destruction with no way out. She saw only one course of action. Skipping lightly across the snow, childlike, she set out to explore.

Back at the stream at the forest edge, Ferensen took stock, preoccupied only with his sister. Where would Morval go? If he knew she was here and alive, the converse must be true. Perhaps she was not yet ready to face her own kind; perhaps she feared she would endanger him. *Perhaps, maybe, perhaps.* He settled on a destination: his own place of martyrdom, the grim lake high in the forest.

The spider, anxious for a first kill in its old form, watched. It recognised the face from the domed ceiling. If it could not have the woman, it would have her mate. But the man was nimble and carried a weapon. *Stalk him,* it thought, *stalk him until he tires. And then . . . like the others so long ago . . .*

When Salt awoke, the snow had slackened to a few isolated flakes. The cold had pockmarked the outside with tiny crystals. He scraped the bubble's skin and took off, but soon the crystals reformed and he was riding blind. With regret at vandalising an invention that had served him so well, he kicked out the entry door. He now had an open view, but at a cost: eyebrows and hair turned white as sensation dwindled. He clenched and unclenched his hands, moving his head from side to side. He lifted first one leg and then the other; he had to keep moving if he were not to freeze to death.

Thanks to Ferensen, he knew where to go. He kept the forest on his left until he came to an immense tree with ropes hanging from its highest branch. Nearby, the telltale patch of sky slid this way and that. He landed the bubble, and as he did so, the power finally failed.

The bloodstained snow suggested much activity, but he found no body and nothing alive, only two shattered cages. He didn't investigate; time was running out. He advanced towards the mixing-point, pausing briefly when a high reedy noise made him look up. The hairline fissures in the sky appeared to be widening from horizon to horizon, and reddening too. *Armageddon.*

By the tree, Salt despaired. The single pulley had broken and the lower branches were too high to climb, even without the handicap of the fragile stem entwined around his arm. He saw no way to access the mixing-point.

He flinched as his upper arm prickled and the bud quivered. Half in wonder, half in horror, Salt saw the mixing-point come to him: slivers of light, oscillating, grey-green in colour, detached themselves – a few at first, but soon the whole mixing-point was on the move, ribbons of light dancing around him. He was trans-figured, numinous. He felt no pain, just a rearrangement of his being – muscle and stem, plant and man, merged and mixed. He felt the single bud explode and multiply as thought gave way to sensory awareness. He could no longer see ground or sky, but *felt* them instead – the texture and taste of earth, the movement of air, temperature.

He and the midsummer flower were one. He was the Green Man, Lost Acre's last hope.

The veins in the sky were now crimson. In the open meadowland, a column of red rose from the ground like a fiery door. Salt felt the warmth calling him. Slowly the Green Man edged towards it, more tree than plant, all foliage and twisted branches covered in flower.

13

The Play's the Thing

Rhombus Smith surveyed the tiers of seats. They'd been well tenanted already by parents, staff and children for the Prizegiving; now they were filling to capacity with those who had only come for the Midsummer Fair play. The Inner Circle, the clump of oaks in the centre of the Island Field, surrounded the auditorium, offering shade to the upper tiers. Beneath the trees, roped-off areas protected the Rotherweird eglantine from trespassing feet in accordance with the *Botany Regulations*.

The Headmaster heaved a sigh of relief. His ghastly duties were almost done. Opposite, in the middle, Snorkel and his retinue sat in an enclosed area. A drape with the Mayoral arms hung beneath it: in all but name the Royal Box.

'School Prize for Art – Miss Vine.'

To the Headmaster's displeasure, Art came last, Science first, for Science made the money. There remained but one award, the social kiss of death in perpetuity, which he reserved for the most obnoxious pupil in the School.

'Last but not least,' said Rhombus Smith in mock-heroic voice, 'the Knapweed Good Conduct Cup goes to—'

On the apron stage behind him a large cave advanced on wheels, propelled by Gwen Ferdy and Ned Guley inside it. Gawgy's costume hung from the roof. They stopped by the tiny cross Oblong had left on the stage – a professional touch, he felt – and turned their attention to the dry-ice machine.

Backstage, behind a plush purple curtain, Oblong gathered the rest of his cast as the unfortunate recipient of the Knapweed Cup made the long walk.

The costumes of the Knight and his page, arranged by Sir Veronal, were splendid: shimmering chainmail emblazoned with weasels rampant, Slickstone's gold, Collier in silver. They carried a long shiny box between them.

'What's that?' asked Oblong.

'The Hammer.'

'May I see it?'

'You will, sir, you will.'

Oblong smiled wanly. He could not afford a showdown, not so close to curtain-up. Angie Bevins, also fitted out at Sir Veronal's expense, looked pretty as a picture in a yellow shift with a green girdle.

'We're gonna fight for you,' said Rodney with a swagger.

'Give that monster what for,' added Collier.

'Oh, Sir Rodney,' Angie simpered.

'Make believe, make believe,' Oblong reminded his cast.

Finch joined them in a long fur coat, moleskin breeches and leather boots. He looked like a rat-catcher. As Rhombus Smith bowed to modest applause, audience conversation dwindled to an expectant hush. Oblong's poetic interests were known; expectations were high. His doomed dalliance with Cecily Sheridan suggested an artistic temperament.

Oblong ambled on stage, as by tradition the Form Master did the introductions. '*The Monster and the Midsummer Maid*,' he declared.

A rhythmic beat started, quiet at first, but gathering volume. Smoke poured from the mouth of the cave as Finch inched forward like a pantomime villain. Oblong wondered if he had been wise to allow the Herald to miss rehearsals, but Marmion Finch brought true surprise. Nobody had expected an adult, let alone the most mysterious recluse in town. Even Snorkel sat up.

Marmion Finch exploited the expectation to the full. He glared. He licked his lips like a vampire come to dine. His delivery was offhand, yet compelling.

> 'Beyond Civilisation's cultured reach
> In a cavernous lair of moss and stone,
> Uncomforted by laughter, love or speech,
> A dark eyed monster sits – and broods – alone.
> The air is so still in the midsummer heat –
> A tune from the band you see standing there
> Drifts all the way to the monster's retreat.
> Where its heart is touched, and the soul laid bare –
> Time to be going to Rotherweird Fair.'

The band struck up a haunting tune. Through the smoke Gawgy emerged, a dragon stained dark by its own smoke, and did a circuit of the stage before returning to the cave. More dry ice, and mild applause.

Marmion Finch turned stage right.

> 'As a village beauty passes the hours,
> Wreathing a necklace of daisy flowers . . .'

Angie Bevins, a model of adolescent angst, did a passable imitation of Ophelia mad, gathering imaginary blooms with one hand, still grooming her hair with the other.

> 'I gather willowherb and rue,
> Bindweed and the cornflower blue . . .'

Collier passed by, warning Angie Bevins of the danger. She checked for split ends by way of response.

Re-enter Gawgy, its plyboard jaws clacking open and shut. Guley and Gwen had rehearsed hard, and the creature had an air of predatory menace. Angie screamed with irritating coyness, the monster closed, and the audience hissed. *A reassuring sign of engagement*, thought Oblong, peering from behind the curtain.

Inside, the costume was stifling. 'They're coming,' whispered Guley from the head. Crouching with her hands on his hips, Gwen could do no more than grunt. In the wings Oblong flapped his arms, pointing frantically. Collier, still carrying the wooden box, looked more railway porter than equerry. Finch continued, unaware of developments behind him.

Rodney Slickstone eyed the monster with loathing – countrysiders, peasants with airs and graces. He had also scanned the audience – no sign of either of his stand-in parents. They clearly thought him incapable of a worthwhile performance. He would show them. He would teach Gwen Ferdy the meaning of respect.

He took out the Hammer and flicked a switch. The Hammer whined like a chainsaw, the edges glinting as they spun.

The music stopped sooner than Oblong's direction dictated. Through Gawgy's narrow slit eyes Guley could not see the knight.

'Help!' shrieked Gwen, 'What's that noise?'

'Run!' shouted Guley, 'Right! Jump left!' They did so as Sir Rodney's first swipe took off Gawgy's right ear.

Megan Ferdy, well placed in the front row, fumbled desperately for the remote control as the knight closed for the kill.

Guley could see himself being cornered in the wings. He had to keep central. 'Reverse!' he cried.

Angie Bevins finally achieved what her director had striven to conjure for weeks – an earsplitting scream – and the audience froze. These were high-level special effects. The music stuttered again as Sir Rodney lunged at Gawgy, and Megan flicked the switch onto maximum power.

The Hammer flew from the knight's hand in a shower of sparks, and Rodney swore as saw-teeth, still spinning, gouged the stage.

Then Gawgy's electrics fused, smoke and sparks engulfing the inside of the costume.

'That's enough, Rodders,' stammered Collier, but Rodney ignored him. He retrieved the Hammer and closed for the kill, fending off Finch with a scything swing. Gwen and Guley, twisting and turning to locate their adversary, tripped over each other, and Gawgy fell in a cat's cradle of sparking wires and the ribbons of a shredded costume.

Nobody moved. This fight was too primal for intervention.

Oblong, gaping in horror at the wreckage of his masterpiece, sensed an alien presence behind him before he heard it – the threshing of leaves in a gale, and a dragging sound, as if a giant broom were sweeping the boards. Past the make-up tent came an apparition: a walking tree, or almost a tree, with boughs where arms would be, a division in the lower trunk for legs, and a ball of dense foliage for a crown. The whole was wreathed in flowers.

Oblong moved to intercept it when he remembered Ferensen's note – '*expect surprises in the theatre, allow all entrances and exits.*' He checked and drew the curtain back to allow the treeman to pass.

The effect was electric. Even Rodney Slickstone stopped and gawped. His finger slid off the power switch and the Hammer went silent. Only Marmion Finch made a positive move: he opened his right arm in a gesture of reverence.

The fragrance of blossom settled on the audience, soothing and rich. Then came a hum, the hum of bees, suddenly everywhere, moving from the flowers of the Rotherweird eglantine in the shadier patches of the Inner Circle to the tree and back.

Megan Ferdy had watched the Green Man pass in astonishment. She had warned her husband of the need for perfect timing. She left her seat and ran to the tent, its sign now up.

Salt in his new extrasensory world could neither hear nor see the bees, but he felt a profound sense of fulfilment as pollen was exchanged between the blossom he carried and the flowers of the Rotherweird eglantine, a millennial marriage recorded in the church tower fresco.

Rodney recovered his bearings. This ridiculous creature with its effeminate flowers and twisted human shape must be the god of the countrysiders. He must bring it down. He did not bother to restart the Hammer. He lifted the weapon and plunged it into the trunk.

Rodney Slickstone had stabbed his share of innocents and had never been worsted, but he felt a flicker of foreboding as the Green Man staggered back, sap bleeding from the wound. A spasm shook the tree. The Hammer, wrenched from his hand, fell to the stage, twisted and useless. Pain knifed through Salt, spiritual as well as physical.

Rodney Slickstone turned to bellow his triumph to the audience: the monster vanquished, countrysiders cringing, their god slinking off in defeat.

But no words came – bees flew into his mouth and nostrils; they did not sting, because they had no need. Air was denied him. His cheeks turned blue, as he tried desperately to cough and spit out his attackers, but they adhered like glue.

Within minutes the bees departed, back to their ordered lives, leaving a body entirely without blemish.

The Green Man had already departed, its gait fast and urgent. A doctor clambered onstage, checked the boy's pulse and shook his head gravely. The audience came to life, most reinterpreting events by stereotype: the tree man as the monster had surely attacked the boy, who had responded in self-defence. The bees had been largely missed, so sudden and violent had been the action. Men and women hurried down from their seats; one grabbed the twisted shaft of the Hammer and others brandished chairs.

'Now!' cried Megan Ferdy, peering from the opened flap of the tent, and they rushed out, clasping an open barrel of the sacred Hammer. The unique aroma of the Hammer mixed with the lingering scent of the Green Man's blossom – all the allure of lotus, ambrosia and forbidden fruit. Gwen and Guley followed behind, carrying trays laden with tiny thimbles of the same brew. Ferdy allowed himself a minute of wonder as he watched the Green Man head for the river.

Snorkel looked at the chaotic scene, appalled – one dead juvenile and a grotesque production, directed by an outsider, where the monster appeared to have won.

Ferdy needed no call for calm, for the aroma was beginning to work its magic. The stage cleared for him. '*The Journeyman's Gist* is open backstage. A little for everyone, and children too – first come, first served.'

'A tot for the tots,' added the Herald, 'and they'll sleep like angels.'

He and Oblong, immune to the Hammer's siren charms thanks to prior exposure, assisted in its distribution.

Snorkel's political nostrils processed the scent. He seized the megaphone as his own resistance faded, just managing to declare, 'Drinks courtesy of the Town Hall!' before joining the surge backstage.

A mouthful sufficed. What the aroma had loosened, the taste swept away – the play, the death of Rodney Slickstone and the entry of the Green Man. Weapons were downed as present anger ebbed away and older wounds eased. Disappointments, bereavements, unrequited love and deepset grudges lost their cutting edges.

The townsfolk, men, women and children, lolled on the grass or swayed like sailors at sea, hammered in their midsummer reverie. High in the auditorium Oblong glimpsed Aggs and Fanguin, together, alone, and oddly immune.

Some two hours later the undertaker broke the good news to the Mayor. 'It appears young Slickstone passed away before or during his performance,' said Mors Valett.

'What performance?'

'He was dressed as a knight. Nerves, I imagine. As for Lady

Slickstone and Sir Veronal, there's no sign of them, and the car has gone.'

Snorkel added his own epitaph on the dead boy. 'Not a death to investigate.'

'Accidental, and a quick burial in all this heat,' Valett agreed.

The Hammer had done its work. Barrels of Sturdy now took over as the pennant of *The Journeyman's Gist* fluttered in the late afternoon breeze.

The Green Man felt the stream about its roots, chill and sustaining, and then the meadow grass beyond. Salt registered the presence of other trees, ancient trees, and then a different presence, eerie and familiar. In the clearing by the white tile the Green Man stopped. The final transformation was quick. The seedpods of the midsummer flower, already mature, burst, and the mixing-point disengaged. Sub-atomic particles rose to the gate in the sky in a seething ball of high energy. The fissure through which the bubbles had passed admitted them and closed.

Salt first examined his hands – skin, cuticles, nails, just as they had been. His clothes and shoes were untouched. An ugly bruise ran down his left shoulder, but Rodney Slickstone's hammer had done no greater damage. A few dead leaves, unique in shape and out of season, were already scattering across the clearing. Nothing else remained of the midsummer flower.

Salt resisted with ease any temptation to test the white tile. He was done with Lost Acre; now more primal urges were at work – hunger and thirst in particular.

Staggering back to the Fair, a familiar voice called from behind. 'I do believe you did it,' said Orelia.

'Nature did,' he replied, before realising she must have returned through the white tile, and that Lost Acre was saved.

'Want to know about Sir Veronal?'

'Not quite yet.'

The pair headed back to the Fair.

At dusk they told their respective stories. The Polks took the fate of their bubbles philosophically. Salt and Orelia held back details, but described the mission as accomplished, thanks in no small part to their transport. Sir Veronal had met a deserved end, they added, playing once too often with the mixing-point. They consumed what remained of the Polks' substantial picnic.

The mood only darkened with a casual question from Bert. 'Any sign of Ferensen? He said he was going in – and didn't expect to be back.'

'Don't worry,' replied Boris, 'Ferensens always come back.'

Ferensen stood in the middle of the mere, its waters frozen and sealed in white. For some time he had known he had a pursuer; only here was he free from cover. On the fringe of the ice he could see movement; too late did he realise that it was Morval's spider, weaving a web to fence him in. The sky was riven with cracks, apparently about to fall in. He raced to the margin, but the high-tensile threads were everywhere. *Better to fight in the open,* he decided.

He did not have to wait long. The creature burst from the trees and made straight for him. Ferensen held his ground and levelled his makeshift spear. The spider circled, spitting, looking for weakness. A line of thread, the material viscous, snagged the blade. The more Ferensen shook the weapon, the more restricted its movement became. The spider began to reel him in until Ferensen had no choice but to relinquish it. Another thread looped round his knee, and he stumbled and fell.

As he did so, the sky transformed and lost all its lines of fracture, turning uniform and intensely blue. A rush of warm air passed over like a blessing, and in a fleeting moment Ferensen glimpsed a single star above the horizon, omen for a new dawn, perhaps. A roll of thunder roared out, flowed by a high-pitched sing-song note, and a series of loud reports. The ice cracked into a grey-white jigsaw as the snow quickly melted away.

There was no time to dwell on Lost Acre's salvation: Ferensen found himself marooned on a large piece of ice with the spider, whose heavier weight tilted the floe, causing water to lap over the edge. The rejuvenated sun beat down. Ferensen, without protection from the warmth, felt horribly exposed.

The spider, now bent on survival, cast threads to adjacent islands in search of stability, but its weight was too great and the ice too slippery without the snow for traction. As the spider skidded into the water, it threw a last line round Ferensen's ankles, dragging him down too.

So dark, so cold, so tired – Ferensen flailed in the water, but his movement felt controlled. He wriggled free from the spider's line as its bulbous body fell lifeless into the deeps below – but miraculously he was not gasping for air. He swam, feeling the water along the sides of his body, the temperature rising and falling according to depth. He slid through fronds and over boulders. The darkness lightened as the ice melted and sunlight broke through. The water was not stagnant but gently on the move over the gravelly bottom.

Half-memories fought for recognition, prompted by this rearrangement of his being. Fleetingly, he found himself looking up through a floating garden to a vast sky, turning through the water by the twist and turn of his body – a fragment of half of his long-forgotten past. Then the other, human, half took over and he saw himself suspended in a cage with a transparent jug beside him containing a snake-like creature, wriggling, shiny and black as liquorice – and then he recalled the agony of the conjoining. The Eleusians carried him through Lost Acre, still ostensibly human, in a net, crying all the while, '*What shall we do with slippery Seer?*'

Of his sister, he could see no sign. They had hurled him in the mere, and as he began to gasp and splutter, so he changed. They had made him an eelman.

He remembered too what lived in the mere: tiny fish like rainbows with razor-teeth. The Eleusians had thrown hooks at him, drawing blood, summoning his would-be killers. Now explanations exploded in his brain – his gift for the weather, his discomfort in heat – and a memory from his other being: a floating garden, the great Sargasso sea.

Then down the lateral line of his ribs came a very present warning: movement that was not his own, all round him, above and below and beside. He had escaped death here before, but how? He frantically ransacked his confused brain for answers as the first searing pain struck his side.

He accelerated around the perimeter of the pond, diving through rocks and weed, but the pursuing shoal was remorseless. Then he remembered a tunnel in the bed of the mere. Trusting to recollection, he dived deep and found the entrance, but his pursuers came with him, savaging him as he took turnings by instinct – right, left, left, straight on. Still he kept going, hunted on land, hunted in water.

What shall we do with slippery Seer?

His determination to cheat his tormentors saved him now, as it had saved him then. At the dead end of the last tunnel, he caught the square of colour – orange-red, the same size and dimension as the black and the white tiles, and also incised with a flower. He plunged into it. They had not pursued him last time and they would not pursue him now, just as the spiderwoman had not pursued Valourhand and Gorhambury. Lost Acre's residents knew their place.

He emerged in a brick tunnel where the Rother first surfaced to the north of the town, close to the start of the Great Equinox Race. He crawled out, covered in mud, bleeding and exhausted, but still himself – just as he had done centuries earlier. He set off home, almost naked, but joyous to feel the dry earth crumble beneath his toes.

*

At sunset on the longest day of the year, great fires were lit on the Island Field to roast carcases pinned on iron spits.

The Journeyman's Gist in its temporary guise of a beer-tent dispensed lavish quantities of Sturdy, replenishing the Ferdy finances and winning new admirers. Snorkel made a speech, rather later than he had planned, although he could not explain quite how the delay had occurred. Such an unparallelled sense of wellbeing could not pass without the Town Hall claiming the lion's share of the credit. For the Ferdys the hyperbole mattered little beside the revival of their fortunes and maintaining the secret of the Hammer.

All agreed it had been a most remarkable Midsummer Fair.

Only Orelia harboured the uncomfortable suspicion that something was horribly wrong.

Old History

It is execution day.

Sir Robert Oxenbridge leads with Hubert Finch; Wynter, ever in search of supernatural connection, follows carrying his cage like Christ did His cross; then come the male Eleusians, young men now, with another cage configured for their special punishment; and flanking them armed guards, as prepared for attack from without as within in this strange and dangerous place. Of Ferox, there is no sign. From Oxenbridge's belt hangs a velvet pouch – the stones, the instrument of execution.

They trudge through the grass in silence.

Slickstone cannot come to terms with the prospect of *tabula rasa*, all that he is about to lose – his command of language, his experience, knowledge and memory, taken back to a drivelling child. Do these fools not understand the difference between deleting the minds of urchins in the cause of progress and deleting those of the chosen few? Laws and ethics were not designed for such extremes.

Beside him a middle-aged man, his manner and dress suggestive of rank, carries a pulley across his shoulder. Affecting bravado, Slickstone asks, 'And what do you do in this company?'

'I design.' The man delivers a judgmental glare: *but not your devilish designing*, it says.

'Weapons? Games? Fishing nets?'

'Houses – I build houses with style and ornament. A town will rise from this wreckage.'

'You have a name?'

'You won't remember it, now, will you?'

'It's a compliment, Master Builder; your name will be the last new fact to lodge before oblivion.'

The man hesitates – might not these fiends reach beyond the grave, or even *tabula rasa*? Then he remembered their victims – the appalling mismatches of human and animal the soldiers had had to put out of their misery. Wynter's sect has instilled enough fear in the innocent. He would not be cowed. 'Banter,' he says, 'Peregrine Banter.'

At that moment the tree comes into view. Slickstone recalls the work it had witnessed, such fine work, to be rendered futile by these over-orderly imbeciles.

Nemesis.

Sir Robert Oxenbridge has seen his share of executions, such is the nature of religious wars and town sieges. A fair and moderate man, he ordered them himself only when clemency had no credibility, when survival represented the greater threat, and when the rule of law prescribed it.

He has seen fanatics on the scaffold and heard their defiant speeches, but he has never heard a performance – for that was the word – quite like this.

Leaders go first. That is the golden rule, both in terms of deterrence and chivalry.

Wynter says nothing during the progress from the town to the white tile to the mixing-point, neither to his gaolers nor to his followers tramping behind to their own terrible fate. He has insisted on carrying his own cage, subservient almost. He does not resist. Indeed, he walks in.

Only as the boom begins to move does Wynter speak. He projects his voice with immense power, but as a statement, not a shout or a scream. 'You know not what you do,' he says – six words bearing a multitude of interpretations, a last mad declaration by a deluded genius, a plea for his own dark brand of science and experiment – or, and this seems more in accord with the confidence of his facial expression, a claim to resurrection.

About that, at least, Oxenbridge has no concerns. Bodies with life and bodies without – whatever is lost between the two does not return to the earthly sphere, and nobody can resurrect from nothing, surely.

The cage swings in with Wynter and swings back without him. Oxenbridge briefly wonders where his constituent parts have gone. The slippery patch of sky glimmers, ruthless and impervious to human command. *Do as you would be done by*. He raises his hand. The cage is changed and the remaining men are brought forward, Veronal Slickstone first.

January 30, 1592. Rotherweird Town.

Snow has fallen in the night, twenty years to the day from Wynter's execution.

Hubert Finch, first Herald of Rotherweird, has reason to rest on his laurels. Walls surround the island and the Manor. A second bridge has been built. A score of houses, each unique in its way, have been erected, all designed and built to last by the energetic Mr Banter. True to his word, Oxenbridge left behind his craftsmen and his soldiers.

The resulting security and quality of building attract wives from villages outside the valley. Finch's rule is respected, as is the law against the study of the past – a suitable price for the promise of a prosperous future. In the hills above Rotherweird a brewer adds hops to his ale, making the finest of beers.

Additional comfort comes with a report from London about the fate of the men sentenced with Wynter and abandoned by Drake in foetid swampland in the Indies. Six of the seven have been found dead. The last is missing, presumed dead.

On this particular morning Finch has a visitor – one of Mr Banter's assistants, Benedict Roc, the sullen but brilliant master carver who has given the interior its unique character – and added a few hidden extras of his own design.

'Master Finch, I am to check the *archivoire*.'

This strange name has been given to the great room in Escutcheon Place that houses what remains of Rotherweird's old history. An archive can be consulted; the *archivoire* cannot, save by the Herald and his descendants, and even they are constrained, as the master craftsman is about to remind him.

'To check what exactly?'

'Her mechanisms.'

'Mechanisms?'

'Her hidey-holes – it is in my orders to confirm their working order, just this once.'

That makes sense. Escutcheon Place holds the trial records and artefacts connected with Wynter's practices in secret compartments; even Finch does not know where these repositories are, nor of what these artefacts consist. Oxenbridge has left him a sealed envelope and a key, to be respectively opened and used in only the direst emergency.

He places a guard on the door and admits the craftsman while he himself checks a new weir south of the Island Field. On his return all looks well. The craftsman has done his work in an hour and left. The guard has seen nothing untoward. The *archivoire* appears as he left it.

Late that night his preparations for bed are interrupted by the watch calling out, 'Mr Finch, you best come quick.'

After a clear day the snow has hardened to the consistency of ground glass and the smaller streams in the Island Field are frozen to the colour of old bones. The master craftsman's body lies on the woodland edge beyond the island stream, shrouded in white, save for the face, where the snow has been scraped away. Blue lines round the neck suggest strangulation.

'The physician says he's been here a good two days,' says the first guard.

'Which is wrong, 'cos I saw him yesterday,' corrects the second.

'I saw him today,' adds Finch, 'but . . .' He pauses. It makes no sense. 'The physician is right: there are no footprints, and the body is covered in snow. There has been no snow since yesterday night.'

'He shook my hand. He were no ghost.'

Finch is puzzled. The craftsman liked only the contact of wood. He would not have shaken hands. He nodded, if you were lucky.

'He is unmarried, Mr Finch, although they say there's a woman and child in Hoy. We can bury him tomorrow.'

Finch decides to close the debate and the risk of rumour. 'He must have slipped on the ice. It happens.'

Back in Escutcheon Place Finch decides against reporting the incident to London for fear of compromising Rotherweird's independence.

A ghost, an anniversary and a murder – surely Wynter cannot reach from the grave, still less an empty one?

Finch neutrally records the incident in his formal record.

The craftsman's workmanship lives on. The dead man's apprentice takes over and excels. The town grows. The name on the craftsman's gravestone fades to disconnected lines.

JULY

I

Home Sweet Home

Valourhand had never before felt so settled. Her fierceness remained, but had been channelled into work – not *teaching* work but *learning* work; here in Lost Acre she had no pupils or timetables to distract her, and no Strimmer to disturb her equilibrium.

Nor had she ever felt house-proud before. The kitchen remained the kitchen, but the large oak table now doubled as a workbench. Here she placed her microscope with its supporting parts, a remarkable variant on the usual outsider contraptions – one of the South Tower's few useful inventions – and her notebooks. All these had been in her backpack when she went in several hours after Ferensen, prepared, if necessary, to fight with and for him. Instead she had found the spiderwoman's lair deserted. She secured the door and bolted the windows, having overlooked them on her first visit, when the shutters had been closed.

The footprints outside suggested that Ferensen had survived and set out into the snowy landscape outside. She reckoned that in such an alien place, she would be more of a handicap than a blessing, so she stayed put.

The wave of warmth at the moment of Lost Acre's salvation penetrated even the solid walls of the lair and she hoped it heralded Ferensen's victory, a hope that strengthened when the spiderwoman did not return and the black tile went dead.

She explored the lair with care, mapping the many passages as she went. The split nature of the spiderwoman manifested itself in disturbing ways: most of the rooms were dark and reeked of butchery, but in one she found a large store of tallow candles of many shapes and sizes – made from the fat of her victims, presumably. At the furthest point from the kitchen she encountered a single door with a complex set of mechanical locks, all numbered. The code turned on a sequence of primes, which once deciphered, revealed what could only be described as an artist's studio: an easel, palette knives, brushes, paints of several types and many colours. The implications she found deeply unsettling. When the bestial half slept, the woman must have dragged their shared body here to paint for as long as the spider's unconsciousness lasted.

Yet who could be the supplier? Who had devised and installed the locks? Indeed, who had brought the library books that had so offended Gorhambury? All the available evidence pointed away from Ferensen. The painting materials came from Alizarin & Flake, the shop in the Golden Mean, and the stock was fresh. A trapdoor at the edge of the room led down into a dark tunnel, which Valourhand had no intention of entering. Wheels within wheels – the company had only scratched the surface of the connections between Rotherweird and Lost Acre.

As soon as she opened the sketchbooks, she recognised the hand behind *The Dark Devices*. The spiderwoman had painted only the local fauna, in orderly sequences. The sketchbooks too were arranged in a particular order. The illustrations brought home to Valourhand the true oddity of Lost Acre: many creatures lived there, bred and evolved without any disruption from the mixing-point – and every now and then something dramatic and new would emerge. Wynter's interfering activities must have distorted the balance.

Valourhand could not draw, but she could measure, observe through her microscope, record and examine. Although at times she yearned for Salt's botanical insights and Fanguin's grasp of biology, she was determined to see how far she could go with her own native wit.

She imposed on herself several rules: she kept away from the mixing-point, to avoid temptation. She did not kill or trap; she studied only the dead – the forest floor and the webs near the lair's front door yielded many carcases that could be matched to one or more of the paintings. Nor did she venture far, keeping within sprinting distance of the front door. She noticed that dawn and dusk were the most dangerous times, and that most creatures afforded her a degree of respect, presumably under the misapprehension that she had ousted the spiderwoman.

She found mushrooms and fruit, and even braved the more palatable-looking dried meat that the spiderwoman had so assiduously stored.

The study gradually softened her misanthropy. She began to respect, even revere, her own species. She hung a few of the paintings on the kitchen walls. She slept beside the kitchen fire, scene of her ferocious fight with its previous owner.

Home, sweet home.

2

Answers and Questions

Old rituals reasserted themselves. The contents of the Manor were meticulously crated up by a brief influx of outsiders, carried over the bridge to a line of waiting lorries and returned to the administrators of Sir Veronal's estate in London. They faced a formidable task: Sir Veronal had died intestate, without wife or descendants. The 'Prohibited Quarter' signs reappeared, and with them the locks. An aberration in Rotherweird's history was shed like a dead skin.

The Journeyman's Gist re-opened with little discernible change. The mysterious death of Rodney Slickstone and the withdrawal of his parents restored tolerance of countrysiders. Collier even sat next to Gwen Ferdy, his mathematics marks improving dramatically in consequence.

Snorkel assisted this return to the old dispensation. The troubling looseness of recent events had coincided with Gorhambury's departure. He wrote a generous letter, by his standards:

I have decided to be magnanimous. You are restored to your duties. Report 7 a.m. sharp on Monday. Lodgings are available in Silent Lane, deductible from salary. Otherwise terms as before . . .

He received a response he judged ungenerous:

Rent is not agreed as deductible, being in lieu of long-overdue pay rise. In
future, holidays will be taken. I am pleased to report Monday if these terms
are acceptable.

Within hours of Gorhambury's return, Snorkel realised what he
had missed, while catching a new note in the town clerk's voice.
Galvanised by the fruits of his Grand Survey of Rotherweird's exterior fittings, Gorhambury found a new lease of life. The in-trays of
the *Sewers and Drainage Committee* overflowed with project proposals.

Between the Inner Circle and the Rother, Salt discovered tiny
seeds in the process of germination. He lifted some and protected
others. For the first time in living memory the Rotherweird eglantine had fruited. He gathered the few surviving berries and froze
them as an insurance against the future.

Only Strimmer felt dejected and defeated. He had lost his precious book, not to mention the promise of real power.

News of Ferensen's return broke via Panjan. Some days later
Orelia received from Ferensen through Boris Polk a grocery list, and
a confidential order for *Proliferate*, the copiers in Old Ley Lane. She
sent back via Ferdy's beer-cart jars of black olives, anchovies, snails
and marrow-bones, as well as several long tubes from the copiers.

Shortly thereafter, invitations in Ferensen's fine hand arrived for
the company to dine at his tower, 7 for 7.30 p.m. The list featured
two additions to those present at the Escutcheon Place meeting:
Aggs and Fanguin, and Ferensen stipulated that Oblong should ask
Fanguin, and Fanguin should ask Aggs.

Happily, Bomber was out when Oblong called. Fanguin appeared
to suspect confidential business, ushering Oblong into his upstairs
study. He offered Oblong elderflower cordial. Oblong placed the
card in front of Fanguin.

'What's this?'

'An invitation to a rural celebration dinner.'

'From whom?'

'A friend of Bill Ferdy's.'

'Why ask me?'

'I understand Flask's notebook helped.' In truth Oblong did not know the reason.

'You mean it did help.'

Oblong nodded. He felt uncomfortable, for reasons he could not articulate.

Enlightenment came from Fanguin seconds later. 'Why not tell me earlier? Who's the skipper, Oblong? Who brought you fame in a coracle? Who came to your tower when you knew nobody? Who had you to dinner? Who gave you the notebook?'

Oblong had the unsettling sensation that Ferensen was teaching him a lesson about friendship. At *The Journeyman's Gist Underground* he had not defended Fanguin when Salt had attacked him.

He had no good answer. 'Well, we're making up for it now.'

'Who's we?'

'You'll find out when we get there. But it's a big vote of confidence, believe me.'

'Rule One: the crew never patronise the skipper.'

'Sorry. But you will have to be discreet, Fanguin.'

The biologist shed his gruffness and smiled. 'I can imagine.'

Oblong belatedly grasped the oddity of the conversation. Fanguin had played with him, rather than ask the obvious questions.

'Guess what Aggs and I wore at the Midsummer Fair?' he continued. Oblong had a snapshot recall of the two of them, swaying together high in the auditorium. Fanguin opened a drawer in his desk and pulled out triple handcuffs. 'Boris provided them. Can you imagine the torment? I'd never smelled such a brew. But I'd also never seen such a feat of Nature. To lose the memory of the Green Man—! Bomber got smashed and can't remember a thing, but yours truly ... Of course I shall come. I look forward to the education. Who knows – poor, sodden Fanguin might even contribute to unravelling this mystery?'

What mystery? thought Oblong as he walked slowly home, a mildly chastened man.

Gorhambury accepted his invitation, but a formal postscript stressed his duties to the Town Hall. 'The leopard reacquiring his spots,' was how Bill Ferdy described it.

Aggs accepted too.

Bert Polk declined, for family reasons.

Only Valourhand did not reply, so confirming what Ferensen had already suspected. Oblong reported that for the last two weeks of term her classes were being taken by a stand-in, at her request. Rhombus Smith had received a note in his pigeonhole on Midsummer Day, which made it clear that she would be back the following term.

On the day of the party the weather broke, showers sweeping in from the west, much to the relief of farmers and window-boxes. In consequence, the tarpaulin covering Ferensen's guests in the rear of Ferdy's beer-cart did not appear incongruous, although those beneath it certainly did.

Fanguin wore white trousers, a blue waistcoat and a straw boater, more gondolier than terrestrial diner, while Aggs, describing her party best as 'bequests and hand-me-downs', had the air of a fortune-teller. Gorhambury dressed for a municipal function. Oblong wore a herringbone tweed suit, which Orelia thought surprisingly dashing and well-suited to his gangly frame. She wore a flared black skirt, inlaid with circles of glass, and a white shirt, with what Oblong took to be curtain rings hanging from her ears, her raven hair held back by a single ribbon. She and Aggs might have been in competition for any clairvoyant business. Salt wore a green tweed jacket, as befitted the Green Man, and (for him) an unusually clean pair of trousers. Jones achieved a bizarre mix of tracksuit bottoms, running shirt and a Rotherweird School athletics blazer. Boris was always Boris, and above, Bill Ferdy was his usual self, so as not to attract attention.

Close to the Ferdy farm, the weather eased into sunshine and the tarpaulins were flung back. The company, hitherto subdued by darkness, revived.

Aggs commenced the thaw. 'Give us the flowers, Mr Salt,' she said, 'I do so love them names.'

Salt did so, leaning precariously out of the beer-cart and pointing, 'Lousewort, cranesbill, greater celandine, burdock, self-heal, sneeze-wort, purple loosestrife . . .' No Latin.

Bill Ferdy led them down past his house to Ferensen's tower. Ferensen appeared in the doorway, arms open in greeting. He wore Elizabethan costume from ruff to velvet buckled shoes – they would have laughed, but somehow his dress fitted the occasion. Orelia knew instantly that they were his, made to fit, and of the period.

They handed over modest presents, except Fanguin, who held back his box, declining all enquiries. Nobody asked about the healing scars on Ferensen's face and hands.

After a round of handshakes and lengthier introductions to Fanguin and Aggs, Ferensen walked his guests to his woodland maze. Bridges swivelled as they passed. Fountains appeared in one place, only to reappear somewhere else. Gates locked and unlocked in complex sequences.

Like Ferensen's mind, thought Orelia, *industrious but tricksy, with a sense of the beautiful too*. She decided that he must have a problem to solve. He was warming them up. As they walked, she outlined to Fanguin what they had learned at Escutcheon Place.

His reaction was unusually thoughtful. 'There had to be something,' he responded. 'There had to be something remarkable.'

Orelia was the first to the narrow arched entrance at the maze's heart. Beyond, seated on a wooden chair, she found the guest they had overlooked: Marmion Finch, who had combined his costume from the Midsummer Fair play with his attire on the night of the fire. He looked like a bandit leader close to retirement.

'Winner's crown,' said the Herald, placing on Orelia's head a garland of laurel, before asking how Sir Veronal had died. She told him; Finch had a seductive manner, when it suited him.

'All connects,' he said.

Reading his face, she did not think he knew how.

Ferensen had harvested freshwater crayfish from the Rother, which he served with anchovies, olives and snails, garnished with garlic, in halved marrow-bones. Other Elizabethan recipes adorned the table, wine too. The plates were wooden or pewter, the pepper mills as old: period flavours for a period table.

Ferensen's tables had interlocked into one, the wheeled book-shelves pushed to the perimeter. Around them trailed a sequence of large blown-up prints of the tapestry's various scenes, taken from Orelia's photographs. It had the uncomfortable look of a record of real events as proscribed by the *History Regulations*. Gorhambury muttered, but no more.

After dinner Ferensen asked everyone to charge their glasses. 'To the redemption of Lost Acre, and to justice done – I give you Hayman Salt and Orelia Roc.'

The botanist modestly waved away the applause.

'I did nothing. I just lay on the ground and watched,' added Orelia.

'The truth needs witnesses,' said Ferensen gently, before raising his voice for an announcement. 'And now for our party game!'

Buoyed by the toasts, Boris, Fanguin (who considered the event a justified exception to his elderflower regime) and Gregorius Jones became boisterous.

'Blind man's buff.'

'Pass the port.'

'Can Boris walk a straight line?'

Ferensen paused for effect. 'It's called: *Who is Robert Flask*? Team game – we pool our knowledge to find the answer.'

'How do we know if we've won?' asked Gregorius Jones.

'It's like my maze: you'll know if you get there.'

'Do *you* know – as in your maze?' asked Fanguin, already intrigued by this mysterious countrysider, whose possessions suggested a polymath with a close interest in all aspects of the natural world.

'No,' replied Ferensen, 'Mr Finch will direct the traffic. Unlike some, I'm sharper when I'm not talking.'

Finch did not stand up. 'Fellow rummagers in history,' he said, 'take a leaf from the schoolmaster's book. Raise a hand to speak, unless I choose you. We do not want a murmuration of starlings. Facts, first; questions, second; informed guesswork, hypotheses and theories, third. No larking about.' He gave Polk, Fanguin and Jones the Finch death-stare. 'This may be serious business.'

Finch paused. He had achieved the silence of an obedient class. He pointed at Boris. 'Tell us about Flask's arrival in Rotherweird.'

'I picked him up at the Twelve-Mile Post with one big suitcase. I saw nothing odd apart from his appearance. He was not inquisitive . . . *then*.'

'Tell us about Flask settling in?' He pointed at Aggs.

'Ever so tidy – not like 'im or 'im.' She wagged a finger at Fanguin and Oblong. 'He always kept his suitcase locked, did Mr Flask.'

Oblong remembered her unconvincing lie at their first meeting. 'Hold it, Aggs, you told me you knew nothing about him.'

'Well . . .' Aggs went red and then white, eyes flashing, ''e bunked off without so much as a "by your leave". I looked after him proper, I did, and 'e goes to Box Street. That's a rat-run, that is. He disowned Aggs; *I* disown *'im*.'

Finch pointed at Fanguin. 'What about Flask in the pub, tongue loosened by Sturdy? Facts, please, facts.'

'Yes, well, we all like a pint now and again,' replied Fanguin defensively. 'Flask did for sure. He became increasingly curious, for ever asking about the prohibited quarter and the Manor.'

'And you, of course, with several pints of Sturdy in the locker,' said nothing,' intervened Boris with a smile.

'Silence!' boomed Finch. 'I saw no hand, Mr Polk.'

Boris blushed like a naughty schoolboy.

Finch turned to Orelia. 'Did Flask visit *Baubles & Relics*?'

'He dropped in occasionally, but never bought. He hunted books. Anything old, anything under the counter – he said to tell him.'

Ferensen intervened. 'We know from Miss Valourhand that he made a point of befriending the North Tower, especially Strimmer.'

Oblong could not resist asking after his chief tormentor. 'Why isn't she here?'

'I've reason to believe she's engaged in scientific fieldwork,' replied Ferensen, 'but she has given me an item of puzzling information, to which we will come to in due course.'

'To resume,' chivvied Finch, and Ferensen did so. 'Flask told Strimmer and Valourhand that a rich outsider called Slickstone would come to the Manor – and that this was an insult to its last owner, a great scientist and the father of Rotherweird.'

'Did he name this "great scientist"?'

'I think Valourhand would have told us if he had. What Flask did do was encourage her to protest at the party.'

Finch turned back to Aggs. 'What of Mr Flask's notebook?'

''e ripped most of it out before 'e went to Box Street.' Aggs controlled herself. ''e left his drawers, spotless save for that book. Wanted me to find it, didn't 'e. So I kept it. Then when he does 'is vanishing act, I gives it to Mr Fanguin.'

'Question to the floor of the house,' said Finch grandly. 'We know the book contained an anagram for Lost Acre and the year of the *Chronicle* entry about the midsummer flower. Anyone here tell him about Lost Acre?'

'Who knew to tell him?' pointed out Boris, again forgetting to put his hand up.

This time Finch let the indiscretion pass. The three who knew – Finch, Salt and Ferensen – all shook their heads.

Oblong raised his hand. 'I contacted Dr Pendle at the British Museum about the *Chronicle*. Pendle said a colleague of mine had already been in touch – surely Flask.'

'But that doesn't answer the question,' Fanguin pointed out. 'How did he know to ask Pendle?'

Oblong suggested an answer. 'He stumbled on the frescoes in the Church Tower. They bear the year 1017 in Roman numerals. They have a Saxon scene and some fairly strange images, which make more sense now than they did.' Then he remembered. 'No, sorry, I'm wrong, Flask didn't go there. I was the first. The dust was ankle-deep.'

Fanguin raised a hand. 'How did Flask know Sir Veronal was coming before Sir Veronal arrived?'

Gorhambury stood up and took a sheet of paper from his pocket. 'A man masquerading as "Paul Marl" suggested to the Mayor that he invite Sir Veronal to restore the Manor. This is his letter. Maybe he told Flask?'

Gorhambury received some mildly approving looks. There had to be a regulation against showing private mayoral communications to countrysiders. The Town Clerk's recent experiences appeared to have widened his view of the public interest.

Gorhambury read out the opening paragraph: '*Your esteemed service merits reward. Rotherweird's singular status is born of a singular secret. There is an ancient treasure, hidden behind an equally ancient hidden gate. The gate will not reveal itself unless the Manor is restored and occupied by the Slickstone family, whose sole survivor is Sir Veronal Slickstone. He is rich beyond avarice and will respond to a well-judged invitation, but on no account reveal to him the existence of treasure. He will lead you there in time. Be sure to emphasise the privilege of being invited in as an "outsider" . . .*'

Gregorius Jones had been lost for some time, but this was the final straw.

'I'm no doubt being dim—'

'*Pas possible,*' chirruped Boris.

Unabashed, Jones continued, 'We talked about Paul Marl at Finch's place. He doesn't exist.'

'New game,' suggested Boris, 'who is Paul Marl?'

Something stirred in Fanguin's brain – an association, a connection, a crossword clue, anagrams, Latin, Flask's weasel . . . 'Wait!' he shouted. '*Wait!*'

He drummed the table for a moment, rallying his facts, before crying, 'Eureka! The Latin for flask is *ampulla*. Add "R" for Robert and you get *R Ampulla*. Jumble the letters and you get Paul Marl. Like "Lost Acre" and "Stole Car". Ergo: Paul Marl is Robert Flask, and Robert Flask is Paul Marl.'

Ferensen's lanterns and candles were taking over from failing natural light. The faces of the company were part lit, part in shadow – Rembrandt faces, *chiaroscuro*. Animation seemed to come to the tapestried landscape – the sails of a windmill turning, sickles sweeping, heads turning and conversing. The gold letters on the spines of Ferensen's books flickered. The past had come to dine.

Oblong added a disturbing detail. 'It was Flask who suggested to the Headmaster that we re-enact the legend of the midsummer flower at the Fair – another anonymous letter, but the same writing as the notebook.'

Finch reeled in the debate with a sober summary. 'So: a person calling himself variously Paul Marl or Robert Flask comes to Rotherweird. He appears to be well versed in our history already. He persuades the Mayor to invite Slickstone to do up the Manor. He provokes a North Tower protest, then vanishes before Slickstone's arrival. He launches the idea of re-enacting the midsummer legend. For good measure he leaves behind a page of a notebook to put others on the trail of Lost Acre.'

Gregorius Jones then displayed his curious gift for developing an argument by stating the blindingly obvious. 'That means he must already know about Sir Veronal's past,' said the athlete.

'But he's not from Rotherweird,' objected Boris.

Orelia corrected him. 'Not from Rotherweird's *present*. The mixing-point confers great longevity, remember.'

'I thought of that,' said Ferensen. 'Courtesy of Mr Fanguin, I have a photograph of Flask from the School magazine. He's nobody I know – or knew. And I knew them all ... I think.' Ferensen was no longer guarding his secret; he knew they knew. 'We need a new angle. Miss Roc – tell them about Sir Veronal's end.'

She told the story – how Ferox the weaselman had taken charge, the confrontation at the mixing-point, the horror in the cage, and the relish with which Ferox had greeted Slickstone's fate – Slickstone, his oldest and closest friend.

'I met Ferox,' said Salt. 'His priority was saving Lost Acre. He knew it faced extinction.' He spoke calmly, his old rage apparently burnt out.

Ferensen took over. 'In the old days Ferox was Slickstone's guide and guard in Lost Acre. He had been there centuries before us. He spoke only Latin until Slickstone taught him English. In Lost Acre they were inseparable.'

'He spoke Latin and English to me,' added Salt.

'Arms and the Man,' commented Finch enigmatically, but everyone understood: Slickstone's choice of a weasel emblem had subliminally come from his time spent in Lost Acre with Ferox, two predators together.

The next contribution transformed the debate. For some time Fanguin had been unusually quiet. Now he stood up and placed his box on the table. 'Talking of weaselmen, what on earth is this?'

He lifted out the skull and rotated it. The snout was narrow and mean, the cranium large and rounded, the teeth pointed and sharp, demonstrably a weaselman.

In Orelia's mind's eye the bony shell acquired fur, the sockets eyes and the sides of the temples ears.

'It's him – I promise it's him,' she said.

'Can't be,' replied Fanguin. 'I found it long before Midsummer Day.'

'Where?' asked Ferensen.

'In the ruined garden of a ruined house.'

'Where?' asked Ferensen again.

Fanguin recalled the schizophrenic tree with contrasting leaves and the ruined property down the dead-end track near Hirstoak. Then the revelation struck. 'There,' he said, pointing.

They all turned to the opening scene of the tapestry: the fatal meeting between Wynter and Grassal, where it all began, superficially innocent, but lethal in context.

'The house is ruined now, the garden overgrown, but the layout is exactly the same. There are "Keep Out" signs everywhere. Flask went there by bicycle. I found the skull in his tent.'

'How did you know it was Flask's tent?' asked Ferensen, a look of intense concentration on his face, as if they were close to the truth.

'There was a crossword – Flask did crosswords for the *Chronicle*. This was a draft, with all the squares, black and white, but only one clue – without the answer. Flask's work in progress.'

'And the clue?' asked Ferensen. 'We already have "Stole Car" and "Paul Marl" – this man delights in scattering clues.'

Fanguin had not forgotten. 'Yet another anagram – a double anagram, in fact. "*Troupes with bad posture*" – seven letters. "*Troupes*" with an "ou", not a double "o".'

Finch's eyes lit up. 'Flasky boy, you're playing us like puppets.'

'I don't get the clue,' mumbled Gregorius Jones, who was looking strangely distracted, reaching over to touch the weaselman's skull.

Oblong obliged. '*Posture* and *troupes* have the same letters. Just like *Lost Acre* and *Stole Car*. The word "bad" before posture is a hint that you need to mix the letters.'

Those present felt faintly sorry for Gregorius Jones, but yet again the athlete had unwittingly opened the way to a deeper truth.

Fanguin followed up. 'Jones has a point – which is the answer? *Troupes* or *posture*? And why should it be either as they're both in the clue?'

'Out of the mouths of babes,' muttered Finch.

Silence. Around Oblong's head spun Flask's notebook, the

weasel's head, the name Paul Marl and much else besides. His brain juddered into life. '*Proteus!*' he cried. 'The answer is *Proteus*. It has the same letters as "troupes" and "posture".'

'And *who* is Proteus?' gabbled Gregorius Jones.

'The god who can forever change shape,' said Finch.

The company took stock as a hideous thought occurred to Ferensen. Sir Veronal had died, forever changing shape. The further they progressed into the clues Flask had left, the darker the puzzle became, and darker still when Fanguin reinforced Oblong's solution.

'That's how he signed his crosswords – Shapeshifter.'

'If you ask me, which I know you ain't,' said Aggs, 'you gotta work out why he beetled off to that rat-hole in Box Street.'

Ferensen sensed another personality behind the devilry. He disclosed the information Valourhand had shared with him by the black tile beneath the library, just as he was about to leave to face his old enemy in Lost Acre.

'There was a charred page from *The Roman Recipe Book* in the grate at Box Street.' They all stared at Ferensen in disbelief. 'Valourhand found it.' Ferensen took the charred fragment from a drawer and placed it on the table. 'We can see on the margin of the page the figure of a jester – nothing monstrous about him. Strimmer told Valourhand that the last page of the *Recipe Book* had ordinary figures in the margin, men and women. So is *this* Wynter's last experiment?'

Orelia felt humbled. Fanguin, Valourhand through the agency of Ferensen, Finch, Aggs, even Jones had made telling interventions in the night's debate, but she had added nothing of note, despite living with old objects. *She* had studied the tapestry. *She* had sold Sir Veronal the stones. She had a feel for the educated Elizabethan mind – fiercely curious with swathes of virgin territory to explore in search of universal truths: the body, the soul, alchemy and the heavens. The focus had all been on Flask. They needed a new angle to progress.

Ordinary figures hardly fitted the reputed wickedness of Wynter's last experiment. Around her, discussion raged about their significance. They might be enemies of Wynter, doomed to die. They might be the subjects of the experiments, though she thought not. Wynter had had no dealings with soldiers, other than Oxenbridge at the end, which had to be too late, and Ferensen had never mentioned a jester. Frustratingly, she felt that she held the crucial evidence, although she had no idea what it might be. She ran through what she knew of Sir Veronal – the visit to the shop, the party, their conversation at the reopening of *The Slickstone Arms*. She remembered how, on this last encounter he had been entirely relaxed, on the verge of victory. Was it something he said? . . . *something he said* . . .

She imagined the inky figures and shuddered. She knew. 'Quiet please,' she said, and the discussion died, such was the edge to her voice. 'I know – not who Flask is, but what Sir Veronal was after, how this page connects with the crossword. At *The Slickstone Arms* Sir Veronal paraphrased Pascal: "*I maintain that, if everyone knew what others said about him, there would not be four friends in the world.*" He said that would be the ultimate gift: to move among those who say they're your friends and discover if they really are. Proteus could – that's what Wynter's last experiment did. He found an arrangement that created a shapeshifter – jester, soldier, nun, whoever. Wynter and Sir Veronal feared treachery above all. Wynter was too late to conduct the experiment on himself, but the book lived on. And—' She stopped, suddenly seeing the significance of what she was about to say.

Ferensen was ahead of her. He went pale as a ghost. 'And if it's in the book, it works. If it works, it was tested on someone. Suppose this guinea pig lived on – he or she would know about Lost Acre; he would know about Sir Veronal. He gambles that if Snorkel uses the word 'outsider', it will trigger a memory despite the *tabula rasa*. He knows about the legend of the midsummer flower. He has been in and out of Lost Acre for centuries. He knows of the millennial threat, and that this is the year – from Ferox, probably. He does not know how to save it, but hopes others will find a way. He plants the idea of a reconstruction with the Headmaster. He cultivates interest wherever he can.'

'He contacted Pendle about the *Chronicle*,' added Oblong, 'and he knew the year was significant, which is why he left it in his notebook for us to find.'

'But the most troubling matter is ...' Ferensen paused, as if aware that his next revelation had even more shocking implications. 'Flask also wanted Sir Veronal destroyed.'

There was uproar around the table.

'How do you know that?'

Ferensen followed up with a surprise question. 'Tell me about Hengest Strimmer.'

'Clever, ambitious, devious,' replied Fanguin.

'That figures,' said Ferensen. 'Now, hear me out. Flask – whoever he is – devises a fiendishly clever plan. He gets Snorkel to lure Sir Veronal to Rotherweird. He leaves the stones for Salt to find – he knows Salt goes to Lost Acre. Sorry, Salt, it's true. Where did you find them?'

Salt grunted. He had found them near the white tile, together, all too obvious to someone using that way in.

'When you take the stones to Rotherweird, Flask is hopeful Slickstone will find them soon enough. As indeed he does. There's another chattel of Wynter's that he has: *The Roman Recipe Book*. He secretes it in the North Tower attic and leads Strimmer to the room, and *only* the room, so Strimmer thinks he has found the book. He persuades Strimmer to confront Slickstone, knowing that will bring them together. The fact Valourhand does Strimmer's dirty work makes no difference. Strimmer and Slickstone are too alike not to share their knowledge. Sir Veronal retrieves the book. But ...' Here Ferensen paused for effect. 'Flask must have altered the stones' position on the last page. This is the original page, which he burned. I'll bet you good money he replaced it with a failed earlier attempt. He knew what it would do.'

More uproar.

Ferensen continued, 'Oh yes, Orelia is right: that is the head of Ferox. So the Ferox you met was Flask, shapeshifting. He wanted to be there when Sir Veronal got justice. Good old-fashioned revenge.'

'Revenge for what?' asked several voices at the same time.

Ferensen turned aside. 'Finch?'

'I told you at Escutcheon Place: when the soldiers came and the Eleusians were broken up, Sir Veronal betrayed Wynter. He gave evidence against his master – treachery, the greatest crime.' Finch knew the passage by heart. He had thought Wynter's words bravado; now he was less sure. '"*The accused sought no pity from the Court. He said he would be back, and that vengeance would be his. He said another would come to pave the way.*"'

'But Wynter is dead,' stuttered Fanguin.

'Yes,' said Ferensen, 'so Flask isn't Wynter, but someone close to him – and very much alive. Consider what we know about him: he's vain. He likes wordplay. He knows about Lost Acre and its secrets. He has been in the mixing-point – why he lives on. He's happy to kill in Wynter's memory.'

He walked over to the first tapestry and ran his finger over the insignificant character standing beside Wynter at his first meeting with Grassal. 'Meet Calx Bole, Wynter's extraordinary manservant. Meet Robert Flask, alias Paul Marl, alias the false Ferox. And I'll tell you why I'm certain. This man always wants us to know he's one step ahead. Aggs – it was your question: why did he go to Box Street? The work on *The Roman Recipe Book* doesn't seem a persuasive reason – why not do it late at night in his original lodgings? Why abandon handsome rooms for nasty ones?'

'Why lose the best general person in town!'

'It's nothing to do with your cleaning, and all to do with his final anagram. This time it's Spanish, not Latin. He wanted to leave a final calling card to sign off his masterpiece. He likes to be admired, but he also likes to tantalise. For Box Street, read Box Calle. Mix the letters and what do we get? Calx Bole.'

Silence. The figure of Calx Bole, as fashioned of coloured thread, appeared to be smiling at them all.

Finch rolled back the centuries. 'I go back to the shapeshifter. We were always in Escutcheon Place, we Finches. We've seen much come and go. The first Herald, my ancestor, Hubert, was ruler in all but name – they had no mayors then. He recorded one horrific incident – I found it tucked away in his History. The master carver who did much work on the *archivoire* visited the house on the twentieth anniversary of Wynter's death to check its secret compartments were in working order. Only he had been murdered two days earlier. A ghost, poor Hubert thought. But it must have been the shapeshifter. And when I used the key, one compartment was empty. I guess it held the stones. And Calx Bole in the guise of the carver, another of his victims, took them.'

'What about the cat with fiery feet?' asked Orelia.

'Bole's creature, Bole's familiar,' replied Ferensen.

'Arms and the Man,'' said the Herald a second time, before reminding them of the cat with fiery feet on the last shield of *The Dark Devices*.

'The cat started the fire,' added Orelia, 'but why?' She answered her own question. 'It – or Flask – discovered that my aunt watched and noted – she must have recorded Flask going to the Island Field at night ... on his way to Lost Acre presumably. I knew there was something odd about the fire. Slickstone took the "Sa – Sl" volume after killing my aunt – not, incidentally, for references to his own name but references to Salt. So why would he start a fire weeks later?'

'I met the cat on Midsummer Eve. Slickstone thought the cat his friend,' said Gregorius Jones, still sounding distant and barely engaged.

'Where?'

'How?'

Questions came thick and fast as the company slowly coaxed the events beneath the library floor from Jones. After explaining the actress' escape, he emphasised that she had made a vow of silence and would not be returning.

'The cat wasn't there to *stop* Slickstone but to be sure he got through,' commented Orelia, who now saw a new problem. 'Why did the cat say to me during the fire, "Do you have the book?" Bole already knew Slickstone had *The Roman Recipe Book*, or that Strimmer did. That was the whole plan. So why ask me?'

Ferensen hazarded a guess. 'I believe Morval kept a volume of Wynter's failed experiments – but why Bole would want that, I don't know.'

The inconclusiveness of the answer unsettled everyone. They could see two narratives. In one, the second volume had little significance; Bole's twin ambitions had been the saving of Lost Acre and revenge on Sir Veronal. He sought this other volume as a memento of his master or out of some private interest. The alternative was altogether darker: Wynter's words about coming back meant what they said, and Bole was the man come to prepare the way. This second volume might assist that objective.

Salt laid their fears to rest. 'Suppose – and it's a mighty big assumption – Wynter could return, he'd be an Elizabethan out of touch with the modern world. He's not Sir Veronal and he's not Calx Bole. He hasn't lived through the centuries like them. He'd be an anachronism. Bole wanted Lost Acre saved – and revenge as a pleasant extra. We may not like his reasons, but I don't mind the end result. This book, I suggest, is closed. Mr Ferensen's first toast was the right one – the redemption of Lost Acre. We humble creatures come and go, but to lose a world . . .'

Fanguin the biologist nodded sagely.

Ferensen looked at the company. He saw old-world virtues –

chivalry, curiosity and pioneering courage to name but three, but also more modern ones – forensic thinking, mechanical invention and inclusiveness – a readiness to embrace countrysiders. He forgave himself a punning thought: they had all brought something to the Fair.

He declared the game over. 'Congratulations. The game is won, and we've learned how to learn from history, how to make history, how potent history can be. But sometimes – like *now* – history should be left to its own devices.'

Ferensen took everyone back to his woodland garden. Paper lanterns hung in the boughs.

Orelia explained to Ferensen how Ferox – or, as they now knew, Calx Bole – had used the stones to separate the spider from the woman, and how his sister had slipped away into the night.

'You saw their separation, I felt it. How did she look?'

'She was young and beautiful.'

Ferensen felt an indefinable pain. He and his sister had been parted for centuries by disfigurement; now they would be parted by age. He suppressed the second question: *Why had Calx Bole rescued her at all?*

Hayman Salt told his legend of the midsummer flower. Boris Polk explained how the bubble worked. Bill Ferdy described the colour and fragrance of the Hammer, and why most would never remember the closing moments of Salt's adventure or Oblong's verse-drama.

And Gregorius Jones absented himself, with Ferensen's leave, disappearing over the fields for a midnight run.

Orelia, untuned to happy endings, held aloof. She returned to Ferensen's room to peer at Calx Bole in the first tapestry, a corpulent man beside the willowy Wynter. She reflected on the skill with which Bole and his familiar had manipulated both the company and Sir Veronal – leaving the stones for Salt and the notebook for Fanguin, bringing Slickstone to Rotherweird and *The Roman Recipe*

Book to Strimmer, encouraging Valourhand to protest to draw Slickstone and the North Tower together, defacing the last page of *The Roman Recipe Book* and even dictating the programme for the Midsummer Fair – all this early on, and in the guise of Flask. He and the cat had then acted ruthlessly to suppress any subsequent threat to the plan – burning Mrs Banter's house and defending Sir Veronal against the attentions of Gregorius Jones. She thought further back. Calx Bole had entered the mixing-point to test the last experiment, so he undoubtedly had courage to match his cunning. Were they right to focus on the possibility of Wynter's return? Might not Bole aspire to revive the Eleusians, now Lost Acre was saved and Slickstone removed? She remembered the mysterious death of her Roc ancestor, the master carver.

'It's time to move on.' Finch spoke quietly.

Orelia turned, noticing that Fanguin's box, still open, no longer held the weaselman's skull. She took Finch's advice and said nothing, but accompanied him to the maze where Boris, an accomplished amateur, was playing the lute as Ferensen demonstrated the galliard's five steps – left, right, left, right and then the cadence, a vigorous jump. That mastered, he added spins and lifts. Aggs, his partner, flushed with pleasure as Oblong dithered over whether to ask Orelia to join the dance.

By all appearances it was a world at peace with itself.

Gregorius Jones ran to his chosen prominence, a summit fringed with birch trees where, half-embedded in the ground, a jumble of flints protruded like spent meteors. He piled up dead branches, crisscrossing them, and balled dead twigs with last year's leaves for tinder. On the top he placed the skull, with a silver Rotherweird coin inside the mouth for the ferryman.

Working a flint against his firesteel, he turned sparks to embers to fire. Gregorius opened his arms in brief prayer for the shade of

Ferox, his centurion and a soldier's soldier, who gave no quarter and expected none.

He ran again as the pyre blazed.

Ferox – requiescat in pace.

Not so far away, in an obscure glade in Rotherweird Westwood, a stream ambles through the trees on its journey to the Rother. Moonlight catches the naked figure in the stream – dryad or naiad? She walks the water, stops, stoops and weighs her catch of stones for size and colour. She lifts a foot and extends the puckered toes, revelling in her own skin.

Below the water the work is almost done. In the silt sits a walled town in coloured pebbles, with towers and walkways, encircled by a river.

'Ferox – requiescat in pace.'

Rotherweird and its citizens
will return in 2018 in

WYNTERTIDE

Acknowledgements

When I suspended writing plays in favour of a novel, I naïvely envisaged a solitary journey without the lessons and pleasures of collaboration. How wrong I was. The depth of paper on the cutting-room floor is a tribute to the contribution of others, if not an indictment of the sprawling character of the early versions. Three in particular helped bring clarity and shape. Charlotte Seymour encouraged me to develop the early history, which proved inspired advice, as well as guiding my search for representation. Enter my agent Ed Wilson and an overdue cull of surplus scenes and minor characters. My publishing editor, Jo Fletcher, then brought to bear her invaluable experience and an unerring eye for detail, further improving the structure and much else besides. I owe Ed and Jo an additional special debt. Both believed in an imperfect script by a debutant which did not fit readily into any one recognised genre, in a world where pigeon-holing appears to be unduly fashionable. The rest of Jo's team have provided invaluable support, not to mention good company, including, in particular, editor Nicola Budd, editorial assistant Sam Bradbury, mistress of the felt tip pen, and publicist Olivia Mead.

I endured my share of rejections, though always courteous and encouraging, and I would like to thank one particular publishing editor who volunteered a perceptive critique, positives and negatives. Megan Barr, Anthony Tobin and Maddie Mogford were early readers of particular note, and my neighbour at work, Jane Kilcoyne, has provided unstinting support throughout. Others have read various drafts at various times, and I am grateful to them all. Sasha, otherwise known as Aleksandra Laika, has devoted hours of toil to fine-tuning her remarkable and atmospheric illustrations, while grasping the spirit of the book from the outset. She is a talent to watch and a pleasure to work with. Ian Binnie of CC Book Production has a masterly eye for a typeface, so enhancing the book as an object, and art director Patrick Carpenter and artist Leo Nickolls have fashioned an eye-catching and original cover, again faithful to the spirit of the book.

My local Caffè Nero provided writer-friendly conditions in the early hours, and often the loan of a pen. But only my wife, children and immediate family have had to live with *Rotherweird* from its tentative first steps to maturity. They have variously read and re-read, encouraged, constructively criticised, proof-read and earthed the lightning at moments of frustration. My debt to them and their patience is beyond words. It is traditional to say that the remaining faults are my responsibility, as indeed they are, but the credit for any qualities the reader may find is very much to be shared.

Andrew Caldecott is a QC specialising in media, defamation and libel law, as well as a novelist and occasional playwright. He represented the BBC in the Hutton Inquiry (into the death of biological warfare expert and UN weapons inspector David Kelly), the Guardian in the Leveson Inquiry (into the British press following the phone hacking scandal), and supermodel Naomi Campbell in her landmark privacy case, amongst many others.

His first produced play, *Higher than Babel*, was described as 'Assured and ambitious . . . deeply impressive debut' by Nick Curtis in the *Evening Standard* and 'Vivid and absorbing and grapples with big ideas without being dry, difficult or patronising' by Sarah Hemming, in *the Financial Times*, but informed by his love of history, which he studied at New College, Oxford, he was seized by the notion of a city-state hiding a cataclysmic secret: the result, *Rotherweird*. 'A history-tragic-comedy all rolled into one', says Hilary Mantel, author of Wolf Hall, and 'baroque, Byzantine and beautiful,' according to M.R, Carey, author of *The Girl with all the Gifts*.

A sequel, *Wyntertide*, is currently taking shape.

Sasha Laika studied figurative art in Moscow, followed by a degree in Graphic Design and Illustration in the UK. A London-based artist for the last 10 years, Sasha creates highly intricate works that draw on imagery from mythology, folklore and religious iconography. Her works are inhabited by mystical creatures that morph between human and animal, and exist in transition somewhere between the worlds of fantasy and reality. She considers *Rotherweird* the perfect subject for her début work as a book illustrator.